NOT AN ORDINARY CLIENT . . .

Angelo Uccello believed in being blunt. "You should get up from that chair and go home," he told Karen. "Drop me as a client. I'll find someone else."

Karen felt as if she'd been slapped in the face. "Why?"

"You a sports fan?" Angelo asked.

"Not really," Karen admitted.

"That's what I mean," Uccello said. "A sports fan would understand. I mean this is the bigs. The majors. The players are all experienced. They know the game, know the other players, know what to expect. You're from another planet, a place where you can walk around like a human being, where you don't have to have six guys with automatic weapons lookin' over their shoulders everytime you leave your house. This ain't your turf. I was wrong to get you involved in the first place."

"Then fire me," Karen said. "But I won't quit."

IMPERFECT JUSTICE

Catherine Arnold

A SIGNET BOOK

SIGNET
Published by the Penguin Group
Penguin Putnam Inc., 375 Hudson Street,
New York, New York 10014, U.S.A.
Penguin Books Ltd, 27 Wrights Lane,
London W8 5TZ, England
Penguin Books Australia Ltd, Ringwood,
Victoria, Australia
Penguin Books Canada Ltd, 10 Alcorn Avenue,
Toronto, Ontario, Canada M4V 3B2
Penguin Books (N.Z.) Ltd, 182–190 Wairau Road,
Auckland 10, New Zealand

Penguin Books Ltd, Registered Offices:
Harmondsworth, Middlesex, England

First published by Signet, an imprint of Dutton Signet,
a member of Penguin Putnam Inc.

First Printing, December, 1997
10 9 8 7 6 5 4 3 2 1

 REGISTERED TRADEMARK—MARCA REGISTRADA

Printed in the United States of America

PUBLISHER'S NOTE
This is a work of fiction. Names, characters, places, and incidents either are
the product of the author's imagination or are used fictitiously, and any
resemblance to actual persons, living or dead, events, or locales is entirely
coincidental.

This book is dedicated to my husband, Harrison DeRoche Arnston, 1936–1996. An author in his own right of nine novels published worldwide, Harry was not only a mentor, teacher, inspiration, and critic for me but for many other writers who learned from his many lectures and courses. He was a very special and giving man. We all need more people like Harry. The world is a lesser place for all of us without him.

ACKNOWLEDGMENTS

Special thanks to Charlotte Douglas and Nancy Yanes Hoffman for their moral support and guidance through the completion of this book.

PROLOGUE

The waiting can be a killer.

Literally.

Karen Perry-Mondori recalled defending a sixty-five-year-old widower three years ago. He was accused of killing a neighbor who enjoyed playing his stereo at full volume all hours of the day and night. The apartment walls in her client's home resonated constantly with the screeching guitars and pounding drums of rock and roll. Her tormented client couldn't watch TV, read, sleep, or even think. Repeated calls to the police resulted in a series of fines, but still the abominable noise continued.

Karen's client had finally cracked, stormed into the other man's apartment, ripped the stereo from the wall, then smashed it over the man's thick skull.

The jury was out for five days. On the fifth day, Karen's client complained of chest pains and was rushed to the hospital. When the jury returned a verdict of second-degree manslaughter, Karen's client was already dead.

Norman Welles, however, exhibited no visible signs of strain. Karen's current client, preferring the quiet dignity of the empty courtroom to his luxurious home, sat stiffly at the defense table, bereft of his usual flunkies, and stared into space, not uttering a word.

The jury had been out less than two days. It was impossible to predict what would happen. It was now clear that neither side in this legal battle had suffered a knockout. Karen felt the pressure mount with each passing moment.

Her small body tingling with tension that had been building throughout this contentious and arduous trial, she clasped her hands to refrain from tapping her fingers. An experienced, highly successful, and therefore sought-after criminal defense lawyer, she'd never developed the ability to relax during important trials, and though she never allowed it to show, murder trials made her especially restive.

Because she passionately believed in the system, Karen sometimes defended, without charge, those accused of breaking the most consequential of the Ten Commandments. In her view, if the system—though badly damaged—failed completely, everyone would suffer. A fervid student of history, Karen believed that living under the rule of reasonable and just law was all that prevented any society from degenerating into fragmented tribal anarchy.

Welles was *not* a pro bono case. Quite the opposite, in fact. Karen was being paid top dollar to defend a man who could well afford her services.

Norman Welles was accused of conspiring to murder his wife, a charge he vehemently denied. Roger Brimley had killed Alicia Welles. Brimley, the epitome of contrition on the witness stand, had freely confessed, claiming that Norman Welles had coerced him into doing the deed when Brimley was psychologically defenseless. Brimley, quite naturally, had been the prosecution's key witness.

Karen had torn his carefully crafted testimony to shreds.

And then the moment of truth was upon them.

The courtroom once again packed, Karen stood stiffly at the defense table beside her client. Welles towered over the diminutive lawyer, a strange smile on his arrogant lips, a cocky gleam in his eyes.

"Has the jury reached a verdict?" the judge intoned.

"We have, Your Honor."

"On the first and only count of the indictment, conspiracy to commit murder in the first degree, how do you find the defendant?"

Karen held her breath.

"We find the defendant . . . not guilty."

The spectators gasped. Some booed. Karen's eyes widened involuntarily. The red-faced judge hammered his bench with the gavel and ordered quiet.

Norman Welles turned to Karen. The gleam in his eyes was like a laser.

"So say you all?" the judge asked the jury.

"So say we all."

"Very well. The defendant is released from custody. This court is adjourned."

In the general hubbub that followed, Norman Welles pressed his lips to Karen's ear. "I knew you could do it."

Karen, taken aback by his comment, forced a smile to her lips. "Congratulations, Mr. Welles. You're free to go. Good luck."

"No need to wish me good luck," he said. "I've been lucky all my life. And damn smart. It's an unbeatable combination."

Karen stepped back and looked into his eyes.

No. She looked through his eyes, into the void where the soul should reside. And what she saw chilled her. For without saying it aloud, Norman Welles was telling her that he was guilty, that he'd just pulled off the perfect crime. It had started with the hiring of a desperate amateur killer and ended with the corruption of a witness, a young, ambitious doctor.

Karen felt sick. The room was beginning to spin. She fought to control the warning muscle spasms in her stomach.

Welles grinned. "I do believe you look disappointed."

And then he moved away.

1

The nightmares had lasted almost a week. Thoughts of the part she'd played in helping a killer go free were driving Karen into a deep depression. Though she'd learned long ago that the law could be capricious, that witnesses often lied, that money could buy those lies, she couldn't shake the melancholy that gripped her. But after a week of mental self-flagellation, her fierce determination lit the fuse to a moribund ability to rationalize and a need to get past this.

Awakened by the latest bad dream and unable to return to sleep, Karen paced the plush carpet of the master bedroom. At five feet two inches tall and 110 pounds, she could roam the room without disturbing Carl, her slumbering husband. She wandered to the second-floor window, and nudged aside the drape. Pushing back tousled, shoulder-length brown hair from her face, she observed an approaching storm, now pounding Tampa across the bay.

As a zigzag of lightning subsided into blackness, the room's dim night-light threw her image against the window, and she stared into penetrating green eyes. Carl claimed her eyes could express a range of emotions that would make an actress proud. And in some ways, she *was* an actress. The courtroom was her stage.

But reason, not emotion, was what she required now. In the Norman Welles case, she had done what she was trained and required to do—defend a client. A more diligent prosecutor might have defused her ploy. Norman Welles was not the first guilty person to be set free by a purposely confused jury, nor would he be the last. To dwell on such injustice could immobilize a lawyer. It was unproductive.

Karen's productivity in terms of billable hours to the firm was legendary. As the most junior of four partners of Hewitt, Sinclair, Smith, and Perry-Mondori, she couldn't allow the disastrous outcome of the Welles trial to affect her efficiency. She would be letting down not only herself, but Brander Hewitt, too.

Brander personally had hired Karen immediately upon her graduation from law school. The cofounder of the firm became her mentor. He nurtured her and eventually convinced the other partners to grant her a partnership.

Walter Sinclair, the firm's other cofounder and the managing partner, was Brander's direct opposite. Walter was a lecher of the highest order until a prostate operation left him impotent.

The early years had been horrible for Karen, a schizophrenic mix of Brander Hewitt's reasoned tutoring and Walter Sinclair's infantile sexual harassment. She had almost quit several times, but something inside urged her to hang on. Walter's ultimate illness seemed the answer to a profane prayer, but not for long. His interest in sex blunted, he became a raging bully and took great delight in seeing his frequent harangues reduce an associate to tears.

Hewitt, Sinclair, and Smith, as it was known before Karen became a partner, was as stuffy a law firm as existed in the misogynistic South. Even now, females accounted for only a dozen of the sixty associates. As a partner, Karen fought to change both imbalances, to offer more partnerships to worthy men *and* women, to bring the firm into the twentieth century before the twenty-first was upon them. Not content with the status quo, she was a constant thorn in the side of Walter Sinclair and Darren Smith, who were opposed to changes. Walter, as the managing partner, had the final say.

Having an even number of people as decision-makers was a time-waster. Having Walter, a tight-fisted, mean-spirited cretin, as the managing partner was just plain stupid. The status quo continued to prevail.

But it couldn't remain that way.

Karen had blossomed after becoming a partner, handling a string of high-profile cases with stunning effectiveness, bringing publicity, income, and grudging respect to the firm. The associates, grinding away under Walter's draconian rule and well aware of the personal rancor that existed between Walter and Karen, expected Karen's increasing prestige would eventually result in greater changes within the firm. They took for granted that a confrontation was inevitable, simply a matter of time before the diminutive lawyer with the growing reputation presented her inevitable ultimatum. Everyone knew it, expected it, some relishing the very thought of it.

They were still waiting.

Unless Karen could shake off her depression over enabling Welles to walk, they'd be waiting a long time.

Karen dropped the drapery, obscuring the threatening clouds. Feeling more purposeful than she had since before the verdict, she climbed into bed. She needed her rest. She had work to do tomorrow.

During that thunderstorm-filled August night, a power substation transformer exploded, leaving a large section of Florida's jam-packed Pinellas County without electricity. The electronic clocks in the upscale Autumn Woods house Karen shared with husband Carl, daughter Andrea, and au pair Michelle ceased operating. As did every other electrical appliance.

Living in a region noted for power outages caused by severe electrical storms had taught the family that alarm clocks required backup circuits. Bedside clocks contained batteries, and in the event of a power failure, the clocks were supposed to continue operating.

The clock in the master bedroom was set to buzz at five in the morning. On days he performed elective surgery, Dr. Carl Mondori rose early, showered, dressed, wolfed down some breakfast, reset the alarm for Karen (who got up at six-thirty), and headed off to the hospital in the predawn gloom.

But not this morning. The clock's battery was dead. There was no alarm. And when Carl's eyes opened at six-thirty, he checked his watch, uttered a curse, and leaped out of bed.

"Why the hell didn't you check the battery?" he screamed at Karen.

It was Karen's fault, of course. Why would an eminent neurosurgeon be responsible?

The battery in Michelle's clock was also dead. Michelle, too, awoke late and disgruntled. She was a treasure, but a very organized treasure. Late getting up, late preparing Andrea for the daily trek to a private, year-round school some twenty miles away, late with Karen's and Andrea's breakfasts, she found it hard to hide her frustration. The young woman was in rare foul humor.

Karen, upset by Carl's ranting and unable to go back to sleep after his hurried departure, felt tired, cranky, and unappreciated. Her hair picked this morning to develop a mind of its own. She finally gave up and tied it back in a bun, giving her fine features an austere cast she normally avoided, and adding five years to her thirty-eight.

By the time she left for the office, her mood was as dark as the morning sky, roiling with tall thunderheads ready to unleash forty-thousand-ampere bursts of electrical energy and torrents of rain. The storm struck with full intensity as she pulled her car onto Highway Nineteen, the cluttered main drag in north Pinellas County, a highway turned monster in a storm, almost impossible to negotiate.

Karen was halfway to the office, driving at a sedate twenty-five in heavy traffic, when a little bald-headed man whose pink dome barely topped the steering wheel of a very long Cadillac pulled out of a side street directly in front of Karen's BMW. Karen's car crashed into the Cadillac's driver's door with a sickening thud. Both cars spun wildly, banging into four other cars before they finally came to rest.

Karen, her face covered with white powder from the air bag's explosion, groped for her umbrella. As soon as she stepped out of the car, a gust of wind ripped the umbrella from her hands and sent it sailing, bouncing along the roofs of blocked cars. She was soaked to the skin in seconds.

She made her way to the Cadillac. Its driver stared straight ahead, unaware the car was stalled, his small hands still trying to turn the steering wheel. He seemed to be in mild shock. The driver's door was pushed in about eight inches, the window smashed, but the man seemed relatively unscathed. Karen saw no blood. A good sign.

"Are you all right?" Karen asked.

The man continued working the steering wheel. Karen reached through the smashed window and squeezed his shoulder. "Are you all right?" she repeated.

He looked at Karen vacantly. "What?"

"Are you all right?"

He fumbled with his ear for a moment, then looked down, as if searching for something. "I've lost my hearing aid," he mumbled.

Karen tried to open the door. It was stuck fast.

"Need some help, little lady?"

Karen turned and looked up into the eyes of two behemoths dressed in shorts and tank tops advertising a local gym. They were all bulging muscles and big smiles. Karen simply waved a hand at the door. "Be my guest."

It was chaos. She stood amid pounding rain punctuated by bursts of blue lightning and thunderous booms while a chorus of horns assailed her ears. Karen, her soaked hair now covering much of her face, was trying to determine if this stone-deaf man of eighty-something was well enough to be left alone for a few minutes.

He was.

As she slogged back to her car, her left shoulder throbbing in pain, the cacophony of sound increased, impatient drivers leaning on their horns as they tried to squeeze past the six cars blocking two lanes of the three available. While the little bald man continued his search for his hearing aid and the two bodybuilders wrestled with the crushed door, Karen observed the fluid leaking from the smashed radiator in her Beemer. She groaned and opened the door. It made a terrible creaking sound. The damage was considerably more than she'd first thought.

She called the Highway Patrol on her cellular phone, then Liz, her secretary, to let her know she'd be late, then stepped back into the deluge and went about the business of jotting down tag numbers and trying to gather the names of witnesses. While Florida had a no-fault accident law, one could never be too careful.

It took two hours for Karen to give the police a report, have her car towed, arrange for a rental car, return home, shower, get dressed, and drive to the office. As if to mock the earlier horrifics of the morning, the sun now shone in all its glory, unobstructed by a single cloud.

When she finally walked through the double doors that separated the inner offices from the law firm's foyer, Walter Sinclair made no secret of his displeasure at Karen's tardiness. In recent weeks, the man, always a grouch, had become increasingly overbearing. "You missed the entire meeting," he said as he followed Karen into her office like a bloodhound on the trail of a scent.

Karen whirled and glared at him. "Would you mind if I checked with Liz before we talk?"

"This is important!" he insisted.

"I'm sure it is, Walter. All right."

Unlike the splendid, leather-intensive offices of the other partners, Karen's was decidedly feminine-looking, tastefully decorated in soft pastel colors and comfortable fabric-covered furniture. It was her home-away-from-home, unobtrusive and warm. Walter's uninvited intrusion was typical of the man. Insensitive and rude, his management style was that of a bully, and getting worse by the day. Over the years, many promising young associates had quit the firm, declaring Walter's guerrilla-fighter persona impossible to bear. Karen's frequent protests to Brander Hewitt elicited promises to speak to his friend and cofounder of the firm. Whatever passed between the two men, if anything, was never revealed, and Walter stormed and growled through each day as before.

And with each passing day, the associates' hopes that Karen would eventually present Brander with an ultimatum grew dimmer. For some unknown reason, their champion was taking a step back from confrontation.

"I'm sorry to be late, Walter," Karen said as she sagged into her chair. "I was involved in an auto accident on the way to work. Didn't Liz tell you?"

"She did." Walter rolled his dark eyes skyward. "A few drops of rain and you women drivers go nuts. You should be restricted to driving in good weather."

With effort, Karen held her tongue. She'd long ago stopped rising to the bait constantly offered by this egotistical misogynist. Well, almost. There were times when he could still push the right buttons.

"What did I miss?" she asked.

"It's not what you missed, it's what *we* missed. To wit, a report on your settlement conference with Gerald Industries. Do we have a deal or not?"

Karen eyes were flashing warning signals. "How am I? Is that what you asked? I'm fine, thanks. A few bruises here and there, but between the air bag and seat belt, I was pretty well held in place. It'll take about nine thousand dollars to get my car fixed, but what the heck. And thanks for asking."

Walter's face reddened. "Liz already explained that you were fine. You needn't make such an issue of it. We were all very concerned about you."

"I can see that. Your concern is touching. As for the settlement, we're getting closer, but no deal yet."

He brightened. "Well, that's progress. I was sure this would wind up in court."

"It may still. They've offered three hundred thousand. I'm holding out for five and our client agrees."

"Do you think that's wise?"

Again, she sighed. "Actually, it's really stupid, Walter. I've spent nearly four hundred hours on this case, so what do I know?"

The look of doom so much a part of him returned. "There's no need to be sarcastic."

"Then don't ask silly questions."

"I see. You're above consulting with your partners, are you? You're now so important, so renowned, that you reign supreme. We mindless peons should know better than to question your judgment."

"Just on days when I'm involved in an auto accident on the way to work," Karen snapped at him. "Your timing is lousy, Walter. Stop being an ass and leave me alone. I hurt all over. I'd like some peace and quiet."

"Did you go to the hospital?"

"No."

"Perhaps you should. Sometimes, there's a residual effect. You might have whiplash and not even know it."

"I appreciate your belated regard. Now, will you please go?"

His face flushed with anger. "There's something we have to discuss."

"What?"

"Liz has a message for you. I wanted to talk to you before she passed it along."

"What message?"

"You received a call from Angelo Uccello this morning."

Karen's jaw dropped. "*The* Angelo Uccello?"

"The same. He was arrested last night. He wants you to represent him."

Karen hadn't had a chance to read the morning paper or catch the TV news. "He's in jail?"

"No. He bailed himself out this morning. Had a banker appear with a certified check for two hundred fifty thousand dollars."

"What's the charge?"

"Drug trafficking. Look, I think it would be a mistake for you to talk to him. Uccello's been shopping for a new lawyer ever since Paul Rizzo died of a heart attack. It was just a matter of time before Uccello got around to you. I'm somewhat surprised he didn't come to you immediately." He shrugged as a belated thought occurred to him. "Perhaps it's because you're a woman. In any case, getting tied up with the Mafia is a bad idea. If you're so much as seen meeting with Uccello, the press will jump all over us."

"I agree," Karen said.

He seemed surprised. "Good. Then that's settled."

"Not exactly. I'd like to hear him out. I'll probably refuse to take his case, but I've never met a real-live Mafia type before. Frankly, I'm a little curious."

Walter nodded. "But we have an understanding, right?"

"We agree that getting tied up with these people . . ."

"Do I have to spell it out?" he snapped.

"You've already made your position clear, Walter. Relax."

He smiled. "I knew I could count on you."

"Always."

As Walter headed back to his office, Karen eased into her desk chair, coddling her injured shoulder. When Norman Welles practically admitted his guilt to her after the verdict, she had doubted a more evil man existed. Preying on

Brimley's desperation over his dying child, Welles had agreed to pay for the girl's bone marrow transplant if Brimley, one of his employees, would murder Alicia Welles. When Brimley's daughter died two weeks after the murder, he'd confessed—and insisted Welles paid him to do it.

In retrospect, Karen was certain Welles had bribed the young doctor to lie on the stand, to testify that Brimley knew his daughter's transplant had been futile *before* he killed Alicia. Karen had based her case—and won—on that chronology of events. The jury believed that Brimley, angry at Welles for not providing better health care for his employees and for paying for his daughter's treatment only in the eleventh hour, shot Alicia Welles and implicated Norman as revenge against his tyrannical boss. Just as Welles had planned.

Norman Welles was evil, all right, and Karen had figured him as bad as they come. Until mafioso Angelo Uccello requested her services. Uccello had a long and colorful history of corruption and run-ins with the law. The more she pondered the two men, the more she longed for her third shower of the day. She felt dirty just thinking about them. So much for a lawyer's objectivity.

Liz came in with a stack of pink phone messages in her hand. Karen's attractive secretary looked perturbed. "You sure you're okay?"

"Aside from a few aches and pains. I hear Angelo Uccello called."

Liz stared at the floor. "He did. Top of the list."

"Did he call me personally or someone else?"

"He called you."

"Liz. Look at me. How did Walter find out?"

Liz lifted her head. "He grabbed your messages off my desk after I told him you were going to be late. I didn't know what to do. I was afraid to grab them back."

"Relax, Liz. I'm not blaming you. Your job description doesn't include getting physical with nosy partners. But something has to be done about that man. He's gone too far. This cannot continue."

Liz sighed in relief. "I'm sorry."

"Don't be. See if you can get Mr. Uccello on the phone. Set up an appointment."

"Right away."

"Anything else urgent?"

"No. The rest of the messages are standard stuff."

"Thanks, Liz."

Liz closed the door behind her. At last, Karen was alone. She rubbed her aching left shoulder, then glanced at the rest of the messages. The clock on the wall read 11:24.

It was going to be a long day.

2

Angelo Uccello lived in nearby Dunedin, in a custom-built mini-mansion on Edgewater Drive that backed directly onto the Gulf of Mexico. The imposing three-story stucco and cedar structure stood on three acres of pine-dotted land protected on three sides by an eight-foot-high wrought-iron fence. Karen pulled her rented car to a stop in front of a small hut at a setback gate and introduced herself to a burly uniformed guard wearing mirrored sunglasses and what looked like a Glock 17. A quick phone call, and she was waved through without a word. Another of Uccello's bodyguards, this one dressed in a suit and tie, waited for her at the front door.

"Follow me," he ordered as Karen exited the car.

She followed the man through the front door into a near-empty expanse of concrete. A wide staircase stood next to what appeared to be an elevator. Obviously, the house had been built after flood control codes had been imposed. What appeared to be a three-story house was, in reality, a two-story. Only a multicar garage and storage room utilized the first floor.

"You wanna take the elevator?"

"The stairs will be fine."

"Suit yourself."

At the top of the stairs, the bodyguard opened thick oak double doors and stepped through. Karen followed. It was like stepping into an art gallery. Paintings of various sizes covered the walls, all of them expertly lighted. Sculptures, from bronzes to marble, some of them reaching almost to the twelve-foot ceiling, were positioned over much of the vast floor space. This private collection was worthy of some small cities.

She followed the taciturn bodyguard, winding her way past the artifacts and into a large home office where Angelo Uccello waited. This room contained the typical office equipment. Two of the office walls were glass, offering a panoramic view of the gulf. The remaining two were covered in eighteenth-century originals. Persian rugs in various sizes covered the gleaming hardwood floor.

Uccello wore a white silk shirt, green slacks, brown loafers, and enough gold chains to snap a vertebra. He held a drink in one hand and a cigar in the other as he waved her to a leather chair, then took a seat behind a large, uncluttered mahogany desk. He was short and heavyset, his arms covered with thick black hair. His round face was pleasant enough. He was bald, which made him look older than his reported sixty-six, and his slightly hooded eyes gave him a rather sinister appearance that was exaggerated when two-dimensional photographs of him appeared in the print media or on television.

"Thanks for comin'," he said. "I shudda come to you, but . . ."

The reasons were clear. As Karen now knew, Angelo Uccello had a long list of enemies. No longer a major player in Florida's illegal drug business, he was still viewed as a competitor by several Miami-based Colombian drug gangs who'd chased him from that once-secure turf three years ago. Were it not for her curiosity, Karen would have insisted he come to her office.

"You're quite welcome," she said.

The wide expanse of glass made Karen slightly nervous. Someone wishing to cause Angelo Uccello serious harm had access and visual sighting from the gulf. As if reading her mind, he said, "It ain't glass. It's two-inch-thick Lexan mirrored on the outside. People can't see nothing. It's also bulletproof. Nothing less than a Tomahawk missile can get through. Besides, I got the gulf covered from upstairs twenty-four hours a day. I got stuff on the roof to take care of anybody gettin' wise. This place don't look it, but it's a fortress. So relax, little lady. Drink?"

"No thanks."

"Good. Let's get to it."

The bodyguard left, closing the door behind him.

"I ain't gonna bullshit you, Counselor," Uccello began. "I'm no angel. I hadda fight to survive ever since I was a kid in New York. I ain't got no manners and I ain't got no patience, I treat you with respect, you treat me the same, that's the deal."

Karen said nothing as his gaze took her in.

"I know how it works," he said. "Everything I tell you is privileged, right?"

"Right."

He nodded. "Rizzo, God rest his soul, was my lawyer for sixteen years. A fine man. I actually cried when that poor bastard died, and I don't cry easy. He was only sixty-two. Too goddam young to die. He was like me, came up the hard way, and I trusted him with my life. There ain't many I do that with.

"Since he died, I talked to a lot of lawyers. Most of them are fallin' all over themselves wantin' my business, but they don't know their ass. The real top-notch guys like Black tell me they're too busy. You gotta lotta press from that Welles case, so I decided to try you. I woulda talked to you earlier, but the fact you're a woman stopped me. I'm being honest here. I don't get along with women too good. Their heads are usually up in the clouds. But I hear you're different."

"Perhaps."

He grinned. "You're already pissed at me. I can tell."

Karen smiled sweetly. "You're typical. Women have their heads in the clouds? Is that what you said? Women have never had their heads in the clouds, Mr. Uccello. Never had, still don't, and never will. It's a myth perpetrated by macho skells like yourself. I don't comment much when I hear it anymore, but you caught me on a bad day."

His eyebrows rose. "Where'd you learn to talk like that? Not in law school."

"I lived in Miami for eighteen years. It wasn't always a picnic."

"Okay. Sorry. I'm a dinosaur. Can't help it. But I do respect you. Your reputation is somethin'. Anybody can get that asshole Welles off is some kinda lawyer."

She felt a twinge. "Let's talk about you, Mr. Uccello."

"Okay. But call me Angelo, okay?"

"If you don't mind, I'll call you Mr. Uccello."

He gave her a look, smiled, then said, "Just so you know, I been involved in both legit and not-so-legit businesses all my life."

"I don't want to hear a confession," she interrupted. "Just tell me why you were arrested."

"For dealin' coke, but this is a bullshit bust, and that's the God's truth."

Karen sighed.

Uccello laughed. "Sounds crazy, eh? Look. I don't know how much you know about me."

"Just what I read in the newspapers."

"Newspapers, eh? They've made you look bad a couple times, right?"

"True enough."

"Then you can't put no stock in what they got to say about me, can you? Fact is, the feds have been trying to nail me since I was a kid. They've never succeeded." He raised his index finger, pointing at the ceiling. "Not *once*!

"They've arrested me dozens of times, but I've never been convicted of a felony, and that drives 'em crazy. I may be uneducated, but I ain't stupid. And Paul, God rest his soul, was one hell of a lawyer. He knew how they operated. So, as soon as he died, the feds figured this was their big chance. They set me up."

"How so?"

"They planted the coke they found in my safe at my vending machine company."

"That's going to be a very tough sell, Mr. Uccello."

"I can't help it. It's the truth. Anybody knows me will tell you I don't do business that way. I ain't stupid enough to keep drugs at my office or in my home. What do they take me for? Now, the bastards are trying to seize my fucking business and put me away for fifteen years, all because some FBI asshole got tired of the game and wanted to take a shortcut. It sucks, lady. But I'd expect as much from those bastards."

"They instituted seizure action?"

"Yeah. I got the papers right here. I got ten days to answer, otherwise they're gonna grab a multimillion-dollar legit business. Maybe that's the whole scam, I don't know."

"Go on."

"Okay. Here's the deal. I'm askin' you to repre- sent me on this one beef. We'll see how it goes from there. You like the way I operate and I feel the same, we talk about a more permanent arrangement. Otherwise, we ain't got much to talk about. I won't expect you to handle the appeals if we lose."

Karen rose to her feet. "Mr. Uccello, you'd better find someone else."

"Whatsamatta?"

"I don't think I can help you."

His face flushed. "Like I said, I'm not too good with women."

"Me being a woman has nothing to do with it."

"What, then? You're a criminal lawyer, ain't you?"

"Not exactly. I'm a criminal *defense* lawyer."

"I getcha. Sorry. So, what's the matter with me? I'm tellin' you the truth. The feds set me up! That don't mean shit to you?"

Part of her wanted to leave immediately. But, as crude as this man was, there was something about him—something intangible and indefinable—that stoked her curiosity.

"Why me?" she asked. "You must have several . . . business associates . . . with good lawyers on their payrolls. Why go outside your normal circle?"

He spread his fat hands face up. "I'll be honest with you. You give me credibility. They don't. This case is going to be heard in federal court in Tampa. You know those people. You got their respect. If this was a legit beef, I'd bring in somebody from New York in a heartbeat. I wouldn't trouble you with it, 'cause I know I ain't the kind

of guy you normally get involved with. But it ain't
a legit beef, and I only repeat myself 'cause it's
the truth.

"They catch me with my hands dirty, I play the
game like everybody else. But this ain't right. I
want them to know up front that we're on to their
game. I walk into court with you beside me and
they know *you* know what's up, 'cause you
wouldn't touch me otherwise. You got that kinda
reputation. You understand?"

For a crook, he was refreshingly candid. Most
of the people Karen represented were criminals.
Most of them lied constantly. Others lavished contrived compliments like confetti at a wedding,
thinking that she, being a woman, a mindless bub-
blehead, would lap it up like a cat with milk.
Some assumed her heralded high win percentage
in court was due to her offering sexual favors to
judges. Such stupid, chauvinistic attitudes failed
to trouble her. She chose cases on their individual
merits, believing that a system requiring proof of
guilt beyond a reasonable doubt was worth protecting, even if it meant defending the scum of
the earth. She'd seen the steady chipping away
at constitutional rights; small, almost unnoticeable
splinters with a cumulative effect, steps taken in
the name of an aroused public fed up with a so-
called epidemic of crime.

In fact, real crime statistics had barely increased—if at all—in twenty years. But as Mark
Twain had observed, quoting Disraeli, "There are
three kinds of lies: lies, damned lies, and statis-

tics." Politicians, if they wished to be elected, had to pander to the popular myth.

Karen let out a deep sigh. "I haven't had the chance to read the FBI report," she said. "I'm not really in a position to give you an answer."

Uccello beamed. "You'll see the FBI report soon enough. And we got a few days before the arraignment. Take your time before you decide. I want you to believe in me. I know that sounds nuts, but that's the way it is. If you take me on, I'll pay you up front. Whatever it takes. You pass and I'll bring in one of the New York boys. And don't worry about the retainer being subject to seizure. I got two other legit businesses making lots of profit. The money'll come from there. You'll be able to prove it if they come after you, which they sure as hell will. This ain't gonna be no picnic, little lady."

She took a deep breath, then said, "Mr. Uccello, 'little lady' is an appellation I find offensive. Please call me Ms. Perry-Mondori. I'll call you Mr. Uccello."

His face reddened. He was a man used to obsequiousness, especially from women.

"You're a tough one, all right. They said that about you. I like that."

Shades of Norman Welles. Karen swallowed hard. "What else did they say?"

"That you don't put up with no bullshit. I can see that for myself. They said you're dead honest. If that's true, you'll be the second honest lawyer I ever met."

"Maybe it's the company you keep."

"Whatever. Ms. Perry-Mondori. Okay? And please call me Angelo. Mr. Uccello was my father, God rest his soul. Every time you say it, I think of him. It hurts. Give me a break."

Karen shook her head at his persistence. "Okay, Angelo. Tell me what happened."

He looked relieved. "The FBI got a search warrant based on a bullshit tip. They went to my vending machine business around seven or so, maybe seven-thirty at the latest, flashed the warrant on my guards, busted into my office, cracked open the safe, then grabbed two bags of coke and the company's books.

"There was no coke in my safe. They put it there."

"How much cocaine did they find?"

"Two bags, two kilos each. And you havin' some experience in this area, you know what that means."

Karen did know what it meant. The sentence for selling 4 kilos of cocaine was the same as for 149 kilos, a minimum of 15 years in prison and a fine of $250,000.

"Where were your guards when all this happened?"

"Outside. The FBI made sure of it."

"Do you use video surveillance at the business?"

"No. I use people. I don't trust most of that electronic crap. Too easy to get past."

"That's unfortunate. It would have been nice if we'd . . ."

". . . had some videos? No way. They would have grabbed them, too."

Karen shrugged. "Well, they had to have something on you to get a warrant."

"They say they've got witnesses who bought stuff from me personally. Bullshit. They say my fingerprints were all over the bag. That's impossible. I never touch the goods. I didn't get this far by being stupid. Twenty years of dealin' and no convictions. Now all of a sudden I get stupid? That make sense to you?"

"You're saying you didn't put the cocaine in your safe?"

"Not now, not ever. I've never used that safe for anything illegal. Never."

"And they took the company books?"

"Yes."

"Anything in the books that can be used as evidence against you?"

He looked directly into Karen's eyes, as all accomplished liars do. "No. The business is strictly legitimate."

Karen stared back at him. "This isn't going to work if you lie to me, Angelo."

He hesitated, then said, "All right. The books are fine. Nothin' to worry about. We use the vending machine business to launder money, okay? But the books balance. All the numbers are exactly as they should be."

"How does that work?"

"Cigarettes and snacks, that's what most of the machines sell. We empty the coin drawer and restock twice a week. Let's say each machine takes in thirty bucks a week. We mark it down as sixty. We inventory from ourselves. In other words, I own the distributor, you understand? That way, we can balance the inventory and make the books look good. We still have to get rid of some overstock. Can't be helped. Some, we give away through another company, and some we dump. But the books balance."

"How many machines do you own?"

"About twenty-five hundred."

"So, you're grossing an extra seventy-five thousand a week? That's almost four million a year. Quite a haul."

He was impressed. "You musta majored in math. We pay taxes on all of it. You happy now?"

"Tell me what happened after they found the drugs."

"They came here to the house and arrested me. I arranged for my bank to bring the bail money after first appearance this morning."

"Okay. You say you never touch the cocaine yourself. How do you explain how your fingerprints got on those bags?"

"I have no idea."

"That's it?"

"No, that's not it. Like I said, they busted my place around seven or so. Freddie put the books in the safe before that, and there was no coke in the safe. I was already home. One of my associates was with me from about six until the feds came here to arrest me around nine-thirty. I was never out of his sight. How the hell could I have put drugs in the safe?"

Karen made some notes. "Who's Freddie?"

"My accountant."

"What's his full name?"

"Fred Hertz."

"And what's the name of the associate who was with you?"

"John Haversol."

"Anything else?"

"That's all I know."

"All right," Karen said, rising from her chair, "I'll do some checking and get back to you. But I want you, Mr. Hertz, and Mr. Haversol to take polygraph tests. Is that a problem?"

Uccello didn't hesitate. "No problem at all."

Karen stared at him for a moment, then said, "Okay."

Angelo was pleased. "Fair enough. I'll wait to hear from you."

The door behind her opened and the stone-faced bodyguard appeared as if by magic. Karen followed him to her car. As she drove toward the gate, she felt a familiar tingling throughout her small body. Another challenge lay before her. Challenge kept her in the game.

Karen drove three blocks, then picked up her cellular phone. A familiar male voice answered her call on the second ring.

"Bill, Karen."

"How's it goin'?"

"Same old, same old. I need a rush job. You willing to work the weekend? Nothing serious, just need you to check on some information."

"For you, I'll fly to the moon. When are you going to wise up, dump that surgeon husband of yours, and run away with me to Tahiti?"

"I'd rather eat live rats."

"Cruel woman. And this from a lady who asks a favor. You got big balls, Karen."

"Don't be crude."

"Sorry. So what you need?"

She told him.

Carl Mondori sat by the pool, a plastic cup of white wine in his hand, watching his daughter Andrea ride the inflatable green alligator from one end of the pool to the other. She used her little hands as oars, throwing up great ribbons of spray as she artfully maneuvered the giant artificial beast, its painted-on smile almost as large as hers. At the age of eight, the child was already an accomplished swimmer, taking to the water like an otter. She spent every spare moment in the pool, even in the winter months when it was too expensive to heat. The coldness never deterred her. She had the constitution of a polar bear.

Carl heard a car come up the driveway and turned to look. To his surprise, he saw a blue Ford slide into the garage. In seconds, Karen appeared at the rear door of the garage and walked toward him, her shoulders sagging, the very picture of exhaustion.

"What's with the Ford?" Carl asked, looking puzzled.

"Hi, Mommy!" Andrea waved from the pool.

"Hi, sweetheart." Karen blew her daughter a kiss, then opened the cooler and poured a small glass of wine for herself. "I had a small problem on the way to work."

"Car break down?"

"Not exactly."

"Not exactly? Then what, exactly?"

"Well, I had an accident. Nothing too serious, but the BMW will be laid up for about two weeks."

He was instantly on his feet, his strong hands gripping her shoulders. "Sounds like more than a simple fender bender. Are you okay?"

Karen winced. "Easy on the shoulder."

Alarmed, Carl pulled his hands away. "You *are* hurt."

"Not really. I just strained my shoulder a bit. A few minor bruises as well. That's all."

"Did you see a doctor?"

"It's not that bad, Carl. Stop being a doctor, will you?"

But he *was* a doctor. A neurosurgeon in fact, specializing in back surgery, a man eight years older than Karen, and her husband for eleven years. He was a devilishly handsome man, with classic European looks, standing six feet tall, all rippling muscles and captivating dark eyes. With his dark hair, thick eyebrows, full lips, and exquisite taste in clothes, he turned heads whenever they attended an infrequent social event. It was something Karen would never get used to.

"I want to examine you right now," he said, his voice filled with concern. "There are often residual effects from an auto accident, symptoms that don't become immediately apparent."

"That seems to be common knowledge," Karen said.

"What?"

"Never mind. May I have some wine first? I'm exhausted. It's been one hell of a day."

He kissed her on the forehead. "I'm sorry I was such a bear this morning."

"Yes, you were. You're forgiven."

"So what happened?"

She told him about the accident, and about the problem with Walter, and then about Angelo Uccello. Carl was stunned.

"The Mafia guy?"

"So they say."

"So they say? There's some doubt?"

"Not about his connections. The question is whether he's on the outs or not. The conventional wisdom seems to be that he's been isolated for some reason."

"That sounds a little scary."

"Not really. If he was really in their bad books, he'd probably be dead by now. I have no idea what the problem is, nor do I much care. But you needn't worry."

"I needn't worry? You're talking about defending some Mafia guy!"

"He's no scarier than some of the other people I've defended."

Carl sighed. "I'll never get used to your work. Why the hell can't you stick to civil cases?"

"You know why," she said evenly.

He was silent for a moment. "Are you going to take the case?"

"I haven't decided yet," she said. "I asked for a copy of the FBI arrest report, but they stalled me. They say it won't be ready until the morning. That's a signal something's wrong right there."

"Meaning?"

"Meaning Angelo Uccello may well be telling the truth."

Carl rolled his eyes. "You can't be serious. The man's a big-time hood!"

"I know. But . . . not all law enforcement officers play by the rules. If they did, there'd be a lot less people in jail. Fact is, cops get frustrated just like everyone else. There was a case in 1982, right here in Florida, where six cops manufactured evidence to put a man way. They got caught. Do you remember the coroner in Texas, the guy who wrote down whatever the police asked him to?"

"I remember you telling me about it, but I forget the details."

"Well, because the man wrote down whatever he was asked to write down, some six hundred people ended up in prison. Now, they're all in the process of getting new trials. Can you imagine the cost? And who knows how many of them are innocent? It happens, Carl. Most petty criminals are pretty stupid, but the really clever ones can make it very tough. Look how long it took them to nail John Gotti. And if some of his closest associates hadn't talked, Gotti might still be free. As for Uccello, the FBI has been trying to bust him for decades and never succeeded. That makes it political, and once it gets political, careers can be over. Maybe somebody got impatient or nervous."

"You want to go up against the FBI? Defend a Mafia guy? Are you sure you understand what you're getting into? The press will have a field day."

She sighed. "Not now, okay? This is one I'll have to run by the partners anyway. I understand my being associated with a reputed mob figure is not exactly a public relations bonanza. But, the truth is, old-line organized crime figures have a more realistic attitude than the new gangs and independents. Some of these South American groups are unbelievably ruthless. I can promise you I'll never get involved with them. But this . . . don't let it concern you."

"Everything you do concerns me," he said evenly.

They both slipped into silence, sipped their wine, and watched their daughter at play, ruminating on a marriage that worked—but not without effort.

It wasn't really a contest of egos, but close enough. Had they both chosen the same profession, it might have been an impossible union. Their initial attraction to one another had been chemical, that marvelously mystical assault on the senses that puts reason and logic in storage. The fact that they were professionals was both an asset and a liability, for Karen had a bone to pick with doctors. There were too many bad ones practicing in Florida, where old age could disguise glaring incompetence. Old people were, after all, expected to die. And Carl, forced to pay over sixty thousand dollars a year in malpractice insurance, viewed most lawyers as vultures, twisting the facts with little regard for reality in order to make a buck.

The chemistry had helped them get past that formidable barrier. That, and hours of intense conversation. Now, there was a less-than-grudging respect and understanding on both sides. Those conflicts that did exist were often fueled by a subliminal need to have complete control. The need for control was unrecognized by either, and there were times when both were left reeling after a bitter exchange of words, wondering what had started it all. Fortunately, these sharp exchanges were rare, and the marriage endured.

Carl beckoned to Andrea. "Time to come in, kiddo. Dinner will be ready soon and then it's homework time."

"We don't have any homework tonight," she called back.

"Don't try and kid me. You have homework every night."

Andrea attended a year-round school, one of

the best private schools in Florida. The school closed for three weeks at Christmastime and that was it. So, for the past two years, family vacations were taken at Christmas.

With both parents working, it was the only way. Leaving Andrea in the hands of a stranger for two months every year wasn't something they wanted. And the child thrived on education. Carl's many passions included education. He'd been tutoring Andrea since she was two. Trying to implant in the child the thrill of learning without unduly pressuring her was no easy task, but Carl was good at it.

For ten months of the year, a car service took Andrea to school and brought her home. For the months of July and August, Carl and Karen employed a French au pair. Last year, the au pair's name was Michelle. Michelle enjoyed herself so much her first year, she begged to be allowed back for a second. And so she was.

Andrea made a face as she paddled her way to the pool steps. "Oh, Daddy, I'm only eight, you know. I'm not supposed to know everything."

That brought a laugh from both parents.

Karen lay on the king-sized bed fresh from a soothing shower. Carl leaned over her naked body, gently kneading her flesh, looking into her eyes and ears, moving her arms and legs, probing, testing, rubbing his lips gently over some ugly quarter-sized bruises on her thigh and arm. Despite her exhaustion, Karen suddenly felt aroused.

Carl had a sexual power unlike anything in her experience.

Still.

It was amazing.

"Well?" she asked.

"You'll live," he said, completing his examination, "but your shoulder is slightly sprained. I want it immobilized for at least a week. I'll zip down to the store and get you a sling."

"Is that really necessary?"

"Absolutely. If you don't immobilize the shoulder, it'll just get worse."

Karen sighed. "Well, at least I don't have whiplash."

"Too bad," he said, laughing, "I hear there's money in whiplash."

"So everyone says."

"Later tonight, we'll conduct an experiment."

"An experiment?"

"Yeah. We'll see how well you can make love with one arm in a sling."

With her good arm, she drew him close. "That's a great idea," she said huskily. "But let's forget the sling for now."

"Dinner's almost ready," he said. "Michelle's been working for hours on this one. You'll make a cook out of her yet."

"I'm not thinking of food."

He kissed her. "Later," he said. "By the way . . ."

"What?"

"Your mother called. She's driving up to Jacksonville to visit one of her distributors. She's stopping in here for a couple of days."

Karen's face fell. "Mother called?"

"Yeah."

"You talked to her?"

"I did."

"When is she arriving?"

"Tomorrow. She called it a spur-of-the-moment decision."

Thoughts of sex vanished as quickly as a soap bubble. "God help us," Karen said.

"It's not that bad."

"Yes, it is. Why on earth would she come here? Did she say?"

"Only that she's driving up to Jacksonville, and it wasn't that far out of the way. She sounded quite chipper. She said she felt guilty for not having seen Andrea in almost four years."

"Mother feeling guilty? Not in a million years."

Carl nodded. "I debated telling you."

"If you hadn't, I would have been very upset. At least I have some time to prepare."

"She really gets to you, doesn't she?"

Karen sighed. "That's the understatement of the decade."

3

"The house looks lovely," Martha Perry said, striding through the living room like a real estate agent assessing a possible new listing. "Just lovely."

Karen waited for the other shoe to drop. She hadn't seen her mother in almost four years. The two women talked on the phone an average of twice a year and had never really tried to bridge the schism that had fractured their relationship twenty years ago.

Like many family disputes, this one appeared to revolve around money, but money was only part of it. The real problem was Martha Perry herself.

She was seventy-five years old now, but looked ten years younger thanks to periodic ministrations by a talented and expensive plastic surgeon. Her dyed-brown hair was carefully coiffed and styled to frame her still lovely face. Tall and slim, she radiated confidence, a self-assurance initially born of necessity.

Fifty-one years ago—three months after the

birth of her son Robert—Martha's husband, an alcoholic dreamer beset by financial problems, ran away, leaving Martha a small and faltering department store, a young son, and a pile of debt. Martha wallowed in self-pity for all of five minutes, then swung into action.

First, she retook her maiden name Perry. Then she talked to the small staff at the store and enticed them into working longer hours for less pay in return for a share of the business. She explained that without their help the store would fold. The war was over, she told them, and there were millions of returning soldiers looking for work. Tough times would be with them for a few years at least. Half wages were better than none in these circumstances. If they went along, she'd give them stock instead of raises and bonuses.

Most of the staff reluctantly bought the deal.

Martha then talked to the bankers, showing them projections featuring lower operating costs and solid profits within eighteen months. "If we close the store now," she told them, "you lose sixty thousand dollars. I don't have a dime to back it up. But if you stick with me and lend us another twenty, you'll get it all back with interest. That would be the smart move, don't you think?"

They did.

She took on six jobs herself, worked twenty hours a day. She spent most of her time on the sales floor, and once Martha got her hooks into a potential customer, they were hers. She combined masterful persuasive powers with what some called hypnotism. Sales soared. The store slid into the black within three months. She paid a premium for scarce consumer goods to ensure adequate inventories and kept her word to the staff. Three years after nearly folding, the store was thriving. The staff now owned forty percent of it. When it became a two-store chain, then three, and finally five stores, some of them—clerks, truck drivers, shippers—became rich. As far as the staff was concerned, Martha could do no wrong.

Martha became even richer, but the staff didn't care. She forced them to work harder than they'd ever worked in their lives, and she kept her promise. That was a new experience for most.

When Martha's husband died in a Los Angeles flophouse in 1948, she refused to have anything to do with his burial. She ordered the body buried in a pauper's grave.

Twelve years after the birth of Robert, Martha, in a moment of weakness and need, had a brief affair with a fast-talking young hustler. When Martha discovered she was pregnant with Karen, she never considered not having the child, nor did she tell the hustler who'd gotten her pregnant that she was with child.

Near full term, she ignored the conspicuous smirks of customers as she went about her business. Anyone who dared to actually comment was greeted with a string of verbal abuse that shut them up in a hurry.

Karen was five years old when she learned she was an illegitimate child. Until then, she'd thought her father was dead. But her half brother Robert, in a fit of pique brought on by some imagined slight, cruelly explained the true circumstances of Karen's birth to her. Karen, confused and frightened, turned to her mother for an explanation.

"It means nothing," her mother told her. "Having no father is better than having a useless one. Consider yourself lucky. And if anyone ever teases you about it, punch them right in the face. You better learn real quick you can't take crap from anyone in this rotten world. You have to be strong. Weak people get stepped on, understand?"

Karen didn't understand at all. When she asked who her father was, Martha slapped her across the cheek. "You are never to ask that question again, understand?"

For a hundred reasons, Robert and Karen were never close. As a mother, Martha was a strict disciplinarian and little else. There were few displays of affection, no reading of stories in bed or explanations of how things worked, visits to the zoo, or making of papier-mâché creatures. Children were just *there*, unfortunately, and it was made clear to Karen early in her life that she was a mistake. She was treated as if her coming into the world were somehow *her* fault. By Robert as much as Martha.

Fortunately for Karen, Martha did possess some small kernel of maternal wisdom. Noting Karen's failure to pass first grade, recognizing the signs of a severely emotionally malnourished child, Martha employed an English woman widowed during the war to be Karen's nanny for most of her young life.

"I don't want people thinking I gave birth to a stupid kid," Martha said by way of explanation.

Aunt Annie, as Karen called the English widow, was the direct opposite of Martha, an affectionate and kind woman, a human storehouse of wondrous knowledge about a million things and eager to share the information as though it were treasure. She became a surrogate mother who presented Karen with a different set of values.

Annie was stout and short. When she walked, Karen could hear the sound of the woman's thighs rubbing together. Karen thought that disgusting. And the odd way she talked! But Annie, with her charm, her kindly blue eyes, her bottomless reservoirs of patience and compassion, quickly won Karen over.

"You are not to blame for your illegitimacy," Annie explained one day, "and what a perfectly dreadful misnomer that really is. You'll learn that society likes to label things, my child. Such labels do more harm than good, so forget about them. You are Karen Perry and you are important because you live on this earth. You are entitled to the same happiness as every other child. You're none the less for not knowing your father. You are one of God's creatures, as precious to Him as any other. Think of God as your father, for he is a father to us all. Always remember that."

Karen said she would.

Annie taught Karen many things. She introduced Karen to the joys of reading; Uncle Wiggly, Red Fox, Black Beauty, and Cinderella became part of the child's life. Annie took Karen to zoos and parks and museums and bird sanctuaries, all the while instilling in her the pleasure of learning. She never forgot a birthday, answered every question asked of her, and defended her employer at every turn.

"Your mother loves you very much even if she doesn't always show it. She was given a bad turn there when her husband left her high and dry. She had to work very hard to provide for you and Robert. You must understand that not all people are alike. Keep in mind it was your mother's idea to hire someone to be with you. And that someone is me. Would someone who doesn't care do that?"

"I don't know."

"Well, consider this. England, where I come from, is filled with children whose parents were killed in the war. Most of these unfortunate children are grown now, and they didn't have a mother or a nanny. They lived in orphanages. You're much more fortunate, and for that, you should be grateful. You must learn to appreciate the good things in your life and set aside the bad things. Dwelling on misfortune is a waste of one's time.

"Your mother works very hard. She doesn't have a lot of time for you, but you've had the great good fortune to live in a nice home your mother has provided. All in all, you're a lucky girl, Karen."

"I guess so. Do you have children of your own?"

It was the first and only time Karen ever saw Annie taken aback by a question.

"Oh, yes," she replied. "Yes, indeed. Two fine boys and a daughter. My boys were pilots in the war. And my girl . . . a nurse . . . in Burma. I'll tell you about them someday. And their father. Oh, yes. We were a family, my child. A wonderful, glorious family."

In typical childish fashion, Karen pressed the issue. "Are they dead?"

"Oh, yes. They're all dead now. Up in heaven with their Father. There was a war, my child. A terrible war. You've been lucky there as well, living in America in a time of peace. This is a precious time for you. My job is to see you make the best of it. And I will, I promise."

It was a promise kept.

The compassionate, caring Annie died when Karen was sixteen.

Karen was unable to speak for over a week. Eventually, she recalled Annie's inculcation, focused on what was good in her life, and pushed the heavy cloak of depression from her young shoulders. Even then, there was an ingrained determination in this young woman, a fierceness softened by compassion.

Thanks to Annie.

While Robert Jameson (for some reason he'd retained his father's name) developed into a cold, unfeeling, driven man, Karen's drive was no less, but tempered by humanity.

Thanks to Annie.

The fragile bond between Karen and her mother snapped when Karen was eighteen. Whereas Robert had received considerable financial support from his mother, including college tuition, law school tuition, and additional funding when he entered politics, Karen was told that her idea of becoming a lawyer was, in a word, stupid. Lawyering was man's work, and even a mother who'd been forced to take over a business started by an alcoholic husband couldn't see why Karen wanted to enter a man's field.

Karen found her mother's thinking ludicrous. Even more ludicrous was Robert's siding with his mother. Karen argued with the two of them constantly, trying desperately to force them, for the last time, to accept her as a part of this dysfunctional family. She failed. She'd been an outsider from the start and would remain that way.

Karen left Miami in a rage at age eighteen, vowing never to return.

She kept her vow.

In the intervening years, in rare moments of reflection, she'd made tentative efforts at rapprochement with both her mother and half brother, to no avail.

Now, Robert was a United States senator and Karen defended criminals for a living.

And her mother was here in Karen's home, acting motherly, feigning affection, as if nothing had happened.

Why?

"Thanks," Karen said in answer to her mother's comment about the house. "You can give Michelle most of the credit. Without her, this place would be a disaster."

Martha fixed her daughter with a withering stare. "Who's Michelle?"

"Our au pair."

"What the hell's an au . . . what?"

"Au pair. It's a French term. Sort of a temporary live-in housekeeper. Michelle is French. She wants to learn the language. We give her room and board. In return, she cooks, cleans, and minds Andrea. This is the second summer she's lived with us."

Martha Perry shook her head. "You young people amaze me. I've been working since I was fourteen. I raised two kids all by myself, built a business all by myself, and even at my age I still work seventy hours a week. I manage to do all my own housework. You young people don't know what it is to work hard."

Her mother's harsh words came as a relief. Now that Martha had dropped the phony affection, hating the woman was a guilt-free exercise.

"We didn't expect you until later today," Karen said, trying to change the subject.

"Well, I would have been here later. I left Miami last night and stayed in some dump north of Ft.

Myers on the way. My plan was to take my time but I was eager to see Andrea. Where is she?"

Of course. Andrea. She was here to see Andrea.

Not in a million years.

"She's out playing with her friends," Karen said. "As I said, we didn't expect you this early. I know she wants to see you just as much. I'll have Carl round her up."

Carl, ignored until now, smiled and said, "Nice to see you again, Martha." His lips were tight, but his eyes were dancing with mirth. While he empathized with Karen's agony—and he truly did—he still took a certain perverse pleasure in watching his wife's customary sangfroid quickly disintegrate in the presence of her mother. The aftermath of the last visit from the insufferable old bat was Karen's renewed appreciation of Carl. He and Andrea were really all she had, and the horrors of a rare visit from Mother made her realize it anew.

"I'll find Andrea," he said, "and then I'll get your bags."

"Thanks, Carl," Martha said as she sat on the living-room couch, crossed her legs and her arms, and assumed her favorite pose; chin up, chest out, rigid, like a queen sitting on a throne, surveying her domain.

She'd always been this way, strident and hateful. Financial success, coupled with personal disappointment, had turned Martha Perry into a bullying tyrant.

When Carl arrived with Andrea in tow, the

child stared at her grandmother as one would a stranger. And why not? Martha called Andrea to come over for a hug. Andrea looked beseechingly at her mother, the expression on her face saying, *Do I really have to put up with this?*

"Grandma came all the way from Miami just to see you," Karen explained.

"Hi, Grandma."

She walked tentatively to her grandmother, accepted a perfunctory hug, then took a step back.

"My, my, but you've grown tremendously," Martha said. "It won't be long before you're taller than your mother."

Karen winced. Another shot about her height.

"I brought you something," Martha said.

"You did?"

"Yes. You want to see?"

"Okay."

Martha reached into her purse and removed a small, brightly wrapped gift that she handed to the child. Andrea tore at the wrappings, opened a small velvet case, and pulled out a thin gold chain. A white, gold-encased cameo danced at the end of the chain. "It's beautiful," Andrea enthused.

"Belonged to my mother," Martha said. "Wear it in good health."

"You shouldn't have," Karen chided, somewhat astonished.

"Nonsense. It's a birthday present. She'll be eight in a couple of months. Still like school?"

Andrea made a face. "It's okay."

She was an actress, this child. She loved school, but she knew that children were expected not to like school. Already, she was learning how to play the game.

"I need the keys to your car," Carl said to Martha. "I'll put it in the garage."

Martha handed him the keys. "You still driving that Jap car?"

"Uh-huh."

"And I suppose Karen still drives the kraut-mobile."

"Mother!"

Martha's eyes flashed. "What? I'm not supposed to speak my mind? I drive a Cadillac. So should you. American workers walking the streets while you two support the very people who tried to destroy us fifty-some-odd years ago. That's another problem with young people. They have no sense of history."

Andrea looked mystified.

"Why don't we all sit by the pool?" Karen said. "We'll have lunch, and then I have to attend a meeting."

"On Saturday?"

"I'm afraid so. It's about the only time the partners can get together."

Martha clapped her hands. "Well, good for you. You're not as lazy as I thought."

As they ate lunch, Martha fixed her cool eyes on Carl. "So, I would imagine you're not too happy with all that's happened in health care."

Carl finished chewing his salad, placed his fork on his plate, and leaned forward. "I think it's just terrific," he said. "We have insurance companies dictating how long a patient stays in the hospital after an operation, as if all human beings were exactly the same with exactly the same healing capabilities. Big Brother is really here, Martha. I shudder to think what lies ahead."

"It'll just get worse," Martha said. "Once the politicians stick their grubby little fingers into anything, you can be sure of disaster. And I include my son the senator among that despicable group. They've all got their fingers in the pie, like always. Even so, I really should plan to drive to Virginia and visit Robert in the next few months."

Karen, her cheeks flushing with anger, asked, "If you despise him so much, why would you drive all the way to Virginia to see him?"

"I don't despise him," Martha said coolly. "Nor do I despise you. You've both disappointed me, that's all. I'm not the first mother that's happened to, and I won't be the last. I wanted my children to amount to something. Lawyers are vermin, all of them. Politicians are all crooks. They steal from hardworking people and hand it over to the rich. There isn't a politician in this country who can't be bought, and that's what's sending this country right down a rat hole."

Karen couldn't hold back. "But you're the one who made it possible for Robert to be a politician. You gave him the seed money for his first campaign. If you hate politicians so much, why'd you do that?"

"Because I thought he was different. He was going to change things, he said. Like hell. At least you married a doctor. I give you full marks for that, Karen. Doctors, even if they do charge too damn much, provide worthwhile service. Lawyers we can live without. Common sense should be the rule, not hundreds of thousands of pages of gobbledygook that nobody understands.

"As for seeing my children," she added, hardly stopping to take a breath, "it's an obligation. A mother should make an effort to see her children. Especially her grandchildren. In the second place, I hate flying. In the third place, I need to get away from the store for a while. So where else am I going to go?"

Carl simply shook his head. This time, his sympathy for Karen was genuine. There was no pleasure in watching her suffer like this. He had the strong urge to throw the old bitch out in the street.

4

There were four of them gathered in the smaller of two conference rooms the firm maintained. This room, located on the top floor of a five-story office building north of Countryside Mall in Clearwater, faced south and provided a marvelous view of traffic-choked U.S. Highway Nineteen. The other conference room was used to impress clients. Larger and more imposing, it overlooked a marina.

Though Karen had asked for this meeting, Brander chaired it, as he did every partners' meeting. His meager thatch of pure white hair was carefully combed across his nearly bald pate. His kind face, soft and pliable, was always full of expression. He never played poker, for good reason. As was his habit, he wore a heavily starched shirt with French cuffs beneath his blue pin-striped suit, probably one of less than a dozen lawyers in all the bay area to do so. These days, even lawyers dressed casually.

Walter was there, of course, and Darren Smith, the fourth partner, a bland-looking man who wore thick black-rimmed glasses that gave him an owlish look. Darren had joined the firm shortly after its creation. While Karen was the most productive of all sixty partners and associates, only Walter openly resented her success.

Karen's soft brown hair was behaving today, falling to her shoulders in a carefully contrived look of breezy nonchalance. "Thanks for coming," she began, after Brander brought the meeting to order and turned the floor over to Karen. "There are two things I want do discuss with you, the first being the Angelo Uccello case."

"You're consulting with us before you decide?" Walter asked, scorn and surprise in his voice.

"Exactly," Karen said.

"Well, that's something new."

As head of the firm's criminal defense department, it was within Karen's province to take the case without consultation, but discretion had often proved the wiser course. Obviously, not often enough to suit Walter.

Brander's cheeks turned red. "Walter, you have the amazing ability to be insufferable at any given moment. Would you be so kind as to allow Karen to make her presentation without interruption?"

Good, Karen thought. That set the stage for item two.

"The FBI arrest report," she began again, "finally arrived in this morning's mail. According to the report, the FBI received a tip from an informant that two of Angelo Uccello's distributors were in town awaiting a shipment of cocaine. The

FBI, assisted by a Pinellas County deputy, raided the motel, arrested the two distributors, and questioned them. The distributors told the FBI that the cocaine had arrived and was sitting in a safe located within the premises of Southern National Vending, a business Mr. Uccello owns.

"The report further states that, acting on the tip, the FBI obtained a search warrant from a federal judge and proceeded to search the office, where they indeed found two bags of uncut cocaine in the company safe. Mr. Uccello's fingerprints were found on both bags. The FBI claims the two men arrested will swear they bought cocaine directly from Angelo Uccello on a regular basis. The witnesses are unavailable to us at this time. The FBI gives no reason for this."

"Sounds like an open and shut case to me," Walter said.

"A little too pat, don't you think?" Karen suggested.

"Not at all," he insisted.

Karen turned to Brander.

"I'm not at all sure we should be defending this man," he said softly. "But before we get too deep into philosophical disputes, I'd like to hear what's on your mind, Karen. You wouldn't have asked for this meeting unless you'd decided to represent Mr. Uccello."

"Not so."

"All right. Assuming you're *leaning* in that direction, would you care to explain your reasoning?"

Karen nodded. "Mr. Uccello makes no attempt at pretense. He admits he's a drug trafficker, admits he's been a criminal all his life, and hints he's mob-connected. Perhaps his reluctance to discuss his association with organized crime is because of its reputed tenets. Perhaps, it's because he's on the outs, as some pundits have presumed. I really don't know. Notwithstanding, Mr. Uccello has been very forthcoming about everything else.

"If we're to believe what we read in the newspapers, he's one of the last of the old families to operate in Florida. He worked in Dade County for most of his career, then came here three years ago. Rumor has it the move was directed by serious threats to Uccello's health. The rumors also claim he's still tied to what's left of the crumbling former Gotti New York family, but there's some confusion about that. One thing's for certain, he's not working alone. It's not his style.

"These days," she went on, "most of Florida's organized crime is run by foreign gangs. Colombians, Koreans, Japanese, and Mexicans. I expect it won't be long before the Russian gangs working New York will spread their wings down here. But at the moment, Angelo Uccello is still a small force to be reckoned with in criminal circles. His legitimate businesses include vending machines, a wholesale cigarette and candy distribution company, imported wine, a catering business, three restaurants, and a chain of dry-cleaning establishments. His criminal activities are confined almost exclusively to drug trafficking and money laundering.

"Until now, he's been arrested many times, but never convicted. Reason? Well, for one, he's very bright. He uses layers of intermediaries as buffers. Those closest to him have been with him a long time and he trusts them. He pays them well and plays it straight. He's not as greedy as some of his predecessors and that's probably the secret of his success.

"Frankly, I find it hard to believe that a man of his experience and cunning would be so stupid as to leave cocaine in his office safe. I've got Bill Castor checking some things for me."

"Who's Bill Castor?" Walter asked.

"Bill's a PI who's done work for me in the past."

"What's he checking?"

"Well, among other things, he's talking to some street people."

"Street people?"

"Yes, street people, the people at the very bottom of the drug-trafficking food chain. Drugs are impossible to distribute without them, and you'd be astonished at how much they know. Bill has taken years to develop connections with these sad folks. He's trying to find out if Uccello has ever done drug business out of his legit businesses before. He's also trying to find out who these so-called witnesses are."

"I still don't understand why you'd want to get near this despicable creature."

Karen sighed. "It's what I do, Walter, I defend criminals," parroting his own words of just a few days ago. It went right over Walter's head.

"Yes," he said, "but this is more than defending a criminal."

"I don't see it that way. Mr. Uccello's regular attorney died recently. Mr. Uccello is of the opinion that the FBI used his temporary legal vulnerability as an opportunity to set him up. He may be right, or he may be just clever. At this point, I'm not sure. But it strikes me that his accusations deserve to be explored. As well, he's offering what amounts to a blank check. That should be of interest to you, Walter."

"It *is* of interest to me. But this business of getting in bed with organized crime figures troubles me. We've never done that before."

Karen tapped her pencil on the legal pad in front of her. "I really don't see this costing us clients. In fact, I see some ancillary benefits."

"How so?" Brander wanted to know.

"Well, in a perverse sort of way, by taking on the feds, we'll ingratiate ourselves with the locals. It's no secret there's considerable enmity between local law enforcement agencies and the FBI. A lot of the locals resent the FBI's high-handedness, interference, headline-grabbing, and especially their seemingly unlimited budget. If Angelo Uccello is lying and is subsequently convicted, we'll have gained nothing. On the other hand, if he's telling the truth and I'm able to prove it in court, we'll pick up a few valuable brownie points with the locals.

"As you know, whenever a local police officer is found to be dirty, the media goes crazy. But when a federal law enforcement officer goes bad, it doesn't get much play in the local press. The locals resent that, and they love it when the feds, incorrectly perceived as Elliot Ness clones, are embarrassed. If it turns out that Mr. Uccello is right, the feds will look bad and a few locals will feel they owe us a favor. You never know when that might come in handy."

"But don't you run the risk of antagonizing the federal authorities? You have to deal with them, too, Karen."

"Less than thirty percent of my cases involve the feds. Besides, dealing with the feds is a different story. You can't really make friends there."

"But you could make enemies."

"True. But if Mr. Uccello is telling the truth, these people need to be exposed. And just for the record, if I do defend Mr. Uccello, it's a one-case deal. There will not be a commitment for permanent representation. So, I really don't see this as being a problem."

"Well, I'm not in favor of this," Walter said. "You can't sit there and tell me that this mafioso is telling you the truth."

"No, I can't. He could well be lying. But if I take the case, I'll take it on one condition: that he *is* telling me the truth. He and two of his associates are to take polygraph tests. If any of them fail, Mr. Uccello will look elsewhere for representation."

Brander's jaw dropped. "He agreed to that?"

"He did."

"I'll be damned."

Karen waited. Brander, after rubbing his chin for a bit, nodded. "I say it's up to Karen."

"Me, too," added Darren.

Walter threw his hands in the air. "So, once again, I'm odd man out."

He was indeed. Always. And in spades.

"Thanks," Karen said. "I'll get right on it."

"You said there were two things you wanted to discuss," Brander reminded her.

It was a golden opportunity for Karen to present her ultimatum. But at the last moment, she changed her mind. She would offer a protest, but not an ultimatum. With her mother still underfoot, Karen had more than enough tension with which to contend. There would be other opportunities to take Walter down a peg. He was a man who provided them daily.

She looked directly at her nemesis as she said, "I don't ever like going behind someone's back, Walter, so here it is. Your heavy-handed management style has cost us some exceptional associates. There are fifty-six associates out there, ten of whom are long overdue for partnerships. We can't keep on like this. This much-too-rapid turnover is costing the firm money and reputation. As unpleasant as it may be, it's a fact we can no longer ignore."

Walter's face turned purple with anger. "That's a gross exaggeration. I've never been heavy-handed with anyone."

"Never?" Karen said. "Let me give you a personal example. Yesterday, I discovered that you went through my phone messages—again. I've complained to you about this several times, without effect."

Walter remained silent. Brander blushed. Darren looked at the ceiling.

"Did you look at Karen's messages?" Brander asked Walter.

"I may have," he snapped. "She was late for work, if you recall. Quite late. I was concerned that some important clients may be—"

"She has a secretary," Brander interrupted. "A very qualified and efficient secretary."

Walter swallowed hard. "That may well be, but . . ."

Brander shook his head. "Karen," he said softly, "if it's all the same to you, I'd appreciate the opportunity to discuss this in private with Walter."

Damn! Why was he constantly covering for the man?

"I have no wish to make this a federal case," Karen said. "I've brought it to the attention of the partners because I believe it's my fiduciary responsibility to do so. As long as you're prepared to present to the partners a resolution to the problem, I'm prepared to let you handle it."

"Very well," Brander said. "I appreciate the consideration."

The meeting was over. Karen stood, forced a smile, and strode out of the conference room, her back straight, her steps sure, chin out, chest out, feeling the heat from three pairs of eyes on her back.

Later that night, as she lay in bed beside Carl, Karen allowed small tears to stain her cheeks. Her shoulder throbbed. Carl, glancing at her, wiped away the tears with a tissue, then kissed her.

"What is it?"

"Nothing."

"Your shoulder?"

"No. It hurts a little, but . . ."

"Your mother?"

Karen didn't answer.

"Why do you put up with it?" he asked.

"Because she's my mother."

"Where does it say you have to be nice to a mother who treats you like shit?"

"You know where."

"I don't think God had Martha in mind," he said. "Maybe it's time you stopped trying to win her affection."

"Is that what I'm doing?"

"It would seem like it."

Karen slammed her fist on the mattress. "Why can't I grow up? Why do I allow her to get to me? Can you tell me that?"

Carl shook his head. "Don't be so hard on yourself."

"I'll try."

"I think there's something else troubling you," Carl said.

"Let's not talk about it."

"Why not?"

"Because you'll be disappointed in me."

"Never. Why would I be?"

"I didn't give the firm the ultimatum."

"Oh, that. I didn't expect you would."

She looked at him in shock. "You didn't?"

"Well, with your mother here, I figure you have enough on your plate."

"But I have to do *something* to stop Walter's hostility toward me. I could try to deflect it if I only knew its source."

"Maybe," Carl said, "he's never gotten over your rejection of his sexual overtures years ago."

"But he's hassled every woman in the office who's been there more than six years. He was a sexual predator of the first order. And now, while those days are past, for some reason he focuses all his hostility on me. So why can't I bite the bullet and put a stop to it?"

He pulled her close. "Would you please stop doubting yourself? Walter probably picks on you because your capabilities threaten him the most. You know what you're doing. You'll choose the right time for an ultimatum. Besides, it's your career. You don't disappoint me, love. You never cease to amaze me."

Karen smiled. "You have a knack for saying the right thing at the right time."

He sat up and looked into her eyes. "Thanks.

Where is this insecurity coming from all of a sudden?"

She laughed. "You have to ask?"

He took her in his arms. "Listen . . . you have to stop this. You're not what I'd call a religious person, though you do try to live by certain tenets. You've always been taught to honor your mother and father. Okay. You honor them, even the father you never knew, but you don't have to love them. You really don't. And you don't have to feel guilty because you don't. Understand?"

"You're a preacher now?"

He groaned.

"I did say I didn't want to talk about it."

"Yes, you did."

"Wanna fool around?"

"No."

"Oh. Okay."

"Well . . . if you really need to . . ."

She gave him a light punch on the shoulder.

The next day, at two in the afternoon, Martha Perry's spur-of-the-moment visit was almost at an end. Her suitcase packed and placed in the trunk of her Cadillac, she asked Karen if they could sit by the pool for a short chat before Martha headed north. Karen, her nerves on edge, ushered her mother to the pool.

"That Michelle is one lousy cook," Martha said.

Karen grit her teeth. "She's not that bad, Mother. She's a terrific housekeeper and great with Andrea. Nobody's perfect."

"Is that supposed to be a slam at me?"

"Of course not. You do your own cooking, your own shopping, your own housework, and still manage to run a business. You have energy to burn. But not everyone's like you. You seem to think they should be. Tolerance isn't your long suit, wouldn't you agree?"

"Maybe not."

They were protected from the sun by the roof overhang, but it was still stifling. Humidity was high and there wasn't a breath of breeze. Karen could feel droplets of perspiration trickling down her neck. "You're sure you won't stay for dinner?" Karen asked.

"Thanks, but no. I better get on the road. I want to make it to Jacksonville before dark."

"I worry about you," Karen said.

"Why?"

"Why? You're not a kid anymore, Mother. Driving all the way from Miami to Jacksonville and back is quite a haul."

Martha bristled. "I'm still young enough to drive wherever I please, even to Robert's, if I decide to go."

Karen seized the change of subject with relief. "What's Robert doing in Virginia, anyway? Congress isn't in session. He usually spends August in Miami."

"He's working on some bills before the next session. Unlike most of those idiots, he actually reads the bills before he votes on them."

"Well, good for him. But if you decide to visit

him, why don't you fly? Do you really hate it that much?"

"Last time I stepped inside an airplane was thirty years ago. The flight was so rough I swore I'd never fly again if we landed safely. We did, thank God, and I've never tempted fate like that since. You can believe all that crap about flying being the safest way to travel, but I'll take a good car any day. At least I know what I'm doing. But before I go, there's something I want to talk to you about."

"Uh-huh?"

"This mafioso guinea. You gonna defend him?"

Karen was stunned for a moment. Angelo Uccello's name had never come up during Martha's visit, but a report of Karen's meeting with him had been on the TV news. Obviously, her mother had heard it.

"You mean Angelo Uccello?"

"Right. The drug dealer, the bastard who makes his living by destroying the lives of children. He should rot in hell. And you should stay the hell away from him."

Karen's cheeks burned with fury. Her mother never gave up a chance to criticize her.

Martha continued her rant. "Do you have to sink to defending that kind of scum? If you don't care what this may do to your career—or to Carl's—can't you allow your mother some small morsel of dignity?"

"This has nothing to do with you," Karen said. "Nothing at all. And I resent . . ."

"I live in Miami, child. That used to be that dago's stomping grounds until the South Americans ran him out of town. But he's still news down there. Adopted native son, and all that crap. Day before yesterday, his arrest was in all the Miami media—then yesterday afternoon the TV news said you'd be representing him. You're in the news a lot yourself, for that matter. Every time you handle a big case, I see your face all over TV and the newspapers. You're building one hell of a reputation. And all my friends know you're my daughter. They ask me how I feel and I lie through my teeth. I tell them how proud I am of my successful lawyer-daughter."

Karen slowly shook her head in awe. "You lie to them. How really remarkable you are."

"You know how I feel about lawyers. I refuse to be a hypocrite. And this is too much. This man is the scum of the earth. To have my own daughter mixed up with him is a disgrace. It's more than I can bear. I've had to be tough all my life, Karen, but I can't take this. I can't take the shame of it."

Karen leaned back in her chair, her mouth open in pure astonishment.

"Well?" her mother said, pushing. "Have I made any impression on you at all? Or is it that you don't care how much I suffer."

Karen took a deep breath. "I defend criminals. I'm sorry that makes you unhappy, but it's my job. The law requires that everyone, no matter who they are, is defended by a competent lawyer. What kind of country would this be if the police simply arrested people and threw them in jail without a trial? Is that the kind of country you want?"

"It would be a hell of a lot better country, that's what. But I'm not talking about this country. I'm talking about you. If you're so hell-bent on being involved with criminals, why don't you prosecute them?"

"Mother, I can't discuss this with you."

"Why not?"

"Because you're impossible."

"I'm trying to tell you that what you're doing is wrong. God! Can't you see it? If you get this bastard off, he's free to destroy more lives! Have you no morals? Have you no sense of right and wrong: Is it the fame and fortune that blinds you to the truth?"

"Mother . . ."

Martha held up a hand. "Not another word. You protect the vultures that feed on people and you think it noble. God! How I wish you'd never been born!"

Karen jerked back as if she'd been slapped. In a very soft voice, she said, "That's always been your feeling, hasn't it? You've hated me from the moment I was born. If you felt that way, why didn't you have an abortion?"

"I don't hate you."

"No? You could have fooled me. All you've ever done is criticize me. I can't ever remember a hug or a kind word. If it hadn't been for Annie, I never would have made it."

Martha lashed back. "I'm the one who put food on the table and clothes on your back, not Annie."

Karen's anger was bubbling over. "You think food and clothes are what's important? Did you ever love anyone, Mother? Did you love my father, whoever he may be, or was that just a quick roll in the hay? And while we're on the subject, now that I'm almost middle-aged, don't you think it's time you told me who he was?"

Her lips formed a cruel sneer as she added, "Or don't you know?"

Martha's eyes widened for a moment. "That's a horrible thing to say to your mother."

"I agree. But you're pretty good at dishing it out. I've been waiting for a kind word from you all my life. I'm still waiting. And I wonder what makes you the way you are. I know I'm not alone. You treat Robert with the same disdain you treat me. God knows why. You were the one who made it possible for him to become a lawyer. So, spare me the anti-lawyer sentiments.

"As for our relationship, I've tried and failed to win your love for as long as I can remember. Well, I've had it. You're always welcome here, Mother, but you can keep your incendiary comments and criticisms to yourself. If you can't treat me with respect, then stay the hell away from me. Understand? I'm just not going to take it anymore."

Martha stood up and stared down at her daughter. "I came here to try and save your miserable ass, but you're not worth it."

"Thanks."

"You're really not. You're arrogant, Karen. I've never liked arrogant people."

Martha turned, walked quickly to her car, got in, slammed the door, and started the engine. The car was halfway down the street before Karen could even move.

Carl came into the pool area and stared at Karen. "What was *that* all about?"

Karen got up and stepped into his arms. "Just hold me, will you?"

5

When the morning alarm sounded, Carl rose quietly from bed, reset the alarm, padded naked to the bathroom, showered, dressed, crept into Andrea's room to give her a kiss, then headed downstairs. All the while, Karen watched him silently through one half-open eye, admiring his muscular body, and groggily refreshing her appreciation for their enduring relationship.

She could hear him talking to Michelle as he ate his breakfast. That was unusual. Carl usually prepared his own breakfast. Maybe Michelle had had trouble sleeping, too. Perhaps Mother's visit had made everyone jumpy. It had certainly shattered Karen's emotional equilibrium. Her mind had been spinning like a top all night, the confrontation with her mother upsetting her more than she could have imagined, stirring deeply repressed emotions almost too painful to bear.

For years, she'd tried to rationalize the reasons for her mother's hostility and her own need to be loved by this cruel woman. She'd even thought of seeing a professional, but set aside the idea. There

were few secrets in the legal community and lawyers who saw shrinks were risking trouble. She'd
seen it happen to others.

"Did you know Don was seeing a shrink?"

"No! Really?"

"Yeah. I saw him going into a shrink's office
yesterday. What do you think it is? Drugs? Booze?
Trouble at home?"

Nosy people.

When it came to matters of the mind, America
was still living in the Dark Ages.

Carl knew there'd been trouble. After holding
her and providing his patented, welcome comfort,
he looked into Karen's eyes and asked what was
going on. She couldn't tell him. "Just a silly argument," she lied.

He knew it was a lie.

It was one of the early tenets of their marriage
that she and Carl not keep secrets from each other,
other than patients and clients. But gradually, that
agreement was discarded in favor of sharing expe-
riences. The act of sharing was uplifting in itself.
The resulting support was another boost. It made
the seemingly intolerable situations bearable, less
forbidding when analyzed by a party once removed. The clear light of rational thought could
often brighten murky, subjective intuitiveness.

But Karen couldn't share this deep pit of sometimes despondent longing with Carl. She'd always
pretended she could handle the complex emotional baggage that cluttered her mind whenever
Mother was in her thoughts. And for the most

part, she put on a pretty good show. But folding herself into Carl's arms had shown him something. He could see that her multilayered, carefully nurtured defensive wall was in tatters.

She felt like a fool. How could she allow herself to be so affected by this insensitive woman? What was the matter with her?

She arrived at the office early and in foul humor. Liz, always the diplomat, simply said good morning and handed her four notes. According to the first note, Brander wanted to see her immediately.

"He's in this early?" Karen asked.

"He was in when I got here," Liz said.

Brander usually arrived at the office at nine-thirty, preferring to wait until the crush of traffic subsided before leaving his home. Karen dropped her attaché case beside her desk, then headed for Brander's office. His secretary gave her a big smile and said, "You can go right in. May I get you some coffee?"

"Coffee would be nice, Bev."

Karen stepped into Brander's opulent office. He was standing by the window, staring out at the bay, his hands in his pockets, looking quite forlorn.

"Good morning, Brander," Karen said, more cheer in her voice than she felt. She wondered if he'd notice the dark pouches under her eyes. When she'd applied her makeup this morning, she'd been more than generous, trying and failing to fix the face from hell.

He turned to face her. "Good morning. Did Bev offer you some coffee?"

"She did."

"Good. Have a seat, Karen."

Karen sat.

Brander, deep in thought, took his time getting behind his desk. Bev rapped on the door, then entered bearing a silver tray and elegant silver tea service. She filled two china cups with coffee, then left the room. Not a word had been spoken.

"Someone die?" Karen asked, trying to break the somber mood.

Brander gave her a weak smile. "You know what this is about."

"I'm sorry. Of course I do."

He seemed to be in pain. "You were very hard on Walter Saturday."

"I meant to be hard on him, Brander. I'm a partner in this firm, and I don't deserve to be treated like some kid still waiting to pass the Bar. Walter has no right nosing around Liz's desk. He's done it before and I've mentioned it before. What am I supposed to do?"

Brander took a deep breath. "Come to me. In private."

"I *have* come to you. Countless times. Nothing changes."

Brander sighed. "You're right, of course. I apologize." He placed his hands on the desk, palms down, struggling to find the right words.

"I'm asking you to bear with me a while longer, Karen. As a personal favor. You see, Walter . . . is going through some . . . personal problems just now. He's shared his problems with me but asked that I keep the discussion confidential. I'm going to honor his request. I hope you'll honor mine."

"I'll try," she told him.

"Good. I appreciate it very much. I realize how frustrating this is to you and I wanted you to know that there are special circumstances involved. I can't say much more."

Karen thought for a moment. "I'm sorry to hear of Walter's problems, whatever they may be. All I ask is that he keep his nose out of my business. Is that too much to ask?"

Brander smiled. "Not at all. I've spoken to him. There won't be any more snooping."

"Thanks, Brander."

Brander sipped his coffee, then said, "Now about the Uccello case . . ."

"If he passes the polygraph test, I'm going to represent him."

"Fine. How many associates will you need?"

"Two. Molly and Jack, if possible."

"I'd rather give you two other associates. You may not be aware of this, but they fight to have the opportunity to work with you. They learn things not taught in school—or most other law firms, for that matter. So, to keep peace in the family . . ."

Karen grinned. "So, now I'm a teacher."

"At the very least, a mentor. Does that bother you?"

"Not at all, just as long as the two people you have in mind are not just sitting and learning. I need help."

"I was thinking of Len Spirsky and Sharon Chin."

"Spirsky? What about the Bar exam?"

"He took it a month ago. The results will be out long before you go to trial, and I expect he'll have passed. He's very bright, Karen. Reminds me of Colin in many ways. As for Sharon, she's worked with you before. You said you were pleased."

Karen nodded. "I was. Okay. Len and Sharon it is. I'll bring them in as soon as I've talked to Uccello."

Brander stood up. "Good. I can't say I'm happy you're taking the case, but I respect your feelings."

"Thanks again, Brander."

Karen stood up and prepared to leave.

"There's just one more thing," Brander said.

"Yes?"

"We no longer represent Norman Welles." He said it with pride.

Karen was astonished. Welles's sizable corporate account with the firm was the reason she'd been asked to defend him. "What happened?"

Brander puffed out his chest. "I asked him to find another firm. He seems to have had little difficulty. We're shipping the files today to Bangor and Wilton. I thought you'd like to know."

"May I ask why? Welles was worth three or

four percent of this firm's total billings, if memory serves me."

Brander took a deep breath. "The air in here smells sweeter, don't you think?"

"It does. But I don't get it. You wanted me to defend that man. You said it was an obligation. Now, right after his acquittal, you decide to dump him? If anything, the timing astonishes me."

"Yes. Well, it's quite simple, really. He was a client, and as a client, we *were* obligated to represent him. To your everlasting credit, you performed at your usual one hundred percent efficiency, and our obligation was met. I was free to act."

"You never cease to amaze me, Brander. You truly are a throwback."

"I take that as a compliment," he said.

"As it was intended."

"Which brings me to something else."

"Yes?"

"You mustn't blame yourself for what happened."

Brander had not commented after the trial, other than to congratulate Karen on her successful defense. It was his custom. Most lawyers like to lick their wounds in private. Comments, however well meaning, are usually an intrusion. The Welles case, a victory, was really a terrible defeat. Karen had never been able to hide her true feelings from Brander. He must have assumed they ran deep, taking time to address the subject in his special way.

"There's no one else to blame," Karen said softly. "It was my idea to offer the alternative scenario, to bring in the shrink, my idea to . . ."

"Stop right there," Brander interrupted. "You did your job. The prosecution team thought they had the case wrapped up because they had Brimley's confession. They didn't work hard enough. They tried to walk this one through. It was wrong. Had they done their jobs properly, you might have lost. In my opinion, the jury would never have had a shred of doubt. You did what you had to do, nothing more, nothing less. That your defense was successful is both a tribute to your proficiency and a damnation of the prosecutor's lack of same. I know you beat yourself up terribly after that trial. Just in case it's still eating at you, I want it clearly understood that I won't stand for it."

Karen lowered her head. "It's better that a hundred guilty men go free than one innocent man be unjustly convicted. Isn't that how it goes?"

"Close enough. That's what sets our system apart, Karen. It may be a cliché, but it's the very essence of our societal soul. May it ever be so."

"Thanks, Brander. But I'm well past it now."

"Well, something's on your mind."

"It shows?"

"Always. You drop the mask when you're with me."

"Hmmmm. Not good."

"I think it is. You need someone in this firm with whom you can be totally candid."

Karen smiled. "This has nothing to do with the job, Brander. My mother dropped by to pay a visit. And you don't want to know."

He looked surprised. "Oh, my. I thought it was . . ."

"What?"

He seemed embarrassed. "Then, you don't know about Dr. Nano?"

At the mention of the doctor whose testimony had clinched Welles's not-guilty verdict, Karen felt electrified. "What are you talking about?"

Brander's eyes widened. He blushed, then ran a hand over his pate. "I just assumed," he stammered, "when you seemed so upset . . . I'm sorry."

"Brander, will you please spit it out?"

He looked stricken. "I imagine . . . it's probably best you don't hear this from someone else."

"Brander, for the last time, what about Nano?"

He looked away for a moment. When his gaze returned to Karen, his eyes were filled with sadness. "I received a letter on Saturday from an old friend. He enclosed a copy of an article that appeared last Wednesday in a New Jersey newspaper. It seems that Dr. Joseph Nano is breaking ground for a new oncology clinic being built just outside the town of Closter."

Karen felt her throat begin to constrict.

"It's going to be called the Nano Clinic," Brander continued, "but the money comes from Norman Welles. That information was contained in an official press release. There was no attempt to cover it up."

Karen sighed deeply. She'd known in her heart that the doctor had lied on the stand, that the entry in his diary was a fake, but there was no proof . . .

There was the lingering thought, more a hope, that she was wrong about Nano. A rationalization perhaps, but a necessary one. Now, she knew the truth. A cold hand seemed to grip her heart.

"They didn't waste any time. How blatant can they get!" she exclaimed. "They're both thumbing their noses at the whole world."

Brander shook his head slowly. "It's terrible, I know. But you know as well as anyone there's no use dwelling on it. Prosecutors rarely go after perjurers unless there's solid evidence, and in this case . . ."

"Damn!"

"I'm sorry, Karen."

"Thanks for telling me," she said. "You were right. I'd rather have it come from you."

"Try not to . . ."

Karen stood up. "I'll try. Have you ever had to deal with something like this?"

"It happens to all criminal lawyers," he said. "Justice isn't perfect, but it's all we have. Remember that."

Karen nodded. "Remember? Remembering isn't the problem. Forgetting is the problem."

Bill Castor didn't look much like a PI. His nickname was Dick Clark, because at age forty he had the face of a teenager, all fresh and wide-eyed and full of boyish excitement. It was a terrific cover. Most people thought of private investigators as serious, cynical, and big. Castor, short and thin, barely cast a shadow, but he had a computerlike mind, the memory of an elephant, and contacts no one else could touch.

"Word on the street," he said, leaning over Karen's desk, "is that your boy was set up all right."

Karen smiled. "As he suspected."

"But it may not be the feds," Bill added.

She gazed at him in awe. "Who, then?"

"The word I get is that a couple of Juan Ramirez's heavy hitters were holed up in a Day's Inn in St. Pete. No names, least not real ones. They were busted by the FBI three days ago, but no charges have been filed, and as far as I can tell, these two are still in custody. Word I get is that they weren't here to deal drugs."

"Juan Ramirez," Karen said. "The Cali cartel, Miami division, right?"

"Exactly."

"Does anyone know what these two *were* doing in town?"

"Not really. One would almost think they were just waiting. Waiting to be busted."

"So they could set up Angelo? Why go to all the trouble? Why not just blow him away?"

"Good question," Bill said. "In the first place, Uccello isn't that easy to get to when it comes to a frontal assault. He lives in a fortress. Rumors are floating around that Uccello has military-grade weapons, including radar, in place on the roof of that mansion of his, just in case a passing boat becomes a threat. I'd say he's close to being paranoid.

"He rarely leaves the place. When he does, it's never on any kind of schedule and he's well protected. Two cars, all the way. The two cars never go in the same direction, and lots of times, Uccello isn't in either of them. He never meets with strangers. You getting the picture?"

"Uh-huh."

"In the second place, the new breed of career criminal operating in this country is a lot more sophisticated. In Colombia, it's a different story. The mobs down there have assassinated over a thousand judges, court officials, cops, and lawyers in the last decade.

"Now the Colombians are moving in on the American mobs big-time, taking over every level of distribution, turning the drug business into a vertically controlled operation just like General Motors. They grow the plants, produce the drugs, package and sell them to their own distributors, who sell them to mob-controlled dealers. No outsiders. But, with this country sick of home-style violence, the tactics here can't be the same. Instead of guns, the Colombians are using guilt to get rid of their competition. Setting up Uccello is clever. It changes the feds' focus."

"And the FBI never looks a gift horse in the mouth."

"Exactly. As for Uccello keeping the goods in his business safe?" He shook his head. "My sources tell me that would never happen. As you suggested, he never comes in direct contact with the stuff."

"What can you tell me about Angelo himself?"

"Well, he's an old-time hood. Used to be part of the Gotti family. Before that, he worked for Paul Castillano. And before *that*, he worked for Tommy Gambino himself. Uccello was Gotti's main man in Miami for years. When Jaunty John went to the slammer, the family fell apart, like all the other old families. Like I said, the old mob is just about done these days. American organized crime has been taken over by foreign interests. Weird, eh?"

"And Angelo?"

"He's still connected to a splinter wing of the old Gotti family, but it's tenuous. Uccello may as well be classed as an independent. These days he spends more time in his legit interests than pushing drugs. He's completely out of prostitution, loan-sharking, and extortion. Drugs R Us is all he's got left, and that's fading fast, thanks to Juan Ramirez."

"So, it's true that Ramirez pushed him out of Miami?"

"Seems so. Uccello left Miami with his tail between his legs. He doesn't have the firepower to start a war. Or maybe he's just getting old."

"Interesting. If Angelo is out of Ramirez's hair, why set him up at all?"

"Because Uccello is still operating. Ramirez wants no competition whatsoever."

"Okay. Makes sense. What about Angelo's personal background? You have anything on that?"

Bill grinned. "Do I ever come here with half a loaf of bread?"

"Never."

"His father was a wise guy, got killed in the forties during a Brooklyn turf war. Uccello made his bones . . ."

"Made his bones?"

"Became a member of the family . . . an initiation of sorts. You have to kill someone, or at least you did in those days. Anyway, Uccello was shipped off to Miami in the early fifties. He set up vending machines for the people down there, assigning locations and freezing everyone else out. Then he became Gambino's third-in-command and started taking care of Gambino's south Florida drug interests. Stayed there until John Gotti eventually took over the family.

"Uccello and Gotti didn't get along too well. Uccello got shoved aside, and when Gotti got busted, Uccello was pretty much out of favor. For whatever reason, Sammy Gravano, the guy who squealed and brought down Gotti and twenty other mob guys, never mentioned Uccello when he sang his long song. Maybe they were pals. I don't really know.

"Sammy's in the Witness Protection Program now and Uccello's here, perhaps the last of a breed. Maybe the feds decided it was Uccello's turn in the barrel. I get the impression Uccello's lost his taste for violence somewhere along the line.

"He was married once," Bill added, checking

his notes. "His one and only wife died of cancer in '92. He's got two kids, both legit, and both estranged from their father. Seems that's the way he wants it. He sent them to boarding schools when they were kids. Never wanted much to do with them, or maybe he just wanted to keep them away from the business. His son is a priest living somewhere in Africa, and his daughter is a nurse in Chicago."

He closed his notebook. "He might be innocent, you know. Wouldn't that be a pisser? You gonna represent him?"

"Yes," Karen said. "I'm meeting with him in an hour. And based on what you've told me, I'll need your help throughout this case."

"I'm yours to command."

Karen smiled. "Great. First up, I want to run Angelo and two of his associates by a polygraph test. You game?"

Castor looked surprised. "He'll do it?"

"If he wants me to represent him, he will. That's part of the deal. I may call on you at a preliminary hearing. It probably isn't going to be allowed, but I'll give it a try. That okay with you?"

"Like I said, I'm yours to command. I have a couple of ideas of my own I want to check out. That okay with you?"

"Of course," Karen said.

"I always did like your style, Karen."

"The feeling is mutual," she told him, her face expressing pleasure for the first time all day.

6

An hour after Bill's visit, a courier delivered a package to Karen. The package came from the U.S. attorney's office in Tampa. Karen opened it and sorted through the contents.

They included a revised copy of the FBI arrest report, a copy of the booking sheet, statements from two men identified as Fito Olivera and Manual Aznar, copies of search warrants, and other incidental information.

Karen picked up the phone and dialed a number.

"U.S. attorney's office."

"Wilbur Brooks, please. This is Karen Perry-Mondori. I represent Angelo Uccello."

"One moment."

Wilbur got on the line. "Karen?"

"Hello, Wilbur."

"What's up?"

"I'd like to meet as soon as possible."

"How about tomorrow morning? Say eight? I'm in court at ten."

Karen groaned inwardly. "Eight it is."

She dialed another number. Bill Castor answered his cellular phone "You're getting to be a pest."

"You said you were mine to command."

"I lied."

"Two names. I need them checked out. Fast."

"Hold it. I'm driving. I'll turn on the tape recorder."

"Okay."

"Fire away."

She gave him the names.

Angelo Uccello greeted her with a look of concern. "You look tired, Counselor."

"Thanks."

Angelo threw his hands in the air. "Sorry. I told you I ain't got much class. But that's between us, right?"

The wounded look on his face was almost endearing. In fact, there was something about this man that Karen liked, something identifiable, something that touched her. And, in recognizing this feeling, she felt troubled. Here was a long-time criminal, a mafia underboss, a cold-blooded killer responsible for who knew how many murders, not to mention drug-induced deaths, whatever—and she was beginning to *like* him.

She found that frightening. What was happening here? Was she losing her sense of values? Had her mother's visit caused that much emotional havoc? Was she losing her cherished ability to separate her work from her personal life?

"So, what's the verdict?" he asked. "You gonna represent me or not?"

"I'll represent you, Mr. Uccello. I'll need a two-hundred-thousand-dollar retainer."

His jaw dropped. "A two-hundred-thousand-dollar retainer? Are you nuts?"

She kept a straight face. "Not at all. Your life is in danger. That's obvious. You live in a fortress, but we all know about fortresses. I'm going to be spending a lot of the firm's money preparing your defense and I don't want to be chasing down some estate lawyer to collect my bill."

He glared at her.

"Just so you know," she added, "this defense will probably run closer to half a million by the time we're through."

The anger disappeared, replaced by a look of dismay. "You talk about me getting killed like it's nothing."

Karen shrugged. "Live by the sword, die by the sword."

"You *are* a tough one."

"You wanted a wimp to defend you?"

"I'll call the bank," he said. "There'll be a cashier's check waiting for you in the morning."

"There's one other condition," she added.

"What?"

"If I find you lied to me, either in the past, now, or at any time from this moment forward, I'll drop you so fast your head will spin. I demand my clients be absolutely straight with me when I represent them. You lie to me once and I'm out. Understood?"

"I haven't lied to you."

"I didn't say you had. And I'm going to hold you to your promise to submit to a lie detector test. You'll be getting a call from a man named Bill Castor. He'll arrange the tests, okay?"

"Fine."

"Good. Now, I have a couple of questions."

"Okay."

"You have security people at your vending machine business, right?"

"Twenty-four hours a day."

"Your own people?"

"Of course."

"And you're saying that when the FBI raided the place, the cocaine was not in the safe, that the FBI placed it there during the raid."

"Exactly. They kept my people out of the office while they searched."

"How'd they get into the safe?"

"It's an old one. Easy to crack. An experienced safe man could figure out the combination in about ten minutes. That's why I never keep anything important in there."

"How long were your security people kept away?"

"Over an hour."

"Where *do* you keep the important stuff?"

He smiled. "Can't say, Counselor."

"Fair enough. Have you ever heard the name Manuel Aznar?"

"Nope. Who's he?"

"The man who tipped off the FBI."

His eyebrows rose. "Where'd you get that?"

"From the FBI. I'm meeting with them and the assistant U.S. attorney tomorrow. You never heard of Aznar?"

"No."

"How about Fito Olivera?"

"Never heard of him."

"You're sure?"

"Positive."

"How about Juan Ramirez?"

There was a pause. "Him, I know."

"Where?"

"Miami. He's a Colombian drug trafficker."

"Is he the reason you moved to Dunedin?"

"Is that what the FBI says?"

"No."

He took a deep breath. "You don't like me much, do you?"

"You're a drug trafficker, Angelo. But even drug traffickers are entitled to a lawyer. By the way, are you married?"

Karen already knew the answer to that question and the ones to follow. She wanted to see if he answered them honestly.

"Was," he said. "She died years ago, God rest her soul. Cancer."

"Any kids?"

"Two. My son is a priest, if you can believe it. I guess he's trying to atone for my sins. Either that or he's a fag. I'm not sure. I have a daughter.

She's a nurse in Chicago. Neither one of them has talked to me in fifteen years. What's it to you?"

Karen shrugged. "Just curious."

"So where do we go from here?"

"I'll be talking to the prosecutor. We'll see just how strong their case is. Then we'll decide. By the way, it might not have been the FBI who set you up."

He seemed confused.

"It could have been Juan Ramirez's people," she said. "And if it is, they may try to kill you if this doesn't work out."

He took a deep breath, exhaled, then said, "They tried twice already. Least I think it was them. And now they've crawled in bed with the feds. And those fuckin' feds . . ."

He dropped his gaze. "Sorry."

Karen pulled a legal pad from her attaché case, made some notes, then said, "Let's start with you telling me everything you know about Juan Ramirez."

Len Spirsky, a recent law school graduate still waiting for his Bar examination results, sat in one chair. Sharon Chin, an associate with the firm for three years, sat in another. Both looked intently at Karen as she gave them their marching orders.

"I'm sorry to have to drop this on you so quickly, but it can't be helped. I need three briefs, and I need them tonight."

The almost-lawyer and the associate started making notes.

"First," Karen said, "I want a motion requesting a show-cause hearing, so we can get more information on the so-called witnesses. Keep in mind this is a federal case, not state. Then, I want a motion requesting reduction in bond to fifty thousand dollars. The third motion will be a preliminary request for a hearing on the seizure question."

She handed Sharon some notes hastily scribbled on a legal pad. "Use these as a guide. If you have a fit of inspiration, go with it. Given the constraints of time, the motions will be short and to the point, but attach a lot of case law."

"You need this tonight?" Sharon asked.

"I'm afraid so."

"When are you meeting with Mr. Brooks?"

"Eight in the morning."

"Would it be all right if we delivered this to you at home just before you leave?"

"You think it'll take all night to prepare?"

"If you want it done right, yes."

Karen looked at Spirsky. "How do you feel about that, Len?"

"Whatever it takes," he said eagerly.

"Okay. When you're finished, bring them over to my house. If it's past eleven tonight, put them in the mailbox. Make sure you have an extra copy handy, just in case."

"Thanks, Ms. Perry-Mondori," they chimed.

"If we're going to be working together, and we are, call me Karen, okay?"

"We appreciate the opportunity," Len said.

Karen smiled. "I hope you feel the same way five months down the road."

"You're still upset," Carl said, moving close to her, rubbing her bare shoulders. "And your shoulder is still giving you trouble. You'd save a week of pain if you'd wear that damn sling."

"I can't work with a sling."

"Have it your way. You look exhausted. I know you always get rattled when your mother talks to you, but this is a little more than usual. Was it anything special?"

Karen, still sitting up in bed at one in the morning, shook her head.

"Nothing special?" he prodded.

"It's just been a really bad few days," she said. "You know, the car, Mother, Walter, the case . . ."

"You work much too hard."

"At times. Like you."

"I remember we talked about that."

"So do I."

"We said we weren't going to fall into that trap again."

"I know."

"So why are we doing it?"

"It just happens, that's all. It's not like I'm trying to make life difficult."

"No? You could have refused to take the case."

Karen rolled her eyes skyward. "That's easy for you to say. I've talked to the man. He may be innocent. Would you refuse to help someone in similar circumstances?"

"If I had your choice? Yes. There are a hundred lawyers in this country capable of giving Angelo Uccello the best representation money can buy."

She turned and faced him. "That many?"

He grinned. "Maybe twenty. Can you live with twenty?"

"I can live with twenty. And what about you, Mr. Cool? I seem to remember a certain John Kelly, a man who stiffed you for an operation you performed. And when he was brought into the hospital for yet another operation, what did you do?"

"He might have died. That's different."

"Is it? If my client goes to jail for twenty years, it's a death sentence. He's no kid."

"But he's a drug trafficker!"

"Granted. But in this particular case, he *may* be innocent."

He sighed. "I don't mean to pick on you."

"But you are. Why?"

"For one, you haven't been wearing your sling."

"I just told you. I can't work that way. I can't drive, do anything."

"Your arm will take twice as long to heal."

"I can't help that."

He shook his head. "Stubborn. God, you're stubborn."

"Granted. Now, what's the second thing?"

"I think the time has come. Now that your mother's out of here, you should lay that ultimatum on the partners. You bring in more income than anyone else in that firm. If you're going to do the bulk of the work, you should be entitled to the bulk of the rewards. As far as I'm concerned, Walter Sinclair is living off the avails of your efforts. He should be kissing your ass, not giving you a hard time. You should make that clear to them."

"I will. The timing is wrong, that's all. There's too much happening right now."

Carl threw his hands in the air. "At least take something for the pain. You'll be up all night."

"If I don't get to sleep soon, I will, promise."

He leaned forward and kissed her. "Love you. G'night."

"Love you, too."

He switched off the light and the room was plunged into darkness.

Karen lay there for five minutes, until she heard the deep breathing that signaled Carl was asleep. She got up and went to the bathroom. She pulled an amber bottle from the medicine cabinet and shook two sleeping pills into her hand.

She hated taking sleeping pills, but one sleepless night was enough.

And she had Wilbur Brooks to face in the morning.

Damn!

7

G. Wilbur Brooks, an assistant U.S. attorney for the Middle District working out of the Tampa office, was a man of towering intelligence. Intelligence aside, his ability to reason was blighted whenever he was called upon to prosecute drug traffickers. Brooks's consuming passion was putting drug traffickers in jail; it was a personal obsession. To Brooks, dealers in illegal substances represented the absolute worst of humanity. They rested at the very top of his hate list, above mass murderers, above serial killers, even above child abusers.

In Brooks's tilted view, these reprehensible creatures were responsible for fully half the crime in America at horrendous cost to the nation. Their list of victims was endless and ageless, the suffering of their victims incalculable, lives forever destroyed, for Brooks was of the opinion that it was impossible to truly rehabilitate a drug user, statistics disputing his position be damned.

Once, he'd actually lobbied the Department of Justice to ask Congress for a law mandating the death penalty for twice-convicted drug traffickers. His plea resulted in a small notation being made in his personnel file to the effect that the man bore watching. He could become a loose cannon in the near future, someone tagged to be shunted to a position where radical statements received little attention. Wilbur, of course, was unaware that he was on the fast track to oblivion.

A tall, portly man disposed to wearing ill-fitting, off-the-rack suits, his dark hair combed straight back from his wide forehead, his small eyes burning with intensity, he also hated the name Wilbur. The G stood for Garth, and for the first forty years of his life, Garth W. Brooks went about his business without giving much thought to names. But when the enormously popular country music star burst upon the scene, Brooks was teased unmercifully, perhaps because he was a humorless man. Garth W. Brooks soon became G. Wilbur Brooks. Those who continued to refer to him as Garth were treated to an angrily delivered five-minute dissertation on the merits of paying attention to a man's right to change his name.

His office was standard government issue, small, with pale green walls. Venetian blinds covered two windows that afforded no view at all. The furniture consisted of a walnut desk, four dirty-brown Naugahyde-covered chairs, and three marred walnut cabinets. A dull brown carpet covered the floor. Altogether, a dingy, depressing place in which to work, it suited Wilbur to a T.

On this morning, the office held three people.

In addition to Brooks, FBI Special Agent Bruce Tasker—the man responsible for the arrest of Angelo Uccello—sat in one of the chairs, while Karen Perry-Mondori sat in another. It was Karen's first face-to-face meeting with Brooks regarding the arrest of Angelo Uccello.

Brooks, leaning forward, his tightly clasped hands resting on his desk, glared at Karen, the author of this complete waste of his valuable time, a woman almost as despicable as the people she represented. Criminal defense lawyers were scum.

Karen understood such attitudes when adopted by lay persons, but she was appalled that a professional, a man charged with upholding the tenets of the criminal justice system, would be so off-the-wall. There weren't many like Brooks, but one was more than enough.

"So," he asked, his voice sounding like rolling thunder, "are you here to talk a deal? If so, forget it. I won't deal when it comes to scumbags like Angelo Uccello."

Karen took a deep breath. She knew the man. Not well, but enough. Karen had tangled with him three times in court, losing once and winning twice. He'd never forgiven her for her wins. Never would.

"I'm not here to discuss a deal, Wilbur," she said.

"So what, then? I'm a busy man."

"Of course you are. I appreciate your taking the time to see me."

"Cut the crap. What's on your mind?"

"I want to depose Manuel Aznar and Fito Olivera as soon as possible. How soon can you set it up?"

Wilbur had a strange gleam in his eyes. "It'll take some time," he said.

"There are rules, Wilbur. Even for you."

Wilbur smiled. "No shit."

"My client claims he was set up," Karen said, pressing on. "I think he's right. He seems to think the FBI set him up. There, I disagree."

Bruce glared at her. "This was no setup. This was a righteous bust."

"Based on a tip from two drug dealers with records as long as your arm? Please."

Brooks was taken aback. "What are you talking about? Neither witness has a record."

"Not in this country," Karen said.

Wilbur's eyes widened. "Care to explain?"

"Both men are Colombian nationals. They have long arrest records there. I think Immigration might be interested in how they came to this country."

Wilbur, stunned by Karen's obvious access to that information, recovered quickly. "Who the hell do you think you are?" he bellowed. "We work for the United States Government. You think we'd let another agency screw up our case?"

Karen smiled sweetly. "It's worth a try, don't you think?"

"Don't waste your time, Karen. And don't waste mine, either. We don't set people up."

"Yes you do. But I never accused you of setting

up my client. I said my *client* thinks you did. One thing for sure. Somebody did."

"Bull! Is that it?"

"Not quite." She opened her briefcase and handed Wilbur the three documents prepared by Len Spirsky and Sharon Chin. "You'll find a motion for an immediate show-cause hearing, another for a reduction in bond, and a third that speaks to the issue of seizure."

"On what grounds?"

Karen fixed him with her laser stare. "I'll address the seizure issue first. My client has never been convicted of a felony. In the eyes of the law, this is a first offense and one that resonates with impropriety. To seize my client's assets at this juncture, even before a preliminary hearing, would fly in the face of the intent of the seizure law. This is America, Wilbur. The constitution, despite the best efforts of those who would try to dismantle it, still means something. Even the Supreme Court has questioned implementation of seizure in cases such as the one we are dealing with now. You'll find case law attached.

"As for the bond reduction, fifty thousand dollars is the customary bond when dealing with first offenses. Angelo Uccello is not a flight risk. His entire net worth is tied up in local real estate and legitimate business operations. We're prepared to release copies of his income tax returns for the past ten years.

"Speaking to the show-cause issue, I expect to have evidence to support my client's assertion that he was set up. I want to depose your so-called witnesses immediately, not when you get around to it, and I want the evidence impounded by the court subject to further examination."

Wilbur was livid.

"You'd be wise to move on this with all due speed, Wilbur," Karen said. "The already tarnished reputation of the FBI doesn't need any more flak. You . . . and the FBI . . . may have been conned. The sooner this gets cleared up, the better for everyone."

"Conned by whom?" Bruce asked.

"I'm not prepared to say at this point. But you should be able to figure it out. Who do Fito Olivera and Manuel Aznar work for?"

"Your client," the FBI man responded.

"Really? For how long? Can they prove it? And who was their previous employer? You're caught in a war between rival factions, sir. You're being used. Don't you see that?"

"You're crazy."

"Oh? Would their former boss have reason to want my client put away? You busted both men a week ago and asked them to roll over. Standard operating procedure. Isn't it odd they picked my client and not their boss? One would almost think you people had something to do with that."

"They say they work for your client," Tasker said. "They have sworn to it under oath."

"Really? And we all know witnesses never lie, right? We'll see how the depositions go."

Wilbur glanced at the documents she'd given

him and threw them on his desk in disgust. "You're a real pain in the ass, you know that?"

Karen opened her attaché case and extracted another brief, one she'd prepared herself. She handed it to Wilbur. "I'd appreciate some civility, Wilbur. We've met in court before. There's no need for vulgarity, and this brief seeks sanctions if you keep it up."

Red-faced, Brooks said, "Excuse me all to hell. You really want war, don't you? What is it? They talk about the short man complex. Maybe women have it, too?"

Karen glared at him.

Brooks sneered back. "We have reason to believe your client has put out a contract on both witnesses," he growled. "I'm not about to expose them until I have to."

Karen looked incredulous. "You can't be serious."

"I'm very serious. You're the asshole's lawyer. That puts you in his camp. I'm not about to let you get near those witnesses until I absolutely have to."

The implications of that insult were so outrageous that even Tasker stared at the floor.

Karen sagged in her chair. Brooks had lost his senses.

"I have a right to—"

"Stick your rights!" he shouted. "You don't get anywhere near those witnesses. Not until we've got them safely tucked away."

Karen turned to Tasker. "Mr. Tasker, you can

expect to be served with a subpoena before the close of business today. You're a witness to this interview."

Tasker shrugged. "What interview?"

"Fine," Karen said, rising to her feet. "You can repeat that in front of a judge. If you want to commit perjury, that's up to you." She turned to Brooks. "I'm seeking sanctions, Wilbur. I don't have to put up with this."

Brooks waved the briefs in the air. "You deliver these to Judge Williams yet?"

"I have."

"Then let's get it on, Ms. Perry-Mondori. You want war, you got war. Let's see if the judge is amenable to talk in chambers, shall we?"

He seemed to be in a real hurry. A surprise. "Be my guest," Karen said.

Wilbur flipped a lever on an ancient intercom. "Susan, get Judge Williams's clerk on the horn. See when he can talk to Ms. Perry-Mondori and myself. Hopefully, at his earliest convenience."

"Yes, sir."

While the call was being made, Wilbur leaned back in his chair and smirked. No one spoke. Then, the intercom beeped. Wilbur pressed the intercom lever. "Go ahead."

"Judge Williams says he can see you immediately if you take less than twenty minutes."

"Tell him we'll be right there."

"Yes, sir."

Brooks stood up. "After you, Counselor."

Tasker stuck out his hand. "Nice to meet you, Ms. Perry-Mondori. I'm sure we'll meet again."

Karen ignored his hand.

Judge Douglas Williams, sans robes, sat at a desk piled high with briefs and bulging file folders, examining the documents Karen had delivered to his clerk just minutes ago. A federal judge for sixteen years, the man had the ability to scan a document and determine the meat of its content quickly. With his gray hair, chiseled face, and military bearing, he looked like a judge. As one of the most senior judges, he was entitled to certain perks, not the least of which was an office that would have done the CEO of a major corporation proud.

Furnished in black leather, chrome, and mahogany, the office screamed lavishness. Its three large windows provided a glorious view of downtown Tampa. A large TV set occupied one corner and a complete stereo system with large freestanding speakers was nestled among the countless bookcases. Leather-bound editions of classic literature shared shelf space with the obligatory law books, row upon row of them. Karen wondered if the judge ever cranked the stereo up to full blast. Quickly she discarded the thought. But why the speakers?

Redundancy personified. A status symbol.

As the judge read Karen's briefs, he nodded several times, then placed the documents on his desk. "Why don't you go first, Karen?"

"Thank you, Your Honor. My client proclaims his innocence. Simply put, he did not place the cocaine in his safe."

"You're saying he was framed? I would have thought you'd be more original. Anything else?"

"I haven't had time to prepare the brief, but yes. Mr. Brooks claims my client has contracted a hired killer or killers to assassinate two witnesses. He's using that as an excuse to delay my deposing them. I'll be asking that he provide evidence to back up his wild claim."

The judge turned to Wilbur. "Wilbur?"

"Your Honor. I'll deal with the assassination plot in due course. It's still under investigation. As for Uccello, he's a known drug trafficker and has been for years. We have corroborating statements from two additional witnesses which we'll present at trial."

Karen stared at him. "What witnesses?"

"You'll be informed," Wilbur said coldly. "Due to circumstances I'm not at liberty to discuss, we haven't completed the arrangements for their testimony. As soon as that's set, I'll furnish you with copies of their statements."

Karen let it go. Brooks might be bluffing. "If my client is such a known drug trafficker, how is it that he's never been convicted?" she asked.

"Because of people like you," Brooks snarled, "lawyers who'd make a deal with the devil himself to get their grubby hands on money gained from the sale of drugs to ten-year-old kids. Scumbags like you, Karen."

Before Karen could say anything, Judge Williams interjected. "Let's not get personal, Wilbur. Fact is, there is an issue here and that issue must be addressed. We'll let the evidence be our guide."

He turned to Karen. "I don't see any evidence, Karen."

She was stunned. "That's why I'm asking for the show-cause hearing, Your Honor. I'll present the evidence at that time."

He shook his head. "Not good enough, I'm afraid. There's nothing here to warrant such a hearing. It's simply the word of your client, and that's suspect. Your request for a show-cause hearing is denied."

"But, Your Honor!"

Thunderclouds formed in the judge's eyes. "I've already ruled on your motion," he growled. "I'm not interested in hearing more argument, Counselor. As for bail, while it's true your client has never been convicted, it's within my province to set bail based on my knowledge of the events surrounding the case. I'll take it under advisement. To be candid, I now see Mr. Uccello as a possible flight risk. I may revoke bail."

Karen was struck speechless.

"As for your complaint regarding Mr. Brooks's purported language," the judge continued, "I'll let you talk to the Bar Association on that one. I don't want personal animosity cluttering up these cases. You will have to take that fight elsewhere. There won't be vulgarity in my court, but I can't control what goes on beyond it."

He seemed pleased with himself. "Finally, as to seizure. The law is quite clear on this point. The Supreme Court has upheld the right of the Government to seize assets prior to trial if there is reason to believe that such assets have been acquired from the proceeds of illegal drug trafficking. The implications are clear in this case. Nevertheless, I'll allow you a hearing on seizure before such seizure is executed. But that's all I can do. Your other motions are denied. If you want to re-present the motions with some evidence attached, I'll reconsider."

Karen sat in the chair, shocked as never before. This wasn't the way things worked, especially at the federal level. Something was terribly wrong.

"Your Honor, with respect to the reduction on bail request, we're entitled to a hearing if you, as you say, are leaning toward revoking the existing bond. I would—"

"Don't lecture me on the law, Ms. Perry-Mondori! I've considerable experience, much more than yourself, and while you may be impressed with the media coverage you receive with nauseating regularity, I'm not. You'll be advised in due course should I decide to reconsider the issue of bail."

It was pointless for Karen to utter another word. This judge was spoiling for a fight, just like Wilbur.

"Very well, your Honor," Karen said. She stood

up, nodded to Wilbur, and left the judge's chambers.

As soon as she was in her car, she called Bill Castor on her cellular phone.

"What's up?" he asked.

"We need to meet."

"When?"

"ASAP."

"Okay. Where?"

"You name it."

"Okay. Chili's. The one near your office. In half an hour. Funny, I was just about to call you."

"What about?"

"I'll tell you when I see you."

"His name is Williams," Karen said glumly. "Judge Douglas Williams. He's been around for years. Never been tainted, no scandals, a real stand-up guy. But something really stinks here."

Bill Castor sipped his coffee, then put the mug down on the table. "Interesting, isn't it? I mean, the bust was hinky in the first place and now you're getting pushed around by the judge. What do you think's going on?"

Karen looked out the tinted window, watched the heavy traffic flashing by. "I don't know. That's why I called you."

"You want me to investigate a judge? You're asking for trouble, Karen."

"I know. I'm counting on you to be your discreet best. If word ever gets out . . . this just isn't done. But I have this terrible feeling in my gut."

Castor sighed. "Okay. But we'll have to do this one off the books."

"No."

"No? Absolutely yes. Unless you want to get someone else. I'm not about to investigate a judge and leave a paper trail pointing back to you. Screw that. It's either off the books or nothing. No compromise, Karen. I'll find a way to make it up."

"I don't . . ."

"Enough."

"Okay," Karen said. "You have something for me?"

"As a matter of fact, I do. First, I've got a man working in Miami. Good man. He's doing some background work on the Ramirez-FBI connection."

Good."

Suddenly Bill Castor laughed.

"What is it?" Karen asked.

It took him some time before he could speak. "Somebody wrote that life is filled with incongruities. Here we have a very straight criminal defense lawyer and an ex-cop cum private investigator busting their butts trying to save the hide of a known Mafia goon. Doesn't that seem a little nuts?"

"More than a little."

"Why the hell are we doing this, Karen?"

She thought about giving her standard speech about preserving the criminal justice system. Instead, she simply shrugged. "I haven't a clue," she said.

He grinned. "I don't think I've ever seen you this steamed."

"It's not funny."

"Sorry. I note you haven't asked me about the polygraph tests."

"You've set them up?"

"Better than that. I've done them. Last night at Uccello's place, the Dunedin Museum of Fine Art. Christ! Some place! Poor old Lester was shakin' the whole time. He's not used to doing tests in the lion's den."

Karen was all ears. "How'd the tests come out?"

"To both Lester's and my complete astonishment, all three people passed with flying colors."

Karen leaned back and took a deep breath. "How good is Lester?"

"The best. He's been through all the usual test-beating scams. He used to be a registered nurse. Now, he makes the customers take a blood test before he gives them the test. That way, he can tell if they took beta-blockers or other drugs."

"And Uccello went for this?"

"Without a murmur. Lester got the blood test results back this morning. That's what I was going to call you about. Unless these three guys have some gimmick Lester doesn't know about, they were telling the truth."

"I'll be damned," Karen said.

"Looks like you've got an innocent client," Bill teased. "How refreshing."

"You don't realize how right you are," Karen said.

"But you haven't heard the best part," he said, grinning.

"There's more?"

"Yeah. It's about garbage."

"Garbage?"

"Uh-huh. It's no big secret that the FBI likes to sort through the garbage of people they're investigating. I kept wondering how the FBI would find your client's fingerprints on the bags of dope if he'd never touched them. So, this morning, I did some sleuthing. Hey, I'm a detective, right?"

"Stop teasing!"

"Okay. The City of Dunedin picks up garbage on Edgewater Drive on Monday and Thursday, usually before eight in the morning. I tracked down the crew with very little trouble. They say nothing was amiss in front of Angelo's house on the twenty-first, a regular pickup day."

"They're sure?"

"Positive. Angelo usually has at least ten cans out there on pickup day. There were twelve on the twenty-first."

Karen looked confused. "But you said . . ."

"I know. A good detective never accepts the obvious. I surveyed the people across the street. Uccello's garbage shed is visible from three houses. I was just hoping to get lucky. You know, old people don't sleep all that well, and the neighborhood is heavy with old people."

"And I'm growing old waiting for the bottom line," Karen said.

"Okay, okay. We got lucky. An old woman by

the name of Carlotta Bensonhurst woke up from a nightmare, sat at the window smoking a forbidden cigarette, and watched as an unmarked truck picked up Uccello's garbage at four-ten. Except they never picked it up. They *exchanged* it. She thought she was seeing things. She didn't tell anyone, and when I asked her about garbage she went white. I thought she was goin' to stroke out on me."

"She saw someone exchange Uccello's garbage?"

"Right. She doesn't know who Uccello is. Never even seen him. But she knows he lives in the house across the street."

"Will she testify?"

"She said she would. But she's confused and scared. I told her we'd keep her name out of it until and unless we absolutely had to. I gave her your name and said to call you if she got concerned. I also told her not to speak to anyone else about this."

Karen leaned back and sighed. "My God. The creep might just be telling the truth after all."

"Could be," Bill said. "You need to talk to your client. See if he ever throws anything out on a regular basis. Plastic bags of some sort would be my first guess. You know, the kind people use to store stuff in the freezer. I can't imagine him handling the cooking, but . . ."

"He's Italian," Karen said quickly.

Bill brightened. "Oh, yeah. He is, isn't he?"

"And you . . ."

"Yes?"

". . . are a genius!"

"How many people live here?" Karen asked, after rushing back to Angelo's house.

He looked puzzled. "Why do you want to know?"

"I have a theory I'm trying to check out."

"What theory?"

He was suspicious. Karen tried another tack. "Who does the cooking?"

Now he was getting upset. "What the hell kind of questions are these?"

"You said you were set up. I'm trying to figure out how it was done. I may have an answer."

He was immediately interested. "Tell me."

Karen shook her head. "Answer my questions first."

"Jesus. How many people live here? Full-time?"

"Yes."

"Fourteen. Counting me. As for the cooking, we have a cook. Everybody eats here. We never leave this place except to go to one of my business offices."

"Let's check out the kitchen."

"The kitchen? What's in the kitchen?"

Karen frowned. "Are you interested in cooperating or not?"

"Jesus! All right!"

Reluctantly, he led her to the kitchen, a room that would have done a medium-size restaurant proud. Gleaming stainless steel covered most of the walls. The counters were real butcher block, not plastic veneer. The kitchen was equipped with everything from a full-sized pizza oven to a closet-sized meat locker. A small Filipino dressed in whites and wearing a tall white chef's hat stared at Karen in total puzzlement. Strangers were never allowed in the kitchen.

"Best Filipino-Italian cook in central Florida," Angelo explained. "Say hello to Paz."

Karen did. "Hello, Paz."

"This is my new lawyer," Angelo explained to Paz.

Paz smiled as if ordered. "Good to meet with you."

"So what are we doing here?" Angelo asked.

"Do you ever cook?"

"Sure. I like to cook. It's a hobby of mine."

"How often do you cook?"

"Jesus. Who cares?"

"Humor me."

"Maybe once a week. Paz is good with everythin' but straight pasta. He'll never learn how to make pasta."

"You make your own pasta?"

"What else? You can't get good pasta nowhere outside of New York or Miami."

"Do you make it by hand?"

"No. I got a machine. A big one. Kneads the dough and cuts it to size. I make a batch, size it, then freeze it."

"Show me."

He went to a large stand-up freezer and pulled

out several freezer bags packed with pasta cut to various thicknesses. "Once I'm ready to cook, I thaw out a couple of bags and cook. I also make a hell of a red clam sauce. Freeze that, too."

"What do you do with the empty bags?"

"What?"

"The bags. What do you do with the empty ones?"

He stared at her for a full five seconds. "I don't get you. I throw 'em out. What the hell else am I supposed to do with them?"

"In the garbage, right?"

"In the garbage, yes."

Karen looked at the bag in her hand, about a foot square and three inches thick. "Would two kilos of cocaine fit in one of these bags?"

It hit him like a punch in the stomach. He slapped his forehead. "Jesus Christ! They went through my garbage! Can you prove it?"

"I don't know." Karen hefted the bag. "This bag is a little big for two kilos, which might make the point. Who takes out the garbage?"

Angelo looked at Paz. "Let's go back to my office."

They went back to his office. Angelo sat behind his desk and Karen took a seat on one of two high-backed leather chairs that fronted it.

"You mind if I smoke a cigar?"

"It's your house," she said. "But thanks for asking. I don't mind."

He used a small device to clip the tip, then held the cigar away from him, rolling it as he applied

a flame to its end. "Avo Uvezian number three,"
he said. "The best. Better than Cuban. These come
from the Dominican Republic."

"I wouldn't know," Karen said.

"No, you wouldn't." He put the cigar to his
lips, drew heartily, then exhaled the smoke
toward the ceiling. The industrial-strength air-
conditioning system whisked the smoke away
quickly. "You're very, very good."

"Thank you. Who puts out the garbage?"

"Paz puts out the garbage."

"This place is patrolled by security people day
and night, right?"

"Right."

"Your own people or hired help?"

He gave her a look. "You have to be kiddin'.
They're all my people. Most have been with me
for years. Why do you ask?"

"Because you've been in this business a long
time. You must know that one of the favorite FBI
tricks is to go through garbage looking for incriminating evidence."

"Of course I know," he growled. "I know my
phones are tapped, and the place is probably
bugged. I have it swept once a week, but the feds
are gettin' very tricky. I don't worry about what
I say to you because I know they can't use it in
court, but I'm damn careful about what I say to
anyone else. I shred every document, and when I
have to communicate, I use a computer. We got
unbreakable codes. Let them try to figure the message out, the bastards."

"You keep all your records on the computer?"

"All except the books. We do those by hand. But everything else, yes. Like I said, it's all in code. They can't break it. I even keep my diary in there. I got a page for every day of my life since I was sixteen. I spent almost a year puttin' all that shit in the files. Then I burned the old diaries."

"What makes you think the codes are unbreakable?"

He grinned. "Because the codes were designed especially for the feds. Most codes use passwords, see? This one uses a pass phrase instead. You can make up a whole sentence, impossible to break unless the pass phrase is easy. The system was designed by a guy named Zimmerman who put it on the Internet for free. A patriot, this guy. Now the feds are tryin' to bust *his* balls. It would take all the computers in the world hooked up together a thousand years to test all the possible pass phrase combinations I could use."

"So tell me," Karen asked, "if you're such a high-tech guy, how is it that a truck exchanged twelve cans full of garbage from in front of your place and your security people never noticed?"

"Is that what happened?"

"Perhaps. If it did, why wouldn't you notice?"

He thought a moment. "Because the garbage goes to a shed by the curb. We don't pay much attention to what goes on outside the front fence. If we did, we'd go crazy. The cops would be marchin' back and forth out there all day long just to drive us nuts.

"We got a real high-tech alarm system that triggers if anything penetrates the perimeter, and that's what we worry about. My people spend most of their time watching what goes on in the gulf. If we're gonna be attacked, that's where it'll come from, not the street."

"Okay."

He scowled. "You trying to say I got problems with my people?"

"I'm just asking questions. The more I know, the better I can defend you."

"So, the bastards stole my garbage, found some empty pasta bags with my prints on 'em, and filled a couple of the bags with cocaine. Real cute. Can we beat this?"

"We're going to try very hard," Karen said. "And by the way, you and your two associates passed the polygraph exam."

He shrugged. "Was there ever a doubt?"

"Not at all," Karen said.

"But you feel better, right?"

"Yes. I feel better."

8

As Karen headed back to her office, she was filled with mixed emotions. While smarting over Judge Williams's biased treatment, she was pleased that Angelo and his two associates had passed the lie detector tests. She was thrilled that Bill Castor had found an explanation for Angelo's prints being found on the bags of cocaine. The thought of federal agents framing her client enraged her. She felt like a good fight, and feeling confident about a client's innocence helped immensely. Perhaps, she thought, a vigorous and successful defense of Angelo Uccello might make up in some way for the injustice that had visited a desperate, disturbed man named Roger Brimley.

No.

Injustice was injustice. Dead was dead. The past was the past. She had to stop thinking about Roger Brimley.

Damn! She pushed thoughts of Roger Brimley aside and mulled over her options concerning the Uccello case. Being on firm legal ground, she could take the matter before the appellate division and ask for a hearing on the legality of Judge Williams's rulings. But that was risky. Federal judge-ships were lifetime appointments, often with thick political strings attached. If the appellate division found in her favor, she would have won a small skirmish, a minor setback for a judge who would now be a formidable enemy. With the case in its infancy, she was leaving herself open to more subtle—but devastatingly effective—retribution.

On the other hand, if Bill Castor found something that would give reason for the judge's obvious bias, what could she do with that information? Confront the judge? That, too, was dangerous. For unless there was solid evidence, she could be held in contempt, perhaps suspended. Judges had enormous power.

She switched on the car radio. Dead silence. Karen usually listened to the news when she drove; both she and Carl were news junkies. The Beemer was being repaired at a shop less than a mile away, and the shop had provided this wreck of a loaner as part of a working arrangement with the Beemer dealership. Karen decided to take a short detour.

The service manager greeted her with a smile. Karen explained the problem with the radio and asked if another car was available.

The smile vanished, replaced by the all-purpose shrug. "Sorry, Ms. Perry-Mondori. All the rest are out."

"Well, can you check the radio? Maybe it's just a fuse or something."

"Sorry," the manager whined, "but we're really backed up. If you like, you could make an appointment for tomorrow."

Karen, like everyone else in America, had some pet peeves. High on her personal list was the lousy level of service provided by those supposedly in the business of providing such service. "Tomorrow?" she fumed. "How long does it take to check a damn fuse?"

The manager sighed, then strode quickly toward the car, jerked open the door, checked something under the dash, popped the hood, checked something in the engine compartment, then slammed the hood shut. "Fuses are okay," he said curtly. "If you make an appointment for tomorrow, we'll take the radio out. We don't fix them here."

"I'd rather change cars," Karen said. "Can you put me on the list for the next available loaner?"

"Why don't you rent a car from Hertz?" the manager said. "The insurance will cover half of it. You lawyers make lotsa money. What's the big deal?"

"Have you ever been sued?" Karen asked.

The now red-faced manager shook his head in puzzlement.

"Ever been arrested?"

"No. Why do you ask?"

"Because . . . if you ever are," Karen said coldly, "don't waste your time calling me."

Back in her office, Karen huddled with her two associates. "I want these motions completely redone," she said. "This time, attach all relevant evidence and at least ten examples of case law for each motion. I'll give Judge Williams so much to read, his eyes will fall out."

Sharon Chin was aghast. "We messed the first ones up?"

"Not at all," Karen said. "The motions were fine, but we're dealing with a judge who seems to have an ax to grind. He threw them all back at me except for the seizure motion. We now have to present motions that are irrefutable. Even hard-nosed judges detest being forced to answer to the appellate division. We have to impress Judge Williams with the merits of our arguments to the point where he will assume that's our next step. I'm working on some of the evidence. Formal statements. So leave these as first drafts."

"Got it," Sharon said, looking relieved.

"And there's another brief we need to file."

They both looked at her expectantly. She explained the garbage theory and told them what she wanted.

"How soon?" Sharon asked.

"ASAP, as usual. The motions won't mean much without the statements, but get started. And call the judge's clerk right now. Find out when the seizure hearing is scheduled. It should be on his docket by now."

"Okay."

The two associates left. Karen picked up the telephone and placed a call to Carlotta Bensonhurst. When the woman answered the phone,

Karen introduced herself. "Ms. Bensonhurst, would it be possible for us to officially depose you sometime today?"

"Depose?"

"Sorry. It's lawyer talk, Ms. Bensonhurst. You've told Mr. Castor what you saw the other night, but we need to have you make an official statement for the record."

"You mean in court?"

"Not at all. It would be at my office."

"But would I have to testify in court later?"

There was an element of fear in the woman's voice that made Karen wary. "Other than Mr. Castor," she asked, "has anyone contacted you regarding what you saw?"

"No, but I don't want to have to go to court. I know I told Mr. Castor I would, but it scares me."

"Courts sometimes scare me, too, Ms. Bensonhurst. Look, I sincerely doubt you'll have to go to court, but there is that possibility. Would you feel more comfortable if I took the deposition . . . statement . . . in your home?"

"I don't know. I really don't want to get mixed up in this. I saw the news on TV. They say that man is a drug dealer. I had no idea that's what he did. I thought he was some rich retired businessman from up north. I'm not so sure I want to get involved in all this."

Karen took a deep breath. "Ms. Bensonhurst, how long have you lived in that house?"

"Why do you ask?"

"Just curious."

"It'll be thirty years this December."

"And how long has Mr. Uccello lived across the street?"

"He moved in there . . . I think it was two years ago. He tore down the old house that stood there and built a new one. It took about a year to build."

"But he's lived there two years?"

"Yes."

"Has he ever caused a problem for you personally?"

"No."

"Has he been a good neighbor?"

"I'd say so."

"Okay. The fact is, you saw something that relates to a criminal prosecution involving your neighbor. Even if Mr. Uccello was a terrible, terrible man, and I'm not suggesting that he is—what you read and hear in the media isn't always accurate—he's entitled to benefit from the truth, and the truth is, you saw something. If you refuse to speak the truth, we're in trouble, Ms. Bensonhurst. The truth is what protects us all in the end.

"I've seen the TV reports and read the newspapers. They paint a pretty dark picture. But even if every bad thing you've read and heard about Mr. Uccello is true, you'd be less than a good citizen if you kept what you know to be true to yourself. I think you know that. If you weren't a good citizen, you'd never have told Mr. Castor what you saw in the first place. So please, let me come over there and get this down on paper, okay? It won't take long. I promise."

There was a pause. Karen waited patiently. Then she heard a tentative, "All right."

When Karen put down the phone, Liz knocked lightly on the door and stepped inside. "There's a man to see you from the Justice Department."

"Justice?"

"Washington, no less." She handed Karen the man's card. Karen looked at it, shrugged, then said, "Send him in."

Karen stood up as Frank Wallace entered her office. He smiled at Karen, then handed her a folded document. As she unfolded it and started to read, he intoned, "It's a summons, Ms. Perry-Mondori."

"I can see that. For what?"

"The Government is requesting seizure of any and all fees paid to you by Angelo Uccello."

Karen smiled at him sweetly. "You're not from Washington, are you?"

He grinned. "We all have our jobs, Ms. Perry-Mondori."

"This constitutes improper service, Mr. Wallace, or whatever your real name is. Service by Ruse is not warranted here."

"If you have a problem with it," he said calmly, "proceed accordingly. Have a nice day."

He was gone before she could respond.

Carlotta Bensonhurst lived in a large plantation-style house that bore signs of age and neglect. The houses on either side seemed to sparkle in contrast, their clapboard gleaming with fresh paint.

The Bensonhurst house looked tired, its ornate gables sagging, its weathered wood gray, its windows dirty, its veranda groaning as Karen and a court reporter waited at the door.

Ms. Bensonhurst pulled back yellowed white lace curtains, peered out, then unlocked and opened the door.

"Ms. Bensonhurst?" Karen asked.

"Yes."

"I'm Karen Perry-Mondori and this is Helen Douglas. May we come in?"

The old woman held the door open. She seemed frail, perhaps in her eighties, wearing a simple white dress that looked as tired as the house. She took her visitors to a small foyer smelling of must and mildew and offered them tea. The two visitors declined. The room was like an oven, a small oscillating fan on a side table making no impression at all. A larger fan suspended from the ceiling was motionless.

The old woman sat in a chair, folded her hands in her lap, and waited, as if for an onslaught. Karen tried to put her at ease. "Thanks so much for seeing us, Ms. Bensonhurst. Helen is a court reporter. She has a little machine in that case called a stenographer's recorder. I'm going to ask you some very simple questions. Helen will take them down along with your answers. In a couple of days, she'll come back with a written record of our discussion and ask you to sign it. That's all there is to it."

"All right."

As Helen started setting up the machine, Karen said, "You have a lovely home, Ms. Bensonhurst."

The woman frowned. "I may be old but I'm not addled, young lady. There's no need to treat me like a retarded person. This house is falling apart and you know it. The city cited me the other day. Either fix it up or I'd be fined, they said. I don't have the money to fix it so I guess I'll have to sell it." She sighed. "I've been holding off so long."

"I'm sorry to hear that."

Carlotta Bensonhurst's eyes burned with sudden anger. "No, you're not," she snapped. "Why should you? You don't even know me. I don't like being old, but I am, and there's not much I can do about it. But I despise being patronized. I won't stand for it. If you plan on having me answer your questions, treat me with respect, not pity."

Karen groaned inwardly. They were not starting well. At least the woman had all her faculties. That was a plus. "So noted," she said. "And I do apologize."

Helen seemed ready. Karen threw her a glance and received an affirming nod. Choosing her words carefully, Karen covered the essentials, then asked, "Do you live here alone?"

"Yes. Have done ever since Charles died in '76, God rest his soul. I have a son in Milwaukee I never see and that's the extent of my family. I guess I might as well get out of this place and move to a condo or something. I do all the housework myself, always have."

She stood up, walked to a side table, pulled a

cigarette from a pack, and lit up. "Charles never liked me to smoke. They say it's bad for you. Hasn't bothered me."

One of the lucky ones, Karen thought. "Regarding the morning of August 21, can you tell me what happened?"

"You mean about the garbage?"

"Yes."

"Well, I don't sleep all that good. Never have since Charles passed over. That night I had this terrible nightmare. Frightened me half to death. I sat up in bed, then went to the window for a breath of air. My house has no air-conditioning as you can tell. It's just too expensive. They wanted ten thousand dollars fifteen years ago when I last checked. I have fans all over the place but half of them are burned out. Can't afford to fix them."

"So, you were at the window?"

"Yes. Charles never allowed me to smoke in bed. He always said that if I wanted to smoke I had to do it by an open window. I guess he was afraid I'd fall asleep and burn us both to death. In some ways, I wish I had. Least I'd be with him now. But I still smoke at the window in case Charles is looking down at me. I wouldn't want to make him angry."

"And what did you see?"

"I was halfway through my cigarette when I saw this truck stop in front of the Uccello place. It wasn't like the regular trucks. It was big enough but it didn't have that thing on the back, you know? The scoop thing."

"Can you describe the truck in detail?"

"How do you mean?"

"You said it was big."

"Well, it was. It was the same size as a regular garbage truck but without the scoop thing. That's what I just said, isn't it?"

"Did it have doors at the back?"

"Yes."

"Do you have some idea of color?"

"It was night. The truck was some dark color, I guess."

"Okay. And what happened when the truck stopped?"

"Well, a man got out of the passenger's side and opened the doors at the back. Then he and the driver did the strangest thing."

"What was that?"

"Well, we're all supposed to put our garbage in plastic bags and then we put the plastic bags inside these big plastic garbage cans. Not just any garbage cans, mind you. The city tells us what kind of cans we have to use. You'd think we lived in Russia."

Karen tried to bring the woman back on track. "So there were two men?"

"Yes. Usually, the drivers throw what's in the garbage cans into the scoop and then put the cans back. But these men . . . they . . . loaded . . . Mr. Uccello's garbage cans onto the truck. And then . . . the strangest thing . . . they took them off the truck and put them back. But the cans were still full."

"How could you tell?"

"Well, by the way they were handling the pails. You know how a person looks different when he lugs something light versus something heavy."

"Okay. Anything else?"

"No. As soon as they put all the garbage cans back, they climbed into the truck and drove off. I thought I was still dreaming."

"Did you see what the men were wearing?"

"They were wearing coveralls. Just like the regular men."

"Were there any insignia on the overalls?"

The woman thought for a moment. "No. I should have noticed that. The regular people have City of Dunedin written on the back. These men didn't."

"And can you tell me what time this took place?"

"It was four-ten in the morning. I remember because I looked at the clock by the bed when I woke up. I didn't know whether to go back to sleep or not. I get up at six. Always have."

"How many garbage cans did you see?"

"Oh, maybe ten, twelve. I didn't count them." She stubbed her cigarette out in a small glass ashtray and placed her hands in her lap again.

"Ms. Bensonhurst, can you . . ."

"I'm not really fond of this Mizz stuff. I've been Mrs. Charles Bensonhurst since 1942. Charles married me just before he went off to war. Would it be too much trouble to call me by my real name?"

"Not at all, Mrs. Bensonhurst. And again, I apologize."

"I notice you use a hyphenated name. I guess that's to show everybody you're a modern woman. I don't mean to stick my nose into your business, but allow an old woman to give you a piece of advice, young lady."

"Okay."

"Until you're ready to accept your husband's name, you're not ready to be a real wife. And that's all I've got to say on the matter."

Karen smiled. The woman was full of spirit. With so many of her contemporaries suffering countless ailments or locked away in nursing homes just waiting to die, this feisty woman was an inspiration.

"You may well have a point," Karen said, her voice devoid of rancor. "I note you're not wearing glasses."

"No need," the woman said proudly. "I had cataract surgery in Tarpon Springs three years ago. I have twenty/twenty vision in both eyes."

Mrs. Bensonhurst was going to make a terrific witness. "Thank you, Mrs. Bensonhurst. That's all I need. Helen will be by in a day or two."

"Very well."

As Helen put away her machine, Karen added, "If anyone from the police, or anyone else for that matter, comes to talk to you, would you let me know?"

"All right. Do you mind if I ask you a question?"

"Go ahead."

"What in God's name has a man's garbage got to do with anything?"

"We live in strange times," Karen answered.

The next stop was the City of Dunedin's waste disposal facility. There, Karen and Helen found the home addresses of the two men who made the regular pickup at the Uccello house. Both were off duty. It took the rest of the afternoon, but they tracked down both men, committed their statements to Helen's little machine, then called it a day.

Karen stopped by her office to answer some telephone calls and check some paperwork with Liz. As Karen and Liz huddled, Sharon Chin rushed into the office, her eyes gleaming with excitement. "We checked with the judge's clerk," she said.

"And?"

"The seizure hearing is set for next Monday at nine. But that isn't the best part."

"Go on."

"Mr. Brooks's office called about an hour ago."

"And?"

"Well, it's a little weird. Liz had me take the call. You don't mind?"

"Not at all. What's going on?"

"Mr. Brooks says he'll arrange for depositions of Special Agent Tasker and Manuel Aznar sometime tomorrow. He says the Tasker depo will take place in Mr. Brooks's office anytime you want. As for Aznar, Mr. Brooks says he'll keep the site a secret until the last possible moment to protect Aznar. He says he'll set up the procedures with you tomorrow during the Tasker depo."

Karen was shocked. "Well, well. I wonder what happened."

"I have no idea," Sharon said.

"They just finished giving us a tough time and now they cave in. That makes no sense."

Liz shrugged. "Maybe it was something you said."

"I doubt that. More likely, someone from Washington is pulling their strings. Hmmm. This might be interesting."

"Well, good luck with the depos," Liz said.

"Thanks, Liz. I better set it up. Call Wilbur for me, will you?"

"Right away."

Brooks was busy, but Karen made arrangements for the Tasker depo with one of his minions, still wondering what had caused such a sudden change of heart. The minion wasn't about to tell her.

Michelle had news of another kind when Karen arrived home, picked up Andrea, and gave her a hug. "Dr. Mondori called," Michelle said. "There's an emergency and he'll be late."

"Did he say how long he'd be?"

"He's not sure. There was a very bad accident involving a bus."

Karen, with Andrea still in her arms, went into

the family room and switched on the TV. While she waited for information on the bus accident, she kept the volume low. "And what did *you* do today?"

Andrea's eyes were shining with excitement. "I did it all by myself, Mommy."

"Did what?"

"I turned on the computer and looked for the ency . . . cla cla . . ."

"Clo . . ."

"Clo . . . pedia?"

"Correct. Very good."

"I found the ica . . . ico . . ."

"Icon?"

"Yes. Icon. I put in the CD, then clicked on the icon and it was right there! I read all about President Washington and then I printed it. Three pages, Mommy! All by myself!"

"That's great," Karen exclaimed. "Where are the pages?"

"In my bedroom."

"Well, go get them. I want to see."

"Okay."

The child scrambled off Karen's lap and hurried upstairs. The modestly priced computer was an early birthday gift. These days, both parents reasoned, it was never too soon to introduce a child to a machine with which she'd be intimately involved for much of her life. Andrea took to it quickly with a child's natural intuitiveness and thirst for knowledge.

Michelle stood at the doorway, an odd expression on her face. "Should I wait dinner?"

"What did Carl say?"

"He said to go on without him."

"Then I guess that's what we better do."

Michelle nodded and started to turn away.

"You okay?" Karen asked.

Michelle's chin was almost resting on her chest. "It's nothing."

It wasn't nothing. And the bus accident was a horror. Struck by a large truck, the driver of which was now suspected of having fallen asleep, the bus had crashed through a highway guardrail and tumbled down an embankment into swampy wasteland. At least ten people died at the scene; fifteen others had been rushed to local hospitals.

Carl would be very late.

During dinner, Michelle gamely tried to make conversation, but Karen could see she was deeply troubled. And when Andrea went back to the computer, Karen stepped into the kitchen and sat at the table, her hands nursing a cup of coffee.

"What's the problem, Michelle?"

No answer.

"Please. Come and sit with me. Talk to me. Maybe I can help."

Michelle took a deep breath, then sat.

Karen lowered her head and tried to peer into downcast eyes. "So?"

"It's just . . ."

Karen patted Michelle's hand. "About going back home next week?"

Michelle nodded. "This is the second summer I've spent with you and Dr. Mondori. It's been wonderful. I've learned so much."

"Yes you have. Your English is outstanding and your cooking is three times better than it used to be."

Michelle smiled. "I was pretty bad, yes?"

"No longer. And we'll miss you very, very much, Michelle. We think of you as part of the family. Your family must be looking forward to getting you back."

The smile faded from Michelle's face. "That's the problem."

Karen waited while the young woman collected her thoughts. "My mother and father have separated. My father has moved in with his mistress. At his age! It's so stupid!"

Michelle was devastated. Karen wanted to hold her close and tell her everything would be all right, but it wasn't the right time . . . or the right message.

"Oh, my," Karen said. "I'm so sorry."

Michelle wrung her hands. "I received a letter from my mother this morning. I phoned. Mother was crying. She said there's no money for my college. When I go home I have to work. And . . ."

She could speak of it no more. She burst into tears.

Karen moved beside her, put her arm around Michelle, and let her cry. After a few minutes of sobbing, the young woman gained control of her emotions and wiped her eyes with a tissue. "I'm sorry."

"No need. I understand how you feel."

"I was wondering . . ."

"Yes?"

"Would it be possible for me to stay with you? I'd work hard. I'd save all my money until I had enough to go to college."

"Have you talked to your mother about this?"

Michelle nodded. "It was her idea."

"Really. Well, I'm not up on the immigration laws, but we have an expert at the office. Let me talk to him. And Carl as well. But, if it makes you feel better, we'd be thrilled to have you stay with us, provided we can do it legally and both your parents approve."

Michelle lit up like a neon sign. "You mean it?"

"Absolutely. But don't get too excited. There's much to consider. I haven't talked to Carl. And you need to think this through. While I do some checking, you do some heavy thinking. If you feel the same way next week, we'll see what we can do. Okay?"

"Okay. *Merci*, Karen."

"Don't thank me yet."

An exhausted Carl arrived home just past eleven. Karen fixed him something to eat and brewed some fresh decaf.

"You heard?"

"The bus?"

"Yes. I worked on a broken neck and two severe head injuries. The hospital was a zoo."

"How'd it go?"

"Too soon to tell. I'll grab a few hours sleep and get back there in the morning. I see you've hit the headlines again."

Karen hadn't watched the late news. "Oh?"

Carl grinned. "You sound surprised."

"I'm not really. I'm just not sure which event made the news."

"It was that kind of day?"

"Afraid so."

"It was a report about the Justice Department moving to seize your fee. What else happened?"

"Nothing serious. As for the fee seizure, don't worry about it. The Justice Department has been hassling defense lawyers who take drug cases for the past three years. It's part of a get-tough policy designed to intimidate defense lawyers who make their living exclusively in drug cases. But the policy now includes almost any lawyer who defends someone accused of drug trafficking."

"Isn't that illegal?"

"Well, it is and it isn't. They have the power to punish lawyers if the lawyers know the money they receive is dirty. I have no quarrel with that. But the feds are using that power indiscriminately, especially in my case. They know well that drug dealers represent less than five percent of my clients. This action is pure harassment."

"But you still have to defend yourself."

"Of course. And I will. In the meantime, the

feds get to make statements to the press designed to make me look bad, hoping I'll drop my client. Lots of lawyers have been harassed to the point of bankruptcy, especially in Miami. Some have even been indicted."

"Are we at risk here?"

"If I really thought so, I'd drop the case."

"Sometimes I wonder."

Karen gave him a look. "Carl, in the Angelo Uccello case, the FBI found drugs worth some seventy or eighty thousand dollars. They're moving to seize a business worth three to four million. And my retainer is almost three times the value of the drugs found. That's called overkill. It'll never hold up in court and they know it, but the whole idea is to scare me off, to scare other lawyers off as well. It's one of the reasons Angelo Uccello came to me. He couldn't get anyone in Miami to defend him. He admitted as much the first time we talked. And he told me they'd come after the fee."

"So, you're not worried?"

"No."

"Well, that's good. Thanks for the sandwich."

She kissed him on the forehead. "You're welcome. By the way, Andrea found her way into the computer encyclopedia all by herself today."

"She did?"

"Yup. She's becoming a real pro."

"Great."

"And there's another piece of news we need to talk about. But it can wait. You need some sleep."

Carl gave her a look. "Good news or bad?"

"From a selfish standpoint, I'd say pretty good."

"And you want me to wait until tomorrow? Forget it. What's the news?"

"Michelle's parents have separated. She'd like to live with us full-time."

"I thought she was entering college."

"She talked to her mother today. Father has left the house to live with his mistress. There's no money for college."

"Geze. What a blow for Michelle."

"Agreed. I have no idea what the immigration laws are, but I could check. How do you feel about it?"

Carl thought for a moment. "Her idea is to work for us to earn the money to go to college here in the States?"

"Exactly."

"It'll take her ten years!"

"Exactly."

"So, you were thinking . . . ?"

"I wasn't thinking anything."

"Sure you were. You have that look. What, guardianship?"

"I don't know."

"But you want her to go to college this year, right?"

"It's that obvious?"

"You're only deceptive when you're being a lawyer. Could she get in?"

"I don't know."

"Does she qualify for student loans?"

"I don't know."

"You're just a fountain of information, aren't you?"

Karen laughed. "She just told me tonight."

Carl finished off the decaf. "Well, whatever you want to do is okay with me. We've been lucky, Karen. Real lucky. Maybe this is a way to pass it on."

"I like the way you think, love."

9

The deposition of FBI Special Agent Bruce Tasker took place in attorney Wilbur Brooks's office. Tasker was a man of average build and unremarkable features. He was represented by a lawyer from the Justice Department named Frank Smith. A court reporter and a video camera operator also attended the deposition. Brooks's mundane office seemed even smaller with such a crowd.

Karen noted the time, place, attendees, and purpose of the deposition, then got down to business. She asked Tasker to state his name, age, how long he'd been with the FBI, what his previous and present duties entailed, the name of his immediate superior, and some other foundational questions. Then she asked, "Mr. Tasker, would you explain the sequence of events that led to the arrest of Angelo Uccello."

Tasker took a deep breath, exhaled, then said, "I received a telephone call from one of my regular informants on the afternoon of August 23. My informant told me that two of Mr. Uccello's distributors were in town, that they were waiting for a shipment of cocaine, and that the cocaine was arriving that night. I, along with three other agents, raided a room at a St. Petersburg motel where we found two of Mr. Uccello's employees. We arrested the two and took them to our Tampa offices for further interrogation.

"Later that same evening, during their interrogations, both men agreed to provide information in return for certain considerations. I told them we couldn't guarantee anything, but that we'd tell the U.S. attorney they'd been cooperative. They then told us that they were supposed to pick up the cocaine at one of Mr. Uccello's business offices that night.

"On the basis of that information, we assembled a force of agents, augmented by a representative from the Pinellas County Sheriff's office, obtained a search warrant, and raided one of Mr. Uccello's businesses known as Southern National Vending, Inc. After a search of the premises, we found two bags of white powder, later identified as cocaine. Each bag contained two kilograms of cocaine. On the basis of that evidence, we then obtained a warrant for Mr. Uccello's arrest. We went to his home, where we arrested him."

Karen made some notes and checked the revised FBI report she'd received earlier. "In your official report dated August 24, you state that the informant's telephone call came to your office at three twenty-three. Is that correct?"

"Yes."

"And this informant is known to you?"

"Yes."

"From where did the telephone call originate?"

"I don't know."

"Is the informant a resident of the Tampa Bay area?"

"I don't know."

"If you don't know where he lives, how can you verify that the tip was valid?"

Tasker took a deep breath. "He's been a valuable tipster in the past. I had no reason to doubt his word."

"And what does he receive in return for these tips?"

"He receives money. The money is mailed to a P.O. box in Miami."

"How'd you come by this source?"

"He came to me three years ago. He said he was involved in the drug business and needed money to get straight. I gave it to him. He's been providing valuable information ever since."

Karen was getting nowhere. She decided to move on. "What were the names of the two men you arrested at the motel?"

"You already know."

"For the record."

"Manuel Aznar and Fito Olivera."

"You said in your report they claimed to be employees of Mr. Uccello. What evidence do you have to support that contention?"

"They said that's who they worked for."

"That's it? No checks, no pay slips, no other evidence?"

"We don't need it."

"We'll see. You said you arrested Aznar and Olivera on the basis of this informant's telephone tip. Do you know how long Aznar and Olivera had been staying at that motel?"

"They'd been there about ten days."

"What were they doing?"

"They were waiting to pick up a shipment of cocaine from Angelo Uccello.'

"When you raided the motel room occupied by Aznar and Olivera, did you find any illegal drugs?"

"No."

"Then, on what grounds did you place them under arrest?"

"On the grounds that they had entered the country illegally. We checked them out. They're both illegal aliens."

"I see. Have you made an effort to have them deported?"

"No."

"Why not?"

"Because they are witnesses to a felony."

"What felony?"

"Drug trafficking."

"By whom?"

"By Angelo Uccello."

"But you said there were no drugs found in the motel."

"That's right."

"And there wasn't time for these two to get the

drugs from Mr. Uccello. So just what is it they witnessed?''

Tasker seemed taken aback by the question. ''Well, they were in contact with Uccello. The deal was set. Then, Uccello changed the time of delivery. He was supposed to deliver the drugs before we raided the motel. He crossed us up.''

''So, in fact, you have no evidence that an actual sale was going to be made.''

''Sure we do. The drugs were still in Uccello's safe.''

''But other than the statements made to you by Aznar and Olivera, there's no evidence that Mr. Uccello was ever involved with these two men, correct?''

''We'll have the phone records of the conversations with Uccello soon enough.''

''But you don't have them as yet. Did you tape record the conversations between your two witnesses and Mr. Uccello?''

''No.''

''Why not?''

''We forgot to bring the equipment with us. There wasn't time to get it before we busted Uccello. We had to move fast. We were afraid he was going to dump the dope.''

Karen took a deep breath, then changed course again. ''Where do Aznar and Olivera live?''

Tasker pulled a small notebook from his pocket and leafed through the pages. ''Both men live in Miami. Aznar's address is 3246 River Drive. Mr.

Olivera lives at 345 North Grand. Both addresses are apartments."

"And when you determined that these two men were illegally in this country, did you determine their nationality?"

"Yes."

"What is it?"

"Colombian."

"Have you determined how long each man has been in this country illegally?"

"Yes. Olivera has been here since 1992. Aznar came here last year. March, I think."

"And when did they supposedly start working for Mr. Uccello?"

"A month ago."

"How did they meet Mr. Uccello?"

"They never met him directly. They were hired by one of Uccello's Miami people, a man named Ernesto Hernando."

Karen stiffened. "That's not on your official report, Mr. Tasker."

He shrugged. "Sorry. Just an oversight. I was in a bit of a rush."

"Where can we find Mr. Hernando?"

"You can't. Mr. Hernando was murdered three weeks ago. Metro-Dade is investigating his death."

Karen shook her head, but said nothing about that little bit of information. "Prior to their claim of being in the employ of Mr. Uccello, for whom did Olivera and Aznar work?"

"They both worked for Juan Ramirez, a known Miami drug trafficker."

"If he's a known drug trafficker, why isn't he in jail?"

"He will be soon enough."

"You didn't answer my question. Why isn't he in jail now?"

Tasker bristled. "Because we haven't nailed him yet, all right?"

"During your interrogation of these two men, Aznar and Olivera, an interrogation during which they freely revealed details of their relationship with Mr. Uccello, did they reveal details regarding their association with Juan Ramirez?"

"No. They refused to discuss it other than to say they worked for him."

"And that's okay with you?"

"Juan Ramirez is not my problem. He's outside my territory. Angelo Uccello is my concern. I've already turned Aznar and Olivera over to our Miami people. I'm sure they'll be trying to learn as much as they can about Ramirez's operation."

"So, both witnesses are now in Miami?"

"I'm not sure where they are. As you well know, Mr. Brooks is making Aznar available to you later today. He could be anywhere. But, officially, both men are in the hands of the Miami office of the FBI. That's all I know."

"But you do have personal knowledge that Mr. Aznar is somewhere in the vicinity of the city of Tampa preparatory to giving a deposition to me?"

"Yes."

"You mentioned some special considerations earlier. Did the special considerations include a staying of deportation proceedings?'

"Yes.'

"And it is your testimony that the reason you turned Aznar and Olivera over to the Miami FBI office is to assist the Miami FBI office to investigate Juan Ramirez, correct?"

"Correct."

"Are you aware of a so-called plan to assassinate Aznar and Olivera?"

"I've heard rumors, that's all."

"From whom did you hear these rumors?"

Tasker's face flushed slightly. "That's confidential."

"Confidential?"

"Yes. All I know is it's possible Aznar and Olivera are in danger. I have an obligation as a law enforcement officer to protect their lives."

"So, you're investigating these rumors?"

"No. That's someone else's responsibility."

"Are Olivera and Aznar in the custody of the Miami office of the FBI to be protected or to assist in the investigation of Juan Ramirez?"

"Both."

"Did you attend a meeting in this very office at which time I discussed the circumstances surrounding Mr. Uccello's arrest with Assistant State Attorney Wilbur Brooks?"

"Yes."

"Do you recall Mr. Brooks mentioning that Aznar and Olivera were in danger?"

"I don't recall any such comment."

Karen glared at the agent. "You're under oath, Mr. Tasker."

"I'm fully aware of that. I do not recall any such statement coming from Mr. Brooks."

Karen sighed. It wasn't the first time a law enforcement officer had lied under oath. Nor would it be the last. "Mr. Tasker, you stated you've been a member of the unified drug enforcement task force for eight years."

"Correct."

"You stated that Aznar and Olivera were in St. Petersburg on August 23 awaiting a shipment of cocaine."

"Correct."

"Did they tell you what they were going to do with the cocaine?"

"Yes. They said they were going to take it back to Miami and distribute it."

"But when you raided Mr. Uccello's business office, you found a total of four kilos of coke, correct?"

"Correct."

"Doesn't it strike you as odd that two men would wait so long for so small a shipment?"

"Not at all."

"How many times have you been involved in raids where quantities of cocaine were recovered?"

"I don't really know."

"Would it be more than a hundred times?"

"Easily."

"Two hundred?"

"Perhaps. Probably close to that."

"What's the largest quantity of cocaine ever recovered in one of these raids?"

Tasker thought for a moment, then said, "I guess it would be the one five years ago. We recovered sixteen tons of the stuff."

"Sixteen tons?"

"Correct."

"What is the estimated street value of that recovery?"

"About three hundred million dollars."

"And what would be the smallest quantity you've ever recovered?"

Tasker smiled. "The Uccello raid."

"Four kilos?"

"Correct. About nine pounds."

"A single bag?"

"No. It was in two bags."

"And the street value?"

"About eighty thousand dollars. Roughly. The price keeps changing depending on the level of competition."

"Pretty small quantity, wouldn't you say?"

"Well, it's our smallest recovered so far, yes."

"How many times have you raided businesses owned and operated by Angelo Uccello?"

"I'd have to think about that."

"Just a rough idea is enough for now."

"Maybe five times."

"Did you ever recover drugs?"

"No."

"Were all of these raids carried out as a result of informant tips?"

"Yes. Ninety percent of all law enforcement arrests are a direct result of informant tips."

"And yet in every previous raid on Mr. Uccello, the tip turned out to be false."

"We don't know that the tip was false."

"If the tips were accurate, how is it that you didn't find what you were looking for?"

"Well, it could be a lot of things. Uccello may have known about the tip, or . . ."

"Or what?"

"Well . . . he's pretty careful. He doesn't always give the correct information to . . ."

"Go on, Mr. Tasker."

Tasker, his face flushed, shook his head. "I don't really know why we didn't find the drugs."

"You were about to say that Mr. Uccello doesn't always give the correct information to his people, isn't that true?"

"No."

"What were you going to say?"

Tasker's lawyer spoke for the first time. "I'm going to object to that. He's already stated he doesn't know."

Karen shot the lawyer a glare, then tapped her pencil on the legal pad sitting in front of her. "Mr. Tasker, doesn't it seem odd to you that a man of Mr. Uccello's experience and guile would be so open with two men who were new to his organization, in that he told them exactly when and where the drugs could be found in his office?"

"I can't say."

"But you are an experienced law enforcement officer specializing in illegal drug trafficking. Have you ever had an experience like this one?"

"Each case is different."

"Isn't it true that your ongoing investigation of Mr. Uccello has provided insights into the way he does business?"

"Yes."

"And it's true, is it not, that this is the first time you've found drugs in any of Mr. Uccello's business offices?"

"That's true."

"And these drugs were worth eighty thousand dollars."

"Yes."

"And two men waited around St. Pete for almost two weeks waiting for this shipment."

"Yes."

"For a shipment valued at eighty thousand dollars."

"I've already answered that question."

"Two men who had previously worked for Juan Ramirez, two men who claim to be in the employ of Mr. Uccello but can't prove it, two men who live in Miami, two men who might have good reason to frame Mr. Uccello."

"We found the drugs in Mr. Uccello's safe, Counselor. The drugs didn't get there by themselves."

"Do you have personal knowledge as to how they *did* they get there?"

"Mr. Uccello placed them there."

"How do you know that?"

"Because his fingerprints were on the bags."

"Did you see Mr. Uccello or anyone else put the bags of cocaine in the safe?"

"No."

"Have you taken a statement under oath from anyone claiming to have seen Mr. Uccello place the cocaine in his safe?"

"Not that I'm aware."

"How long did it take you to open the safe?"

"Ten minutes."

"Who actually opened it?"

"An FBI locksmith."

"Who was in the room when the safe was actually opened?"

"I'm not sure."

"Why not?"

"I just don't remember."

"Would it refresh your memory to see your initial report?"

"Yes."

Karen showed him a copy of the report. "Does that refresh your memory?"

"Yes."

"So, who was in the room when the safe was being opened?"

Tasker was getting frustrated. "I was there, and Detective Chalmers . . . Robert Chalmers . . . from the Pinellas County Sheriff's Office, and Special Agent Ronald Trencher, and the safe man, Agent Jack Carroll."

"And where were the other FBI agents?"

"Outside, making sure the security guards were all accounted for."

"Why was Detective Chalmers on the raid?"

"Because we try to involve local law enforcement officials in our raids."

"But Southern National Vending's office is in Clearwater. Isn't that the Clearwater Police Department's jurisdiction rather than the Pinellas County Sheriff's Office?"

"Technically, yes, but Clearwater agreed to let us handle it this way."

"They were advised?"

"Yes."

"That isn't on your report either, Agent Tasker."

"Another oversight."

"Given your experience, could any competent locksmith open that safe in ten minutes?"

"I guess they could."

"So it wasn't a safe designed for maximum security?"

"I don't know what it was designed for."

"To the best of your knowledge, did either Mr. Olivera or Mr. Aznar contact Angelo Uccello directly while they were staying at the St. Petersburg motel?"

"Yes."

"How?"

"By telephone."

"But you don't yet have telephone records to confirm such conversations took place, isn't that what you just said?"

"Not yet. We'll have them soon enough."

"Were the calls made from the motel?"

"No. The calls were made from a pay telephone."

"Where?"

"Near the motel. We've requested records from all of the pay telephones in the area."

"Why didn't Olivera and Aznar use the motel phones?"

"They didn't want records available."

"They were unaware that pay telephone records are just as available?"

"They thought that pay phones were inviolate."

"Really."

"That's what they said in their statements."

"I see. Where exactly were Mr. Uccello's security guards while the safe was being opened?"

"I told you. They were in another part of the building."

Karen made a note. "They were inside, not outside?"

"Some may have been outside. I wasn't paying attention."

"How many FBI agents attended the raid on the vending machine business?"

"Twelve, I think. Yes. It was twelve. Plus the detective from Pinellas."

"Who was in charge?"

"I was."

"So, while some agents were in the office opening the safe, where were the other agents?"

He was getting angrier. "I told you that. Some were guarding Uccello's security people. Others were searching the premises."

"Did you find illegal drugs other than those found in the safe?"

"No."

"Once you had the drugs, what did you do?"

"We called a judge and obtained a telephone warrant for the arrest of Angelo Uccello. We then went to Mr. Uccello's home and arrested him."

"All of you?"

"No. Some of the agents stayed behind to make sure none of Uccello's people warned him."

"And when you arrived at Mr. Uccello's home, what did you do?"

"We told the guard at the gate we had a warrant for Mr. Uccello's arrest. The guard opened the gate. We then proceeded to the house and told another guard about the warrant. About that time, Mr. Uccello appeared in the garage and surrendered."

Karen made a note. "So, as soon as you identified yourselves as FBI agents and announced you had a warrant for Mr. Uccello's arrest, it was a simple operation. You met no resistance."

"None."

"Mr. Tasker, though it's inadmissible in court, would you be willing to take a polygraph examination?"

Smith held up his hand. "Don't answer that."

Karen smiled. "I didn't think so."

Smith scowled. "I resent the implication, Counselor."

"There's no implication, Mr. Smith. Mr. Tasker is a liar, plain and simple."

Smith leaped to his feet. "This deposition is over!"

"You bet it is," Karen said, glaring at Tasker. "We'll see you in court, Mr. Tasker."

Tasker simply smiled.

Karen was standing at the elevator door when Wilbur Brooks came up beside her, a stupid smile on his face.

"What is it?" she snapped.

"You do know how to piss people off."

"He lied."

"Bullshit. You want to talk to Aznar?"

"Of course. You were going to let me know, wasn't that the deal?"

"It was. He's at your office as we speak, waiting for you. I figured your client would refrain from blowing away half your people to get at Aznar, so if you tip Uccello off now, it won't do you much good. Of course, he might try and take Aznar out when he leaves your office, but I doubt it. In any case, you can tell him for me we've got thirty people hoping he'll give it a try."

Karen wanted to slap his arrogant face. Instead, she simply stared at him. "I always considered you as slightly Neanderthal," she said softly. "But it's more than that, isn't it?"

"Fuck you," he said, sotto voce, as he walked away.

*   *   *

Manuel Aznar was a slight man of thirty-one, dark-complected, with dark, brooding eyes. He spoke no English, so the deposition required the services of an interpreter. Because of the mutual distrust that had grown like wildflowers in an untended field, Karen was unprepared to accept any translation offered by the prosecution's interpreter, so she provided her own. That meant that a total of nine people crowded into Hewitt, Sinclair's small conference room: Aznar, of course, his Miami-based attorney Ruben Estavez, a representative from Wilbur Brooks's office, Aznar's interpreter, a court reporter, a TV camera operator, Karen, Karen's interpreter, and Sharon Chin.

Outside, the temperature was rising to its midday high of ninety-five as it did almost every day in the summer; dark, roiling clouds could be seen building strength over the gulf, soon to sweep onshore in an explosion of light, sound, wind, and rain.

Karen tripped quickly through the obligatory stipulations, then focused her attention on Aznar. "Mr. Aznar, when did you first meet Angelo Uccello?"

"I've never met him," was the translation.

"Then how can you claim to be one of his employees?"

It was a trick question. Aznar's attorney would have none of it. He objected even before the translation. "That's an improper question, Counselor. Argumentative."

Karen, satisfied that everyone was awake, nodded. "Withdrawn," she said. "Mr. Aznar, what is your occupation?"

After the translation, Aznar answered in Spanish. His interpreter said, "I am an auto mechanic." Karen looked at her own interpreter, who nodded. The same procedure was used for each succeeding question.

"Where do you work?"

"Miami. South Florida Auto Repair."

Karen looked at Aznar's lawyer. "Mr. Estavez, would you please remind your client that we have a copy of the statement he gave to the FBI? We'd like to get past the posturing if we could."

Aznar's attorney whispered in his client's ear. Aznar nodded, then spoke. The translation was, "I sell cocaine for Angelo Uccello."

"How long have you been selling cocaine for Mr. Uccello?"

"About a month."

"How did you come to sell cocaine for Mr. Uccello?"

"I was contacted by a man named Ernesto Hernando in Miami. He asked me if I would like to work for Mr. Uccello. He offered me more money than I was getting, so I said yes."

"Where and when did you meet with Mr. Hernando?"

"It was sometime in late July. I was at work at the auto shop. Mr. Hernando came to see me."

"Had you ever met Mr. Hernando before?"

"No."

"When he started discussing cocaine, how did you know he wasn't a police officer?"

"Because of the way he talked. If he was a cop, he would have been guilty of entrapment."

Karen fought to keep the smirk off her face. It was obvious that Aznar had been carefully coached. This deposition was going to be a complete waste of time. "Really," she said. "Are you a lawyer, Mr. Aznar?"

"I object to the question," Estavez said.

"Withdrawn. How long did Mr. Hernando talk with you?"

"About a half hour."

"And after that half-hour discussion, what did you do?"

"I went to see my boss and quit."

"Just like that?"

"Yes."

"And this took place in late July."

"Yes."

"Who owns the auto shop?"

"Juan Ramirez."

"Is he your boss?"

"Not there. He never comes there. I told Aldo. Aldo runs the auto shop."

"But you also work for Juan Ramirez, correct?"

"I did, yes."

"Selling drugs?"

"Yes."

"How long did you sell drugs for Juan Ramirez?"

"About a year."

"How did you come to sell drugs for Juan Ramirez?"

"I knew him in Bogota a long time ago. When I came to America I looked him up. He put me to work."

"Were you friends?"

"In Colombia?"

"Yes."

"We were friends."

"Were you involved in the drug business in Colombia?"

"Yes."

"For whom did you work?"

"Juan Ramirez."

"So, in fact, you've worked for Juan Ramirez for many years, correct?"

"Correct."

"Isn't it a fact that you've never worked for anyone other than Mr. Ramirez?"

"Just Angelo Uccello."

"But, in actual fact, you've never met Mr. Uccello."

"Correct."

"Nor have you ever sold drugs purchased from Mr. Uccello. Correct?"

"Well, not yet."

"You say you were planning to, but no actual transaction ever took place, did it?"

"No."

"Was it your idea to come to the United States?"

"Yes."

"While you were in Colombia and Mr. Ramirez was in Miami, you were still working for Mr. Ramirez?"

"Yes."

"So you've been working with a man who was a friend for many years, correct?"

"Yes."

"And then Mr. Hernando comes along and talks to you for a half hour and you decide to work for someone you've never met, is that your testimony?"

"Yes."

Karen shook her head in amazement. "When you were in St. Petersburg, you stayed at a motel, correct?"

"Yes."

"With Fito Olivera?"

"Yes."

"And you set up the deal with Mr. Uccello, correct?"

"Yes."

"How did you do that? Did you go to see him?"

"No. We called him on the phone."

"From the motel?"

"No. We used a pay phone."

"Why?"

"We didn't want any records of the calls."

"Where was the pay phone you used located?"

"I don't know, exactly. About three blocks from the motel."

Karen turned her attention to Howard Briscoe, the man from Wilbur Brooks's office. "I'd like to ask for a short recess. Mr. Briscoe, could you and I chat for a moment in my office?"

"Sure."

Karen turned back to the group. "This won't take long, I'll have coffee sent in."

Briscoe was a tall, good-looking man in his early thirties. Karen had never met him before today. She showed him to a seat, then went behind her desk. "Off the record," she said.

"Sure."

"How long have you been with the U.S. attorney's office, Mr. Briscoe?"

"I've been with Justice four years. I came here five months ago."

"So, you've been a government lawyer for four years?"

"Right."

"Have you been paying attention to what's going on in the conference room?"

"Of course."

"What do you make of it?"

"How do you mean?"

"Please, Mr. Briscoe. This room isn't bugged. We're off the record here. What the hell is going on?"

He shrugged. "I have no idea what you're talking about. As far as I can tell, you're asking questions and getting answers. Aznar seems cooperative to me. What's the problem?"

Karen sighed. "Mr. Briscoe, do you know who Juan Ramirez is?"

"Sure. He's a big-time drug trafficker in Miami."

"Okay. We have a man sitting in the conference room who claims to have worked for Juan Ramirez, his friend for many years, and then jumps ship after a half-hour discussion with a man now dead. Surely, this must seem a tad weird to you."

"You can never tell with drug dealers."

"Oh? You really believe that Juan Ramirez is going to sit still while this guy goes to work for the competition?"

"I can't say. I've never met Juan Ramirez."

The anger building within Karen was bubbling just beneath the surface. She fought to keep it there. "This isn't a game, Mr. Briscoe. No jury, even a jury biased against people involved in the drug business, is going to buy this. Jurors aren't stupid people."

Briscoe shrugged. "What do you want from me?"

"A little candor, for one."

Briscoe leaned forward, a silly smile on his face. "I'll give you candor, Ms. Perry-Mondori. You said this isn't a game. You couldn't be more wrong. This *is* a game, and the bad guys are winning. But we've decided to level the playing field. Finish your deposition. Defend your client. Do your thing. We'll worry about how it looks to a jury, if it gets that far."

"What does that mean?"

Briscoe shrugged. "Maybe your client will confess. Maybe he'll drop dead of a heart attack. Who knows what the future holds?"

Karen glared at him for a moment, then stood up. "Have it your way, Mr. Briscoe."

"It's not *my* way, Ms. Perry-Mondori. It's the way things are, and it'll get worse before it gets better, looking at it from your perspective. We're damn well sick of beatin' our heads against the wall. Scum like your client aren't going to be able to hide behind their lawyers much longer. The gloves are off."

Karen just stared at him.

"You want candor, I'll give you candor," Briscoe continued. "These people are going down, all of them, along with those who help them stay out of prison. Whatever it takes, understand? Until now, the war on drugs has been an empty phrase. No longer. Now it's a real war. And we're gonna win it hands down."

"No matter what it takes? Is that what you said?"

"Exactly. This country is being destroyed by the insidious influence of the drug culture. It sucks our children dry of incentive and motivation; it's already trashed our social services, wrecked a million lives, and is about to bring the entire country to its knees. We've got politicians screaming that all this crap should be legal. Why? Because the criminal justice system is hamstrung by constraints imposed by the Constitution, a document created by men who had no idea we would be facing a war where the weapon was drugs.

"There are those who want this country to fail. The Chinese and the fat-cat Arabs are pumping heroin into this country like never before. The dictatorial South American countries, along with Mexico, are laughing in our faces as they watch us snort their nose candy. No bombs, no guns, no missiles. They'll destroy us with powders.

"Well, we're not going to let it happen. We're going to fight back, not sit on our cans and wring our hands while the asshole politicians shoot off their mouths and do nothing. We're going to stop this invasion by whatever means. If you don't like it, tough. If you want to stay healthy, step aside. Try and protect men like Uccello, and you're putting yourself on the front lines, lady. People on the front lines should expect to get hurt."

Karen leaned back in her chair, stunned. "That's quite a speech, Mr. Briscoe. Reminds me of other speeches I've heard from zealots who think the Constitution is simply a piece of paper. Well, it's not. It's a basis for the way we live, and despite the attacks, it'll hold us in good stead."

"We'll see."

Before Karen could respond, Briscoe stood up and strode out of the room.

Karen got up, walked to the door, closed it, then returned to her desk. She breathed deeply until she felt confident her temper was under control.

10

By the time Karen reached Angelo Uccello's house, the storm that had been brewing in the gulf for hours swept ashore with full fury. But this time she was able to stay dry, for one of Uccello's guards opened the garage door and let Karen park her car inside.

Upstairs, Uccello, standing by the window, greeted her with a smile and a wave of the hand holding the ever-present cigar. "Getcha anything?"

"No thanks."

A flash of lightning and a clap of thunder that shook the building made Karen duck involuntarily.

"Pretty close, this one," Uccello said calmly. "It'll pass in a few minutes."

"Thanks for letting me park inside," Karen said, taking a seat by Uccello's desk.

"No problem. How'd it go today with the depositions?"

Karen took a moment to collect her thoughts. "I'd like to say it went well, but the truth is . . ."

". . . what?"

"I'm confused."

"You gonna explain that, or do I gotta figure it out on my own?"

"I almost believed you when you told me you were framed," Karen said, breaking one of her own cardinal rules. "I don't know why I did, but I did. Then, after I learned the results of the polygraph tests, I was convinced you were framed. Now, after talking to the FBI and Aznar, it's so obvious I find it an embarrassment. I feel ashamed."

Angelo stared at her in total astonishment. "Why should *you* feel ashamed?"

"Never mind."

Suddenly he smiled. "I get it. I forgot you were a Girl Scout. Things ain't so simple, eh? Good guys versus bad guys. Used to be an easy call. Now, you're all confused."

"I'm no rookie," Karen retorted. "I've been doing this awhile. That's why you hired me, remember? I'm well aware that bad cops can manufacture evidence. But they usually know what they're doing. This frame is so utterly shameless it boggles my mind. It's as if they conceived the idea in a hurry . . . but then . . . Aznar and Olivera were in town for days before it went down. It just doesn't make sense. Did you ever receive a phone call from either Fito Olivera or Manuel Aznar?"

"Never."

"Ever talk to them in person?"

"Never."

"Did you ever receive a phone call from someone not known to you that . . ."

He waved a hand to stop her. "Listen . . . I
don't talk to nobody I don't know. One of my
people screens all my calls. You know that."

"Well, could either of those two men have
called and talked to your . . . person?"

"No. We get those goddamn phone salesmen
like everybody else. We hang up. We hang up on
anyone we don't know. What are you drivin' at?"

"The feds are claiming Aznar talked to you on
the telephone. There'd have to be phone records
of those calls. Why would they lie so stupidly if
they can't back it up?"

He snorted. "They lied about the cocaine, didn't
they? What's so different about some phone
calls?"

He had a point. "Who was Ernesto Hernando?"

Angelo took a seat behind his desk. The expression on his face soured. "Ernesto was my
negotiator."

"Negotiator?"

"Yeah. There are times when we all have to
make deals with people. Ernesto was real good
at making deals. He could discuss things without
gettin' personal, without gettin' mad. He was the
best. Better'n me."

"He lived here?"

"Yeah."

"What was he doing in Miami?"

"He was trying to make a deal with Ramirez."

"What kind of deal?"

He gave her a look. "You really need to know this stuff?"

"I don't need to know everything, but I have to know everything that relates to this case if I'm to defend you properly. I don't like surprises, Angelo."

Angelo looked away for a moment, puffed his cigar, then stubbed it out. "I can't tell you everything you want to know about this case."

His comment took Karen by surprise. "I'm your attorney. My job is to defend you, and I can't do that unless I have all the facts. I refuse to go into court with half a defense."

He looked almost melancholy as he said, "Then, I think maybe you should drop this thing."

Karen wasn't sure she'd heard him right. "You mean you won't answer my questions regarding Hernando?"

"No. I mean you should get up from that chair, turn around, go back downstairs and get in your car, then go home. You should drop me as a client is what I'm sayin'. I'll find someone else."

Karen felt as if she'd been slapped in the face. "Why?"

He seemed angry. "Because this ain't for you. I'm not sayin' you're not up to it. I know you're good. It ain't that. This just ain't for you, that's all. We got serious problems here, complicated situations. Unless you been in the business for the last ten years, you ain't never gonna figure it all out. And maybe you don't want to know."

"Don't try to read my mind, Angelo."

"You got ideals. Sometimes it's better if you don't know things. Like if your husband is messin' with another woman. Would you want to know about that?"

"Let's keep my husband out of this, okay?"

"I'm just makin' a point. There are times when not knowing beats knowing. This is one of those times, that's all I'm sayin'. You a sports fan?"

"Not really."

"That's what I mean. A sports fan would understand."

"Understand what? You're talking in circles."

"I mean that this is the bigs. The majors. The players are all experienced. They know the game, know the other players, know what to expect. You're from another planet, a place where you can walk around like a human being, where you don't have to have six guys with automatic weapons lookin' over their shoulders every time you leave your house. This ain't your turf. I was wrong to get you involved in the first place."

She stared at him with mixed emotions. Part of her wanted to get up and walk out. Another part of her wanted to see this to the end. Voices echoed in her consciousness. The voice of a man named Briscoe talking about war; the voice of an FBI agent named Tasker laughing when she called him a liar to his face; the voice of Manuel Aznar as he spoke his carefully crafted lines, his face expressionless, the lines uttered from memory.

And faces. They shimmered before her eyes, a

collage of visions; the arrogant Brooks, the equally arrogant Tasker, an angry Judge Williams . . .

"I've never dropped a client unless they lied to me," Karen said. "Not ever."

"Maybe now's a good time to start," he said.

"Then fire me. That's your right. But I won't quit."

"Why not?"

"Because I believe in the system. It's all we have. If we don't protect the system, we're done. I have an eight-year-old daughter. I don't want my legacy to be anarchy."

Angelo's face hardened. "You wanna be around when she's nine?"

"What does that mean?"

"The truth? It means you could be dead in a month—or less—if you keep on with this."

Karen shuddered. "If you're trying to frighten me, you're succeeding."

"I'm trying to tell you how it is, that's all."

"They're going to start killing lawyers? Who? Ramirez?"

"Not Ramirez. The feds."

"That's crazy!"

"You think so? They put lawyers in jail, didn't they? And not all those guys were guilty. You know it and I know it. Killin' them is the next step."

He banged his fist on the desk. "They talk about the war on drugs. Big deal. There's a war on, all right, but it ain't no war on drugs. It's a war to decide who's gonna control the distribution of drugs in this country. It's been comin' down for a long time. Now it's here, and the feds are into it up to their stinkin' eyes. Like I said, this ain't for you. My people don't put our women in the trenches when there's a war goin' on, and I ain't about to start now. I can't make it any clearer, can I?"

"So, you want me to drop you as a client because I'm a woman, is that it?"

"Exactly."

"Tell me what's going on, Angelo. You owe me that much."

"And then?"

"And then I'll decide."

He grimaced. "I tell you, you ain't gonna believe it."

"Maybe I will, maybe I won't. But, aside from failing to tell me at the outset that you've been using your vending machine business in a money laundering scheme, you haven't lied to me yet."

His response was almost a whisper. "No, I haven't."

Karen waited.

Angelo fiddled with a cigar and paced the floor, thinking. Finally, he looked at her and asked, "How much do you know about the illegal drug business?"

"More than you might think," Karen answered. "I know that despite the best efforts of everyone involved in law enforcement both here and abroad, we manage to stop less than five percent of the illegal drugs coming into the country, a figure that has remained constant despite the government's best efforts over the years.

"I know about the Colombian cartels. I know that a lot of people have died during internecine warfare that threatened to destroy Colombia. What else?"

Uccello discarded the cigar in his hand, took a fresh one from a small humidor on his desk, played with it for a moment, then put it back. "Let me tell you about the drug business," he said gravely. "The two biggest drug problems we got in this country are booze and smokes. Both of 'em kill more people every year than all the illegal drugs put together. If you think I'm trying to snow you, check it out yourself."

Karen sighed. "If you're trying to justify what you do, please don't. I'm not interested."

"You want to know about the drug business or don'tcha?"

"I want to know about the cocaine business, yes. I could care less about cigarettes and liquor. They happen to be legal products."

"That's the whole point!" he bellowed. "If you'll get off your high horse for a few minutes, I'll tell you why."

Karen, her cheeks burning, waved a hand. "All right. Talk."

He glared at her. "Don't give me that pissed-off look. You said you wanted to know. Do you or don't you?"

Angelo was manipulating her and she knew it. She found his insight into her character disturbing. "Go on," she said.

He leaned back in the chair, gazed at her for a few moments, then started talking. "Fact is," he began, "the families—all of 'em—got started during Prohibition. You know about Prohibition?"

"Of course."

"Well, until Prohibition, the mobs were really disorganized, fightin' among themselves all the time, nobody really in charge. When Prohibition came along, there was so much easy money to be made, the mobs started to get their act together. It was stupid to be killin' each other when there was enough dough for everybody. So, they got together and started settin' up territories. It worked real good for a long time. A lot of people made a lot of money, including one two-faced son of a bitch named Joe Kennedy."

He stopped and stared at her. "You know who I'm talkin' about?"

"Yes."

He smiled. "You know your history, huh?"

"Some."

"Did you know the mobs got that son of a bitch son of his elected?"

"I've read stories to that effect."

"It's true. Everybody knows. The Chicago mob put him over the top. And then his brother, the double-crossin' . . ."

"Can we get back on point?" Karen interrupted.

He waved his hand again. A true Italian. "All right, all right. When the Government realized they couldn't stop people from drinkin', they made booze legal again and the mobs hadda look for another way to keep the cash comin' in. And they did. No problem. And the feds, they did okay, too. About ninety percent of the cost of a bottle of hootch or a pack of smokes is taxes. Ever wonder why they don't make drugs legal and tax the hell out of them?"

"It's not the same."

"No? Tell me the difference between a guy who sits in the corner and drinks cheap wine until he passes out every night and a guy who pumps heroin into his arm all day. Where's the goddamn difference? Both are abusin' themselves, right? Both are near useless, right? So where's the difference?"

"Well . . ."

"Well what? One's legal and one's illegal? Is that what you're gonna tell me? Big deal. Listen to me. Nothin' they can do about drinkin'. And they know damn well there ain't nothin' they can do about drug users either. Somebody wants to use drugs, they're gonna find a way. That's all there is to it. Half the commercials on TV are drug commercials. Walk into any supermarket and you'll see more goddamn pills than you can count. No way you're gonna stop people takin' drugs. No way! They almost shove the pills down our throats."

He leaned forward, his eyes like lasers. "Let me tell you something. Four hundred thousand people die from smokin' every year, did you know that?"

"I've read the figures."

"Did you know another two hundred thousand die from bad livers, car crashes, or gettin' heads bashed in in fights or bein' shot by a wife or husband? All from booze. Did you know that?"

"What's your point?"

"I'll get to it. When you add in all the other people who suffer because of booze, it's a hell of a toll, but there's no way the government is ever goin' to get involved in stoppin' drinkin' again. They learned their lesson.

"Here's the point. You know how many people die every year because of illegal drugs? Less than thirty thousand a year, and that's countin' all the turf wars and all the kiddie crime."

Karen rolled her eyes skyward. "Your point is irrelevant. Cocaine, heroin, and marijuana are illegal drugs. If zero people die from using them, it doesn't make them less onerous. We have to live by the law of the land. Trying to rationalize legalizing these drugs serves no purpose. It's not going to happen."

"You're not really listenin'," he said angrily. "I'm not tryin' to do nothin' but explain to you what's going on. If you'd stop interruptin' all the time, maybe I could get you to understand that."

Karen was tiring of being lectured. "All right!" she said harshly. "Then get on with it."

"I will. Everybody knows alcohol and smokes cause more deaths, more injuries, and more problems than all the illegal drugs you'll ever find. And the only reason the feds don't get serious about illegal drugs is because too damn many feds are makin' too damn much money from it. The moment they make it legal, the money stops rollin' in."

He stabbed his chest with a thick forefinger. "The bastards learned it all from *us*, don't you see? The families showed them how it was done, and now they want us out!"

Karen shook her head. "You can't seriously believe . . ."

"Damn right! The feds are takin' over the business."

"The FBI is taking over the drug business? Is that what you're saying?"

"No. There are some people—CIA, FBI, DEA—dirty. Maybe they work on the outside, maybe not. Maybe the Government is part of it, maybe not. I don't know. But what I do know is these guys—these people—are runnin' the show. Ramirez is *their* guy."

"I don't believe it," Karen said.

He threw her a malicious sneer. "Just like I figured."

"They couldn't keep something that big a secret. It's impossible!"

"You think so? You remember Manuel Noriega?" Angelo asked.

"Of course."

"The man was busted in 1989. Convicted of drug trafficking, right? He was the CIA's man in Panama. Everybody knows it. He got greedy, so we invaded his country, killed a few hundred people, then dragged his sorry ass back here. On the day he was sentenced, he stood there and told the world what was goin' on. Nobody believed him either."

He leaned forward. "But it's all true. Now, Ramirez is the CIA's man. The CIA helps Ramirez oper-

ate because they're takin' five percent of his action.
That's about five billion dollars every year! In cash!
You know how many countries you can buy with
five billion dollars a year? They do what the hell
they want, where they want, when they want, without no congressional committees lookin' over their
shoulder. Jesus! Not even Congress knows what the
hell's goin' on. They don't wanna know.

"And the FBI? They've known about this for
years. Can't do zip. So, some FBI agents decided
they wanted a piece of the pie. Some of them got
it. The whole situation is nuts. The straight guys
are trying to bust the crooks and the crooks have
to be careful who they kill. Too many bodies pile
up and the people in Washington get nervous. It's
crazy. Nobody knows who to trust. The guy
you're talkin' to might be a crooked fed or a
straight fed. Who's to know?

"I used to be a part of it, so I know what I'm
talkin' about. I was workin' for Gotti then. When
John went down, I was left out in the cold. I got
the hell out of Miami rather than fight. Now, I get
my stuff from a Mexican I've been doin' business
with for twenty years. Him I trust. And only him.
But Ramirez isn't happy with that. He wants me
buyin' from him. He don't want nobody else
doing business with me or anybody else in the
entire East.

"So I sent Ernesto down there to talk to Ramirez. I offered Ramirez a kickback. Ramirez had
Ernesto killed to let me know that wasn't the deal
he was lookin' for. Now he's after me big-time,

'cause I refuse to do business with the bastard. He set me up and the feds are helpin' him because the feds are as dirty as he is.''

Karen leaned back in her chair and shook her head. ''If they're out to get you, why not quit?''

He glared at her. ''This is America. No foreigner is gonna tell me how to make a livin' in my own country. Not now, not ever.''

''And you know who these people are?''

''Some.''

That took her breath way. ''Then why are you still alive?''

''Because of my diary. I been keepin' a diary for fifty years. It's all on file in my computer. And it all comes out in the *Miami Herald* the day I die. They know that.''

Karen shook her head. ''Do they know your diary is in your computer?''

''No. All they know is I got notes on everythin' that ever happened.''

''And this person at the *Herald* has a copy?— Is the copy encrypted?''

''Yes, and he'll receive the password if they hit me.''

''I don't understand. If they're afraid of what's in your diary, why would they kill you now?''

He paused for a moment, then said, ''I don't think they give a shit anymore. They're gettin' more powerful by the day. They figure they can get past it. And they probably can. The only reason they want me in prison is so some con can stick a knife in me there. Keep things neat.''

Karen took a deep breath, then exhaled. "It has to be more than that. When's the last time you checked on your friend, the one with the copy of your diary?"

"About a month ago."

"Better check again."

Karen stood up and walked to the window, thinking. The storm was weakening fast. The once-black sky was now a dirty gray, with a thin blue line visible just above the horizon far out in the gulf. She turned and faced Angelo. "This story you just told me, how much of it can you back up?"

"What do you mean?"

"How much can you prove?"

"All of it."

"Then there's a way to make all of this stop," Karen said. "At least for you."

He didn't answer.

"You've been at this a long time," she said. "Your children are grown, your wife is deceased, and you're essentially alone. How much money does one person need? You're cooped up here like a prisoner anyway. You said yourself it's not much of a life. Why not change it?"

"What are you talkin' about?"

"I'm talking about you telling what you know to people in Washington, people we could trust. I'm suggesting you name names, get all this out in the open, help clean it up, and then becoming a protected witness like Sammy whatshisname. You don't have that many years left. Twenty, twenty-five? Why not live them in comfort? Why not enjoy life? Why continue to be hunkered down in this fortress waiting for the bomb to go off?"

He shook his head. "You can't trust nobody in Washington. If they aren't on the goddam take, they can't keep their mouths shut. They see a TV camera and they start shootin' their mouths off about everything. Bunch of greedy, crooked bastards. At least I know I'm a crook. I been a crook all my life. But I don't run around pretendin' I got everybody else's interests at heart. If I start talkin', I'm a dead man."

"But Sammy seems fine. You said yourself . . ."

He held up a hand. "Forget that. Sammy could be dead for all we know. You think they'll announce it?"

"Well," Karen said, "I'm not dropping the case. If you want to fire me, then do it, but I'm *not* going to abandon you."

"You're a stubborn woman."

Karen smiled. "Others have said that."

"It's true."

"Then fire me."

He glared at her for a moment, then shook his head. "You're not only stubborn, you're stupid."

She grinned. "Go ahead. Insult me. I still won't quit."

He shrugged. "I've said my piece. I'm tired. I need some sleep. You want to keep on with this, go ahead.

"It's your funeral, Counselor."

11

Jack Dougherty, the firm's immigration expert, handed Karen a folder when she arrived back at the office. "Have Michelle fill out the forms marked with a red slip," he said. "Then have her parents sign, notarize, and return the forms I've marked with a yellow slip. Finally, you and Carl need to fill out the forms I've marked with a blue slip. Once that's all done, I'll file with Immigration."

Karen leafed through the forms in the folder. "My God!"

Jack grinned. "Yeah, I know. It'll take a few hours. But it has to be done. Got to keep those bureaucrats busy. In the meantime, I've already filed for a special temporary student visa. Michelle can start at Eckerd next week if she wants."

"How'd you manage that?"

He shrugged. "Nothing to it. The alumni association owes me a couple of favors for some pro bono work. While Michelle's attending Eckerd, she can be working on an application for another college if she'd rather be somewhere else. But she'll be earning credits all the while. Seems to me it might work out. Isn't Andrea's school about three blocks from Eckerd?"

"It is. You think of everything."

He grinned. "You're too kind."

"Suppose Immigration . . ."

"Relax. She's in. Even criminals get two years free ride if they appeal deportation. Michelle has nothing to worry about. And, just for the record, I think what you're doing is terrific."

"Thanks, Jack. I can't wait to tell Michelle."

As the door closed behind him, she buzzed Liz on the intercom. "Get me Senator Robert Jameson's Washington office. If he's not there, try his home in Warrenton, Virginia. I want to speak with the senator personally."

Her earlier conversation with Uccello prompted her to contact her brother, something she hadn't done in over a year. It had been four years since she'd actually seen him, except on television— usually in his capacity as chairman of the Senate drug oversight committee.

Liz's voice crackled over the intercom. "Senator Jameson's on line one."

Karen's hand shook as she picked up the receiver. Their interaction had always been unpredictable, at best, and she had no clue how he'd receive her call. "Robert?"

"Hi, Karen. To what do I owe the pleasure—"

"Business, Robert." She didn't pretend affection. Their relationship had passed that point decades ago. "Mind if I ask a question that requires an honest answer?"

"Not at all." He was a strong, virile man with a booming voice and the hubris required of anyone in public life. But on the telephone at this moment, he sounded tentative, wary.

What the hell. If he'd called her, she'd sound the same way. "Suppose . . . just for the sake of discussion, and with the understanding that this is absolutely confidential . . . okay?"

"Absolutely."

"Suppose I had a client . . . who wanted to come forward . . . say to appear before some Senate committee. Yours, perhaps. Let's say he has evidence that ties in directly with illegal drug dealing in this country. And let's say this evidence is very, very strong stuff. Real high-profile stuff. It might mean wall-to-wall TV coverage, that kind of thing."

"You have my full attention," he said. "Go on."

"What would you suggest he do? Who would he contact? He wouldn't want to make a mistake and tip his hand to one of those small minority who take advantage of situations, if you catch my drift?"

Robert was silent for a moment. "Well . . . I would suggest you work through me. I know who to place you in touch with."

"Could you guarantee he'd be safe?"

"The honest answer is no," he said gravely. "But we would try very, very hard. The truth is, we can't even protect the president, as any president will tell you."

"Thanks for the honesty."

"You're welcome. Is there a chance that . . ."

"Not at the moment. I just thought I might as well ask the question . . . in case later, I have to move fast."

"Call me, day or night. You have my home number?"

"Yes. Thanks for your help."

"No problem. And, Karen . . ."

"Yes?"

"It was good to talk to you."

She sat, holding the receiver, stunned by the sincerity in his voice, long after Robert hung up.

The family, except for Andrea, spent the evening filling out forms. Michelle was, as expected, overjoyed. It was decided she'd take a liberal arts course for the first year before deciding on a major.

By the time Karen climbed into bed, she was exhausted. Her shoulder throbbed. Sleep eluded her.

After tossing and turning for half an hour, Carl sat up, turned on the light, and glared at her. "Take a pill," he ordered.

Karen threw back the covers and sat on the edge of the bed. "No more pills," she said. "I don't want to start becoming dependent on pills to get some sleep."

"But you're in pain! When did you start worrying about becoming an addict?"

"I'm not worried about becoming an addict."

"I see." He stared at her back for a moment,

then touched it gently. "Okay. We'll talk. What is it?"

"Tomorrow. We'll talk tomorrow. I'll go downstairs and read a while. You need your sleep."

He reached forward and held her wrist. "Now. I don't mind listening. Really. What is it?"

"The truth?"

"I think I can handle it."

"Okay. Try this. I think I'm losing my mind," she said.

He rolled over, his back to her. "Let me know when you want to get serious."

"I *am* serious."

He sat back up. "Okay. You think you're losing your mind. Why?"

"Because I'm not thinking right."

"That's usually a strong sign," he joked. "Could you be a little more forthcoming?"

She sighed. "I find myself actually liking this guy."

"What guy?"

"Angelo Uccello."

"You're *not* serious."

"See what I mean? I must be losing my mind. How can I feel some measure of affection, however small, for such a man? What's happening to me?"

"I'm a neurosurgeon, not a shrink. Perhaps . . . nah, forget it."

"No, please. What?"

"Okay. Maybe it's because he's Italian. You have an affinity for Italians."

"Oh, Carl. Be serious. I'm trying to tell you . . .

it really bothers me. Here's a man engaged in one of the filthiest businesses in the world. He supplies the drugs that end up in schools where ten-year-olds start experimenting to impress their peers. So many lives utterly destroyed and he doesn't have a scintilla of remorse. He went on and on today about drugs versus cigarettes and booze, telling me how drugs are the lesser of the three evils."

"Well, he's right about that."

"That makes it okay?"

"Not at all, but if you want to discuss the destruction of lives, alcohol wins hands down. That's not the way the media plays it, but that's the reality. But I digress. What is it about this guy that makes you like him?"

Karen shook her head. "I can't imagine. That's what scares me."

Carl thought for a moment, then said, "You were right. Now is not the time. We'll talk tomorrow."

"You think I'm going crazy?"

"Nope. I think you're confused. Look at everything that's been thrown at you in a matter of days. You wreck your car, your mother visits and gives you nothing but a hard time, and then there's that wonderful news out of New Jersey about Dr. Nano. What do you expect? You're a strong woman, Karen, but the events of the last few days would overwhelm anyone. You want my advice? Take some time off. You need a rest. We both do."

"I can't."

"You mean you won't."

"I mean I shouldn't."

He stared at her, a look of hope in his eyes. "Which means you might?"

"Let me think about it. What's your schedule?"

"Nothing that can't be postponed for a few days. All I need is about three days notice."

"Really?"

"Really. Why don't we take off for a long weekend? Aruba, maybe, or St. Thomas."

"We've been there."

"Well, how about some island we've never seen, where we can lie in the sun and drink powerful mind-altering fruit drinks. It'll give you time to sort it all out. You always do eventually, but you've got too damn much on your plate this time."

"You really mean it, don't you?"

"Absolutely. Just give me the word and I'll make the reservations."

"I'll give it some serious thought," she said. "I really will."

"Good."

"Maybe after the seizure hearing. Michelle could look after Andrea, take her to and from school, work her classes to fit the schedule. It could work. God! I'd love to get away."

He smiled. "See? You're not going crazy."

"Don't be too sure."

"One thing for sure," he said softly, "you will go nuts if you don't slow down."

12

When Karen arrived at the office in the morning, Bill Castor was waiting. He looked like the cat who'd swallowed the canary as he chatted with Liz, who looked on the private investigator as somewhat of a god.

"Well, it's about time," Bill said as Karen approached Liz's desk.

"Glad you're here," Karen responded. "You have some info?"

"Have I ever failed you?"

"Pride goeth before the fall, they say."

"I've already had my share of falls," he said with a laugh. "I've earned the right to be cocky."

"I guess you have at that. It must be good stuff. You look mighty pleased with yourself."

"It is . . . and I am."

"Okay, let's talk."

Liz handed Karen her mail. "We need to talk when you have a chance."

"If it's important . . ."

"It can wait," Liz said, her voice about an octave lower than normal.

"Sure?"

Liz nodded, the grave look on her face serving only to intensify Karen's curiosity. It would have to wait.

As Bill sat across from Karen's desk sipping coffee, the detective reported on the progress of his investigation. "First, the bad news. I'm still working on my Miami connection. All I can tell you so far is that Juan Ramirez is *the* man when it comes to cocaine coming into Florida. Nobody else even counts. Ramirez is so wired in, he's got city cops patrolling his neighborhood to make sure he isn't bothered. Can you believe it?"

"At this point, I'll believe almost anything."

"Wait till you hear this," he enthused. "The guy's so high profile, his house had become a tourist attraction. The buses were driving by, the drivers giving the spiel. 'Ladies and gentlemen, if you'll look to your right, you'll see the eight-million-dollar, sixteen-room house owned by Juan Ramirez, one of this country's biggest drug dealers. Who says crime doesn't pay?' I love it. But I guess Ramirez didn't. So he tells the cops to ixnay the buses.

"And they do. The cops made the buses take a hike. They're actually protecting the guy! And I'm trying to nail down some other rumors that are so outrageous I'd rather not even mention them at this point."

Karen offered a weak smile. "You amaze me."

"Why?"

"Your contacts. You have contacts everywhere. How'd you manage that?"

"No big thing. When I started in this business I knew I'd need contacts, so I attended every PI get-together in the country. Even some conventions out of the country. I networked like crazy, kissed ass, provided a lot of pro bono information to out-of-towners just to have a few markers out there. Over the years, they began to trust me. Now, I tap those sources when I need to. Good PIs know the lay of the land. So do good cops. I've managed to maintain a few friendships from my cop days, too. Long as you play it straight . . ."

"Anything on Judge Williams?"

"Ahhh. The good news. Seems the judge was found consorting with a hooker in Daytona Beach two years ago. The local cops kept it quiet, but somehow, Wilbur Brooks found out. And I guess he also found a way to let the judge know his secret was out. Ever since, the judge has leaned over backward to help good ol' Wilbur. I've gone over all the public records where Judge Williams was handling Wilbur's cases. Wilbur is batting a thousand. Surprise!"

Karen shook her head in dismay. "What is it with men, anyway?"

"Some men, if you don't mind."

"Point taken."

"Maybe Judge Williams is such a lousy lover his wife won't give him the time of day. Ever think of that?"

"Gee . . . no."

Bill handed Karen a file folder. "My report. I have her name, her shoe size, her bra size, her phone number, favorite foods, favorite celebrities, sleeping habits . . .''

Karen grinned. "Mr. Efficient."

"I don't believe in doing half a job. Her name is Melody Pickett. Kinda cute, actually. Twenty-four, independent. Works the small conventions. She's still at it."

"So Judge Williams leaves himself open to blackmail. Any sign that Melody is cashing in?"

"None. But she hasn't been busted in two years. The judge could be her ticket, but I doubt it. More likely someone else in Volusia County. So, tell me. How do you handle this one?"

"I'm not sure. Does Melody use drugs by any chance?"

"Little coke now and then. Occasional user, or so I hear."

Karen brightened. "That's the answer, then. Give me her address and phone number."

"Care to fill me in?"

"Nope."

"Okay. You don't need her bra size?"

Karen gave him a look.

"It's in there anyway. Thirty-six D. Just so you know I wasn't kidding."

"Bill . . ."

"Okay, okay. I should have a full report for you on the Miami situation in about a week."

"Good. As I said, you are, in a word, amazing."

"Thank you. I feel the same way."

"Humility becomes you," Karen said, shaking her head. "There's one more thing."

"Uh-huh?"

Karen handed him a list of names. "The men on this list are all FBI agents. I'd like you to do complete background checks on all of them."

Bill took the list. "What am I looking for?"

"Someone who has more money than he should. If you find one, make sure it isn't an inheritance or lottery win, something like that . . . And if it isn't, see if you can trace the source."

"This is going to take some time."

"That's okay."

Bill pursed his lips, then said, "You know, if I ever get in legal trouble, you're the one I'd call."

Karen smiled. "You're too smart to get in trouble."

As soon as Bill left, Karen called in Len Spirsky. "I want you to go to Daytona Beach right now," she said, handing him a copy of Melody Pickett's address and phone number. "I want you to find this woman immediately."

Len looked confused.

"She's a hooker," Karen said. "And you're a customer, got it?"

Len took a step back. "Excuse me?"

Karen grinned. "I don't mean for real, so relax. That's how you make contact. Give her five hundred dollars in cash up front to get her attention. Then tell her you're preparing for a criminal case involving a man named Angelo Uccello. She probably won't know who he is and that's fine. Tell her it doesn't matter. When you take her statement, you keep asking her if she's ever met him, ever bought drugs from him, ever so much as laid eyes on him. You keep at it for half an hour. Have the statement typed and signed. She'll cooperate because she's admitting to nothing. If she signs the statement, give her another five hundred in cash. Bring everything back to me by the morning."

"I don't get it," Len said. "If she's got nothing to do with the case, why are you doing this?"

Karen smiled. "We go to court Monday morning on the seizure motion. You'll find out then. But if you don't have that statement in your pocket, I'm in deep trouble. Understand?"

"Not really."

"You will."

Liz rapped lightly on the door and stuck her head in. "You have a telephone call?"

"From whom?"

Liz looked at Len, then at Karen. "It's important, Karen." Always on her toes, the secretary didn't want to divulge the name in front of Len. Len took the hint and stood up. "I'm outta here."

With Len gone, Liz said softly, "It's your brother."

"Robert?"

Liz nodded. "Senator Jameson, calling from Washington, line two."

Liz quietly left the office, and Karen reached for the receiver. "Robert, is something wrong?"

"Relax," he said in his booming voice. "No family emergencies. I have some information on the matter we discussed yesterday."

She grabbed a pencil. "Go ahead."

"I don't have time to discuss it now, but I'll be in Miami Saturday for a fund-raising dinner. I was wondering . . . would you mind if I came by to see you at your home on Sunday? Just for an hour or so."

Karen was having trouble breathing. "You want to see me?"

"Yes, I do. I had intended to call you for weeks, and your call yesterday convinced me . . . Look, I turned fifty-one a couple months ago . . . and . . . I'd rather tell you in person. It's time we talked, Karen. I mean, really talked."

"Sunday?"

"Yes."

"What time?"

"Well, I have to be back in Virginia by ten. Say three or four in the afternoon? And, for both our sakes, this meeting would be confidential. I'll be arriving in a regular car. No entourage. One of my staff will bring me there, but he'll sit in the car while you and I chat."

Robert's voice vibrated with a quality she'd never heard in it before—vulnerability.

"Sunday's fine," Karen said, totally confused. "I'll look forward to seeing you."

"I know you don't really mean that, but I'll take it. See you Sunday. And thanks, Karen."

He hung up before she could answer. She leaned back in her chair, strange thoughts rambling around in her head. And then Liz stepped into the office and closed the door.

"What's up?"

Liz wore a hangdog expression on her face. "I hate to sound like a tattletale, Karen . . ."

"What?"

"Walter. He went through your mail this morning. This is the first chance I've had to mention it."

Karen leaped to her feet. "He went through my *mail*?"

"Yes. He grabbed the envelopes right off my desk and quizzed me on each one. I told him he'd have to talk to you. He seemed . . . almost deranged. He's been sitting in his office most of the day, talking to no one. Then, he left about an hour ago. I think there's something seriously wrong, Karen. I thought you should know."

"You did the right thing, Liz. And there is something wrong. Thanks for bringing it to my attention."

Liz turned and left the office. Karen waited a few minutes, then headed for Walter's office. The door was open. Walter's secretary informed Karen that Walter had gone home early, just as Liz had said. Karen, her eyes blazing with fury, strode purposefully toward Brander's office, past his startled secretary, and into his office. Brander, huddled at a document-covered worktable with a client, peered at her over his half glasses, shock evident on his face.

"Sorry," Karen said immediately. She wheeled and left as quickly as she'd come. She went back to her office and buried herself in work. Twenty minutes later Brander tapped on the door and poked his head in. "May I?"

Karen waved a hand. "Please."

Brander stepped inside, closed the door, and leaned against it. "What was *that* all about?"

"Walter did it again," Karen said coldly. "This time, he went through my mail and quizzed Liz on each and every letter. This has to stop, Brander. You said he had some personal problem. Well, whatever it is, it needs much more attention than it's getting. I'm not going to tolerate this kind of behavior for another second."

Brander looked crestfallen.

"I don't mean to be insensitive," Karen continued, "but I can't work this way. Either you do something about Walter or I'll hand in my resignation. I mean it, Brander. I'm sorry, but that's the way it is."

Brander studied her face for a moment. Then, as he realized he could stall no longer, he said, "I understand. I'll take care of it."

Senator Robert Jameson, the junior senator representing the State of Florida, arrived without fanfare at the Mondori residence at 3:10 in the midst of another violent afternoon thunderstorm. Karen, watching from the living-room window, saw the black car pull up to the curb, saw Robert exit from the passenger's side, unfurl an umbrella, and semi-duckwalk to the front door. Karen opened it before he could ring the bell.

"Hi!" he said cheerily.

"Hi, yourself. You should have parked in the driveway."

"Well . . ."

"Come in, please."

Robert left the umbrella in the small alcove and stepped inside.

"Your shoes are soaked. And look at your trousers!"

Robert looked down. "Indeed."

Carl padded up behind Karen. "Hello, Robert. Nice to see you again."

"The pleasure is mine, Carl."

The two men shook hands.

"You'd better get out of those shoes," Carl said. "Socks, too. While you're at it, I'll get you a pair of slacks. We can hang those up for you."

Robert slipped out of his shoes, took off his socks, then followed Carl to the back of the house. When he finally made it back to the family room, he was wearing a pair of Carl's old brown slacks. The incongruity of a U.S. senator dressed in brown slacks, a starched white shirt, a very conservative tie, a blue suit jacket, and bare feet was too much. Karen burst into laughter. "You look so silly. You could at least take off your jacket."

"No, no," he protested. "I'm not the shirtsleeve type. I feel naked without the jacket. I really do."

He looked thinner than she remembered. And older than his fifty-one years. His closely cropped hair was graying, the skin on his face slightly mottled, his eyes surrounded by tiny folds of flesh that hadn't been there before.

"It's been a while," he said, as if aware of her examination.

"That it has. Can I get you anything?"

"Coffee, if you have it."

"Decaf or regular?"

"Regular."

Karen stepped into the hallway and asked Michelle to make some coffee. When she returned to the room, Robert was seated on one of the sofas. Karen sat in an identical sofa across from him. "It really is good to see you," Karen said.

"Thanks. You, too. How've you been?"

"Fine. Working hard. Andrea'll be back in a bit. You haven't seen her in four years. She's grown a lot."

"I'm sure."

"How's Claire?"

"Fine."

"And the boys?"

"Great. Both in college. One soon-to-be doctor, one soon-to-be lawyer. And I'm not even Jewish."

No, Karen thought. But still a bigot. She'd heard his vile bigoted talk when she was a child, his comments parroting those of their mother. But when he became a politician, that kind of talk was uttered in private, among trusted friends.

"So . . ."

"Yes. My reason for wanting to see you."

Karen could feel the tension building within her

small body. "You have some information for my client?"

"I'll get to that in a minute. As I said on the phone," he began, "something happened a while back. No one knows and I'd like to keep it that way."

"Okay. What was it?"

"I had a mild heart attack."

"Oh, my."

"It's all right. I'm fine, really. The doctor said it was just a warning. My cholesterol is much too high. I need to take my medication, exercise regularly, and watch my diet, that's all. But it scared me, Karen. It scared the hell out of me. I was fortunate in that it happened while Congress was on vacation, I was able to keep it quiet.

"In any case, I was lying in my hospital bed, all kinds of crazy thoughts running through my mind. I thought about Claire and the boys, and how I've really been a lousy father and husband. And then, for some reason, I thought about you and what a perfect asshole I'd been to you ever since you were born. I was rather overcome with remorse.

"So . . . I did something I've never done before. I guess I was pretty scared. Whatever, I made a deal with God, if that's possible. I prayed. I told God if he let me live, I'd try to make amends to everyone.

"Two days later, I was fit. I've already turned over a new leaf with my family. As for you, this is step one. Frankly, I'm here to ask your forgiveness, Karen."

Karen was stunned for a moment. And then, as if a plug had been pulled, the tension drained from her like so much dirty bathwater.

He'd been frightened, and now he wanted forgiveness.

There was a time when she would have walked over cut glass to hear those words, would have done almost anything to gain a tiny morsel of affection from a half brother who treated her so cruelly or, worse, with cold indifference. She'd loved him once, not knowing why, hating herself for being stupid and weak, but loving him anyway. And then the love had turned to hatred. Eventually, the fires of hatred died, like an untended furnace in the dead of a northern winter, the tangle of emotions blunted by logic and intellect, a mature Karen realizing that expending such precious energy was like throwing money down a sewer.

Now, he was just someone she knew.

To forgive him meant as little as not forgiving him.

She stood up, walked to where he sat, and kissed him on the cheek. "You're forgiven."

He looked astonished. "Just like that?"

"Just like that."

"No hard feelings?"

"Of course," she said, smiling. "I'm a human being, after all. But you're still forgiven. We'll see what we can do about the hard feelings."

Michelle brought the coffee tray into the room.

Karen made the introductions, and Michelle left. "Now that I've got that off my chest," Robert mused, "I don't know quite what to say."

"You're sure you're okay? I mean the heart trouble."

"I'm fine. Really."

Karen sat beside him, looking like a midget in comparison. They had the same mother, but they were very different people. Robert was cold and calculating, always had been, even now with his sincere manifestation of his obsessive need to keep his life in order. He was probably unaware of the demons that drove him. Here was a barefooted man who refused to take off a suit jacket for fear it made him appear less important, and completely unable to see the silliness of it all.

If there was an ounce of humanity left in the man, it was only because it was contained within the spermicidal DNA of his father. And in truth, there was some humanity buried deeply within him. Having followed Robert's political career, Karen was aware that he'd stuck his neck out several times in support of worthy legislation that flew in the face of the very special interests whose calculated largesse kept him in the Senate.

That took enormous courage. More than Karen would have expected from such a man.

"Does Mother know about your heart attack? She was here a few days ago and didn't mention it."

"God, no. She'd be the last one I'd tell. You know Mother."

"Too well. Did you see her in Miami?"

He nodded. "She attended the fund-raiser last night. Looked in the pink. Sat at the head table, in fact. She never mentioned a word about seeing you. Never mentioned you at all, come to think of it."

Karen leaned back on the sofa. "I don't get it. She certainly talked enough about you when she was here."

"Anything good?" he asked, smiling.

"No, as a matter of fact. She says you're just another sleazy pol, yet she actively supports you."

"It's just for appearances," he said. "I have a solid core of boosters in Miami. Mother figures it would look odd if she didn't appear supportive. But when we're alone, she spares me nothing. Her invective is something to behold. She hasn't mellowed much. What was the purpose of her visit to you?"

Karen thought for a moment. "She said it was obligatory, that she hadn't seen Andrea in a while, or me, for that matter. Felt it was her duty, she said. She's planning a visit to you for the same reason."

"Really."

"That's what she said."

"Strange," he said. "Mother's never been a slave to duty before. How was she when she was here?"

"Her usual irascible self. She was giving me a hard time, as always."

"About?"

"The work I do."

"Defending criminals."

"Exactly."

"All of them or someone in particular?"

"Someone in particular, actually. At the moment, I'm defending a mafioso drug trafficker. Mother said she'd read about me defending him in the newspaper. She told me she was ashamed of me, that I'd caused her embarrassment."

"I read about it in the paper."

"Angelo Uccello. Ever hear of him?"

A jolt of what appeared to be discomfort flickered across his face before Robert looked away for a moment.

"Familiar name," he answered with sincerity, making her wonder if she'd imagined his reaction. "She came up here to dissuade you from defending the man?"

"Yes."

"Because she was embarrassed?"

"Yes."

"That's impossible. Nothing embarrasses Mother. Nothing!"

"I know. But what other reason would she have?"

"I can't imagine," he said. "I might accept that she really wanted to see you and Andrea. But . . ."

"Yes?"

"That just doesn't sound like Mother."

"My feeling exactly."

"Well . . . getting back to this Mafia client of yours for a moment."

"Yes."

"He ties in with the other matter I wanted to discuss with you. Just between us, and I mean that sincerely, you should know that the Justice Department is going after every lawyer who defends these people, going after them hard. You're liable to run into some problems."

Karen gave him a harsh look. "Interesting. You, a United States senator, and those words roll off your tongue as if they were nothing. Do you realize what you just said?"

"I do," he said. "And I make no apology. Drugs are robbing this country of its future. We have to get tougher."

"And the ends justify the means?"

"In this case, yes."

Instantly suspicious, Karen looked deep into his eyes. "Would the fact that I'm representing Uccello have anything to do with your visit today?"

Robert held up his hands as if in surrender. "None. I swear. I'm here to keep a promise I made to God."

"Really. When you took your oath as a member of the Senate, you made another promise to God. You don't seem very concerned about keeping that one."

He looked hurt. "Let's not fight about politics. You know we'll never agree."

"Okay. Mind if I ask you some questions about the war on drugs?"

"Not at all."

"I've been hearing rumors that many of those

charged with the responsibility of stopping the illegal drug traffic are dirty. True?"

Robert took a moment to answer. "There are always those who will take advantage of a situation. We're on top of it. Investigations are proceeding."

"Investigations? How serious?"

"I can't say, Karen. I really can't. I've said too much already."

"But I can still contact you if my client—"

"So it was—Uccello—you called me about?"

"No—a lesser-known client."

"But tied to Uccello?"

"No. This is a different case."

He frowned. "You're representing two drug dealers? My, my. You really are asking for trouble."

"You didn't answer the question, Robert."

"Yes, of course, contact me. How soon . . ."

"It's all hypothetical at this point."

"Maybe you should talk to Uccello."

"It's *not* Uccello."

Robert frowned. "I don't mind telling you, it would certainly make things easier for you in the long run if you were successful in getting him— your client—to come forward."

"Easier, how?"

"Like I said about the Justice Department playing hardball with lawyers who defend drug dealers. You'd earn some points there."

"What kind of points?"

He shrugged. "I can tell you this," he said. "During the past few years, the Justice Department has been very successful in persuading some very important people engaged in the drug trade to come forward. In every case, dozens of convictions were secured and a tremendous number of previously untouchable traffickers have gone to prison, both here and abroad. Those who came forward have been given new identities and relocated. It's a program that works very well."

"Then why is it," Karen asked, "that the traffic in illegal drugs has increased?"

He gave her a look. "Those figures are subject to interpretation."

"Of course. But the bottom line is this: The price of a kilo of cocaine is less than it was five years ago. What does that tell you?"

He stiffened. "I really shouldn't be discussing this with you, Karen. As much as I'd like to . . ."

"Sure."

"Look, if I can be of help . . ."

"I'll let you know," Karen said coldly.

He stared at her for a moment, then said, "I came here to ask for your forgiveness, Karen. I had no ulterior motives. And I fully realize that one trip isn't going to bridge the gap between us. I'm going to work on that, if you'll let me. It's important to me now. I realize how selfish that sounds, but I'm being as honest as I know how.

"I was cruel to you when we were young. I took my cue from Mother. I wanted to please her. I'm still trying to please her, dammit. I don't know why, but I am.

"This isn't easy for me, Karen. Humility is not my long suit. If you'll just give me a chance, I'll try and prove my sincerity."

"The door is open," she said. "And I do appreciate you coming to see me. I really do."

"Thank you."

"I'd like you to keep this thought in mind, Robert."

"Yes?"

"If I ever do come to you and if it turns out I shouldn't have, I'll hold a press conference that will put an end to your political career."

His face flushed. "You needn't make threats, Karen. I would never do anything to hurt you. I know I have in the past, but . . . You can trust me, Karen. I swear it."

"Robert certainly looked spooked today when you mentioned Uccello." Carl massaged Karen's sore shoulder gently as she sat on the edge of the bed.

"You saw that?"

"I was halfway into the living room before I realized your conversation was personal. You told Robert about Uccello just as I turned to leave."

"I thought I'd imagined his discomfort." She twisted to look at Carl, then winced at the twinge in her shoulder. "But if he knows Uccello, why did he deny it?"

Carl shrugged. "Maybe he's only seen the name

somewhere, like his drug oversight committee reports.''

''Or maybe he knows something he's not sharing.''

''Like what?''

''Like the Justice Department's building a case against my client.''

''That would be good, wouldn't it?'' Carl abandoned the massage and pulled her toward him. ''After all, Uccello's a known drug trafficker.''

''Yes, but . . .''

He held her at arm's length and scrutinized her face. ''You really do like the old guy, don't you?''

She could never hide anything from Carl. He knew her too well. ''I just don't want to see him framed. If they can convict him on solid legal evidence, so be it.''

''Then why are you frowning?''

''Because I can't figure out why my mother made such a scene over Uccello. I've represented worse criminals.''

''Did you tell Robert about your mother's objections?''

''He couldn't explain them, either.''

''Why don't you ask her?''

''Call Mother?'' The thought sent a chill down her spine.

''Martha's a night owl. She'll still be up.''

He settled back against the headboard and watched as Karen dialed the Miami area code and her mother's number.

Martha answered on the third ring.

"Mother," Karen said, "I've been thinking about your visit . . ."

"Is that why you're disturbing me this time of night, to tell me your thoughts?"

Karen bit back a bitter reply. If she antagonized her, Martha would tell her nothing. "You seemed extremely upset that Angelo Uccello is my client. I'm just trying to understand the basis of your objections. Is there something you haven't told me?"

Dead silence filled the other end of the line.

"Mother, are you still . . ."

"You may not care about your reputation, but I care about mine. I've spent seventy-two years building it. Unless you drop that Mafia creep's case, don't bother to call me again."

Karen flinched at the crack of a receiver slamming into the cradle before the line went dead.

"Well?" Carl asked.

"Exactly what I should have expected. No answers, only more rejection."

"Come here." He tugged her down beside him. "I know just the cure."

13

At exactly 9:03 on the last Monday morning in August, Judge Douglas Williams appeared in the doorway connecting the courtroom to his chambers, swept majestically up the three steps leading to his perch, sat down, slammed his gavel, and waited while the bailiff announced that court was now in session.

Since this was a hearing, there were few spectators in this prosaic, small courtroom, among them two TV reporters and two reporters for local newspapers. Angelo Uccello was not required to be in court, so the level of interest was low.

"All right," the judge said impatiently, "let's get on with it. We have a show-cause hearing in the matter of order number TMD-377475, with regard to the forfeiture of property belonging to Angelo Uccello, a resident of Dunedin, Florida. Is Mr. Uccello represented this morning?"

Karen stood up. "Karen Perry-Mondori, representing Mr. Uccello, Your Honor. My associate is Sharon Chin. I'm also accompanied by Len Spirsky, a paralegal."

"Very well."

Because Len had yet to be "called" to the Bar, he had to sit in the section behind the defense table. Sharon sat next to Karen.

"And the Government?"

Wilbur Brooks rose to his feet. "The United States is represented by assistant U.S. attorney for the Florida Middle District Wilbur Brooks, Your Honor."

The judge nodded. "Mr. Brooks, how long do you anticipate this will take?"

Wilbur, a look of supreme confidence on his face, replied, "Less than an hour, Your Honor."

The judge looked at Karen. "Ms. Perry-Mondori?"

"I anticipate three days, Your Honor, but it could take longer if Mr. Brooks intends a lengthy cross-examination of my witnesses."

The judge glared at her. "Witnesses? This is a show-cause hearing, Counselor. We're here to deal with the right of the Government to execute forfeiture, not to try a case."

Karen stood her ground. "I understand, Your Honor. But the facts of this case are these: My client is innocent of the charges against him."

Brooks leaped to his feet. The battle was truly joined.

"Your Honor," Brooks thundered, "under Title 21 of the U.S. Code, Section 853, the Government is entitled to seize property and/or assets used in any manner or part, to commit, or to facilitate the commission of the felony for which the defendant is charged, provided that the Government has a substantial probability that they will prevail at trial. The Government may seize the property when there is probable cause to believe that the subject property may not be available at the time of conviction. Under those provisions, the Government is entitled to proceed with forfeiture prior to trial, and the Supreme Court has upheld that right. Probable cause is the only issue here.

"The defendant is a known criminal, a member of a long-established organized crime fraternity for over thirty years. We have probable cause. To allow this hearing to be used as nothing more than an opportunity for counsel for the defense to trot out a bunch of liars and thieves simply to obstruct justice would be an affront to this court and to the entire criminal justice system."

The judge nodded, then turned to Karen. "I have to agree. I see no need for witnesses."

"May I be heard on this issue, Your Honor?"

He scowled. "If you must."

"Thank you, Your Honor. With regard to Section 853, the defense wishes to present evidence to support a claim that there existed at the time of the claimed commission of the felony . . . and that there exists to this day . . . a conspiracy to deprive my client of his constitutional rights. To wit, that my client was framed. There is *no* probable cause. There does *not* exist a substantial probability that the assets were used in the commission of a felony, other than felonies committed by agents acting on behalf of the United States Government or other interests."

Judge Williams leaned forward, fire in his eyes. "That's enough! Where do you think you are, Counselor?"

"I'm in a United States District Court, Your Honor. I'm fully aware of the gravity of my statements. I'm also prepared to prove, here and now, the veracity of the claims. Further, I submit that there is no probable cause to believe that the assets as set forth in the information will *not* be available should a conviction be obtained.

"Finally, my client has never been convicted of a felony. Not ever. This charge which has brought us here today, as trumped up as it is, is still a first offense. The law treats first offenses with deference and the Supreme Court has upheld the wisdom of such deferential treatment The intent of the seizure law was to discourage those engaged in the business of drug trafficking to the exclusion of all other criminal activities. As for the property the Government wishes to seize, it has a value of over four million dollars. The street value of the drugs found on the property is, at best, eighty thousand dollars. To seize such a property in light of the amount of illegal drugs found would be a gross misapplication of the forfeiture statute."

Wilbur's jaw dropped open, his face flushed with anger.

Karen, warming to the fight, went on. "In order to rebut the Government's contention that seizure is justified, we are placed in the position of having to prove the defense's case here and now. Only then will my client obtain due process. We are not here to litigate the legality of the U.S. Code. We are here to prove that, in this specific case, the code does not apply, and we can't present a defense unless we are allowed to present witnesses."

The judge was staring at her, his eyes emitting a death ray. His fury distorted his features, not a pretty sight. Karen, her exterior calmness hiding the bubbling emotions that percolated within her, took it a step further. "Your Honor is no doubt aware that the court may receive and consider at probable cause hearings evidence and information that would be inadmissible under the Federal Rules of Evidence. That's what we ask of this court at this time."

Judge Williams was beside himself. "I don't need some lawyer from across the bay coming into my court first thing on a Monday morning and giving me a lecture on the law. You're about one step away from contempt, Counselor. I won't warn you again."

"I didn't mean to . . ."

"Just put a cork in it, Counselor. Right now!"

Karen stood mute.

The judge glared at her some more, then held out his hand. "You have a list of witnesses?"

Wilbur exploded. "Your Honor!"

"Quiet!" the judge yelled back.

Karen said, "I do, Your Honor."

"Let's have it."

Karen picked up two typed sheets of paper

from the table, handed one to a stunned Wilbur Brooks and the other to the judge. Both men perused the list for a moment. Then, the judge's head snapped up as if pulled by an invisible string. "I'll see counsel in chambers," he growled.

Brooks and Karen fell in step behind the judge as he hurried to his chambers. The judge took off his robe, hung it up, then sat behind his desk. The barest hint of country and western music emanated from the giant stereo speakers. Brooks, still red-faced, stared at the speakers. The judge glared at Karen. The court reporter poised her long fingers over the keys of her stenographic machine.

"Who is Fred Hertz?" asked the judge.

"He's my client's accountant," Karen answered.

"What's he got to do with this?"

"He's prepared to testify that he locked the company books in my client's safe at six twenty-five on the evening of August 23. There were no drugs in the safe at that hour."

"And who's John Haversol?"

"He's a security guard. He works for my client. He's prepared to testify that my client was never out of his sight from six-ten to nine twenty-six on the evening of August 23. These two witnesses alone make the case for my client. But we have several more."

"I can see that. Most of them are employees of your client, which brings up the question of veracity. Who the hell is Jane Doe?"

"Jane Doe is obviously a pseudonym for a witness who requires protection, Your Honor. Under the circumstances, I fear for her safety. I'll need to make certain arrangements with the Department of Justice before I can reveal her name."

The judge was enraged. "What exactly are you trying to intimate, Counselor?"

Karen, her own eyes blazing with anger, dropped all pretense."I'm not intimating anything, Your Honor. I'm flat out declaring that my client was framed by federal law enforcement officers. I have the evidence and I'm going to present it, either here or in another court. You'll note that I have deliberately avoided speaking to the media as a token of my respect for those officers who are not involved in this travesty. This case is an utter disgrace, an affront to the criminal justice system, and those responsible must be forced to answer for their actions.

"You mentioned veracity. If you'd like to discuss the question of veracity, you'll note in our motion for discovery that the Government's entire case begins with a tip from an informant. Subsequently, based on statements made by Fito Olivera and Manuel Aznar, a search warrant was issued allowing my client's business to be raided.

"In their statements, both Olivera and Aznar claimed to have contacted my client by telephone. I've asked several times for copies of phone records substantiating these claims. We assume the records are in the possession of the Government. We still don't have them."

She glared at Wilbur. "Perhaps no phone calls were made."

"Enough!" the judge shouted. "Just who is Melody Pickett?"

He was clever in his own mean-spirited way. He'd asked about some other witnesses first so as not to make it obvious that *this* was the name that had captured his attention.

"She's a prostitute, Your Honor. From Daytona Beach."

The judge's eyelids flickered. "What's she got to do with this case?"

Karen chose her words carefully. "She's prepared to testify to matters that have a bearing on this case. Just like the others."

Out of the corner of her eye, Karen could see Wilbur staring at her. Then Wilbur looked at the judge, a helpless expression on his face, as if to say he was not the one who'd spilled the beans about the hooker. Judge Williams answered Wilbur's look with a look of exasperated resignation.

There was danger here. Real danger. If the judge decided to call Karen's bluff . . .

No. Karen could see it on his face. The judge wasn't going to take the chance. She felt her heart skip a beat.

"I don't have time to hear a parade of witnesses," the judge said, his voice more a tortured moan of frustration.

Karen, infused with confidence, pressed her advantage. "Your Honor, the meter on forfeiture has been running since the day my client was indicted. The Government has ten days to put up or shut up. If I'm not allowed to proceed and my client's property is seized, he will have been denied due process. I would have to . . ."

The judge waved a finger at her. "Don't you dare threaten me!"

Karen said nothing more. She waited as the judge, his rage near the boiling point, took a deep breath. Then he turned to the court reporter. "We'll take a short recess, Angela. I'll get back to you."

The court reporter nodded and left the room. There was silence, save for the muted sounds coming from the stereo speakers, a plaintive wail of a man claiming to have lost his wife to a no-good traveling man.

After what seemed like an eternity, Judge Williams sighed, then said, "You think you're pretty damn clever."

Karen kept a straight face. "I'm just defending my client, Your Honor."

He snorted. "You and Uccello belong together in the same sewer. You're scum. Nothing but scum."

"I take exception, Your Honor."

"You can take all the exception you want. Write a letter to the appellate division. Call a press conference. Do whatever the hell people like you do. See if I give a shit. You're still scum."

Karen said nothing. There was no point. Neither the judge nor Wilbur would ever let it be known Judge Williams had uttered such words. And the transcribed record of what had been said before would be sanitized before symbols became words.

Turning to Wilbur, the judge said, "I'm recusing myself from this case, Wilbur. I don't need this crap. My suggestion is you find another judge real quick. Seems Mr. Uccello has hired himself a lady lookin' to make trouble for a lot of decent people. Not a smart career move, if you ask me. But, there it is. I don't have the time and the law is clear."

Wilbur's eyes betrayed him. There was no point in arguing, and he knew it.

"Let's get back in court and be done with this," the judge said.

And so they did.

Judge Williams granted Wilbur's motion for a continuance, recused himself, slammed his gavel, and left the room. Wilbur moved just as quickly, leaving the courtroom without a word to Karen.

As Karen drove Len and Sharon back to Clearwater, the two young associates were still confused. Karen explained what had taken place in chambers. "It's a small victory," she said. "Another judge will be assigned, and we start all over. But since the feds have to execute seizure within ten days of issuing the order, there's not much time for Wilbur to get his ducks in a row. Which means the feds will probably drop the seizure ball."

"I understand that much," Len said. "What I still don't understand is why the judge recused himself."

"No?" Karen asked. "You sure about that?"

Len thought for a moment, then brightened. "The hooker?"

"Perhaps."

"But she has nothing to do with this case."

"You know that," Karen said, "and I know that. But it's possible Judge Williams doesn't know it."

"But why . . ."

And then, like a sunrise, the dawn of realization. "I'll be damned!" Len exclaimed. "The judge and the hooker, right?"

"It's just a rumor," Karen said. "Probably no truth to it."

"But you never asked me to talk to her about the judge. I don't get it."

"I didn't ask you to talk to her about the judge for good reason. Whether or not the judge has a relationship with a hooker is irrelevant. Then again . . ."

"Isn't that illegal?"

"How is it illegal?"

"Well, he must have thought you were going to expose him."

"If he did," Karen said, "he was wrong."

"But that's still blackmail!"

"How so?"

"Well . . . you were going to call her as a witness. That's what frightened the judge. But she couldn't testify to anything. And if you went public, you could be in deep trouble, no?"

"Perhaps," Karen said. "But you're missing the point. I never threatened to link the judge with Melody. All I did was put her on my witness list.

If the judge had let us play it out, I couldn't have called her. He should have known that, but he was too shocked after learning we'd contacted her. He wasn't thinking straight. Neither was Wilbur. We took a chance and it paid off.

"On the other hand, if we'd been forced to make an issue out of the judge's rumored relationship with Melody, we could do it another way that would fully satisfy the ethics canons. Had we done so, it would look pretty bad for both Judge Williams and Wilbur Brooks. There would have been an investigation. Neither one of them wanted that. It was easier to let the judge wash his hands of this case."

Len shook his head. "Boy. There's more to this lawyer stuff than they teach you in law school."

"Lesson number one," Karen said. "Be prepared."

"I hear you."

Karen clicked the car radio on-off switch, forgetting the radio didn't work. Perhaps it was providence, for had she heard the news being broadcast at that very moment, she might have been crushed.

The law office's main work area—the pit—grew strangely silent when the trio arrived. Heads were bowed as if buried in files, telephone conversations became whispered, eye contact studiously averted. Clearly, something was up. Karen made a beeline for Liz's desk. "What's going on?"

Liz looked dreadful. "Can we talk in your office?"

"Sure."

They went into Karen's office. Liz closed the door, wrung her hands for a moment, then leaned against the wall.

"What is it, Liz?"

"I don't know how to tell you this."

"Well, sooner or later . . ."

"It's Walter. He shot himself early this morning. He's dead, Karen."

The words took time to register. Liz seemed faraway, her voice echoing in the distance. Crazy, wrong. The room began to spin. Karen grabbed her chair, then slowly sagged into it, her lungs screaming for air. Liz swam back into focus.

"Walter . . . He shot himself?"

Liz wiped a tear from the corner of her eye. "The news was broadcast just after nine-thirty. You must have been on your way back from Tampa. Did you come in the back way?"

"Did I . . . yes."

"Good. You avoided the press. They're camped out front looking for you. We've had to stop answering the phones."

It made no sense. "They're looking for me?"

"Yes." Liz brought a hand to her face. "Oh, God! This is so . . ."

"Why? Why would Walter do such a thing? And why is the press after me?"

"That's the really bad part, Karen."

"The bad part?"

"The radio and TV stations have been giving this so much attention . . ."

"What happened, exactly?"

Liz took a moment to answer. "This morning, Walter took a gun from his bedside table and placed it at his temple, then pulled the trigger. He did it right in front of Eleanor."

Karen brought her hands to her face as if to shut out the horrible vision. "Oh, my god! How awful!"

Liz, almost numb, continued her litany of disaster. "Eleanor was hysterical, naturally. And when she found the suicide note on the bed, a note blaming you for ruining Walter's career, she talked about the note to the police *and* the press."

Karen found it difficult to breathe. "A note . . . blaming me? For what?"

"She was hysterical, Karen. She didn't know what she was doing. A reporter stood outside Walter's house less than a half hour ago and read the letter aloud. It was terrible."

"What was in the note?"

"Walter wrote that you'd ruined him, made it impossible for him to carry on. He said you did it because you . . ."

"Because I what?"

"Because you wanted his job."

"That's not true."

"Of *course* it isn't. He was sick, Karen. Sick and crazy, too. Look at the way he's been acting lately."

Karen rubbed her forehead. "This is terrible. I have to see Brander. What must he be thinking?"

"He's not here," Liz said.

"What?"

"He left as soon as he heard the news."

Karen, slipping into mild shock, stood up and wandered, rather than walked, about her office. Two vases filled with colorful fresh-cut flowers, routinely changed every second day, seemed bizarrely out of place. She sagged back into her chair, looking utterly despondent and bewildered. Liz rummaged through the credenza and found what she was looking for, a bottle of vodka left over from a recent celebration. "I'll be right back," she said. "Don't you move a muscle."

Karen nodded numbly.

Liz was back with glasses and ice. She poured two stiff shots and handed one glass to Karen. "Drink this."

Karen drank. "I can't believe it," she said. "All I asked is that he not be managing partner. Why would he kill himself because of that?"

"It wasn't that," Liz said. "It was his health. It has to be his health. Maybe he had a nervous breakdown or something. He was a sick, mean, rotten man, Karen. You know that. We all knew it. Maybe he was dying. Maybe he had a brain tumor. But he wanted to stick it to you, the bastard. A hateful man. I'm not sorry he's dead."

Karen looked away. "You don't mean that, Liz."

"Yes, I do."

"No you don't. That isn't you. Walter was a

jerk, but I had no idea he harbored such hatred, no idea he was that far gone. Brander mentioned something about a personal problem, but never gave me details. Had I known it was this bad I wouldn't have made an issue of Walter's management style. God help me, I would have kept my big mouth shut."

"I'm so sorry, Karen. What can I do?"

Karen stood up. "You can call Angelo and tell him the feds are delaying the case. Tell him I'll call him tomorrow. Then go home, Liz. That's what I'm doing. We'll see how things are tomorrow."

"If it's all the same to you, I'll stay. We're in a mess here. Nothing I can't handle. By the way, Carl's been calling. He says it's urgent. I guess he heard the news."

Karen sighed. "God! I can't talk to anyone just now. I've got to get out of here. If anyone calls, I've gone for the day."

"What about Carl?"

"I'll see him later."

"And the press?"

"No comment. Absolutely none!"

Karen strode out of her office, down the hall, into the service elevator, and outside the building.

She didn't go home. She left her car in the parking garage to escape the media, and found her way to the nearby lake on foot.

And then, the full impact of what had happened hit her with full force. Her heart began to pound.

Beads of sweat formed on her forehead. She was having trouble breathing. She felt faint.

She sat on the sand for a few moments resting her head between her knees until the dizziness faded. Then she slowly rose to her feet and started walking. She stopped and took off her shoes, then continued walking along the thin wedge of sand, oblivious of her shredding panty hose or the sun's heat on the back of her neck. All she could feel was the heaviness in her heart.

She was no stranger to cruelty, she told herself. She would learn to live with this.

She had to.

But she knew it would take a while.

God! Already it was unbearable. She let the tears roll down her cheeks unfettered. Her body shook with deep sobs.

And then she threw up.

She walked and walked until her legs and feet screamed in pain. She finally checked her watch and was astonished to learn she'd been at it for over two hours.

She made it back to her car without encountering the press. When she arrived home, a few reporters were nearby, being held at bay by security guards. Carl must have hired them, she thought. She parked the car in the driveway and ran inside the house. Carl was waiting. He looked angry as he took her by the arm and almost dragged her into the den, closing the door behind him.

"What's the matter with you?" Karen asked.

"I'm a little upset."

"I can see that. About what?"

"About the way you carry the weight of the goddamn world on your back."

"Where's Andrea?"

"I asked Michelle to take her to the park. I've been waiting for you for almost an hour. Why the hell didn't you return my calls?"

Karen couldn't bear to look at him. "I couldn't talk to anyone. I just had to walk for a while."

"Alone, right? You have this monumental crisis and you couldn't share it with me? You think I could stay at the hospital knowing what the hell you're going through?"

"Stop picking on me," Karen yelled. "I feel bad enough as it is."

"I see. So you're going to waste time feeling sorry for yourself, is that it?"

She was shocked by his insensitivity. "I'm entitled, dammit."

"The hell you are."

She glared at him. "Why are you being so cruel? It would be nice if you offered some understanding."

"And it would be nice if you leaned on me once in a while instead of trying to handle everything alone. You should have called me, dammit. You could have saved yourself a lot of agony."

"What would I say to you?" Karen said bitterly. "Walter's dead and I drove him to it."

"Nonsense! Walter killed himself because he knew he was dying. It had nothing to do with you! That's why I've been trying so hard to contact you!"

"But . . . the note . . ."

Carl took a deep breath. "Jerry Sanford has been Walter's attending oncologist ever since Walter's prostate operation. I called Jerry as soon as I heard about that goddamn suicide note. Then I tried to get you at your office. I even tried your beeper, but you must have turned it off."

"I did. I was just . . . walking. I was stunned."

"Listen to me. Walter was diagnosed with pancreatic cancer two months ago. Jerry would have told me back then but he couldn't because Walter wanted it kept secret. Damn! *That's* why Walter killed himself. He knew he was doomed. And the bastard never told Eleanor. That's why she foolishly released that fucking insane letter to the press. She had no idea he was ill again. Walter kept it from her, like everything else in his life.

"And Walter, the stupid idiot, wanted one last chance to dump it all on you, the only person in his life he'd never been able to intimidate. That's why he wrote the note!"

Karen, astonished, stared at the wall.

"He was a cruel, vengeful bastard, Karen. You knew that! We *all* knew how eaten up with hatred Walter was. So why should you be surprised when he reaches out from the grave with his hatred?

"Even Jerry, who has more compassion than any other doctor on staff, had a hard time dealing with him. He said it's hard to show understanding for someone who has none for anyone else."

"*Jerry* said that?" She struggled out of her daze, like a diver breaking the surface.

"You should have called me back the moment you heard about that stupid note. I told Liz it was urgent, dammit!"

"She told me. I wasn't thinking. I'm sorry."

Carl ran his fingers through his hair. "Brander's been over there most of the day. He's called here three times looking for you."

Karen felt weak. "Oh, my," was all she could say.

Carl was still furious. "Brander knew. He's known for the past two months. He was the only one Walter could ever talk to. As soon as Brander heard the news, he knew something was screwy. He rushed over to see Eleanor. He told her the truth and asked her to release a second statement to the press. Eleanor immediately agreed. You can't imagine how badly she feels. Her statement is going out now. By tonight, everyone will have the facts."

Karen took a seat on the sofa and buried her head in her hands. She felt Carl's arm around her shoulder. "Next time, share," he said softly.

"I'm sorry."

"And I'm sorry for yelling at you. I was just so damn frustrated. I knew how upset you'd be." He slammed his hand on the sofa. "Jesus! We really do need to get away."

She couldn't look at him. "I know," she mumbled. "The sooner the better. I'm a wreck."

"You're a human being," he said, his anger spent. "This had to have hit you right between the eyes."

"It did. And you're right. We have to get away, Carl. The sooner the better."

He pulled her close. They held each other, not saying anything.

The phone rang. Carl pulled away and picked it up. "It's for you," he said. "Brander again."

Karen got to her feet. "Bless his heart. I'll talk to him."

At last, an invisible hand lifted some of the concrete blocks from her shoulders.

14

Many Americans regard all lawyers as vermin. Many Americans are cynical. Some very cynical Americans believe nothing of what they read in newspapers and magazines or see on TV and little of what they see with their own eyes. They think they're being fed a steady diet of lies from all quarters, be it government spokespersons, politicians, or anyone with a modicum of power and/or influence.

When Eleanor Sinclair recanted her earlier public statement with a second one acknowledging that her terminally ill husband had written his suicide note as a final, desperate act of vengeance for some imagined wrong, there were those who perceived the second statement as one crafted by some "spin doctor" from up north. Even within Karen's law firm, there were some who thought that way. Karen could see it in their eyes when she arrived for an emergency meeting of the partners on Tuesday morning.

Brander looked drawn. Walter, a cofounder of the firm, was his friend. Walter's death and the resulting swirl of negative publicity surrounding it was a heavy burden. Brander had done everything he could to counter the damage and had no time to grieve. Like a small boat in roiling sea, the firm's reputation was foundering. A personal tragedy was now sordid fodder for public consumption. Damage control was uppermost in Brander's mind. Once that was achieved, he'd take time to mourn Walter.

"Well," Brander said, opening the meeting, "this is indeed a sad day. But we must move on. I'd like to start by suggesting that we close down on Thursday so that everyone can attend Walter's funeral."

Karen and Darren nodded their approval.

"I'd also like to suggest that nothing decided today be made public until after Walter's funeral."

"Agreed," Darren said.

Karen nodded her agreement.

"Good. Now, do either of you have some suggestions?"

"I have one," Darren said quickly.

"Let's hear it."

"I think Karen should drop Angelo Uccello as a client."

Karen said nothing. Brander steeled himself. "Why?"

"Because it reflects badly on the firm. I realize we've defended criminals before, even drug dealers, but at this time, and with this particular client, we leave ourselves open to the worst kind of publicity. It reached its zenith last night. I taped all the news broadcasts. In reporting Walter's death, every single station also mentioned the Uccello case. And if the Government prevails in its bid to have Karen's retainer seized, it'll all be for nothing. I think dropping Uccello is the first order of business."

Brander looked at Karen. "Karen?"

"First, I'd like to express to both of you my heartfelt condolences on the death of your friend and colleague. It's no secret that Walter and I weren't close and I won't pretend now that we were. But he was a cofounder of this firm and a good friend to both of you. Despite all that's happened, I feel badly for you on the loss of your friend, and I wanted to say that."

Brander was touched. "Thank you, Karen. Very much."

Darren said, "I'd like to say something about that."

Brander nodded.

"I realize you've already talked to Brander about this, but I want to express to you my apologies, on behalf of Walter, for the terrible experience you have been forced to endure. I'm sure you appreciate now that Walter was not in his right mind, that he knew he was dying, and that he was terrified of the pain associated with that pending event. Whatever animosity he displayed to you, Karen, was never personal. Walter, like all human beings, was flawed. In his case, his attitude toward women lawyers was abominable and unacceptable. I can assure you that Brander and I both tried very hard to change these attitudes, but Walter was not a man to change his mind about anything.

"He was a good lawyer in his own way and a good partner in other ways. But his treatment of you was unforgivable, and we never should have allowed it to reach this point. If anyone, other than Walter himself, is responsible for what happened, it is Brander and myself. As I said, I know Brander's had his say. I just wanted to have mine."

Karen nodded. "Thanks, Darren."

"All right," Brander said, "we have business to discuss."

Karen turned and faced Darren again. "Okay. As for Angelo Uccello . . . let's assume we do drop him. What sort of message does that send to potential clients?"

"I don't really care," Darren said.

"I see. What you're really suggesting is that we drop the criminal law department."

"I didn't say that."

"No, but that's what we'll end up doing if we start dropping clients. As you well know, criminal law represents sixty-five percent of our net revenue. Criminal law isn't pretty, Darren. At times, it can be downright ugly. But, we're either going to offer our services to those charged with crimes or we're not. You can't pick and choose."

"Yes, you can."

Brander tapped a pen on the table. "We are not going to drop Mr. Uccello. Let's move on. Karen?"

Mildly surprised by Brander's assertiveness, Karen said, "All right. First, I'd suggest that we hire a media consultant immediately." She opened a file and removed a page. "I have a list of companies that have done good work with other law firms and come highly recommended. I know we've never done this before, but Darren's right about the negative publicity. We need to counter it quickly."

Brander looked as if he'd swallowed something disgusting. "A media consultant? Have we reached that point?"

"I think we have," Karen said.

"Darren?"

"Well, if we're going to keep handling people like Uccello, we'll need a media consultant on staff full-time."

Brander's face reddened. "Let's stick to this issue. Are you in favor of hiring a media firm immediately for an indeterminate period of time or not?"

"Obviously, I'm in favor," Darren said.

"Fine. We'll do it. Karen, do you have some other suggestions?"

"Yes. I think it's time for a complete overhaul of this firm. I'd like to see at least four people made partner. It's long overdue. Two of them should be women, but I can live with one. Then, I'd like to see our entry-level salary for new associates raised at least ten percent. And while we're at it, a ten percent raise for all associates. As I've said before, our turnover is horrendous. We're not competitive and that makes us little more than a training ground for other law firms, which is more expensive for us in the long run. Other than that, I submit that we have no choice but to simply weather this storm with the help of the media consultants. And I accept either of you as managing partner."

"How about yourself?" Brander asked.

"It's not for me, Brander."

Brander looked at Darren. "How about you, Darren?"

Darren straightened up in his chair. "I think I can handle it."

"It's settled then. Now as to the new partners, how do you feel about that?"

"I think Karen's right on that issue."

Brander looked surprised.

"I know I've spoken against it in the past," Darren said, "but look at us. Three people. It's not enough."

"All right. Which four?"

It took an hour, but they finally agreed on the four people to be given partnerships.

Two of them were women.

At two o'clock in the afternoon on that same day, Karen received a two-page fax from Wilbur Brooks. She read it, uttered an oath, balled up the fax, and threw it into a wastebasket, then told Liz to tell Len Spirsky and Sharon Chin to come to Karen's office. When they arrived, Karen had the TV set turned on.

"What's up?" Len asked.

"You're about to see your government in action," Karen said.

"I don't get it."

"You will. Sit and relax, both of you. Wilbur Brooks is getting ready to hold a news conference."

By the time the two young attorneys were settled in, the local station had broken away from regular programming to cover the news conference. After a short introduction by the TV news announcer, Wilbur Brooks, flanked by two FBI agents and Assistant State Attorney Ben Gastner, stood grim-faced at a lectern festooned with microphones and stared into the TV camera lens. The presence of an assistant *state* attorney at this press conference signaled what was to come. Karen gave the TV set her full attention, the back of her mind already working, calculating, planning.

"After careful consideration," Wilbur began, not looking too happy about such consideration, "and after consultation with law enforcement agencies within the State of Florida, the U.S. attorney has decided to allow the State of Florida to proceed with the charges against Angelo Uccello. Pursuant to that decision, my office has turned all relevant evidence over to the Pinellas County Sheriff's Office for further action.

"We've taken this action for two reasons: The state attorney for Florida's Sixth Judicial District has asked that he be allowed to prosecute this case because the defendant is a resident of Pinellas County, the crime occurred in Pinellas County, and a member of the Pinellas County Sheriff's Office took part in the arrest. The state attorney is of the opinion that local prosecution of local criminals charged with crimes that are committed locally is more in keeping with the State's obligation to protect and serve. And we agree.

"Second, this is an opportunity for federal authorities to demonstrate that we, contrary to popular myth, are working with local law enforcement agencies in a joint effort to rid our communities of the scourge of drug trafficking. By turning this case over to local authorities, the federal government gives much more than lip service to a pledge made years ago.

"Trafficking in illegal drugs is a national problem. If each and every county, with the assistance and cooperation of federal law enforcement agencies, roots out and destroys the cancer that exists in their communities, we can—and will—win this war. We must prevail, for to fail means the possible loss of an entire generation."

Smiling for the first time, Wilbur closed with, "Now, I'd like to turn this over to Assistant State Attorney Ben Gastner, representing the State of Florida."

Ben Gastner, tall, lean, and clear-eyed, nodded to Wilbur and stood in front of the cameras. "We will present the evidence to the Grand Jury this week. Should an indictment be handed up, and we have no doubt it will be, we will vigorously pursue the prosecution of Angelo Uccello. I'll have more to say after the Grand Jury has announced its verdict."

Karen pressed a button on the remote control and the TV set blinked off.

"I don't get it," Sharon said.

Karen took a deep breath, exhaled, then smiled.

"What you've seen here is a sham. Pinellas County didn't ask for this case; it was dropped on them. It happens more times than most people realize."

"But why?"

"Well, I think we have them a little nervous. We're claiming our client was framed. There are times when that kind of defense is simply a ploy, but in this case, it's not a ploy at all. Uccello *was* framed. The question is by whom? Uccello says the feds and Juan Ramirez are in bed together. That's quite an accusation and one that's very difficult, if not impossible, to prove. So, we're left with the questions: Are the feds really protecting and helping Juan Ramirez? Are these just some rogue agents or is this something much more sinister? Whatever the truth might be, I don't think Wilbur Brooks wants those questions on the table in open court.

"For another thing, drug cases are tougher to win in federal criminal court. The standards may seem the same, but they aren't. Dropping this case into the state's lap has given the feds a very big edge, one they didn't have in federal court."

"How so?"

"Well, for one, we're prohibited from calling any of the FBI agents as witnesses because they have immunity. For another, the feds can let Olivera and Aznar flee to Colombia where we can't touch them. We are now facing a much less complex case without being able to call the witnesses we need. And without those witnesses, we'll have a much tougher time proving it was a setup. All in all, a pretty clever move by Wilbur Brooks, I'd say."

"What do we do now?" Sharon asked.

"Destroy that immunity.

"First, you go down to federal court, dig up the document confirming the charges have been dropped, and get our client's bond back. They're holding some accounting ledgers that belong to our client as well. Get them. That's number one. While you're doing that, I'll make some phone calls."

"Okay."

Karen watched her two associates leave, then headed for Brander's office. She brought him up to date on the Uccello case, then said, "I have a request."

"Yes?"

"I want to take a few days off."

"Now?"

"Immediately after Walter's funeral. I need some time. I'd like you to shepherd Len and Sharon while I'm away."

"Karen, I haven't done criminal defense in years."

"I know that. Uccello will probably be arrested sometime this week, but the arraignment won't be for at least two. I'll be back long before that. You can handle the bail hearing with Sharon. I'll explain things to Uccello.

"I have to get away, Brander. I simply have to."

He looked at her for a long time before he finally nodded his approval.

* * *

Uccello was just finishing up his lunch when Karen was ushered into his office.

"So," he said, wiping his lips with a white linen napkin, "my condolences on the loss of your partner. Press tried to make you look bad, the bastards. You okay?"

"I'm fine," she said.

"This Sinclair guy. Musta been some kind of nut."

"Let's talk about you," Karen said.

"You mean about the feds getting out of my face? Sounds good to me. I rather face the locals any day."

Karen shook her head. "Don't get too excited. What they've done hurts us. You're sure to be arrested by the local authorities. There'll probably still be a trial, unless we can stop it."

Uccello looked totally confused. "I don't get it."

"I think I do," Karen said "We're getting too close to something. The feds don't want to chance exposure, so they're letting the locals carry the ball. The law allows federal agents immunity from being called as witnesses as a result of doing their jobs. That means we can't call them, which really screws up our defense. This way, there's a better chance of getting a conviction, at least in their eyes."

"What about them seizing my business?"

"As far as the federal warrant is concerned, it's a dead issue. Under Florida law, the locals have the right to ask for seizure, and they may."

"In other words, we're back to square one?"

"It would appear so."

He banged a fist on his desk. "The bastards. They're tryin' to wear us down, that's what. If this doesn't work, they'll do somethin' else. Am I right or am I right?"

"You may be right."

"So what do we do now?"

"We wait to see what happens. You'll probably be arrested this week."

"Terrific."

"I have something else to tell you."

"What?"

"I might not be here when you're arrested. I'm going away Thursday for a long weekend. Brander Hewitt, along with two associates working with me, will take care of things."

"You're gong away?"

"I need some time off."

"Now?"

"Yes, now. Brander's very capable."

"I'm sure he is, but . . . what happens if he screws up?"

"He won't."

"But if he does . . . where can I find you?"

"You can't."

"That's just great!"

Karen's jaw tightened. "Listen to me. This is going to be a long drawn-out process. If I'm to be of any use to you whatsoever, I need time to recharge my batteries. I've had a tough couple of weeks. Now, if this isn't acceptable, you can fire me and find someone else."

He held up his hands. "There's no need to get hysterical."

"I really hate that word, Angelo. What's it to be?"

He shrugged. "You need some time, you need some time. What can I say?"

"Fine. I'll be in touch as soon as I get back."

"Fine."

She placed a business card on the desk. "This is Brander's card."

"Great. Just great."

"Look, I'm not abandoning you. I'm talking a few days vacation, that's all."

"I heard you."

"While I'm gone, I'd like you to go through your diaries and pull out anything you think might have a bearing on this case."

"You gotta be kiddin'. You want me to go through my diaries?"

"What's wrong with that?"

His eyes rolled back in their sockets. "There's thirty megs of stuff in there."

"So?"

"So? You expect me to go through thirty megs of documents and pull out . . . didn't I tell you that every file is encrypted?"

"Yes, you did."

"Don't you understand? That means every file has to be decoded before you can read it. Then, it has to be encrypted again. I ain't got time for all that."

"But you said you had names and dates that were relevant."

"I do."

"Angelo, we need that information. We're going into court trying to prove—"

"Forget it. I'm not ready to let the feds know what I got on them. Not yet, anyway."

Karen, exasperated, said, "Well, do you have a better idea?"

"As a matter of fact, I do."

"Okay. What is it?"

"If I give you the diaries, they're protected by the same client/lawyer privilege as everything else, right?"

"Yes."

"You can't do nothin' with 'em without my say-so, right?"

"Also true."

"Okay, while you're away, you leave your laptop with me. I'll transfer copies of all the files onto your machine. Then *you* can take the time lookin' for whatever it is you want. I'm payin' you enough."

"What about the password?"

"I'll give you your own password when I transfer the files. What password would you like to use?"

Karen thought for a moment. "Angelo, I don't have the time either. The only way this would work is if my associates worked on this. They're bound by the same rules I am, so don't worry about that."

"Can you trust them?"

"Absolutely."

"Okay. Then that's what we'll do. But I want your word that nothin' gets out unless I say so, and that the files stay encrypted except when you've got one of 'em open."

"Okay. But I may need to use some of them at the hearing."

"What for?"

"The prosecution is going to present witnesses who will testify under oath—lie, in fact—that they bought drugs from you directly. I want to be able to rebut that testimony. Having your diary on hand is the perfect rebuttal because the court knows we can't anticipate what dates will be discussed."

He shook his head. "That stuff is dynamite. You'd have to block out some stuff before you use what you need. The only way I'll let you do that is if you bring the laptop to court. We can pull the file you need right there."

"Okay. I can live with that."

"I'd have to see each page first."

"That's okay."

He thought about it for a minute. "As long as you keep everything encrypted, okay. If the feds grab your laptop, and they damn well might, it's no good to them as long as the stuff stays encrypted. They can't use it. That's all I care about."

"No problem," Karen said. "I'll leave my laptop with you now. And I'll see you when I get back."

He threw his hands in the air. "I'm about to be

arrested again and you're takin' off. What if the locals deny bail?"

"They may, but I doubt it."

"Just so you know, I think your timing stinks."

"So noted. And just so you know, if I waited until the right moment to take time off, I'd never do it."

She turned on her heel and headed for the door. He called after her. "Karen?"

"Yes?"

"You were right."

"About what?"

"I tried to contact my friend, the one with a copy of my diary? He's been dead for a month. Died in a fire. Cops say the propane tank beside his house exploded. No foul play."

"I'm sorry," Karen said.

"He musta gone to them. There's no other way they'd know he existed. No way. I guess he figured I was goin' down anyway, so he might as well try and make a buck."

"Again, I'm sorry."

"Have a great vacation," he said, his voice thick with sarcasm.

"I will."

"Hey!"

"What?"

"You never told me what password you wanted."

Karen hesitated, then said, "Let's use the words 'imperfect justice.'"

15

Karen felt like a kid. It was wonderful. She was in the master bedroom, packing for a four-day vacation; four days of being a wife and lover without the added responsibilities of mother and professional. Four days with this gorgeous hunk of humanity who was her husband, four days of fun and relaxation, and sex, and more sex.

She needed this escape, hungered for it, and could hardly wait to get to the airport. At the same time, there was the looming specter of Walter's funeral, scheduled for eleven o'clock the next morning. She had to be there. Absolutely had to be, knowing she'd be subjected to stares, glares, whispers, and a few cruel verbal jabs.

Eleanor had asked that Karen stand with the family. It was her way of making amends for Walter's final truculent act, an act that could have been devastating to Karen's career. By making a public display of her support for Karen, Eleanor was showing the world what she thought of Walter's cruelty. It as a lovely and courageous gesture, but Karen politely and gratefully declined. The family deserved to grieve without intrusions from outsiders, however well intentioned.

Karen wasn't going to let the funeral dampen her enthusiasm for the trip, no matter what.

She heard the door chime's musical tune. Her head automatically turned to the room's alarm system/intercom unit, one of eleven in the house. It was force of habit. She heard Michelle ask who was there and then the answering voice of Jennifer Steel, president of the homeowners association.

Karen walked to the intercom and said, "I'll be right down, Jennifer."

When Karen reached the bottom of the stairs, Jennifer was standing there, wringing her hands.

"What's the problem?" Karen asked.

"I hope I'm not disturbing you."

"Not at all. Carl and Andrea are doing something with the computer in the den. Why don't we go into the kitchen?"

"Okay."

"Coffee?"

"No, thanks."

Jennifer was an architect by profession, but seemed to spend most of her time helping manage the affairs of this upscale community, 280 upper-middle-class homes, independently owned, but managed by an association and a board of directors created to maintain harmony in the community's appearance, be it in the color of the house and/or the landscaping. There was a thick document given to all homeowners that covered almost every aspect of home ownership, and enough rules and regulations to choke a horse. But under Jennifer's able leadership, the association worked well. There was little friction.

"We have a real problem," Jennifer said as she took a seat at the kitchen table, "and Laura is away for another week." Laura was the association's attorney.

"Well, I'm going away myself," Karen said.

"Oh. Well, I just need an opinion, that's all."

"I'll try. What is it?"

"You know the Taylor place has been vacant for almost a year. They've lowered their asking price three times, but still nothing."

"Of course." The Taylor place was a four-bedroom ranch-style house across the street from the Mondori house. "What about it?"

"Well . . . the Taylors have rented it out, completely furnished. I guess they're getting desperate. That's not the problem, though. The rules say you can rent as long as it's for a minimum of seven months."

"And?"

"Well . . . it appears they rented it to a single man. All the papers were in order and the man's credit was good, so the board approved it without giving it much thought. But now I suspect the man's running a business out of his house."

"What makes you think that?"

Jennifer seemed surprised by the question. "You haven't noticed anything weird?"

"No. I've been a little busy. I've hardly had a chance to look out the window. Why? What should I be noticing?"

"Well, the man who rented the house has a live-in friend, another man. And the two of them have other friends. The renter moved in a week ago and there's been a stream of men coming and going ever since. Usually at night. Who knows what's going on in there?"

Karen nodded. "And you're worried that they're operating some kind of business?"

"Exactly. Worse yet, it could be some kind of boiler-room scam. If it was legitimate, why not rent office space? It would probably cost less."

"Okay, let me ask you some questions. Other than men entering and leaving the house, has there been anything else unusual going on? Like loud music, wild parties, things like that?"

"No. They're very, very quiet."

"Have any of the neighbors been bothered in any way?"

"No. Not so far."

"So, what are you worried about?"

"They're not what we want here. This is a development for families. If they're conducting a business, they're breaking the association rules. I want them out—before our property values are affected."

Karen nodded. "Do you have any evidence they *are* doing business out of the house? What do you know about them?"

"Mr. Fielding, the man who signed the lease, is about forty, I guess. The other men seem to be about the same age. That's all I know about them—except for their strange schedules."

Karen took a deep breath. "You said you wanted

an opinion. Well, here's mine. There's nothing you can do. There's nothing you *should* do without solid evidence."

"But—"

"Look, if the man's not doing anything wrong except keeping odd hours for himself and his friends, you could cause a real rift in neighborly relations by antagonizing him."

Jennifer shook her head. "I don't know . . ."

"Once Laura gets back, talk to her, but I suspect she'll tell you the same thing."

"You really think so?"

"Consider this: Just because men gather doesn't mean they're operating a business or doing something illegal. Ever been to a Kiwanis or Rotary club meeting? I think you're overreacting, Jennifer. Relax."

"You're not much help, you know?"

"I'm sorry, Jennifer. Perhaps Laura will have a more attractive suggestion when she gets back. She's the expert on homeowner association law, not me."

"I was hoping . . ."

"I know. But truth to tell, this may be premature. Are there a lot of men coming and going?"

"Well . . . not a lot. It's almost like shifts. Mr. Fielding and his . . . companion . . . seem to work all day. They usually get to the house together about eleven or so."

"At night?"

"Yes."

"They're gone all day?"

"Yes. Then, in the morning, two other men show

up and Mr. Fielding and his friend leave. There's another pair that shows up around five."

"Every day?"

"For the last week."

Karen shrugged. "Well, it's certainly odd behavior. Tell you what, bring me a copy of the application Mr. Fielding provided. I'll have the private investigator who works for me do a background check and see if there's . . ."

Jennifer gushed. "Oh, would you?"

"Sure."

Jennifer pulled a folded sheet from her handbag. "I brought it along."

"I'll see what I can find out. I won't have an answer until I get back, though."

"That's okay."

"Well, I better get back to my packing."

Jennifer took the hint.

Karen put the folded sheet in her handbag. She'd give it to Liz at the funeral and ask Liz to have Bill do some checking.

Just to keep the peace.

Karen and Carl flew to Bermuda—Carl's choice; he kept the destination a secret until the last moment—immediately after Walter Sinclair's well-attended funeral. They were lucky to get seats on any airplane, this being Labor Day weekend. Were it not for Carl's near harassment of the travel agent and a fortuitous cancellation two days before flight time, the couple would have had to choose some other destination.

The sun was just beginning to set as the MD-11's

spindly-looking landing gear dropped free and its small wheels kissed the asphalt runway on St. George's Island. They took a cab across the bridge to the main island and the Elbow Beach Hotel. They registered and were escorted to a luxurious two-room suite on the fifth floor that faced the ocean. They quickly changed into relaxing clothes, then headed for the now-darkened beach.

It was a glorious night, cool and moon-bright, the sky ablaze with stars. They sat on the deserted beach and let the gentle breezes caress their skin like a thousand invisible feathers. Bermuda was but a few hundred air miles from home, but it felt like half a world away. Already, Karen could feel some of the tension draining away.

They walked and walked until exhausted, then slept until ten the next morning, had breakfast served in their room, then explored the Front Street shops in busy Hamilton. They held hands and smiled at each other like new lovers, watched like kids as a huge cruise ship tied up across the street and disgorged chattering tourists dressed in garish, multicolored outfits that seemed as foreign to Bermuda as bad manners. Then, it was back to the beach and a dip in the chilly waters of the mid-Atlantic.

That night, and the next, they made love unhurriedly, by candlelight, the distant sounds of steel drum bands and gently rolling surf drifting through the open balcony door. Carl, a patient, unselfish lover, was especially spectacular on this trip, and there were times when Karen wanted to scream at the top of her lungs to express her ecstasy. It had been years since she'd experienced such powerful orgasms, each one more potent than the last. The world vanished as she and Carl gave themselves to each other, collapsing in one another's arms, struggling for air, their bodies covered with perspiration and the uniquely pungent smell of passionate sex.

She slept like a log every night. In a dreamless state. Awakening slowly, every muscle in her body limp from relaxation. Even her sore shoulder was returning to normal.

It was magic.

They talked about nothing and everything, as when they'd first met, like two strangers getting acquainted. In fact, they were getting reacquainted, and both realized it. The press of business and parenting—or was it simply a rut—had imposed its ugly list of needs on both of them for far too long. Once before, they'd recognized the danger. That time, they'd flown off to Canada with Andrea, watching her delight at discovering snow for the first time. But this retreat was for them alone, and none too soon.

They rediscovered all the wonderful things in each other that had drawn them together in the first place. They laughed more in two days than they had in all the previous six months. They watched the little children in their tidy uniforms gather at the schools; observed the gentle people of Bermuda as they served their guests with unfailing charm and politeness.

Fully aware that much of the island nation's economy depended on tourists, the natives exhibited patience and sincere civility to even the rudest of visitors. To Karen and Carl, it was as if they'd taken a step back in time.

They rented motor scooters and explored this magical place, just the tip of a volcanic mountain descending fourteen thousand feet to the ocean floor, winding their way through narrow, labyrinthian, flower-laden, redolent roads cluttered with small cars—rationed one to a household and unavailable to tourists because of the paucity of highways and parking space. This was a country that steadfastly refused to resign itself to what most Western nations saw as inevitable.

Bermuda was, for Karen and Carl, an Eden.

By the third say, the couple had surrendered themselves to the slow pace. And it was that same day, while sitting on the beach, their already tanned skin darkening perceptibly, that Karen startled her husband with a remark he'd been praying to hear ever since their marriage.

"Maybe I *should* give it up."

It came out of nowhere, in the middle of a discussion about old whaling ships. Carl rolled over on his side, the pink sand sticking to his gleaming skin, propped his head on one hand, and stared at Karen with those dark eyes that always drew her in. "Give up what?"

"Criminal law."

"Great idea," he said, placing his head back down on a towel and closing his eyes.

"I mean it," Karen insisted.

"Good. I've been asking you to give it up for years."

"I know."

"Well, that's settled, then. What will you do? Family law? Corporate?"

"You're teasing me."

"Of course I am."

"I'm trying to be serious," Karen said firmly.

"Okay. Let's talk about it."

"I thought that's what we were doing."

He sat up. "Okay. Let's look at the facts. We've both been doing very well financially. Andrea's trust fund is established. We have a healthy investment portfolio. We live in a nice house in a good neighborhood, have a limited but enjoyable social life, all the comforts, all the whiz-bang electronics. We have our health, and we're still relatively young. A lot to be thankful for, I'd say.

"On the other side of the ledger, because of what you do, your name is mentioned in the newspapers about once a week, usually in a negative context. Half the people in the Tampa Bay area recognize you on sight, and not all of them are asking for your autograph. You've been spat upon three times if I remember correctly. Threatened at least four times. Punched once, but you socked the shit out of that bitch, so I guess that one doesn't count."

Karen laughed. It had been quite spectacular, her one and only fistfight. A woman she'd defended on a check-kiting charge—pro bono, no less—was found guilty. As soon as the verdict was announced, the woman turned and punched Karen in the stomach. Before the bailiffs could react, Karen's temper exploded and the lawyer threw an uppercut that some witnesses claimed lifted the woman right off her feet. She collapsed in a heap on the floor while the bailiffs and jury applauded.

Karen was mortified.

But only for a few minutes.

The press dubbed her the "Battling Bantam." It took several letters beseeching them not to do so before they retired the appellation.

"At the moment," Carl continued, "you're escaping the week from hell, a week that would put most people in a rubber room. So you're asking yourself the question: Why the hell am I busting my butt? It's enough that your husband has to, if only because we do need some income and men are supposed to work because it's in the rule book, but . . . you don't really have to work, right?"

"That's what I've been thinking," Karen said. "I should be spending more time with Andrea. I feel very guilty about that. I'm becoming like my mother, letting Michelle be the parent."

"Bad example," Carl said. "Annie saved you. If you'd been raised by your mother, you'd really be a basket case."

"That's not the point. I want us to raise Andrea."

She finally had Carl's full attention. He looked at her intently. "You're being a tad hard on yourself. You spend a lot of time with Andrea. We both do. I don't think she's suffering. All Michelle does is take her to and from school, when you get right down to it."

"Except when we both have to work a weekend."

"That doesn't happen very often."

"Lately, it's been happening much too often."

Carl said nothing.

"I'm tired of the stupid games, Carl. I got into this business because I was an idealist. I thought I could make a difference. But I make no difference. No one can. The system grinds along untended, uncared for, falling apart in big chunks. No one gives a damn. It's all a joke."

"All true," he sighed.

"Take this Uccello case. Either he's lying or he isn't. If he *is* lying, all I'm doing is helping him continue to sell drugs to people who should be spending what little money they have on treatment."

"I thought you put him through a lie detector test."

"I did. But the questions concerned *this* case. Even then, you never know. The machines are not infalliable, nor are the operators. And Angelo is no fool. But even if he's innocent of this charge, he's still a drug trafficker."

"Okay," Carl said. "Let's look at the facts. If Angelo Uccello dropped dead tomorrow, would less people use drugs?"

"That's not the point."

"But it is something to consider."

Karen thought for a moment. "Didn't you once tell me drug addiction is a genetic predisposition?"

"I did, and it is. They've found the gene locus, too. In twenty years, through the miracle of genetic engineering, they'll be able to treat addiction in an entirely new way. Be it drugs, booze, cigarettes, whatever, addictive personalities will be successfully treated without all the pain and suffering of withdrawal. The ethical questions that remain seem to focus on the morality of voluntary or involuntary treatment. I suspect that by the time the treatment is ready, they'll have answered that question. In any case, Mr. Uccello and his friends will be out of business. No one will want to buy his product."

"I won't hold my breath."

"You have a right to be a cynic, but genetic engineering is going to change everything. Trust me. But, getting back to Mr. Uccello and his ilk, nothing is served by you quitting the business. Not really."

"But," Karen argued, "I'm helping him destroy a few more lives."

"Is that how you see it?"

"Yes. And besides, I'm looking at what appears to be a conspiracy. The Government of my country working in concert with drug traffickers. I'm not at all sure I want to face that kind of reality."

"I wouldn't say it's the Government. I'd say it was some people working within the Government."

"I wish that were so. But the more I learn of this case, the more it appears the whole drug enforcement bureaucracy is looking the other way. Otherwise they'd do something."

"Maybe they are doing something," Carl said. "Maybe the results of what they're doing aren't yet obvious."

She stared at him. "You? An apologist for the Government? I never thought I'd see the day."

"I'm not being an apologist. I'm simply suggesting that you may be hearing one side of the story, that the other side's position isn't available . . . yet."

"In any case, this is a lose-lose situation, don't you see?"

"I see exactly."

"Good. And, as I said before, it bugs me that I like this guy. How the hell is it possible for me to muster up even a milligram of affection for such a man?"

"That's easy," Carl said. "It seems to me that he's the only guy in this whole stinking mess who's actually being straight with you. Okay, so he's a drug dealer. Very, very bad. But it's never black and white with people. I'm not apologizing for him either, so don't get the wrong idea, but why waste time kicking yourself because you don't hate him? Enough of that."

"All right."

"And I fully support your decision to get out of the criminal law business."

She looked into his eyes. "Why do I get the feeling you're humoring me?"

Carl sighed. "Karen . . . I'd be thrilled if you decided to stop being a criminal defense lawyer because you really wanted to quit. I really mean that. But let's be honest. You're not in it simply because you're an idealist. You're in it because you know you *do* make a difference.

"Remember Jack Palmer? That poor guy would be in jail today if not for you. You believed in him. A public defender might not have, given the weight of the evidence pointing toward his guilt. Caroline DeFauldo and her sneaky husband would be walking around free. Now, they're both in jail where they belong and Jack is the free man. That's justice, and you're responsible for it.

"How many people would be dead broke if you hadn't gone to bat for them and sued the hell out of those who would have screwed them into the ground. There has to be *some* satisfaction in knowing you've been instrumental in helping a lot of folks, and it's that satisfaction that keeps you going."

He pointed to the ocean. "Why are we here in this lovely place? Because you've had things pile up at a frightening rate, that's why. You've been visited by your mother and brother, causing all kinds of emotional turmoil; you've had a partner commit suicide, a man you despised for good reason. You feel guilty about hating a man who was truly a bastard even before he got ill; you're in the middle of a dirty trial, defending an old mafioso who's trying to scare the hell out of you . . . Jesus! There's no way I'd be able to stand that kind of pressure. But to quit? Uh-uh. You'd end up hating yourself. You know it and I know it.

"You love what you do. You may not enjoy all that goes with it, but you get the same kind of gratification when you win one that I get when I see someone walking pain-free for the first time in years. In our own way, we're junkies, too, Karen. We thrive on accomplishment. We need that constant rush. That's the biggest thing we have in common, when you get right down to it. That and sex."

"Please don't talk about sex right now."

"Why not?"

"I'll want to make love to you again."

"Ready when you are."

"Later. We are discussing my career."

"Okay. To sum up, Counselor, you give all that up, and you'll wilt like a rose in a sauna. I don't think that's what you really want. And you know I'm right."

She hung her head in silence. After a few moments, Carl put his arm around her and pulled her close. "You okay?"

"You're crazy, you know?"

"Why?"

"Because you see right through me."

"And you through me. Let's have no more talk of business. We're here to get the hell away from business, remember?"

"Okay."

"I love you, Karen."

"I love you, too. Wanna make love?"

"Here?"

"I'm game."

Carl looked at the crowded beach. "Maybe we should go back to the room first."

Karen kissed him, then said, "Yeah. Maybe we should."

16

The Beemer was ready.

Just sitting behind the wheel gave Karen a sense of normality. And taking it for a test drive before signing off on the bill was like being with an old friend. With its fresh paint and new parts, it not only smelled like a new car, but the repair had eliminated a few annoying rattles and creaks from the past. The car felt solid.

And the radio worked.

Karen arrived at the office in great spirits—renewed, refreshed, and bolstered by Carl's whole-hearted support. After hounding her for years to quit criminal law, he'd shown his true colors the first time she seriously considered it. The depth of his support was a wonderment to Karen, for though she'd always thought of Carl as a treasure, she'd never fully appreciated how great a treasure he really was. When the chips were down, he was more interested in her well-being than his own. She felt more loved than ever before.

Bermuda had turned out to be more than a vacation. It was a special experience in many ways, like falling in love all over again. Just thinking about it now gave her a tingle.

Now back to work, the first order of business was a meeting with Brander on the Uccello case. He brought her up to speed quickly. The Grand Jury had handed up an indictment in short order. Angelo Uccello was arrested immediately, his bond set at two million dollars. Karen knew that wouldn't stick. It was just the judge's way of tweaking Karen's nose for not attending first appearance.

"The good news," Brander said, obviously distressed that he'd been unable to convince the judge to lower bond, "is that, for some unknown reason, the state is not pressing for property seizure. So that's one issue you'll not have to face."

"That *is* good news," Karen told him. "One less issue is appreciated. Thanks for standing in for me, Brander."

"You're welcome. How was the vacation?"

"Wonderful. As soon as I have some time, I'll give you a full report."

"Where'd you go?"

"Bermuda."

"Ah, yes. A lovely place. Well, it seems to have done you a world of good. You look terrific!"

"Thanks. What did you think of Angelo?"

Brander shook his head. "He's not what I expected at all. He hardly said a word to me, kept referring to me as Mr. Hewitt, was helpful and quite courteous throughout. I will say he was quite concerned about being in jail until his first appearance. If I had to make a guess, I'd say he's in great fear for his life."

Vacation was over. Karen felt the familiar adrenaline surge.

"His bodyguards were everywhere," Brander said, reflecting. "It seemed to me they were expecting trouble. And that's a great concern, Karen. My concern, quite naturally, is for you."

"There's not much I can do about it," Karen said. "I'm not a fatalist, but I doubt anyone would risk killing or injuring the man's lawyer, igniting the full fury of the criminal justice system."

"I hesitated to mention it," Brander said, "but you should be aware."

"I am. How did Angelo post bond?"

"He put up the house and business." Brander rubbed his hands together. "Well, enough of that. There are four new partners now very eager to shake your hand."

"You told them?"

"Yes. The official announcement will come tomorrow, but, as you suggested, I let them know Friday. At the same time, we initiated the new salary scale. There are a lot of smiling faces out there, thanks to you."

"Thanks to the three of us."

He held up his hands. "Not in the least. This was your idea, Karen, and if it reflects badly on the bottom line, you'll soon realize just how much it was your idea."

"You'll have to give it some time, Brander."

"I will. You estimated two years. I'll give you that." She smiled. "Then, I'll have no excuses."

"Exactly. Oh, and the media consultants are hard

at work. They interviewed Eleanor again and prepared a press release in the form of an article that re-
volves around the general issue of terminally ill
people and suicide, sort of a human interest approach. Buried within the article is Eleanor's reaffir-
mation of the true intent of Walter's suicide note. The
media people say it'll take repetition of this theme to
completely undo the damage. They seem to know
what they're about. And they want to interview you
as soon as possible."

"I'm not sure that's a good idea," Karen said.

"I'll leave the decision to you."

"Thanks. I better get caught up with Liz."

"One other thing before you do."

"Yes?"

"Len Spirsky passed the Bar exam. The results
were posted yesterday. He's walking on air."

"That's great."

"We'll be having a small gathering Friday night."

"I'll be there."

"Welcome back, Karen. We missed you."

"Thanks. I'd like to say I missed all of you as well,
but the truth is . . ."

"Yes, yes," Brander said, grinning. "Before you go,
let me give you back your laptop. Uccello gave it to
me the day after you left. I gave it to Sharon and she
transferred the files onto her computer. She and Len
have been hard at it ever since."

"There's a lot of files to go through. Fifty years'
worth."

Brander walked to a closet, reached in, and
grabbed a small leather case that he handed to Karen.

"If what Mr. Uccello claims is true, you have a bomb-shell here. What are your plans?"

"I'm not sure, yet."

"Well, good luck."

The mail was heavy, as were the messages. Requests from newspeople were thrown away. Normally, Karen cooperated with the press, sometimes even used them, as do most lawyers, to plead her case to the public. But not this case.

"Bill Castor called," Liz told Karen. "He said he'll be here early. He says he has some very important information."

"Great. Send him in the moment he arrives. In the meantime, send Len and Sharon in here."

"They're practically foaming at the mouth to see you," Liz said.

The two associates had been working exclusively on the Angelo Uccello diaries almost the entire time Karen was away. Their efforts bore much fruit. Sharon had a thick file in her hands.

"Before you start," Karen said, "I want to congratulate Len on passing the Bar."

"Thanks."

"Now you can sit in the pit."

He grinned. "I'm looking forward to that."

"So, how'd you make out?"

Sharon gave the report. "This was quite a chore. Mr. Uccello's diaries are in fifty separate directories, each with twelve subdirectories, one for each month, and file for each day. We couldn't possibly decode and reencrypt all of them, so we had to use the rough dates provided by Mr. Uccello."

"He gave you a list of dates?"

"There was an envelope in the laptop case addressed to Ms. Perry-Mondori's associates. We figured it was okay to open it."

"Go on."

"Well, it was a note from Mr. Uccello. He gave us a list of dates which he said were as close as he could remember, like September 1987, and spring 1958 . . . stuff like that. So we had to decode as many as fifty files in order to find a particular reference."

"And?"

Sharon beamed. "So far, we have a total of forty-five names: one senator, eight Miami cops, four DEA agents, three Customs agents, eleven CIA agents, two judges, seven FBI agents, five lawyers, and four Justice Department investigators. In each case, Uccello has documented their relationships with either himself, members of the old Gambino family, or Juan Ramirez."

Karen tried to keep her voice level as she asked, "What's the senator's name?"

"Stewart. He's from California."

"What's his connection?"

"Why don't you read the diary entry?" Sharon suggested.

Karen's heart started beating again. She held out her hand. "The folder contains the hard copies?"

Sharon handed her the folder. "Yes."

"You didn't let anyone know about this?"

"Just Brander."

"And the files are still encrypted?"

"Yes."

"These are the only hard copies?"

"Yes."

"Good. Let's keep it that way."

Karen flipped through the pages. Each was headed with the name and position of the contact. She found the one marked "Senator Stewart" and began to read.

"January 23, 1987. Met with Senator George Stewart today at the Hilton. Had breakfast with the little prick. He owns a small ranch in Texas handed down from his daddy. Land ain't worth much except it lies on the border between Mexico and Texas. A perfect spot. There's a narrow, unguarded road that runs right across the border.

"The asshole met Gotti in New York and pitched him on the idea. Says we could bring drugs in through his property. He's got a big barn where we can load and unload trucks. The nearest neighbor is five miles away, and the nearest Customs office is fifty miles away. Stewart says all he wants is twenty grand a month. Gotti figures it's almost a good deal and asked me to meet with him. I told John I was worried it was a setup, but he says it ain't. So, I was supposed to tell the senator we'd give him five grand for every load we brought across. I was also to tell him that if we ever got busted he was a dead man.

"I told him. He bought the deal. After he left, I looked at the chair he was sitting in. The little prick had pissed his pants."

Karen let out a low whistle. "This is incredible."

"We thought so, too."

"Are the rest like this?"

"You bet. Some are even better."

"You did well. Keep at it. There's got to be more."

"We will."

"And thanks, both of you."

Bill Castor arrived ten minutes later. As usual, the detective was a treasure trove of information.

"We got one," he said, his Cheshire cat grin firmly in place. "Guy's name is Trencher. Ronald Alvin Trencher. He's been with the bureau for twelve years. Worked Miami until a year ago. Now, he works out of Tampa."

Karen remembered his name in the FBI report. "He was in the room when the safe was opened," she said.

"That figures."

"Hold on."

Karen picked through the folder Sharon and Len had just provided. Trencher's name was there. She quickly scanned the diary entry.

"November 11, 1992. More FBI assholes getting their share of the pie. Ballard introduced me to a new guy today. Name's Trencher. Ballard's been trans-ferred to Washington. A promotion, no less. Ain't that great! The guy's been ripping us off for three years and he gets promoted. Trencher seems okay. From the way he acts, this ain't nothing new to him."

Karen closed the folder.

"What's that?" Bill asked.

"Just some notes. What about Trencher?"

"Well, as you know, Trencher was one of the guys

in on the raid. According to the FBI report, he and two other FBI agents were inside the room holding the safe."

"And Detective Chalmers from Pinellas."

"Right. You look surprised. How come? You were the one who suggested these guys might be dirty."

"I know. But you're saying only one was dirty. I expected a different name."

"Bruce Tasker?"

"Yes."

"He checks out okay. He's not above breaking a few rules to make an arrest stick, but if he's making extra money, I can't find it."

Tasker's name was not in Angelo's files either. Karen wondered why. He couldn't possibly be straight. "Okay," she said, "tell me about Trencher."

"I was about to."

"Sorry."

"No problem."

Bill read from his notes. "He's married, three kids, lives in a small rented house in Carrolwood. Drives a government-issue car, wife drives a three-year-old Ford, and there's nothing to indicate he lives beyond his means, except . . ."

"Quit teasing. Go on."

"Okay. His parents are both alive. Listen to this: Until three years ago, his parents lived in a dump in some Wisconsin farm town. Now they live in a four-hundred-thousand-dollar condo in Kingman, Arizona. Mother never worked and father was a teacher. Both are on small fixed incomes, but the condo was purchased with cash. Parents told the developer they'd saved the money by skimping for thirty years. Said it was their dream."

"I'll bet."

"That isn't all. Trencher has a brother named Harold. Harold used to be a sales manager for an electronics distributor in Carson, California. Now, he's got his own thriving business in Irvine. Calls it HFT Electronics. Started the business two years ago. Initial capital was three million, supposedly borrowed from friends, except none of the friends are on the board of directors. If I lent a guy money to start a business, I'd sure as hell want to keep an eye on my investment, wouldn't you?"

"Absolutely."

"Seems Harold travels a lot, especially to Switzerland and the Netherlands Antilles. He has no business interests in either country, but, as you know, both countries are havens for laundered money."

"You think he's doing it for more than just his brother?"

"You got it. Harold's the courier for more than his brother, which means we're dealing with an organized group."

"Wheels within wheels, and no one's the wiser?"

"Not so far. Harold lives in a million-dollar house with live-in help. He drives a Rolls, and nobody out there knows his brother is an FBI agent. He listed himself as an only child on all the papers he signed for both the house and the business. Parents backed him up, according to the credit reporting agency."

"Nice family."

"Yeah. I managed to obtain copies of phone records that show at least two calls a week being made between Harold and Ronald Trencher. All the calls to Ronald were made direct, but all the calls *from* Ronald were made from pay phones. Cute, huh?"

"Cute. He looks dirty to me. How'd you manage to get all this?"

"We all have our secrets, Karen."

"Right. And the others? Tasker?"

"Like I said, all the other agents check out okay. That doesn't mean they're clean, just that I can't find it if it's there."

Karen rubbed her temples. "Tasker and the safe-cracker have got to be dirty. That deposition was a crock. If Trencher did this alone, he would have to make sure all the other agents were out of the room when he put the coke in the safe, wouldn't he?"

"Not necessarily."

Karen leaned back in her chair and stared at the ceiling. "Angelo has a theory that everything changed after Noriega was busted. He says that was the signal for the CIA to start taking over the drug trade. It was also the signal for the good guys to start breaking the rules to get what they wanted. Any truth to that?"

"I picked up something which I'll get to in a moment. Did you know that almost fifty former Justice Department lawyers have quit in the past five years?"

"No."

"Some of them have gone to work for the cartels, while others have gone into private practice. And a few have simply disappeared. No one seems too concerned. Uccello could be right.'

Karen sighed. "We need to get close to one of those FBI agents and get the real story."

Bill shook his head. "They're not going to talk to us. Even if they knew one of their own is dirty, they'd want to handle it in their own way."

"Fine. But let's make sure they know what we know."

"And if they're dirty? Bad idea. You'd be in serious, serious trouble if you talked to the wrong side. You can't take that chance, Karen. Things are bad enough already. But you can call me as a witness at the hearing. I can testify to what I found out."

"But that would leave you hanging out to dry."

"Not really. It's public record then. No point in coming after me."

Karen thought for a moment. "You sure you want to do this?"

"No, but it has to be done."

A wave of melancholy swept over Karen.

"You okay?" Bill asked.

"I'll be all right. It's just . . ."

"What?"

She sighed, then said, "I was just thinking about Bermuda."

He handed her another file folder. "This won't help. As I said, I picked something up. I had a long talk with two retired Miami cops who now live there. They are two very bitter retired Miami cops. According to them, the CIA is bringing more cocaine into this country than the bad guys. And there are more than a few FBI guys and Miami cops involved. It's not common knowledge, but close.

"There've been about six major task forces working on this. All have failed, primarily because each task force has at least one person tied in to the action. People are getting frustrated. It may explain why they're going after lawyers so hard."

Karen tapped a pencil on her desk. A thought was percolating in the back of her mind. "How well do you know these retired cops?"

"I just met them."

"I see."

"Why?"

"Forget it. Just thinking out loud."

"You'll find everything in my report. It's not pretty, Karen. Not pretty at all."

Karen nodded. "Once again, you've come through with flying colors. I really appreciate your work, Bill."

"Thanks. Make sure you pass those thoughts along to your accounts payable people when they get my bill."

Karen grinned. "I'll do that."

"Oh, by the way, on your Mr. Fielding?"

"Who?"

"The guy who moved in across the street?"

Karen nodded. She'd completely forgotten. "Yes?"

"I checked him out. At least I tried to."

"And?"

"This is going to sound crazy."

"What?"

"Well, he doesn't have much of a history. I ran him through the DMV and a few other agencies. I can't find any school records, can't find his place of employment, and his credit records only go back three years." He had a silly look on his face. "If I had to make a guess, I'd say he's a protected witness."

Karen's jaw dropped. "You can't be serious. The feds do a better job than that!"

"I know. I think he might be one of Florida's. We do it, too, you know. But they sure didn't do a very good job on this guy. All I can tell you for sure is he bears watching. He isn't who he says he is. And as far as those people coming and going, I haven't a clue what that's all about, unless . . ."

"What?"

"Maybe the feds are keeping an eye on you?"

"From across the street? What would be the point?"

Bill shrugged. "I have no idea. I can dig some more if you want. Say the word."

"This is a matter for the homeowners association," Karen said. "I'll give the information to them and they can handle it. I have enough to do."

"It doesn't bother you that this guy is living across the street from you?"

Karen shook her head. "Not really. If it was someone planning to make trouble, it would have already happened. And it can't be the feds. Makes no sense. Just a coincidence, I'd say."

Angelo Uccello was formally arraigned September 12. Karen drew a judge she knew and respected, one she'd appeared before dozens of times. She knew the assistant state attorney almost as well. Ben Gastner was a dedicated, hardworking, typically underpaid lawyer who bore no personal animosity toward defense attorneys making ten or twenty times his salary. Ben was unfailingly polite in and out of court, a man who played by the rules, who rarely raised his voice or resorted to cheap theatrics. If Wilbur Brooks had a polar opposite, it was Ben Gastner.

Ben regarded juries as conscientious and intelligent. His attitude was dangerous, in that juries tended to bond with this gregarious prosecutor.

But there was no jury to impress at this arraignment.

"Not guilty!" Angelo Uccello boomed when asked to enter a plea.

The courthouse was surrounded by police wearing bulletproof vests. The police were surrounded by Angelo's small army, all of them legally armed, all equipped with communications gear, looking like Secret Service officers with their earpieces, sunglasses, and hard faces. And the media people were everywhere. For some reason, Uccello was being portrayed as the last of the old guard, his position in the order of things falsely elevated from mere underboss to don. The public still had a fascination with mob figures and the media was going to make the most of this one.

"A plea of not guilty is entered," Judge Robert Ham said. "You wish to address bond, Mr. Gastner?"

"The State requests that the established bond of two million dollars be continued, Your Honor."

The judge nodded, then looked at Karen. "Ms. Perry-Mondori?"

"As Your Honor knows," Karen said, "'Mr. Uccello was under a much lesser bond while subject to appear at trial in federal court, Your Honor. He made no attempt to flee. He is a pillar of the . . ."

"I've read your brief. Can you live with two hundred thousand dollars?"

"We'd prefer ROR, Your Honor."

"I'm sure you would, but the charge is a felony. I'm not about to release him on his own recognizance. Bond is hereby reduced to two hundred thousand dollars. Anything else?"

"Yes, Your Honor. We request a preliminary hearing at the earliest possible time."

"How much time will you need, Counsel?"

"We anticipate the hearing will take one week, Your Honor."

Judge Ham's eyebrows rose. "One week?"

"Yes, Your Honor."

"Why do you need that much time for a probable cause hearing?"

"Your Honor, under the federal immunity laws, the FBI agents involved in this case are not subject to subpoena. It is the defense's position that these officers were not operating as agents of the government at the time they participated in the arrest of my client, but rather that they were acting in their own interests and that of other private parties. We are prepared to offer evidence to support our claim.

"If the court should ultimately rule in favor of the defense's position, we would submit that the officers are then subject to subpoena and can be forced to testify. Their testimony is key to our case, Your Honor."

Judge Ham leaned back in his black leather chair. "You're telling me you can prove this?"

"I can, Your Honor, but only if I'm allowed to present the testimony of the witnesses."

"So, what you're really saying is you need to have these protected witnesses testify to prove your contention that they can be forced to testify. Sounds like a Fifth Amendment issue to me, Counsel."

"I realize that, Your Honor. However, we have depositions from one of the officers and the witness whose statements to the FBI initiated the raid. If the court will entertain a motion to have those depositions be made part of the record and allow us to present other relevant testimony, the court will have enough information to make a ruling on the immunity question. We are confident we can show we have ample probable cause to pierce the immunity statute."

"You realize," the judge said, "that in the event I rule you have provided probable cause to proceed on the issue of piercing the shield of immunity, my ruling is subject to litigation in federal court?"

"I realize that, Your Honor. I have no choice in the matter."

The judge turned to Ben. "What's your position, Counsel?"

"Your Honor," Ben said, "the law is clear on this point. To circumvent the immunity laws in this case would set a dangerous precedent. We oppose the introduction of any evidence relative to statements or actions made by any federal officers involved in this case. This is now a state action. The Grand Jury has handed up an indictment and we are acting on that indictment. While there was federal involvement in the arrest, there is no federal involvement in the state's presentation of the evidence. Therefore, the issue of whether or not their shield of immunity should be pierced is moot."

Judge Ham looked at Karen. "Mr. Gastner has a point."

"Your Honor, the State cannot help but mention the involvement of federal agents during the presentation of their case. They may not choose to call certain personnel as witnesses, but the fact is the original tip resulting in the arrest of Fito Olivera and Manuel Aznar came from a federal source. Both Olivera and Aznar are federal witnesses unavailable to us, but they are the ones who pointed the FBI and the Pinellas County Sheriff's Office in the direction of the defendant. Without federal involvement, my client would not have been arrested the first time.

"The Grand Jury's indictment comes as a direct result of evidence gathered by federal agents. Again, there would be no case without it. It's impossible to isolate them from this case and remain fair to the rights of my client."

Judge Ham thought for a moment, then said, "I'll see counsel in chambers."

Judge Ham's chambers were cramped and cluttered. Not a stereo in sight. The white-haired jurist

leaned back in his chair, put his feet up, and grim-
aced. "Had a plantar wart removed last week.
Hurts like hell. So, what's this all about, Karen?
There's more here than meets the eye."

"Your Honor, the evidence I'm prepared to
present strongly suggests that my client was
framed."

"A novel defense," the judge said, smiling.

"In this case," Karen said, "the facts speak for
themselves."

"Okay, let's hear what you have."

"Thank you, Your Honor. One: The raid on my
client's business was carried out after the FBI received information from an unknown informant
that two men, Fito Olivera and Manuel Aznar,
were waiting to receive a shipment of cocaine
from the defendant.

"Two: Both Olivera and Aznar claim they work
for the defendant. They further claim that they had
contact with the defendant, and that this contact
was made by pay telephone near the motel in
which both men were staying. But the telephone
company has no record of any telephone calls
made to my client from any pay phone within a
mile of the motel. Nor does the motel have any
record of calls made from the room occupied by
the witnesses to my client. That alone impeaches
their statement. Their claim that they work for my
client is a complete lie.

"Three: The raid on the defendant's business
took place at approximately seven-thirty p.m. on
the evening of August 23. The state contends that

two bags of cocaine bearing the defendant's fingerprints were found inside the company safe. But I have witnesses who will swear there was no cocaine inside that safe at six twenty-five p.m., that the defendant was at home from approximately six-ten p.m. until the time of his arrest, and that he was accompanied by an associate during that period of time. Therefore, he couldn't have placed the cocaine in his safe.

"Four: By his own admission, in statements made to the FBI and in a deposition given to me, Manuel Aznar stated that he has worked for Juan Ramirez for many years and that he just began working for the defendant, a few weeks before the raid. As I have already stated, there is no evidence to support his claim that he ever worked for the defendant, but there is a plethora of evidence to support the contention that Aznar is still in the employ of Juan Ramirez."

"Who is Juan Ramirez?" the judge asked.

"He's alleged to be the Cali cartel's head man resident in the U.S., Your Honor. He has reason to want my client either in jail or dead."

"I see. That's why we have so many goons out there."

"I'm afraid so. It's also the reason the media has taken such an interest in this case. They're expecting a show."

"Let's hope they don't get one. Go on."

"Given all this, the evidence will support our claim that the cocaine found in the defendant's safe was placed there while the raid was in progress."

Judge Ham leaned forward, his eyes gazing at Karen intently. "Your scenario could only happen if the FBI was involved in this alleged frame. Is that what you're saying?"

"That's exactly what I'm saying, Your Honor. And if I can prove the FBI agents were involved, and I'm sure I can, they lose their shield of immunity."

The judge thought for a moment, then looked at Ben. "What's your take on all this, Ben?"

Ben thought for a moment, then said, "Can we go off the record for a moment?"

"Sure." The judge motioned to the court reporter, who left chambers.

Ben took a deep breath, then said, "I'm somewhat mystified, Your Honor. With all due respect to Karen, if this is a frame, it's the dumbest frame I've ever seen. It's possible, I suppose, but I have my doubts. More likely, Karen's witnesses are lying through their teeth. I'm left with the fact that cocaine was found in the defendant's safe. I have witnesses who will testify that they have purchased cocaine from the defendant during the past three years. That establishes the defendant as a drug trafficker. I think all this other stuff is a smoke screen."

"We could answer some of the questions," Karen countered, "if Your Honor will order that the bags containing the cocaine be examined by the Florida Department of Law Enforcement. I've left a brief with your clerk, Your Honor, outlining the reasons we're requesting such an examination. If the results are as I suspect, it might point us all in the right direction."

"What exactly are you after?" the judge asked.

"The defendant's garbage was stolen early in the morning of August 21. We have a witness. It is our contention that two empty freezer bags previously used to store pasta were found in the garbage, and that these bags were filled with cocaine, then subsequently placed in my client's safe during the raid. The freezer bags bear the defendant's fingerprints. If they also contain traces of pasta, that would indicate that the defendant didn't necessarily touch that cocaine."

Judge Ham made some notes. "Let me get this straight. You're seriously suggesting that the FBI, in concert with a rival drug trafficker, set up your client?"

"Exactly, Your Honor. And I'll share this with you. I believe that the reason the U.S. attorney dropped this case into Mr. Gastner's lap is to prevent testimony supporting my contention from being heard."

Judge Ham looked at Ben, then expelled some air. "I'll tell you what, Karen. You give me copies of all statements made by your witnesses. I'll examine them, and if I think your position has merit, I'll schedule the preliminary hearing. You'll have to leave it with me. If I rule against you, you can take it to the appellate division, but I doubt they'll overrule me. Can you live with that?"

"I can, Your Honor."

"You realize, of course, that if I grant your request, we're all going to be under one hell of a microscope. You're sticking your neck out a mile. The FBI will not be pleased."

"I understand, Your Honor."

"Anything else?"

"Just one thing." She turned to face Ben. "When the cocaine was taken from my client's safe, a set of accounting ledgers was also seized. My client needs those ledgers to run his business. If you're not prepared to return them at this time, can you at least allow my client copies?"

Ben nodded. "No problem, Karen. I'll take care of it."

"Thanks."

Ben scratched his head. "Since we're off the record here, mind if I ask you a question?"

"Not at all."

"Are you playing some game here? You can't really believe that a group of FBI agents is dirty. One, I could understand, but the whole bunch?"

"It may just be one or two, Ben. I'm not sure. But I'm sure that the cocaine was planted."

"For all our sakes," he said quietly, "I hope you're wrong."

Back in the courtroom, Judge Ham announced he would review a series of statements presented by the defense. He told Karen and Ben that his answer would be forthcoming within a week. The formal arraignment of Angelo Uccello was over.

Karen watched as her client left the courtroom surrounded by his bodyguards, her heart in her mouth, wondering if Angelo would live long enough to be there for the hearing. Judging by the security measures being taken, he was in great fear for his life.

Copies of the vending machine business's accounting ledgers were waiting for Karen when she reached her office. Naturally curious, she gave them a cursory inspection. She was stunned to learn that the business had contributed over six hundred thousand dollars to local charities—most of which served the homeless—during the last year.

All of the donations were anonymous.

She leaned back in her chair and listened as some of Angelo's words echoed in her mind, words he'd offered during one of their many discussions.

"Not so simple, eh? Good guys versus bad guys. Used to be an easy call. Now, you're all confused."

He was smiling when he spoke those words. Mocking her in a way. But he could see her confusion even then, a confusion that was intensifying with each passing day.

On impulse, Karen picked up the phone and called one of the charities listed in Uccello's books. After some introductory skirmishing, she asked some pointed questions and received some direct answers.

The donations were real.

*   *   *

Three days after the arraignment, Judge Ham's clerk telephoned Karen's office with the news that the preliminary hearing would begin on October 5. The rules of the engagement would be faxed within the hour.

She would not be allowed to call any witness subject to federal immunity laws, but would be allowed to present evidence allowing the judge to make a ruling concerning their future availability.

It was exactly what she expected.

A small shudder ran down her spine. There was no turning back. And once the details of this case became known, the media would seize on it with relish.

The road ahead was littered with land mines.

Even knowing it, she had to move on.

17

Reporters from all media packed the small courtroom. Extra bailiffs watched everyone inside the room while Pinellas County sheriff's deputies, both uniformed and plain-clothed, prowled the halls and exterior of the building, augmented by Angelo Uccello's small army of thugs.

The drive-by shooting of one of Angelo's men at the Edgewater mansion the previous night had heightened both security and media interest.

Angelo sat quietly at the defense table, bracketed by Len Spirsky, who seemed in awe of his semi-celebrity client, and Sharon Chin, who was doing her best to look unfazed by it all. Angelo wore a suit and tie for the occasion, kept his face expressionless, and spoke only when spoken to. He was not the high-profile criminal he'd once been. He looked old and washed up.

Judge Ham acknowledged the presence of the parties to the action, then told Ben Gastner to call his first witness.

"The people call Detective Robert Chalmers."

Detective Chalmers took the oath, then the witness chair. Ben quizzed him on his background and length of service, then got to the meat and bones. "Detective, would you tell the court where you were on the afternoon of August 23 at approximately three p.m."

"I was in my office."

"Would that be within the Pinellas County Sheriff's Office complex on Ulmerton Road?"

"Yes."

"And did you receive a phone call from FBI Agent Bruce Tasker?"

"Yes."

Ben was asking blatantly leading questions, but Karen held her tongue. This unimportant detail was going to come out eventually. She preferred to save her objections for more important matters.

"Please tell us the nature of that telephone call," Ben asked.

Karen rose to object. It wasn't smart to allow an opposing attorney to walk all over court procedure. There was a limit.

"Objection, Your Honor," she said softly. "Hearsay."

"Sustained."

"I'd also ask that counsel be directed to refrain from asking leading questions," Karen added.

Judge Ham gave her a look, then nodded at Ben. "Proceed."

Ben got the message. "What did you do after you received the phone call at three p.m. on the afternoon of August 23?"

"I made arrangements to meet with some FBI

agents outside the offices of Southern National Vending on Belcher Road in Clearwater. It's a business owned by the defendant."

"And what was the purpose of your meeting with the FBI agents?"

"I was there to assist them in a raid of the premises as set forth in a valid search warrant."

"And did the raid take place?"

"Yes it did."

"What, if anything, did you find when you raided the premises?"

"I found two bags containing a white powder which was subsequently identified as cocaine. Also, a set of books for the business."

"How much cocaine did you find?"

"Four kilograms."

"And after finding this cocaine, what did you do?"

"I accompanied the FBI agents to the home of the defendant, where he was arrested."

"Did you personally arrest him at that time?"

"No. The FBI agents arrested him."

"What did you do?"

The detective shrugged. "I went home. My job was to accompany the FBI on behalf of the Sheriff's Office."

"Why? What did they need you for?"

"It wasn't that they needed me. It's procedure. This is now a common practice within the law enforcement community. Local and federal agencies cooperate as much as possible. It prevents accidents, such as undercover local officers being involved in gunfights with undercover federal officers. It's happened too many times. So now, when there's a raid going down, we try to keep in touch and coordinate the activities."

Ben looked at his notes. "Did you subsequently have reason to personally arrest the defendant?"

"Yes."

"And why was that?"

"The U.S. attorney turned the case over to the Pinellas County Sheriff's Office after the Sheriff's Office made a request. After a complete investigation, the case was presented to the Grand Jury. The defendant was indicted. I was assigned the task of taking him into custody."

"Getting back to the raid for a moment, did you personally see the bags of cocaine found on the premises at Belcher Road?"

"Yes I did."

"Have you had an opportunity to follow the chain of custody of that cocaine, based on official reports given you by the FBI?"

"Yes."

"Would you describe to the court that chain of custody?"

"Yes. After the cocaine was seized, it was taken to FBI headquarters in Tampa. It was tested and then stored in the secure evidence room. It remained there until the case was given to the Pinellas County Sheriff's Office. At that time, the FBI turned the cocaine over to me. I placed it in the secure evidence room at our headquarters. Then, upon receipt of a court order, I delivered the cocaine to the Florida Department of Law Enforcement Laboratory in Tampa where some additional tests were made. Once the tests were completed, I took the evidence back to the Sheriff's Office secure evidence room. Then, I brought it to court with me today. It's in the evidence pen."

"Can you say with certainty that the chain of custody has never been broken?"

"Yes, I can."

"Thank you, Detective. That's all I have."

Judge Ham made a note, then said, "Your witness, Ms. Perry-Mondori."

"Thank you, Your Honor."

Karen moved to the lectern and placed her notes on it. Gripping the lectern with both hands, she posed her questions. "Detective, you testified as to the chain of custody involving the cocaine seized at the Belcher location. You stated that your testimony was based on your reading of official FBI reports, correct?"

"Correct."

"Also, if someone, for whatever reason, decided to borrow that cocaine from the FBI's evidence room and then put it back two hours later, you'd have no way of knowing, would you?"

"That couldn't happen."

"But, in fact, you can't really testify to the accuracy of the FBI report, can you?"

"I have no reason to doubt . . ."

"That wasn't the question, Detective. I ask that the answer be stricken."

"Detective, can you say with certainty that the chain of custody was never broken?"

"Yes. I checked the procedures. They were followed to the letter. There's no way the chain of custody was broken."

That was exactly what Karen wanted to hear.

"Thank you," she said. "What time of day was Southern National Vending raided?"

"The raid started at approximately seven-thirty p.m."

"And what time did you arrive at the home of the defendant?"

"It was about nine-thirty."

"So, it took two hours to complete the raid, is that correct?"

"No. It took about twenty minutes to drive from the Belcher location to the defendant's home."

"Okay. Would it be fair to say that the raid took about an hour and a half?"

"Yes, that would be fair."

"Would you please describe to the court exactly what took place from the moment you arrived at the premises on Belcher until the time you left."

"Yes. Well, I arrived at the premises at about seven p.m. Actually, I wasn't exactly at the location, but about a block away. That's where I met the FBI people. We discussed what action would be taken, put on vests, then dispersed to our assigned positions. At exactly seven-thirty, we entered the premises from three directions. We disarmed the security guards and took them outside the building. Then we conducted a search of the premises. One of the FBI agents placed the cocaine in an evidence bag. We then took statements from various security guards and employees. After that, one of the FBI agents placed a call to obtain a telephone warrant, and after it was received via fax, we headed for the home of the defendant."

"Did any of the security guards offer any resistance whatever?"

"No."

"Were any of them arrested?"

"No."

"And when you arrived at the home of the defendant, did he offer any resistance?"

"No."

"With the court's permission," Karen said, "the defense would like to place into evidence defense exhibit number one, a rendering of the floor plan of the Belcher premises."

"Go ahead," Judge Ham said.

Len picked up a large poster board from the evidence pen and placed it on an easel where it could be seen by the witness and the judge. "Is this a fair representation of the floor plan of the Belcher premises?" Karen asked.

The detective looked it over, then said, "It seems right."

"Fine. Now, you'll note the area marked in red. Is the safe located in that room?"

"Yes."

"How many people were in that room when the FBI agents opened the safe?"

"Four."

"Who were they?"

"I was there, and FBI Agent Bruce Tasker, and FBI Agent Ronald Trencher, and FBI Agent Jack Carroll. Agent Carroll is the safe expert."

"Where were the company security guards at this time?"

"Most were outside the building. A few were in the area marked in yellow."

"Were any of the security guards in custody?"

"Not exactly. They were being questioned."

"And none of them was in the room while the safe was being opened?"

"Correct."

"But you were."

"Yes."

"How did Agent Carroll manage to open the safe?"

"He used a stethoscope. He kept turning the tumbler and listening. Every so often, he would make notes. Then he pulled the handle and the safe opened."

"And how long did all this take?"

"About fifteen minutes."

"So, it is your testimony that you, Agents Trencher, Tasker, and Carroll stayed in that room for the entire fifteen minutes, correct?"

"That's correct."

"During that period of time, did you speak to the FBI agents?"

"Some, sure. I mean we were all there together.

But we were paying attention to Agent Carroll and his progress."

"What did you talk about?"

"I don't recall."

"Do you recall who started the conversations?"

"No I don't."

"But you do recall that there were conversations."

"Yes."

"Did anyone leave the room, even for a moment?"

"No."

"You all just stood there while Agent Carroll worked on the safe for fifteen minutes."

"That's right."

Karen turned to the judge. "With the court's permission, the defense would like to offer into evidence exhibit number two."

"Go ahead."

Once again, Len reached into the evidence pen and pulled out another poster, which he placed on the easel. The poster displayed a large photo of a safe.

"Is this a fair representation of the safe located on the Belcher premises?"

"Yes."

"There are some numbers beside the photo representing the safe's height and width. The height is listed as five feet three inches, and the width as three feet six inches. Is that a fair representation of the size of the safe?"

"Yes."

Once again, Karen faced the judge. "With the court's permission, the defense would like to offer into evidence defense exhibit number three, a cardboard likeness of the safe."

"Go ahead."

This time, both Len and Sharon were needed. They removed a large, paper-wrapped box from the evidence pen, removed the paper wrapping, and placed the cardboard safe on the floor near the witness chair. The exhibit was a cardboard duplicate of the safe shown in the earlier photograph, painted the same color, even down to the gold-leaf trim and the manufacturer's name. It looked like an actual safe, except this one weighed about ten pounds instead of two tons.

Karen asked, "May I approach the witness, Your Honor?"

"Go ahead."

Karen took a position directly in front of the witness stand. "To the best of your recollection, does this cardboard exhibit fairly represent the shape, size, and color of the safe at the Belcher Road location?"

"Far as I can tell, yes."

"With the court's permission, I would like to ask my associate to stand by the exhibit and respond to directions from the witness."

"That's fine," the judge said, leaning forward, his interest keen.

Len Spirsky stood by the cardboard safe and removed a stethoscope from his pocket.

"Detective Chalmers, you said that Agent Carroll wore a stethoscope, correct?"

"Yes."

"Mr. Spirsky, would you please position the stethoscope as we discussed earlier."

Len plugged the rubber-tipped ends into his ears and the pickup plate near the combination dial.

"What was Agent Carroll wearing?" Karen asked the witness.

"Wearing? I don't understand the question."

"You said earlier that the agents were wearing bulletproof vests. Was Agent Carroll still wearing his vest?"

"Oh. Yes."

Karen looked at the judge. "With the court's permission, we'd like to have Mr. Spirsky don a vest."

Judge Ham nodded. Len Spirsky opened the door of the cardboard safe, extracted a bulletproof vest, and put in on, strapping it tightly around his torso with the Velcro straps provided.

"Was Agent Carroll wearing anything over his vest?" Karen asked Chalmers.

"Yes. He wore an FBI windbreaker."

Karen looked at the judge. "With the . . ."

Growing impatient, the judge waved a hand. "Go ahead."

Once again, Len reached into the safe and pulled out a dark blue windbreaker with large yellow letters on the back spelling out FBI. He put on the windbreaker. The door to the cardboard safe stood wide open.

"If your Honor pleases," Karen said, "we would like to note for the record that the exhibit is empty at this time."

"So noted."

"Thank you, Your Honor."

Len closed the safe door.

"Now, Detective Chalmers," Karen continued, "Mr. Spirsky will take a position in front of the exhibit. I'd like you to stand in a position similar to where you were standing at the Belcher Road location."

Chalmers climbed down from the witness stand and stood about six feet behind Len.

"Fine. And please indicate where the other agents were standing, if you would."

Chalmers looked to his left. "Agent Tasker was on my left, and Agent Trencher was on my right."

"How far were you standing apart?"

"Not far. Less than a foot."

"And were you all standing behind Agent Carroll?"

"Yes."

"Now, would you please direct Mr. Spirsky so that he assumes the same position Agent Carroll was taking when he used his stethoscope to figure out the safe's combination."

"Okay."

It took a few seconds. Finally, Len was in position, crouched down, his head close to the safe door, one hand holding a stethoscope near the combination dial, the other hand slowly turning the dial.

"Detective Chalmers," Karen continued, "you testified that it took fifteen minutes to open the safe, correct?"

"Yes."

"And you were in the room the entire time, correct?"

"Yes."

"And when the safe was opened, you saw, with your own eyes, two bags of white powder inside the safe."

"Correct."

"And this powder was subsequently identified as being cocaine, is that correct?"

"Yes."

As Len Spirsky flung open the fake door to the fake safe, Karen pointed to the exhibit. "Would the bags of white powder look anything like the bags of white powder we now see *inside* our exhibit?"

The fake safe door was open. Len Spirsky was standing up, a stony expression on his face. Two bags of white powder sat inside the safe.

Detective Chalmers's face was as white as the powder. Judge Ham looked furious but said nothing.

"Detective," Karen asked, "did you see Mr. Spirsky place those bags in our cardboard safe?"

Ben was on his feet. "Objection!"

"Sustained," Judge Ham boomed. "I'll see counsel in chambers."

*   *   *

"I'm not amused by your little demonstration," the judge fumed as they gathered in chambers. "Explain to me why this shouldn't be stricken from the record."

Karen sat stiffly in her chair. "As Your Honor knows, the defense claims the defendant was framed. Detective Chalmers testified that he and three FBI agents were in the room when the safe was opened. He also testified that he engaged in conversation with two of the agents while the third took fifteen minutes to crack the safe. When the witness helped Mr. Spirsky position himself exactly as Agent Carroll positioned *himself* while working on cracking the safe, Detective Chalmers testified that he and the two other FBI agents were standing *behind* Agent Carroll.

"All we are attempting to do is demonstrate that Agent Carroll could have placed the cocaine in the safe without the knowledge of Detective Chalmers or the other two agents. The evidence we intend to present later will show that at least one of the FBI agents knew full well that the cocaine was going to be planted, but for now we'll assume neither of them knew. We will also stipulate that we believe Detective Chalmers was not a party to this, that the conversations in which he was engaged were designed to draw his attention away from the safe.

"Since Detective Chalmers is the only witness involved in the raid we are able to bring to the stand, we have the right to impeach his testimony.

We have proven that the witness cannot say with certainty that the cocaine found in the safe was not put there in a fashion similar to the one depicted in our demonstration. We were able to plant the cocaine in front of the witness and the court, with no one the wiser.

"By establishing what *could* have happened, we're laying a foundation for what we believe actually did happen. Once we present all our evidence, the purpose of this demonstration will become crystal clear. As I've stated to Your Honor before, we are faced with the daunting task of proving the defendant was set up in order to pierce the immunity shield. Given that context, I would submit that the demonstration was in order.

"Prior to the demonstration, Detective Chalmers agreed that the exhibits fairly represented a depiction of the Belcher offices and the safe itself. I happen to know, and will present as evidence if required, that Mr. Spirsky is smaller in stature than Agent Carroll.

"There were no cheap theatrics employed here, Your Honor. All we did was demonstrate what could have happened. There's nothing unfair in that."

Judge Ham turned to Ben. "She's right, Ben. She laid the foundation. It has to stay unless you can give me a reason why it shouldn't."

"I can't do that unless I'm allowed to call the three FBI agents as witnesses," Ben said.

"That's not possible at this time."

"I realize that. There's no jury to impress, Your Honor. I leave it in your hands to weigh all the evidence."

The judge turned to Karen. "Karen, I'm going to direct that you not engage in any more of these kinds of demonstrations without my prior approval. By that, I mean we'll discuss any planned demonstrations in chambers prior to them being placed into evidence. This hearing is less than twenty minutes old and I can already read tomorrow's headlines. You may be within your rights, but I think you're playing to the media, and I don't like it one bit. Are we clear on this?"

"I take exception, Your Honor."

"Noted. But are we clear?"

"Yes, Your Honor."

"Very well. Let's get back in there."

As they walked back into the courtroom, Karen found it difficult to keep from smiling at her young associate. Len Spirsky had practiced his sleight-of-hand for hours until getting it just right.

Once again, he was learning the value of preparation.

18

The hearing resumed with Ben Gastner offering the bags of cocaine found in Angelo Uccello's safe into evidence. His next witness was a fingerprint expert from the Pinellas County Sheriff's Office forensics lab, who testified that the fingerprints found on the bags of cocaine matched those of the defendant's, whose prints had been on file with the FBI for some thirty years.

When the witness was turned over to Karen, she said, "We have no questions at this time, Your Honor. We reserve the right to cross-examine this witness later."

The judge's eyebrows rose. "Very well. Mr. Gastner, call your next witness."

Ben's next witness was a pathologist who testified at some length regarding the tests done on the cocaine itself to verify that it was, indeed, cocaine. He also testified as to the handling of the evidence, step by step, in an effort to prove the chain of custody was intact. Karen had hoped Ben would take that approach, because it was just as important to the defense to prove that the chain had not been broken. She'd raised the issue with Detective Chalmers for that very reason.

To everyone's surprise, Karen did not cross-examine.

It was time for lunch.

Karen, Len, Sharon, and Angelo left the courthouse and climbed into a large motor home parked in the court complex parking lot. Uccello had rented the luxurious house-on-wheels for security reasons, but it was as subtle as a circus. He didn't want to chance eating in the court cafeteria for fear of assassination, but a small plane loaded with a few small hand grenades would find this motor home a tempting target.

The blinds were closed and the two rooftop air conditioners growled incessantly. Outside, Angelo's army ringed the vehicle with Pinellas County deputies helping keep the press at bay. Angelo picked at a light salad, prepared by Paz. Len and Sharon joined him, but Karen had no appetite.

The setting was bizarre. Karen kept waiting for the sound of a low-flying airplane. The circumstances of this case were beginning to make her paranoid.

Angelo pushed his salad away. "I can't eat this slop. Those bastards—why'd they have to shoot Lucky? He was the best damned bodyguard I ever had."

Mention of last night's drive-by shooting did nothing to restore Karen's appetite. Machine-gun fire had wakened the sleepy Dunedin neighborhood just minutes before Lucky's hulking, bullet-riddled body had been discovered between the street and the compound, where he'd been completing a perimeter check. No one saw the shooters or their vehicle, and no suspects had been apprehended.

"I'll tell you why they shot him." Angelo's face darkened with rage, and he shook his fork in Karen's face. "It was a warning—to you as well as me. You shoulda got out while you had the chance."

Len and Sharon exchanged uncomfortable glances.

"We've been through all this," Karen said.

"Then the sooner this trial's over, the better." Uccello's angry shout filled the motor home. He narrowed his eyes. "What happens now?"

"The prosecution has three more witnesses to present," Karen said. "One will present evidence that you are the sole owner of Southern National Vending—which ties you to the drugs found in your safe—and the other two are convicted felons, former employees of yours, still serving time. They'll testify that they bought drugs from you, thereby establishing the fact that you are a drug trafficker."

"I told you all about those guys," he bellowed.

"I know you did. I have the information."

"Why would they testify against me now?" Angelo asked with a growl. "They didn't shoot their mouths off when they were busted."

"Could be any number of reasons," Karen told

him. "They've been working for Juan Ramirez the past two years, right?"

"Right."

"Okay, maybe they were reached by some of Juan Ramirez's people serving time in prison. Maybe they were told they better cooperate or else. Or they might have been offered a reduction of sentence by the feds, even though this is no longer a federal case. More likely, it's a combination of both. You're the one who thinks the feds are working with Ramirez."

He gave her a hostile look. "You don't?"

"Perhaps some of them."

Angelo slammed his fist onto the table. "This ain't like the old days. In the old days people were stand-up guys. They didn't pull this stuff even if they were workin' for a competitor."

"Right," Karen said. "They just stuck an ice pick in your back."

"I ain't paying you to be a smart-ass. I'm paying you to git me outta this mess." He leaned forward, his face inches from hers, and she could smell the garlic on his breath. "You'd better have somethin' good up your sleeve, Counselor. I'm losing my patience—fast."

Her temper flared. "You'll get your money's worth."

With a sinister smile, he asked, "You gonna eat them new witnesses up like you did the detective? You really took him apart with that toy safe. That was something!"

"You can thank Len for that," Karen said. "It was his idea."

Len swallowed nervously and shot Uccello a hesitant smile. The man's bad humor had them all walking on eggshells.

"No," Karen said. "I'm going to try and stop the other witnesses from testifying at all. They were in jail when you were arrested. They have nothing to do with this case and are, therefore, irrelevant."

"Will that work?"

"Probably not. Even though Judge Ham is a fair man, he'll let it in."

"Then what?"

"Then we'll see. Normally, we'd make a motion to the effect that there's no probable cause to bind you over for trial. But that's not why we're here."

Angelo's scowl deepened. "Then what's the fuckin' point? I'm paying you to keep me outta jail."

He shoved away from the table and began to pace the motor home, like a tiger in a too-small cage. Len and Sharon averted their eyes to their plates.

Karen took a deep breath. "Let's save our battles for the courtroom. We're here to present our own evidence and get a ruling that allows us to force the FBI agents to testify at your trial."

"But," Angelo stopped and confronted her, "if you make that motion and the judge says it's all over, we don't even need a trial. Ain't that right?"

"That will never happen," Karen told him. "The

Grand Jury indicted you. Cocaine was found in your safe. No judge is going to stop the prosecution from taking this to trial. It would be political suicide. Remember, this hearing is our idea."

Angelo shook his head in frustration. "Just another game," he complained.

Karen, as usual, jumped to the defense of the system. "Not totally, Angelo. Let's face it, you've never been convicted of a felony because the system gives you certain rights. In most other countries, you'd be arrested, tried, and convicted all on the same day. So be thankful you live in this country."

He gave her a strange look, but said nothing.

An official from Tallahassee testified that Southern National Vending, Inc., was a private commercial enterprise solely owned by Angelo Uccello. Karen had no cross.

The first of the two prison inmates was called at two-thirty. Karen rose to her feet to object. "Your Honor, this witness was in jail at the time of the alleged incident involving the defendant. He has no knowledge of the alleged incident, was not a party to it, and his testimony is therefore irrelevant."

Ben Gastner had been doing his homework. Stung by the embarrassing demonstration of this morning, he turned Karen's triumph into a defeat. In rebuttal, he said, "Your Honor, I'm aware that evidence of past crimes is usually inadmissible at trial. However, in this case, we are using this witness to provide foundation showing a pattern of wrongdoing by the defendant. Since the defendant has never been convicted of a felony, it behooves the people to present witnesses who can verify that the defendant *could* be involved in drug trafficking. Just as counsel this morning demonstrated that drugs *could* have been placed in the defendant's safe by other than the defendant, we have the right to demonstrate that the defendant *could* be capable of trafficking in cocaine. By presenting this witness and others, we can show a pattern of criminal activity which gives us probable cause to bind him over for trial."

It was the reference to Karen's cardboard safe that turned the tables. The judge, after giving it about ten seconds of thought, ruled that Frank Bagalia could testify.

Bagalia was a swarthy man of thirty, mean-looking, insolent, and angry. He still wore his prison clothes, as if to remind everyone he was incarcerated. As he took the stand, he glared at Angelo. Ben walked him through his testimony.

"How long have you known the defendant?"

"Nine years."

"And during that time, did you ever have occasion to purchase illegal drugs from the defendant?"

"Sure. Lots of times."

"Can you give an example?"

"Sure. When I got busted two years ago hustling a load of cocaine in Miami, it was Angelo's stuff. I bought stuff from Angelo all the time, maybe once a month. He was my regular supplier. Still would be today if I was out."

So much for rehabilitation, Karen thought.

"How did you pay for the drugs you bought from the defendant?"

"Cash. It was always cash."

"And did you deal with the defendant directly?"

"Sure. I never dealt with nobody but Angelo."

Beside her, Karen heard Angelo whisper in her ear, "He's a liar."

She patted his arm. "I know that. Relax."

Once the witness was hers, Karen asked, "You said you'd done business with the defendant for nine years. Correct?"

"Yeah."

"And it was always with the defendant?"

"Yeah, like I said."

"And you mentioned you were arrested two years ago."

"That's right."

"What was the name of the law enforcement official who made the arrest?"

"I don't remember."

"Was he a member of the Miami police department, the DEA, the Florida Department of Law Enforcement, the FBI, or any other agency?"

"I don't recall."

Karen pulled a copy of the arrest report from her desk, asked the judge if she could approach the witness, and did so. She showed Bagalia the report. "To refresh your recollection, please read this report."

Bagalia read it.

"Do you see the name Bruce Tasker anywhere on that page?"

"Yes."

"Who is Bruce Tasker?"

"He's a fed."

"An FBI agent?"

"Yeah."

"Is he the person who arrested you?"

"Yeah. I remember now."

"Thank you. After you were arrested, booked, and arraigned, you were out on bond until your trial, correct?"

"Yes."

"And isn't it a fact that you were acquitted of the charges?"

"Yes."

"And then you were arrested in April of this year, correct?"

"Yeah."

"Do you remember the name of the arresting officer who arrested you in April?"

"No."

Again, Karen brought forward an arrest report and showed it to the witness. "Does the name Jack Silver appear on that page?"

"Yeah."

"Is Jack Silver, a sergeant with the Miami-Dade special task force, the man who arrested you?"

"Yeah."

"And it was that charge that led to a trial, at which time you were convicted and sent to prison, was it not?"

"Yeah."

"And when you were arrested in April, you were found to be in possession of illegal drugs, correct?"

"Yeah."

"Is it your testimony that you bought those drugs from the defendant?"

"Of course. I said I never sold for anybody else."

"But in Jack Silver's report, which you've just read, he indicates that you refused to divulge the name of your supplier, isn't that right?"

"Yeah."

"Why didn't you?"

"Because I was afraid Angelo would have me killed."

"I see. But you're testifying now. You are no longer afraid?"

"No."

"Why is that?"

"Because I learned in prison not to be afraid of nobody."

"Isn't it a fact that you've lived in Miami all your life?"

"Yeah."

"Are you aware of the fact that the defendant moved to this area three years ago?"

"Yeah, I know."

"So, when you bought drugs from the defendant, did you come here, or did the defendant come to Miami?''

"I came here."

"Where did you stay?"

"I don't remember."

"According to your testimony, you did business with the defendant at least a hundred times. Would that be a fair number?"

"I don't keep count. It was a lot of times."

"Could it have been a hundred times?"

"Maybe. At least fifty."

"All right. Can you remember the details of just one of those fifty transactions?"

"Whaddayamean details?"

"I would like to know one date, location, time of day, how many people were there, what cars were used, how much money was involved, who said what to whom . . . Details. Just one time. Can you remember one transaction in detail?"

The witness thought for a moment, then said, "Sure. I bought ten kilos from Angelo on February 20."

"This year?"

"Yeah."

"Where?"

"Here."

"Can you be more specific? Where exactly did the transaction take place?"

"It was at some motel. I don't remember the name of the place."

"A motel. You can't remember where. Why is it you remember the date so well?"

The witness smiled for the first time, like he'd just passed some sort of test. "I remember because it was my birthday."

"February 20 was your birthday?"

"Yes."

"And you're positive you bought drugs from the defendant on that date."

"Absolutely."

Karen looked at the judge. "May I have a moment?"

"Go ahead."

Karen walked to the defense table and asked Angelo to use the laptop. She wanted his entry for February 20. Angelo's fingers raced over the keys. In less than a minute, a printed sheet of paper emerged from a portable printer. Angelo looked it over carefully, making sure the page contained no incriminating evidence, then handed the sheet to Karen.

Karen faced the judge. "With the court's permission," she said, "we'd like to enter this diary entry as defense exhibit number four."

Ben was on his feet. "Objection. Irrelevant. If counsel wants to enter a diary as an exhibit, they should enter the entire diary. This is out of context."

"This is for the purpose of impeachment, Your Honor. The rest of the diary is irrelevant, but this entry, which covers the date in question, is relevant in that it impeaches the witness's testimony."

"Overruled. Proceed."

"May I approach the witness?"

"All right."

Karen, the sheet of paper in her hands, stood five feet away from the witness. "You said you were sure the date was February 20 because it was your birthday. Are you still certain you met with the defendant on that date?"

It's a strange thing with liars. Even when confronted with evidence that makes their story impossible to believe, they never back off. Bagalia was typical. "I'm positive."

"I'd like to show you this diary entry. For the court's edification, the defendant keeps a daily diary on his home computer, Your Honor. He makes entries which are then encrypted. We've just decoded one of the entries, the one relating to February 20, and we're prepared to give an offer of proof that this is indeed a true copy of the original entry. As Your Honor knows, we had no way of knowing in advance what date the witness would choose."

"Go ahead," Judge Ham said.

"Now, if you'll read over this entry . . ." She placed the sheet in front of the witness. He began to read, then stopped. "This is phony."

"What makes you say that?"

"Well, it says here that Angelo was in the hospital gettin' his gallbladder out. That can't be right. I was with him that day."

Karen smiled. "No you weren't, Mr. Bagalia. And we can get the hospital records to prove it if need be."

Karen returned to the defense table. "May I have a moment, Your Honor?"

"Quickly, Counsel."

"Yes, Your Honor."

Karen leafed through voluminous notes provided by the always thorough Bill Castor. Castor had done a background check on both prison-held witnesses, but there was nothing relating to that specific date. Karen decided to take a chance. It was Bagalia's birthday. He had a girlfriend. That meant the odds were good that he'd been partying on his birthday.

"On February 20, you were in Miami," she said confidently. And then she chose her words very carefully. "Would you be surprised if we brought forward a witness to testify that you spent the night with her?"

Bagalia took the bait like a hungry grouper. "That's crap," he screamed.

Judge Ham leaned toward the witness. "Watch your language, Mr. Bagalia."

"Sorry, Judge, but this . . ."

Karen pressed her attack. "Isn't it a fact that FBI Agent Bruce Tasker offered to make a deal when you were arrested two years ago, that he told you if you gave him the name of your supplier, he'd reduce the charges against you?"

"No. He never offered no deal."

"Then what brings you to this court today?"

"I ain't lyin'."

"That wasn't the question. Why are you here?"

"I was asked to testify by the FBI."

"What was the name of the FBI agent who asked you to testify?"

"I don't remember."

Karen removed another sheet of paper from her table. "According to the prison visitor's report, FBI Agent Bruce Tasker visited with you twice in September. Are you denying you had conversations with Agent Tasker?"

"I guess not."

"Did Agent Tasker offer you a deal if you would testify today?"

"No."

"Then how is it you're here?"

"Like I said, he asked me."

"And you, a man who refused to reveal the name of his supplier when he was arrested, decided to testify simply because you were asked? Is that your testimony?"

"Well . . . yeah. I'm just doin' my civic duty, that's all. Some FBI agent came to see me up in Stark and told me my supplier had been busted. He said it was my duty to come here and testify."

"And that FBI agent was Bruce Tasker, correct?"

"I don't really remember."

Karen looked at the judge plaintively. "Your Honor, do I really have to keep doing this? It's clear this witness is unable or unwilling to tell the truth."

Judge Ham had heard enough. "I agree," he said. "The witness is excused. The witness's entire testimony will be stricken as unresponsive. I'll refer the matter to both the state attorney and the U.S. attorney for possible action.''

Karen nodded. ''Thank you, Your Honor.''

''And I'll see counsel in chambers. Both of you.''

Clearly, Judge Ham was upset, but this time, his anger was directed at Ben. ''How long did you spend with this witness before you brought him into my courtroom, Mr. Gastner?''

''A few hours, Your Honor. I apologize to the court. I was going on information given me by the FBI.''

''What information?''

''Transcripts of interviews with the witnesses. I was told that the testimony had been corroborated. Obviously, there is some miscommunication here.''

The judge sighed. ''Miscommunication? Is that what you call it?''

The judge looked at Karen. ''Karen, do you intend to move for dismissal?''

''As Your Honor knows, I'm obligated to so move.''

''I understand. I also understand that's not what you're after. The purpose of this hearing, as you've described it, is to allow you to present evidence that will enable you to pierce the shield of immunity that protects federal law enforcement officers. Well, at this point, I'm prepared to go along with it.''

''Thank you, Your Honor.''

The judge turned his attention back to an embarrassed Ben. "Ben, other than your next witness, do you have anything further?"

"No, Your Honor."

"In that case, I suggest you rest. We'll let Karen make her motion for dismissal. I'll deny it, and we can get on with the business at hand. That okay with you?"

"Yes, Your Honor."

The judge turned back to Karen. "Are you ready to proceed with your first witness?"

"I am, Your Honor."

"Very well. Looks to me like this hearing will be a lot shorter than you anticipated."

"Yes, Your Honor."

Paz Mindinaro looked completely different in a suit and tie and without the tall chef's hat. He was about Karen's height and no more than ten pounds heavier. He took the witness stand, his gaze darting about the courtroom nervously. Karen ran through the preliminaries, then asked Paz about pasta.

"Have you ever seen the defendant prepare food in the kitchen of his home?"

"Yes. Many time."

"What does he usually prepare?"

"Pasta. Mr. Uccello say I don't make good pasta. He make his own."

"And how does he make his pasta?"

"He use eggs and flour . . . not regular flour but a special flour call semolina . . . and some salt and olive oil and little water. He put all this in a machine. Then, after the machine knead the pasta, it comes out the end in strips, either fettuccine or linguine, sometimes both. Mr. Uccello folds the strips and put them in plastic freezer bag. He freeze bags."

"And when Mr. Uccello takes one of those bags from the freezer to use for dinner, what does he do with it?"

"He take the pasta out of bag and put in boiling water."

"What does he do with the empty bag?"

"He throw away."

"Where?"

"In garbage."

"Does he allow you to touch the bags when he uses them?"

"Never. he fussy about his pasta."

"Does anyone else in the house touch those bags at any time?"

"No. Just Mr. Uccello."

"Does Mr. Uccello use any freezer bag or does he prefer a particular brand?"

"Oh, he buy nothing but SuperSeal freezer bags. He say they are the only one thick enough."

"Have you ever seen him use anything but a SuperSeal freezer bag?"

"Never."

"And how long have you worked for Mr. Uccello?"

"Six years."

Karen walked over to the evidence pen and retrieved the bags of cocaine previously entered into evidence by Ben. She handed the bags to Paz. "Do you see a name embossed on the top of these bags?"

Paz looked them over carefully. "Yes."

"Would you tell the court what it says?"

"Yes. It say SuperSeal freezer bags."

"Is this the same size and type of bag Mr. Uccello uses when he prepares pasta?"

"Exactly the same, yes."

"Thank you, Mr. Mindinaro. That's all I have."

Ben Gastner looked pained as he cross-examined Paz for thirty minutes, a cross-examination that led nowhere.

They were done for the day.

19

According to the local media, Angelo Uccello was being railroaded. This was a highly unusual stand for the media to take. Crime lords were unsympathetic characters to begin with, especially in an area of the country with far too much drug-related crime, and yet this long-time Mafia hood was being portrayed as a man getting a bad rap. It was an astonishing turnaround for the local media, most of whom presented reports of criminal activity in Napoleonic Law fashion—those arrested were guilty until proven innocent.

Karen had achieved much without benefit of a single press conference.

Questions were being raised about improprieties on the part of the federal government and the Pinellas County Sheriff's Office. Ben Gastner, now under the gun, gave a very defensive interview at which time he took great pains to explain that this case had been handled by the FBI from the start. If there were improprieties, the Pinellas County Sheriff's Office was not to blame. At the same time he said, "I'm not suggesting there are improprieties. There are times when witnesses lie for reasons of their own. Sometimes, they simply like to be in the spotlight.

"The facts of this case are irrefutable. The FBI found two bags of cocaine in the defendant's safe, and both bags bore the fingerprints of the defendant. The defense may have practiced a little trickery in court today but that doesn't mean the cocaine wasn't found exactly as was specified in the information. For the defense to imply that an entire squad of FBI agents is corrupt harks back to another case that received national attention not long ago. As far as I'm concerned, the defense is being disingenuous at best."

Karen switched off the television set and turned off the light. Carl was already asleep.

She wouldn't be long joining him. She was sleeping much better these days. The papers had arrived from Michelle's parents and Michelle was now a college student, driving Andrea to and from school as well. The timing couldn't have been better. Michelle was as happy as Karen and Carl had ever seen her.

The case was going well, with Judge Ham giving Karen all the room she needed. Even Ben, press conferences notwithstanding, was leaning over backward to make this less arduous than it might be. He seemed to have serious questions in his own mind.

And across the street in the house rented by the mysterious Mr. Fielding, unnoticed by a tired lawyer drifting off to sleep, there was another changing of the guard.

"Please state your name and occupation," Karen asked her first morning witness.

"My name is George Gilbert, and I'm a forensic pathologist with the Florida Department of Law Enforcement."

"Which branch, sir?"

"I work in Tampa."

Karen took ten minutes to establish the witness's expertise and length of service, then asked, "Did you have occasion to examine two bags of cocaine marked as evidence package TYB-3644 in the matter of United States versus Angelo Uccello?"

"Yes I did."

"And how was it that this evidence was given to you?"

"It was as a result of a court order."

"Were precautions taken to ensure that the chain of evidence was unbroken?"

"They were."

"And to the best of your knowledge, was the chain of evidence broken at any time?"

"It was not."

"Very well. When you examined the evidence, did you find anything inside the bags other than the cocaine?"

"I did."

"And what did you find?"

"I found traces of egg, semolina flour, salt, and olive oil."

"And based on those findings, do you have an opinion as to what those ingredients were used for?"

"I would say they were used to make pasta."

"Where in the bags were the ingredients found?"

"There were traces all over. The traces were clinging to the inner surfaces."

"Were the traces on top of or beneath the cocaine?"

"The traces were beneath the cocaine."

"Can you therefore offer an opinion as to when the pasta was placed in the bags?"

"Yes."

"And what would that opinion be?"

"The pasta was placed in the bags before the cocaine was put in the bags."

"Thank you, Mr. Gilbert. No further questions."

Ben had to cross. He asked a lot of questions, but in the end achieved nothing.

Karen called Carlotta Bensonhurst to the stand. The frightened woman moved slowly as she took the oath, then sat in the witness chair, her long, bony fingers wringing a small white handkerchief. Karen took the woman through her testimony with great care, testimony almost identical to the information she'd given Karen during her deposition.

She was a terrific witness, obviously had no ax

to grind, just an honorable, decent woman living out the last days of her life with pride and as much dignity as a heartless society would allow her. When she spoke of seeing the strange events that occurred on the night of August 21, it was with conviction and certainty.

On cross, a shaken Ben Gastner tried to rattle her, and the old woman took an immediate and profound dislike to the prosecutor. His questions were designed to impeach her, and that's exactly how she received them. She was a woman who thought anyone questioning her word had an ulterior motive. And when Ben decided to question her eyesight, she took him apart.

"There's a man standing by the door at the rear of the room," Ben said. "Do you see him?"

"Yes."

"Can you describe him?"

"Certainly."

"Please do so."

"He's about fifty, with brown hair and brown eyes. He's balding slightly. He's about six feet tall and one hundred and eighty pounds. He's wearing a white-on-white shirt and a blue tie that has small American flags embroidered on it. He's . . ."

Ben almost choked. "That's enough," he said. "Thank you. No further questions."

Even Judge Ham smiled.

Karen called Fred Hertz to the stand. He testified about leaving the books in an empty safe at 6:25 P.M. on the night the raid took place.

Ben thought he could win one here. After all, Fred was an Uccello employee.

"You testified that you've worked for the defendant for several years."

"Correct."

"You're not married."

"True."

"You have no relatives other than a niece, correct?"

"True."

"You live in a small apartment near the premises, correct?"

"Yes."

"What is your annual salary?"

"Objection," Karen interjected. "Irrelevant."

"Foundation, Your Honor."

"Overruled," the judge said. "You may answer the question."

"My salary is thirty-six thousand dollars a year."

"Do you have any other income?"

"No."

"So, in fact, you are dependent on your employer for your paycheck, true?"

"Yes."

"And if your employer asked you to lie in order to keep your job, you'd be in a tough spot, wouldn't you?"

"Objection!"

"Sustained."

Ben, flustered, asked, "Do you regard your employer as a friend?"

Before Karen could object, Hertz answered. "No. I regard my employer as a criminal."

Ben rocked back on his heels. "Have you ever told him so?"

"Many times."

"And yet he keeps you on the payroll. Why would he do that?"

"You'll have to ask him, but I suspect it's because I'm a good accountant."

Ben scratched his head. "You testified that you regard your employer as a criminal. Why would you continue to work for someone you regard as a criminal?"

"Why not? I'm not in the judgment business, I'm an accountant. There are many large corporations I also regard as acting in a criminal fashion. In fact, if I refused to work for anyone I regarded as criminal, I'd have a difficult time finding work anywhere."

Ben tried a few more questions and then gave up.

After another tension-filled lunch in the motor home, Karen called John Haversol to the stand.

"What is your occupation?"

"I'm a security guard."

"How long have you been a security guard?"

"Twenty-three years."

"And how long have you worked for the defendant?"

"Twenty-three years."

"What was your occupation prior to becoming a security guard?"

"I was a police officer."

"For whom?"

"The Miami Police Department."

And how many years did you work for the Miami Police Department?"

"Eight."

"What were the circumstances under which you left that position?"

"I was working vice. My partner and I received a call that a prostitute was selling marijuana out of a trailer on Tamiami. We got a search warrant and went over there. We had the suspect in custody and were searching the place. I entered a darkened room and saw someone in the corner crouched down low, with a gun in his hand. I shot him. He was a kid of eight. The gun was a toy. The kid died. I was fired."

"What happened after that?"

"I got drunk and stayed that way for a year. Then Angelo offered me a job if I straightened out. I got straight and started working for him."

"Where were you on the night of August 23 between six p.m. and nine-thirty p.m.?"

"I was with Angelo. Once a month Angelo and me, we play rummy. I was up three hundred bucks when the cops showed up and busted him."

"Was the defendant ever out of your sight during that time?"

"No."

"You're sure?"

"I'm positive."

"And where did this rummy game take place?"

"In Angelo's den. He's got two full-size pool tables in there, a wide-screen TV, a poker table, a couple of pinball machines, and some video games. All us security people live in the house, so he makes sure we have lots to do in our off hours."

"Thank you, Mr. Haversol."

It was Ben's turn. He was about to ask a question, then changed his mind. "No questions."

Judge Ham looked at Karen. "Call your next witness."

"We have no more witnesses, Your Honor. We'd like to rest at this time."

The judge nodded to Ben. "You wish to make a closing statement, Mr. Gastner?"

"Yes, Your Honor."

Ben went to the lectern and checked his notes. Then he said, "Your Honor, as I understand it, the purpose of this preliminary hearing is to determine two issues: The first concerns the issue of probable cause to hold the defendant over for trial. And the second is to determine if there is reason to believe that the FBI agents involved in the finding of cocaine on the premises owned and operated by the defendant were acting in their official capacity as law enforcement officers or as private citizens.

"I would submit that the evidence supports our position that probable cause exists in the first instance. Despite the dramatics offered by the defense, the facts are clear. Cocaine was found within premises owned and operated by the defendant.

"As for the second issue, the law is clear. Should you find that the federal agents were acting outside their official capacity, that issue must still be decided in federal court. Accordingly, the prosecution asks only that you rule on the issue of probable cause, and asks that the defendant be held over for trial. We suggest no changes in the present bond."

Karen was not surprised. Ben was preparing to distance himself from this travesty.

"Ms. Perry-Mondori?"

"Thank you, Your Honor. As Your Honor knows, the defense has been unable to call certain witnesses because of the immunity statute. We feel that had we had the opportunity to call these witnesses, we would have been able to prove beyond any doubt that my client is innocent. As I said in chambers and in this court, we need those witnesses to prove our case.

"I submit that we've provided enough evidence to allow you to issue a ruling that the immunity shield has been broken, and that we should be allowed to call these witnesses if there is a trial. To be candid, we see no need for a trial. We would ask that Your Honor rule that there is not probable cause to hold the defendant for trial, and that the charges be dismissed forthwith.

"Thank you, Your Honor."

Judge Ham made a note, then leaned forward.

"Normally, I'd take this under advisement. But in this case, the evidence presented by both sides makes it clear that this issue cannot be resolved unless all the parties are heard from.

"I am therefore ruling that there is probable cause to bind the defendant over for trial, and that the defense shall be allowed to call all witnesses who were parties to the raid that occurred on August 23.

"The law allows those protected by immunity to challenge my ruling. Therefore, we will not set a trial date until the federal officials have either accepted the defense subpoenas, or in the event they are challenged, a federal court has ruled on their legality. At such time, I will hear testimony from both sides as to the setting of a trial date.

"Should the federal court rule that the shield of immunity may be pierced, a trial date will be set. Should the federal court rule that the shield of immunity *cannot* be pierced, we will revisit the probable cause issue. I will entertain a motion from the defense and hear argument at that time. Frankly, I do not feel the defendant can be assured of a fair trial unless all witnesses are heard from.

"The defendant will remain on bond, which is hereby reduced to fifty thousand dollars.

"This court is adjourned."

He banged his gavel and retreated to chambers. Karen walked over to Ben's table and shook his hand. "That was very magnanimous, Ben. Thank you."

"No big deal. I'm not going to fight you on this

until the feds get their act together. They're the ones who busted him. They're the ones with the shaky witnesses. We never should have gotten involved in this mess. There's something going on here and I don't like it."

Karen smiled. "One would almost think you believe my client is innocent."

"Don't kid yourself. He's as guilty as hell. He's also very clever. And so are you."

"You really believe he's guilty?"

"Absolutely. He's been a mobster his whole life, for God's sake. You and I both know he's been dealing drugs for decades. So what's the big deal here? Four kilos of coke? Twelve FBI agents raid a place to recover four kilos of coke? That's crazy. Five tons I could understand, but this? I just don't understand it. And then, when it looks like the feds will get egg on their face, they dump it on us, like we've got nothing better to do with our time.

"You know what bugs me? Your client belongs in jail. But because the feds really screwed this up and because he can afford someone like you, he'll probably walk, just like he's been walkin' all these years. I think that stinks. It's no wonder the public thinks the system is a joke."

"You sound a little bitter."

"I am. I'm fed up. Just between you and me, I'm making some inquiries. I've had it. Maybe you might . . ."

"Drop me a note," Karen said. "But not until after this case is over, understand?"

"I hear you."

*　　*　　*

Karen arrived home early for a change. She was alone in the big house. She took a swim, then lay by the pool catching the rays of a benign early evening sun. There was a light breeze coming in from the gulf and the humidity had dropped slightly. It was almost bearable.

She tried to relax, but couldn't. She wanted to watch the news, but passed. She'd wait until the eleven o'clock edition.

Michelle arrived with Andrea. Both decided to have a swim. Then Carl showed up and joined them.

They ate outside. Carl barbecued some ribs, while Michelle prepared fresh corn on the cob. It was like a picnic. As Michelle and Andrea left to tend to homework, Karen filled Carl in on her day.

"I heard about it on the car radio," he said. "The way they described it, the prosecution seems ready to throw in the towel right now. Does that mean there won't be a trial?"

"No. There'll be a trial all right. These are just the first skirmishes. Even if Ben quits the case, and he might, they'll assign someone else."

"So, now you have to go back to federal court?"

"Right."

"This is like a tennis match. Crazy. A waste of taxpayer's money."

"I won't argue. When it comes to conflicting jurisdictions, things can get sticky."

"Why bother?" Carl asked. "Can't you come to some arrangement with the state attorney? It seems to me they'd welcome an opportunity to back away from this mess. Wouldn't they agree to a fine or something?"

"They might, but Angelo won't hear of it. He wants to keep his record of no convictions intact."

Carl shook his head. "Macho crap."

20

The Mondori household alarm system was very sophisticated, as might be expected in an upscale house located in one of the more exclusive developments in all of Pinellas County.

There were three levels of sensitivity, each with unique sounds and colored lights, emitting and flashing simultaneously in every room in the house. Should a myopic bird fly into a window without breaking it or some other disturbance trigger the vibration sensor, a low-pitched tone would sound for a second and an orange light would flash for ten seconds. In the event a window or door was ajar when the alarm was activated, a medium-pitched sound would signal and an indicator on each intercom/alarm panel would flash, a small green arrow on a mini-diagram of the house pointing to the offended area.

The third level of security was serious stuff. If a door or window was penetrated while the alarm was armed, a red light would flicker and a high-pitched squeal lasting ten seconds would alert everyone inside the house. At the same time, an alarm would sound at the security company head-quarters. If the security company didn't receive a satisfactory reply to their immediately placed telephone call to the Mondori household, the po-lice were notified that an unauthorized entry was now in progress.

When it happened, Carl was helping Andrea with her homework. Michelle was downstairs in her room doing homework of her own. Karen was soaking in the bathtub, letting the hot and silky water work its magic on her aching, tense muscles. She lay back, resting her head on a folded towel, closed her eyes, and felt the physical and psycho-logical damage generated by a full, busy court day slowly slip away, as unenduring as the day's accu-mulation of dust.

And then she heard an unfamiliar sound, the alarm's high-pitched squeal signaling a break-in. Her gaze went immediately to the intercom/alarm panel near the door. For the first time since they'd lived in this house, the red light was flashing, the beacon continuing to screech its frightening warning.

Panicked, her first thought was of Andrea. She had to get to Andrea. Nothing else mattered. She leaped from the tub, quickly wrapped herself in a thick towel, and headed for the door. It opened before she reached it. Carl threw open the door and came into the bathroom, Andrea in his arms, a wild look in his eye. Without a word, he thrust Andrea into Karen's arms and closed the door, then pushed the white rattan dresser against it.

The phone started ringing.

"Don't answer it," Carl shouted.

Two thoughts immediately entered Karen's consciousness. Andrea was safe, and Carl was taking complete charge. Somehow, the fear slowed its upward track.

Andrea looked at her father, then her mother. "What's happening?" she asked, pure terror evident in her young eyes.

The alarm's squeal, having completed its ten-second warning, turned quiet, but the red light kept blinking ominously.

"The burglar alarm has gone off," Carl explained to Andrea, trying to keep his voice even. "We're going to stay in the bathroom until the police arrive. It's probably a false alarm, but you never . . ."

His words were cut off by the sound of a scream.

A woman's scream.

Michelle!

"Everyone down on the floor," Carl ordered. "Lean against the dresser."

Karen, her heart in her mouth, did as she was told, her body still wrapped in the towel. Andrea started to cry. Carl put his hand over the child's mouth, held her close, then said, "Try not to cry, sweetheart. The longer it takes them to find us, the better. Let's not make a sound."

Andrea stopped crying. "Who are they?" she asked. "What do they want?"

"Burglars," Carl said. "The police will be here any minute."

Suddenly there was the deafening sound of gunfire that made both Karen and Carl jerk back. Two, three, four shots. Then another scream, this one a man's, then two more gunshots, and two more, three, four more in quick succession.

There was a war going on just beyond the bathroom door.

Impossible! Karen thought. This can't be happening. It has to be a nightmare.

It was no nightmare.

The three of them huddled together by the dresser, terrified, wondering, worrying. They heard the sound of a man moaning and then another gunshot, this one just outside the door.

God! Could they beat their way through the door? Would they fire shots through it?

They lay as flat on the floor as they could, straining to hear what was happening. There were no more sounds, just deathly silence. All they could hear was the sound of their own heavy breathing.

Karen was assailed by terrible thoughts. Uccello had warned her she might be in danger. Was this what he meant? That killers would attack her in her own home? Kill her and her family? Wipe them out? She thought he'd been exaggerating, trying to frighten her for no reason.

But no.

This was real.

Oh, God! Help us!

And still, it was quiet.

The phone started ringing again. Carl repeated his earlier command. "Don't answer it."

Karen's heart was banging so hard against her rib cage she was sure Carl could hear it. Andrea fought valiantly to fight her tears. She sniffled and sobbed, then pushed part of Karen's towel against her mouth to deaden the sound. Karen had never been more proud of the child, or of Carl. He was so brave, so in control.

He would save them somehow.

They stayed like that for five minutes, fighting the rising sense of panic.

And then they heard the welcome sirens. One, two, maybe three police cars were approaching. And then, the sound of screeching tires. In front of the house. Shouts from outside the house. Then more shouts. From inside.

The police were in the house. Karen could feel it.

After what seemed like an eternity, there was a knock on the bathroom door. Someone shouted, "This is the police. Anyone in there?"

"We're here," Carl called through the door.

"Okay. Good. How many of you?"

"All of us. Three. My wife, me, and our daughter. But Michelle. Oh my God, Michelle is in her room."

"All okay in there?"

"Yes."

"Great. You're Dr. Mondori?"

"Yes."

"Okay. Everything is cool, but we want you to stay in there for a bit. We have some things to do before you come out."

Carl looked at Karen. "What things?"

"You have a young daughter?"

"Yes."

"We don't want her to see this. Could you cover her eyes when you come out? But don't come out yet."

Karen could hear people running up and down the stairs, then more shouts from outside the house, more cars arriving. The reflections of the flashing lights on the outside of the bathroom window gave it the bizarre appearance of a Christmas decoration. All the while, the three of them were breathing hard, feeling shocky, their limbs weak, the heavy stink of fear still with them.

They waited five more minutes. Then another voice. "This is Detective Herb Holloway. You in there, Karen?"

Karen recognized the detective's voice. She'd known him for years.

"Yes."

She was surprised at the reediness of her voice.

"Okay. You can come out now. But please don't let Andrea see this. We'd like you to proceed directly to the family room. We can close the door and talk. Okay?"

"Okay," Karen said.

"I have to warn you. There are two bodies on the stairs and another downstairs in the foyer. Things are pretty messy out here. We can't cover the bodies until the M.E. gets here. So be aware. Ready?"

Three bodies. God! Who were they? Michelle? What had happened to Michelle!

"Okay," Karen said.

As Carl moved the dresser away from the door, Karen put on a terry-cloth robe and cinched it tightly around her body. Her hands shook. Carl took a small towel and blindfolded a now very stoic Andrea. "You okay?" Carl asked Karen.

"I don't know," she replied honestly.

"How about you, sweetheart?" Carl asked Andrea.

Andrea's teeth started chattering. She simply nodded.

Carl took Andrea in his arms, then opened the door. Three uniformed deputies greeted them, along with Detective Holloway.

The house was crawling with police.

"This way," the detective said.

He guided them past the mutilated bodies of two men. One of the bodies was less than five feet away from the bathroom door, the other crumpled on the stairs. The detective steered them past the blood spattered all over the walls and the carpeted stairs, past the deep gouges in the walls and the ceiling of the hallway and stairway, down to the main floor and the foyer where another body splayed crookedly . . .

Oh, God! Michelle!

Karen could see that most of her face was gone.

Karen let out a scream that frightened the still-blindfolded Andrea.

Andrea yelled, "Mommy!"

"It's okay, sweetheart. Mommy's all right."

Karen felt Carl's strong hand on her arm, pulling her past the unspeakable horror, into the family room, the door closing behind her, the three of them alone with Detective Holloway.

Carl placed Andrea on one of the sofas, then sprinted to the bar, poured some liquor into two glasses and handed one to Karen. She gulped it down. Carl drank deeply, then attended to Andrea, taking her pulse. "She's in mild shock," he announced.

He turned to Holloway. "Detective, give me a blanket, will you? There's a closet in the hall."

The detective moved quickly.

"I have to get my bag," Carl said softly. It meant he'd need to pass the carnage twice more. When he returned, he pulled a syringe from his bag, stuck it into a small vial, then gave Andrea a shot. He stroked the child's brow until she stopped shaking.

"What happened?" Karen finally asked Holloway.

Detective Holloway sat on a chair and opened a small notebook. "You have no idea how glad I am to see you folks alive."

"Michelle's dead?"

His face told the story. "I'm sorry."

Karen started to sob. "What happened here?"

Carl stood beside her, a syringe in his hand. "I'm going to give you a mild sedative," he said.

"No. I want my wits about me."

"Karen, you're in shock. We all are."

"I don't care. No shot."

Carl gave her a look, then moved back to the sofa and Andrea.

Holloway seemed dispassionate as he tried to explain. "Best we can tell right now is that two intruders smashed the glass panel beside the front door, reached in, threw back the dead bolt—the key was still in the lock—then entered the house. Michelle must have come out of her room to see what the noise was all about. Too bad. They gunned her down in the foyer. Shot her three times. They were using silencers."

Karen heard the words, but they seemed unreal. There was evidence of gruesome death throughout the house, and yet . . . She seemed divorced from it all. She wasn't calm, far from it, but she was removed, as if she'd somehow been shoved inside the television set, an actor in some low-budget movie, forced to speak lines, forced to . . .

She looked around the room. It was familiar, part of her home. She looked at Andrea lying on the sofa, Carl still stroking her forehead. Her daughter, precious daughter, terribly shaken, as disengaged as Karen. And Carl, a rock. How she loved him.

Karen sat beside the sofa and took them both in her arms. "I love you both so much," she said.

"I love you, too, Mommy."

"Me, too," Carl said, his eyes filled with sadness.

Karen turned to Holloway. "We heard shots," she said.

"So did your neighbors," the detective replied. "The shots you heard were not fired by the intruders. The shots you heard came from at least two other guys."

Karen was stunned. "What two other guys?"

"The way it looks right now, the two who broke in were assassins. Both were using semi-automatics with silencers. We've recovered the weapons. The assassins were halfway up the stairs when two *other* men stormed in and started shooting. A whole series of shots were exchanged. The two assassins were killed, and as near as we can tell, your saviors never suffered a scratch. We don't see any blood outside the house."

"Our saviors?" Karen asked numbly.

"I'd call them that. Wouldn't you? If it wasn't for them, you'd all be dead."

"Who? How? Where?"

Holloway took a deep breath. "Two men from across the street. They're long gone now. We have witnesses who saw two men leaving your house after hearing shots fired. The witnesses thought the men they saw were the killers. The two ran from your house to a car parked in a driveway across the street and bailed out in a hurry." He scratched his head. "One of the witnesses says that car's been there a few days. He thinks the two men were living in the house. You know anything about that?'

Karen felt a jolt of adrenaline. At the same time, her brain started functioning again. "Two men?"

"Yeah."

"Their car was in a driveway across the street?"

"Yeah. Like they were neighbors. Been here a few days. You know them?"

It was all so incomprehensible.

"Mr. Fielding?" Karen asked.

Holloway nodded. "That's the name of the guy who rented the place, according to a witness. You know him?"

Karen didn't answer. Bill Castor had said Mr. Fielding was a phony. Karen was convinced his presence had nothing to do with her. She thought it a homeowners association problem, hadn't given it another thought.

God!

What had really happened here?

"You'd better have someone check inside that house across the street," Karen said.

"It's being done as we speak," the detective told her. "There's another car parked right in front of your house. It's on the hot sheet. Probably used by the bad guys. We'll get rid of it after the crime scene people check it out."

There was a knock on the door and a uniformed cop stepped inside. He whispered something to Detective Holloway, then left.

"The M.E. is here," Holloway said, "but this is

going to take some time to clean up. How would you like us to handle it, Karen?"

"I have no idea."

"Well, I can direct you to a service that'll come out here on a moment's notice and . . ."

"I have to see Michelle," Karen said suddenly.

"You sure?"

"Yes. You need someone to ID her body."

"I can do it," Carl said.

"No!" It was almost a scream. "This is my responsibility. This happened because of me. Because of what I do. Michelle is dead because of me!"

Carl took her by the arm, then held her. He whispered into her ear. "This is not your fault. You don't know that this had anything to do with any of your cases, and even if it did, it's still not your fault. It's the fault of whoever sent those bastards out here."

Karen pulled away. "I have to see Michelle," she cried.

Carl was about to stop her.

He let her go.

Karen stepped out of the room and hunched down by Michelle's shattered body. Hot tears rolled down the lawyer's cheeks. For the past few days, Michelle had been as happy as Karen had ever seen her, anticipating a new life, looking to the future with optimism and enthusiasm. And now . . .

One of the bullets had gone through her left eye, another just below her mouth. The third had hit her right chin and blown most of the back of her head off. The girl's face was a bloody pulp, but there was enough to know it was Michelle. Karen took one of the girl's small hands in her own and kissed it. "I'm so sorry, Michelle."

All the while, cops came and went. Some took pictures. Others gathered evidence, the men and women of the crime scene unit doing their jobs, their hands covered with rubber gloves, using powerful flashlights to find items that they then placed in evidence bags.

The house had been invaded once tonight. Now, by necessity, it was being invaded a second time.

Karen retreated back to the den like a wounded animal.

"I think we should stay in a hotel for the night," Carl said to her. "Maybe a couple of nights."

Detective Holloway looked pained. "Ah . . . if it's all right with you, we'd rather you didn't do that until we have some kind of handle on what went down here tonight. The attack was so intense, they may try again. We'll be here in force for some time. Why don't you try and get the child to bed? You're a doctor, right?"

"I am," Carl said. "And you can go to hell. My family is getting out of this house within the hour. I expect you to give us an escort to wherever we go, and I expect you to keep your mouth shut about it. Understand?"

Holloway sighed. "If that's what you want . . ."

"That's what I want."

"Okay. We'll need some time to get things set."

"Within the hour, Detective."

"Okay. Look, they've got sheets over the two bodies on the stairs, so if you go upstairs, I'd still suggest . . ."

Carl cut him off. "I'll take care of it."

Andrea was half-asleep from the powerful sedative given her by her father. "Can you handle this alone for a while?" Carl asked Karen.

Karen simply nodded.

"I'll pack some things."

"Okay."

Karen was alone with Detective Holloway. He wasted no time filling her in, one professional to another.

"Both guys who busted in here are Latino," he said quickly. "ID makes them from Miami. My guess is they're Ramirez's people. Not good, Karen. It means he wants you dead. We can protect you only so far. You're going to need some serious help from now on."

Karen nodded numbly.

"As for your neighbors across the street, we figure they were hoods, probably Uccello's boys keeping an eye on things in case something like this went down. The house over there is a mess, lots of empty beer cans and TV dinner containers. No fresh prints anywhere. Oh, and two sets of binoculars. They were pros, Karen. Looks like your client was worried about you. We're tearing the place apart now, but I doubt we'll ever make an ID. The witnesses didn't really get much of a look at them, it was dark, and the car has probably been ditched by now.

"We'll want to talk to Uccello. You want to be there?"

Karen wasn't listening anymore. She was dialing Uccello's number on the telephone.

"Yeah."

"This is Karen Perry-Mondori. I want to talk to Angelo, now!"

"Hold on."

Angelo came to the phone. His first words were, "You and the family okay?"

His words were instructive. They meant he knew there'd been an attack. It meant the men living across the street *were* his people. They'd already reported back.

It meant . . .

"We have to talk," she said. "Tonight."

"Not tonight. I'm goin' to bed."

"Tonight!" Karen insisted. "I almost died tonight. My child and husband could have been killed. My . . . friend . . . is dead, a young, sweet girl slaughtered like an animal by other animals who were prepared to kill everyone in this house. I'm coming over there in a couple of hours, because this can't wait. If you fail to see me, you'll rue the day. Understand?"

There was a pause.

"I'll be waiting," he said. "Make sure the cops give you an escort."

"They want to talk to you as well. But I get you

first. We'll talk, and then I'll be with you when they ask their questions."

Karen hung up the phone. "That was privileged communication," she said to Holloway.

"Gotcha."

"What was the name of that cleaning crew?"

It was past midnight when the first of two late-night caravans left the Mondori address. The first consisted of five Pinellas County Sheriff's Office marked cars, each carrying five people. It wound its way through darkened streets without flashing lights or sirens, covering the five miles between Karen's house and Uccello's in record time.

The second caravan was made up of four cars. Carl, Andrea, and a half-dozen suitcases were headed for a hotel in St. Petersburg. Karen would join them later. Already, private security guards hired by Carl were heading for the hotel. They'd take up their positions before he and Andrea arrived. Carl wasn't satisfied with police protection. He wanted to be sure there'd be no repeat attempt on Karen's life.

The house was far from empty. The crime scene unit was almost done. Three bodies, now in plastic body bags, were placed in an ambulance and taken away. Four people dressed in overalls bearing the logo of a local cleaning service waited patiently for permission to start the work that would remove all vestiges of the horror that had visited this place just hours before.

And the curious, along with the media, some of

whom had stood outside the house for more than two hours, still lingered in the street, talking, shaking their heads, gossiping, speculating, angry that such brutal violence could infect even this neighborhood.

The first caravan stopped at the gate leading to Angelo Uccello's residence. Karen got out of one of the cars and walked through the opening in the gate under the watchful eyes of two of Angelo's goons. The police cars remained. Karen strode to the house and took the stairs to Angelo's living quarters. The door opened before she reached it.

Angelo was sitting behind his desk, a drink in one hand, a cigar in the other, looking almost the same as the first day they'd met. It seemed like years ago, not weeks. And because of that meeting, her life was forever changed. Shock and anger were evident on Karen's face.

Angelo stood up as she approached. He looked melancholy. "I'm real sorry about your maid," he said solemnly.

Karen nodded.

"Have a drink?"

Karen sat. "No."

"At least you're okay."

"Am I supposed to thank you?"

He shrugged. "Only if you want to."

"You knew this was going to happen."

"I didn't *know*. I thought there was a possibility. I tol' you that. I asked you to get off this case. When you refused, I figured I better set up some protection for you."

Karen fought the sudden urge to cry. "I do thank you," she said. "I mean that."

"I know you do."

"We might all have died."

He expelled some air. "We still might. That's the hell of it."

"This can't continue," Karen said.

He nodded. "I don't blame you for bein' upset. No judge is gonna give you action for quittin' on me now."

"That's not what I mean," she said. "I'm not worried about a judge. And even if I did quit, it wouldn't make much of a difference. They won't stop until we're all dead, Angelo. You know it and I know it. You were always dangerous to them, but now they know I'm just as dangerous. And I don't live in a fortress."

She looked around the room. "I refuse to live like this. I refuse to go through life being guarded by men with guns twenty-four hours a day. I won't do it. And I won't place my family in that position. I won't allow my husband to worry if I'm still alive while he's trying to concentrate on an operation. I won't allow myself to wonder if my child will be kidnapped, or worse, at any given moment. That's not a life."

He shrugged. "There's nothin' we can do now. Once we're on the shit list, they won't let it rest. All we can do is try and protect ourselves."

Karen shook her head. "That's not good enough. You're talking defense. I'm talking offense."

He puffed on his cigar. "You mean me talkin'? No way. I already told you I ain't about to do that."

"Why not?"

"Because that means I'm dead for sure. Once I tell 'em what I know, it'll take too long to round everyone up. There'll be fifty guys after us. And they can't protect me while I'm talkin'. They can't protect me *or* you or your family. You can't trust the feds. You should know that by now. You can't trust nobody."

"So," she said, making no attempt to hide her mounting anger, "this is it? My family and I have to spend the rest of our lives being protected? That's your answer?"

"You shoulda got out when you had the chance," he said.

"Well, I didn't."

"I'm sorry, Karen. I really am. I'll give you all the help I can. My boys did good tonight. I knew they didn't stop the maid from gettin' killed, but they moved as fast as they could."

Karen stared at the ceiling. The vision of Michelle's mutilated face swam before her eyes. "If we'd been in the family room, we'd all be dead."

"So, I'll change the setup. We'll put some people right outside your door."

Karen sighed. "Why did they run away tonight?"

"Too much to explain. They ain't exactly cops. They could still face charges. So we thought it was better to make sure they can't be nailed. And they can't. No prints, no weapons, no nothin'. The cops will never tie my guys to this even though they know it was them. Knowin' and makin' something stick are two different things."

"You're the expert, right?"

"I've done good so far."

"You're not listening to me, Angelo. I'm not suggesting we debate the merits of you putting an end to this. I'm telling you there's no choice."

His eyes narrowed. "What's that mean?"

"What it means is that you're going to tell the Senate Drug Enforcement Oversight Committee everything you know. And I'll be sitting right beside you, making sure you get full immunity and a new life."

"The hell I will."

"You must. Surely you must know that Senator Robert Jameson is a high-ranking member of that committee."

"I know about him."

"Well, he happens to be my brother. He owes me something, and this is how he can clear the books."

Angelo blinked once. That was it.

And at that precise moment, Karen realized that Angelo Uccello knew Robert was her brother. The carefully kept secret was no secret to Angelo.

"So he's your brother," Angelo said derisively. "Big deal. He's one man."

"But he's clean, at least as far as being tied to the CIA or Ramirez. Or is he?"

Angelo stared at her for a moment. "Yeah, he's clean."

"Then he's the one."

"No."

Karen sighed. "Then you leave me no choice."

Angelo leaned forward, his gaze intense. "What's that mean?"

"I had two of my associates go through your diaries looking for material that might prove helpful at your trial. You've seen the results already. We were able to blow the testimony of that so-called drug trafficker right out the window.

"While we were sorting through your files, we came across some of the names you'd hinted at earlier. We found forty-five, but I'm sure there's more. With you backing up your diaries, you can put them all away, Angelo."

"I tol' you, I'm not gonna do that."

"Then I will. I'll turn over copies of your diaries to Robert. He'll make everything public. The media will make this the biggest story of the year. The FBI will have to pull out all the stops in a complete investigation. Once they're armed with names, places, and dates, the drug task force can make their case and shut this operation down.

"That's the only way my family will ever be free again. It's the only chance you and I have of survival."

"You can't do that!" he screamed. "I gave you that information for a reason. It's privileged! Nobody can use it. You told me that yourself."

"I know. But they can still use the information

if they can prove it came from someone else. I'll find a way to make that happen."

He was on his feet, his face flushed, his heavy-fisted hands leaning on the desk. "You'd do that to me? You'd cross me like that?"

"In a heartbeat," she said. "I want my family to have a life, don't you understand?"

"You won't have no life!" he yelled. "You'll be dead. All of you! You think they'll let you get away with this?"

"We have to try, Angelo. We're sure to be killed if we don't stop these people. I'd rather go down fighting than cowering. I would have thought you'd feel the same way. Why else would you have kept that diary in the first place? You *knew* this day would come!"

He simply stared at her.

She glared back at him.

"They told me you were tough," he said finally.

His comment broke the tension. Karen almost laughed. Instead, she smiled at him. "You wanted a wimp to defend you?"

"What exactly do you want me to do?" Angelo asked.

She told him. It took fifteen minutes to cover it all, and Angelo had some ideas of his own. They negotiated, then negotiated some more. "I need more names," she said. "I need them all, Angelo."

"Even the ones already dead?"

"Even those. I want you to be able to show the pattern of corruption."

"You want me to show what?"

"You heard me."

He shook his head. "I give you the go-ahead on this and that list will be on the front page of the *Times* within two days."

"No it won't. I'm not like you. There are a few people I *do* trust. And they're the only ones who will have access to this material. They will *not* leak it. They'll know that by doing so, they've killed me. And if my trusted friends get me killed, I'm better off dead.

"No, I take that back. I don't want to die, Angelo. I really don't. But if you fight me on this, that's what's going to happen. And you'll be the one responsible. Do you really want to go to your grave knowing you were responsible for getting me killed? Remember, it was you who came to me in the first place. It was your idea I should have a copy of the diaries. This is your doing! You can't just walk away from it!"

He held up his hands in surrender. "Christ! What a pitch."

"Well?"

"All right! Jesus Christ! I'll work with you. I'll do the whole number, if only to shut you the hell up."

The words were harsh ones, but Karen knew him by now. He was looking for leadership, looking for someone to show him the way. And she was doing it.

"We have a deal then?"

"Yeah. For whatever that means. You don't keep your promises, lady."

That one was a low blow. And it hurt. "We've kept Detective Holloway waiting long enough," Karen said crisply. "He wants to talk to you."

"I can talk to him alone."

"Not a good idea. You should have your lawyer present."

"I've talked to cops before without lawyers. I'm a big boy now."

"What's the problem? You're angry with me? Don't let your anger interfere with your judgment."

"Enough already! Go home, Karen. This is my area of . . . what do you call it? Expert something?"

"Expertise?"

"That's it. This is my area of expertise. I've been doin' this longer than you been alive. Shove off. You got what you came for."

"Okay, Angelo. And thanks."

He laughed. "For what? Just remember this was your idea. If we all get killed, it's your fault."

There was the strangest twinkle in his eye.

"If we all get killed, it won't matter much whose fault it is," Karen retorted.

He grunted in satisfaction. "Now, you're startin' to get the message."

21

By the time Karen and her police escort reached the hotel Carl had chosen as their temporary living quarters, it was almost four in the morning. Three men dressed in civilian clothes lingered near the entrance to her fourth-floor room. One of them moved to block entrance. "Mrs. Mondori?"

"Perry-Mondori," Karen corrected him.

"Sorry. I need to see your ID."

"Who are you?" one of the cops asked.

"We're with Global Security, Officer. Dr. Mondori hired us."

"So you say. I'd like to see your ID."

The security officer showed the cop his badge and ID.

"Next time," Karen said, "why don't you have that ready before someone has to ask for it?"

"We don't normally do that, ma'am. We have to be ready to move fast. People who don't belong up here get real antsy when we ask to see their ID. I was told to expect you, but all I really knew was that you were short. Sorry."

Satisfied, Karen pulled out her ID and showed it to him. He nodded, then moved away.

Karen tried the key in the lock but the door was double-locked. Before she could knock, she heard Carl's voice. "Karen?"

"Yes."

Carl opened the door and Karen stepped inside, leaving the private and public cops to sort out just who would be providing protection. Carl immediately took her into his arms. "Am I glad to see you," he exclaimed. "I've been worried sick."

"I told you I'd be okay," she said, hugging him back.

"I know. But there are times . . ."

Karen looked around the room. She was surprised to see Carl still fully dressed and the room brightly lighted.

"It's a two-bedroom suite," Carl explained. "Andrea's asleep, but I'm worried about her. She's still in mild shock. I want to get her in to see Leo in the morning."

"Maybe Leo can come here," Karen said.

"Better yet," Carl said. "I keep forgetting. This is going to take some getting used to."

Karen, exhausted, sat on the sofa and leaned back. "Thank God, Andrea didn't see Michelle like that. But she knows what's happened. She has to be terribly traumatized. Which room is she in?"

"The door on the right."

Karen got up, walked to the door, opened it silently, then went inside. She stood over Andrea's bed, listened to the sound of the child's even breathing, pushed some stray hair away from her eyes, kissed her lightly on the forehead, then left the room.

Carl was out on the balcony staring off into space. Karen joined him.

"She'll be okay," Karen said. "She's a strong kid."

"I still want Leo to see her."

"So do I. I may want to talk to him myself. God! What a night!"

The breeze had picked up. The moon was hidden by thin clouds. Flashes of muted lightning flickered dully in the distance. Under other circumstances, it might have been a romantic setting, but Karen and Carl were still struggling to deal emotionally with the horror of violent death.

In their own home.

Someone had tried to kill them all.

The initial shock had worn off, leaving in its place an altered sense of being. Something that had no place in their highly organized lives was suddenly there, uninvited, intruding, omnipresent, threatening to appropriate all conscious and unconscious thought.

Like a cancer, a malignancy of terror. For Andrea, even more than themselves. If they were killed and Andrea lived, what would happen to their child? When coupled with the sense of loss at the death of Michelle, the burden was crushing. Never again would they view their comfortable home in the same light. Never again would they take lives for granted.

Would they be forced to move in order to start again? And though neither had mentioned it, the thought crossed both minds.

Probably, Karen thought.

The cleaning specialists could make things look as they were; remove the bloodstains, change the carpet, repair the walls and ceilings, disguise the stink of sudden death—but they could never erase the memories.

"I talked to both of Michelle's parents," Carl said. "I made it a conference call, which is not easy to do in France. I was on the phone over an hour."

"They both must have been devastated."

He hung his head. "They were. Naturally, I tried to express how sorry we were, but I think they blame us. They rambled on for ten minutes about what a terrible country America is, with all its violence. I could hardly disagree.

"They want her body shipped home. I told them I'd take care of it. You'll have to get someone in your office to look after the paperwork. Michelle's parents are airmailing the documents within a few hours."

"I'll get Liz over here in the morning," Karen said. "She'll take care of it. I have a ton of things for her to do."

She started to weep. Carl held her close. "Michelle was like another child," Karen sobbed. "I'll miss her so much."

"Me, too. How will we ever replace her?"

"I can't think about that right now."

"Sorry. I'm being a jerk. How did it go with your client?"

Karen stopped sobbing. "Well, on that score, I have very good news. He went for it."

Carl stepped back and stared at her. "He did? That's incredible!"

"I'm as astonished as you," Karen said. "He resisted at first, but when I told him I'd release his diaries if I had to, he folded. He started out being angry as hell, but when I left, I had the feeling he was actually relieved."

Carl shook his head. "Unbelievable! I've been up all night worrying, chewing my nails down to the quick. When you told me what you were planning, I had visions of him killing you on the spot."

"Not with the place surrounded by police," Karen said. "Detective Holloway was waiting right outside the gate. I knew I was safe."

"But will he change his mind down the road? Will he really cooperate?"

"All the way. He has to. He has no other choice, and he knows it."

"You're sure he won't change his mind?"

"I'm sure."

There was a light knock at the door. "Who would that be?" Karen asked.

"I'll find out," Carl said. He strode to the door and asked the question. It was Detective Holloway. Carl opened the door.

"I'm sorry to trouble you, Karen," Holloway

said. "But one of our guys is on the beach keeping surveillance. He saw your lights were still on."

"It's okay," Karen said. "What is it?"

"I thought you'd want to know. We just heard from the Miami police. They found the bodies of Fito Olivera and Manuel Aznar two hours ago. Both died from multiple gunshot wounds. Looks like Ramirez is tightening up the ship."

Karen sagged. "I thought they were back in Colombia."

"Guess not."

Would the killing never end? she wondered. Or was this just the beginning of a bloodbath?

"Well, good night," the detective said. "Be sure to throw the dead bolt."

"Detective?"

"Yes?"

"You told me you'd protect my client. I hope you weren't just making small talk. If Ramirez has gone this far, he has to be after Angelo."

"I know. We're pulling out all the stops and getting full cooperation from both the FBI and the Coast Guard."

Karen's hand flew to her mouth. "You didn't tell them . . ."

"No, no. All we said was that he was a marked man. I told everyone I didn't want anything happening to him on my watch. As far as anyone knows, we're just doing our jobs. The FBI doesn't know. I won't let you down, Karen. I told you that."

"I know you did. I'm just a little shook up right now."

"And so you should be."

"How did your interrogation go?"

He gave her a look. "What do you think?"

"That bad?"

"He knows nothing. Sure. We've been over that house with a fine-toothed comb, but there's zilch to tie him in. We'll have to mark this one as still open."

"Thanks," Karen said. "For everything."

Holloway scratched his head. "You know, he must really care about you to do what he did."

Karen didn't answer.

Holloway threw her a smile, then left.

Karen and Carl went back to the balcony. Then, suddenly, Carl pulled her back into the room, closed the door, and pulled the drapes. "I think we better get used to being less visible."

Old habits were hard to break. Karen sat on the sofa, feeling miserable.

"So what happens now?" Carl asked.

"I'll call Robert first thing in the morning. I'll let him make the arrangements. I'm sure we'll have it all set by tonight."

"What about you? Are you going to Washington?"

"I have to, Carl."

"Then we're coming as well."

"You can't. You have patients. And there's Andrea."

"I have three doctors who can fill in for me. I'm not going to let you go to Washington by yourself, not under these circumstances. No way. And I'm not letting Andrea out of my sight until this is over. She can't go to school anyway. Not without a dozen guards. She couldn't take that. And I won't allow her to be exposed without them."

Karen stroked his cheek. "This could take weeks to resolve."

"I don't care."

"It's me they want, not you or Andrea."

He grunted. "You're not thinking straight, Karen. What better way to get to you than through Andrea or me?"

He was right. On both counts.

"Okay," she said. "We'll go as a family. You can tutor Andrea. She won't miss anything."

Carl nodded. "God! I'll be glad when this is over. I'd go crazy if I had to live like this." He gripped her arm. "Promise me you'll never, ever, take a case like this again."

Karen nodded. "I promise."

"What about security in Washington?" Carl asked. "How will we handle that? Maybe we could stay with Robert. No one knows you and Robert are related. He's probably got security in place anyway."

Karen didn't answer. She was staring off into space, thinking.

"What is it?" Carl asked.

"Angelo knew Robert was my brother."

"He did?"

"Yes. He didn't say so in so many words, but when I mentioned Robert's name, his eyes betrayed him for just an instant."

"It may not mean much. Maybe he checked you out before he hired you. He's a very careful guy. That would make sense."

"It would, except there's no record in either Robert's background records or mine indicating we're related. We both made sure of that years ago. I've done several checks since, and there's nothing of which I'm aware."

Carl started pacing the floor. "If Angelo knows, others may know. That means . . ." His voice trailed off.

"What is it?" Karen asked.

Carl looked at his watch. "I just had a weird thought."

"What?"

"Not now. Tomorrow is a full day. We both have to get some sleep. I'm too exhausted to think straight."

He handed her a pill. "Take this. I'll take one as well. We have to get some sleep."

"Yes, Doctor. Can I ask what it is?"

"No."

She kissed him. "I'm very glad I'm married to you. You might have saved our lives this day. You moved so quickly. I was just standing there, not knowing what to do."

He kissed her on the nose. "No more. Sleep. Doctor's orders."

They woke early, their nerves on edge, their minds still reeling. Karen got on the phone to Robert while Carl woke Andrea.

When Robert came to the phone, his first words

were, "Thank God you're all right! I've been try-ing to find you, but no one would tell me where you were. I kept telling them who I was, but it didn't matter."

"How did you know?"

"How did I know? Are you serious? It's the lead item on the national news. Has been since late last night. Claire's been beside herself. You're sure you're okay?"

"I'm fine. We're all okay."

He sighed in relief. "I'm so glad you called."

"Robert, I need your help."

"Yes?"

"My client wants to come in and I want you to be our mediator. Will you do it?"

Without hesitation, he said, "Of course."

"This won't be easy."

"I wouldn't expect it to be. What exactly do you want me to do?"

She told him.

"I'll be back to you before the close of business today," he said. "I'll arrange everything."

"Remember," she said, "this has to be handled with extreme caution. If word leaks, we're dead, and that is no exaggeration. I hope you under-stand that."

"I do, and I'll move carefully. This is right up my alley, Karen. Don't worry. You'll come here and stay with Claire and me. You must. I'll make arrangements for added security."

"Thanks, Robert. I was counting on you."

"I won't let you down, Karen. Not this time."

"I know you won't. See you soon."

"I'll call you this afternoon."

"Okay."

Carl came out from Andrea's bedroom.

"How is she?" Karen asked, hanging up the phone.

"She'd not doing as well as I'd hoped," he said. "I'm going to call Leo right now."

While Carl made the call, Karen went into Andrea's bedroom. Andrea held out her arms for a hug.

"You okay, sweetheart?"

"I'm scared, Mommy. Those men might come back."

"They won't come back. Daddy explained that last night. Besides, we have policemen protecting us."

"But they might come back. They might! They killed Michelle. They wanted to kill us. I know they did! They'll come back."

"No they won't. Mommy and Daddy will make sure of that. Besides, we're going to Virginia to see your Uncle Robert."

"When?

"Either today or tomorrow."

"What about school?"

"You can miss a few days. Daddy will help you with your studies."

That cheered her up some.

Carl poked his head in. "Leo'll be here in less than an hour. I invited him for breakfast."

"Good. You stay with Andrea for a moment. I want to check the news."

"Okay."

Karen closed the door to the bedroom and switched on the TV, keeping the volume low.

It was just as Robert said. The story was the lead item.

"Noted Florida criminal defense attorney Karen Perry-Mondori," the announcer said, "narrowly escaped death last night during what police are calling a home invasion. A maid was shot to death during the attack which took place just after nine last night in the central Florida community of Palm Harbor, some fifteen miles west of Tampa.

"According to Detective Herbert Holloway of the Pinellas County Sheriff's Office, two men, as yet unidentified, smashed through a glass window near the front of the house and opened the door from the inside. They then shot the maid, identified as Michelle LaBlanc, a French national living in the United States under a student visa, mortally wounding the woman.

"In a bizarre twist, the home invaders were confronted by two as yet unidentified men who witnesses say lived across the street from the Mondori address. After a fierce gunfight during which at least thirty shots were fired, the two home invaders were killed. We have no word on the fate of the as-yet-unidentified neighbors, who are still being sought by police.

"Local authorities have refused to release any other information on this terrifying incident. Calls to both the Mondori household and the law firm of Hewitt, Sinclair, Smith, and Perry-Mondori have not been returned.

"Karen Perry-Mondori represents Mafia drug lord Angelo Uccello, scheduled to stand trial later this year for drug trafficking. At a recent preliminary hearing, Ms. Perry-Mondori claimed that her client was framed and asked the court for permission to subpoena the federal agents who were responsible for planning and executing the raid that resulted in her client's arrest. The judge allowed her request, while at the same time ordering Uccello held over for trial. It is unclear at this time whether federal officials will allow the subpoenas to stand because of laws that protect federal officers from having to testify at state trials.

"Also unclear is whether the home invasion was connected to the Uccello trial. Police refuse to speculate, but it is known that two potential witnesses at the pending trial were assassinated last night in Miami. Fito Olivera and Manuel Aznar were found murdered, gangland style. Miami police have made no official statements regarding their deaths, but a source close to the investigation tells UBC news that their deaths are definitely related to the Uccello trial.

"We'll keep on top of this story and bring you more details as they develop."

Karen, satisfied that there'd been no leaks so far, showered, dressed, then made several phone calls. It was going to be a very busy day.

22

Dr. Leo Zimmer joined the family for room-service breakfast. The doctor talked animatedly with Andrea, his conversation designed to elicit indications of the child's feelings. The skilled psychiatrist was especially good with children and managed to put Andrea at ease in very short order.

Later, with Andrea in the bedroom with Carl, the doctor told Karen, "She'll be fine. It'll just take some time. You'll need to keep reassuring her for a while." He smiled. "Just as you need such reassurance yourself."

"In spades," Karen said.

"Well, as for Andrea, I wouldn't worry. She's reacting quite normally at this point. She ate her breakfast, and that's always a very good sign."

He pulled at his beard. "Expect her to break into tears for no apparent reason at some point in the future. She may cry for as long as an hour, or she may exhibit some other type of abnormal behavior, such as temper tantrums. That's the release. On the other hand, don't be concerned if none of this happens. Andrea has a very strong personality and may react to this trauma in a different way. If you see no change within a week, let me know. A few sessions will help, I'm sure."

Karen wanted to tell him they were going away, but couldn't. "Thanks, Leo."

"Not at all."

The rest of the day was filled with hurried meetings. Karen met with Brander, Liz, Len, and Sharon, while Carl met with his secretary, operating nurse, and two doctors. The room was as busy as Grand Central Station.

Finally, preparations were complete, and the family was ready to leave. As if on cue, Robert called at three in the afternoon.

"The arrangements are set," he said. "For security reasons, I'd rather not discuss them with you over the telephone. All I can tell you is that an FBI special agent will be there within the hour."

Karen felt a chill run down her spine. "An FBI agent? Robert, are you . . ."

"Please don't be concerned, Karen. I'm quite conversant with your situation. The man is completely trustworthy. I'll explain everything in due course. Just get your things together as quickly as possible."

"We're already set," she said. "You're absolutely sure about . . ."

"Karen, I'm sure."

"Okay." But her voice lacked conviction.

"Karen?"

"Yes?"

"Remember that conversation we had in your home?"

"Of course."

"I meant what I said then, and I mean it now. I won't let you down this time."

"Okay."

A half hour later there was a knock at the door. One of the security guards told Karen that an FBI agent was here to see her.

Karen looked at Carl, took a deep breath, then told the guard to send him in. "And I want you to stay with my daughter in the bedroom," she added.

"Yes, ma'am."

When Bruce Tasker walked through the door, Karen almost fainted.

"You!" she yelled.

"Take it easy," Tasker said quickly. "I'm on your side."

Karen slumped to the sofa. Carl looked confused. "You know this guy?"

Karen nodded. "He's one of the agents who raided Angelo's place."

"Jesus!"

"Listen to me," Tasker exclaimed. "I've been working undercover for months as a member of the special task force investigating possible CIA, FBI, and DEA involvement in drug trafficking. Just so you know, I'm fully aware the drugs found in your client's safe were planted. I helped make that happen. I had to, don't you see?"

Karen simply stared at him.

Tasker chuckled, trying to put her at ease. "I heard about that demonstration you put on in court. You had it exactly right. You're quite a detective, Ms. Perry-Mondori."

"What about the other two agents who were in the room with you?"

"They're dirty, working for Ramirez, as you probably figured out. The cop from Pinellas is okay, hasn't a clue. Ramirez tried to take you out because he knows he can't get to Uccello this way. The case is lost. Now, Ramirez is trying to scare Uccello into running for it. But he never dreamed Uccello would run to the Senate committee."

Karen expelled some long-held air. "What about all that stuff with Wilbur . . . and the depositions?"

"I was working undercover. I was playing a character, if you will. There was nothing I could do, no way to let you know. Surely, you can understand that."

"It'll take a little getting used to," Karen said. "What *about* Wilbur, anyway. Is he part of this charade, a bad guy, or just terminally nerdy?"

Tasker chuckled again. "Wilbur is just obsessed. He hates drug dealers. Would he break the law to put one in jail? Yes. Has he? Probably, though I don't know for sure. But he isn't part of this."

"You're sure?"

"I'm sure."

"And Briscoe?"

Tasker blushed with anger. "He's dirty."

"I had a feeling," Karen said.

"Look, we'll deal with it. Right now, we have more important issues. I've been assigned to get you to Washington. You'll just have to trust me."

"That will take some getting used to as well," Karen said. "Tell me, why did Wilbur dump the case?"

"We're wasting time."

"I want to know."

"Because I wrote a report to Justice advising them to drop this case. It was becoming clear the case was lost. If you were allowed to take it all the way, it would most certainly have risked additional exposure to those of us on the task force. We had to break away."

Tasker took a deep, frustrated breath. "Listen, we have to get moving. The attorney general gave me this assignment personally. If anything happens to you or your family, it'll happen to me, too. Do you really think the entire U.S. Government is involved in this mess?"

"I'm beginning to wonder," Karen said. "The CIA is obviously dirty all the way to the top. That can't happen without government knowledge. Who's left to trust?"

"You're wrong. CIA involvement in illegal drugs is limited to a small group of rogues operating outside the knowledge of the head honchos."

"Bullshit! You can't hide five billion dollars a year's worth of unauthorized foreign aid."

"What makes you think the money's being used for foreign aid?" Tasker snapped. "You're a lawyer. You know better than to make judgments until all the evidence is in. For your information, most of that money is sitting in offshore banks. Are you so cynical you think everybody's dirty? How the hell can you operate with that attitude?"

"That's enough," Carl said, his hands balled into fists.

Tasker raised his hands defensively. "Take it easy, Doctor. You pop me one and you'll break a hand. Not too smart for a surgeon."

"I won't take it easy," Carl said angrily. "We damn near got killed last night. I'm not in the mood to stand by and listen to some asshole give my wife a hard time."

"Sorry," Tasker said. "Look, it's a touchy thing with me, this business of working undercover, knowing some of my colleagues are working with drug traffickers. It'll take the bureau years to recover from this. Years! A lot of good men will take it on the chin for no reason."

"My heart bleeds."

Tasker looked at Karen, his eyes pleading. "Enough, okay? You'll get your chance to lay it all out. Right now, we have to get you out of here. There's a Justice Department plane standing by at Clearwater Airport. I'll take you there now. Some other agents will pick up Mr. Uccello and bring him to the airport separately. We'll all fly to Washington together. Once there, you'll part company with your client. You'll be staying with Senator Jameson at his home. That's been arranged. As for your client, he'll be housed at Quantico. That's a Marine base—"

"I know what it is," Karen interrupted.

"You'll have complete access to your client whenever you want it. The hearings are being scheduled as we speak. Best guess is they'll start next week."

"The sooner the better," Karen said. "What about the attorney general?"

"He's agreed to meet with you tonight. Unless you think that's too soon. After what you've been through . . ."

"Tonight is fine," Karen said firmly.

"Good. There's just one more thing."

"What?"

"We've not talked to your client. Under the circumstances, we thought it best that the information come from you. You need to call your client and tell him we'll be by to pick him up in half an hour. He'll have to come alone. We can't have his bodyguards along on this trip. If he refuses to come, we can't force him and this whole thing goes by the boards. We'll still take you to Washington, but as far as the hearings, there wouldn't be much point."

"I disagree," Karen said. "There are some things of which you're unaware. With or without my client, those hearings will be held."

Tasker's eyebrows rose. "Okay. Well, first things first. Why don't you give your client a call?"

Karen picked up the phone. When Angelo came

on the line, she said, "Everything's arranged. Some people from Justice are with me now. They'll be coming by to pick you up in half an hour. And it's just you and a suitcase, Angelo."

There was a long pause. "You sure about this?"

"As sure as I can be."

"Your brother set it up?"

"Yes. I talked to him a few minutes ago."

"All right," he said. "Tell them to drive right into the garage. The door will be open."

"I'll tell them."

She put down the phone and turned to Tasker. "He's ready."

Karen, Carl, Andrea, and Tasker climbed out of the car and hurried aboard an unmarked plane parked inside a service hangar at the rear of the airport. Tasker introduced them to a man dressed in civilian clothes. "Special Agent Barnes."

"Can I get anyone a drink?" Barnes asked.

The plane was an executive four-engine jet, with luxurious brown leather seats and all the other accoutrements. The small galley between the cockpit and the bulkhead would have done a commercial plane proud.

Karen and Carl ordered martinis for themselves and a diet Coke for Andrea.

The car bearing Angelo arrived almost as soon as the drinks were served. Angelo, wearing sunglasses and a silly-looking hat, scrambled aboard as another FBI agent stowed his luggage.

"Okay, folks," Barnes announced, "we're ready to go. Let's strap ourselves in."

Angelo looked over at Karen. "I hope you know what you're doin'."

"Me, too."

"This your husband?"

"Yes. And my daughter Andrea."

Karen made the introductions. Angelo, his eyes filled with pure venom, glared at Tasker. "You're one of the feds who set me up. I oughtta take you apart right here."

Karen grabbed Angelo's arm. "Not now, okay? For Andrea's sake. I'll explain everything en route. It's okay."

"It's okay?"

"Yes."

He sighed. "Can I smoke on this crate?"

"Sorry," Barnes said.

"Why do I feel like I'm already in prison?" Angelo asked.

The plane's four engines started to whine. The pilot taxied the plane to the end of the runway, waited for less than ten seconds, then pushed the throttles forward. Karen was pushed back in her seat as the plane gained speed.

And then they were in the air, banking sharply to the left, then leveling off, now rising steeply. Karen could see Autumn Woods receding out the right window just before they entered some low cloud.

The plane reached cruising altitude quickly. Angelo said nothing, just sat and stared out the window.

Karen watched as Carl conversed with Andrea. Clearly, he was still worried about her. As was Karen. And why not? Even though Leo had seemed to penetrate the protective wall, it was firmly back in place again.

Karen wondered if things would ever be as they once were.

The sun was just setting as the plane touched down at Dulles Airport in Washington. It taxied to a remote section of the airport and stopped. When the door opened, two men immediately climbed aboard. Special Agent Tasker introduced the two FBI agents to everyone, then suggested all but Karen and Angelo disembark. "You two probably need to confer," he explained. Karen was touched by the consideration.

Now alone in the plane with Angelo, she started to detail what was to come. He held up his hand to stop her.

"What's the matter?"

"This plane is probably bugged," he said.

"It might be, but so what?"

"I'd just feel better if I knew we couldn't be overheard."

Given everything, his paranoia was justified. Karen switched on the overhead TV set and turned up the volume. "Feel better?"

"Yeah. So what happens now?"

"I'm meeting with the attorney general tonight.

I'll tell him you're prepared to testify but only under the conditions you and I have discussed. You'll be happy to know that Tasker was working undercover. He told me the drugs were indeed planted, so they have nothing with which to charge you. They can't keep you here against your will."

Angelo was shocked. "Tasker told you that?"

"Yes."

"Son of a bitch."

"I'll know more after my meeting with the attorney general. I'll call you."

"The guys in the car said I was goin' to stay at Quantico."

"Correct. It's the safest place right now."

"How come I couldn't have some of my people with me?"

"Because it complicates matters. They can't carry weapons outside the State of Florida anyway. No one wanted to risk taking a chance of some unforeseen incident. They want to present you in the best light possible."

"Okay, Counselor. You've made it this far. We'll see just how far you can push it."

"Good. I already have your phone number. I'll give you the number where I'm staying. You can call anytime. The lines will be secure. Remember, my brother is a U.S. senator. That helps."

"I guess it does. They tell you when the hearing might start?"

"Next week. Once the hearing's over, they'll take you somewhere where you can relax for a few months. Then, after you testify in court, they'll put you in the program permanently.

"On the other hand, if they fail to meet our conditions, we have a decision to make. And that's a decision I'll leave entirely to you."

"Okay. Let's get this over with."

They left the plane. Karen was escorted to a waiting helicopter and Angelo to its twin. As Karen climbed the small steps, she could hear Andrea crying. She sat beside her daughter and stroked her hair.

"It started as soon as she sat down," Carl explained. "I guess Leo knows his stuff."

Karen kissed her daughter on the cheek. "It's okay, sweetheart. We're going to visit your Uncle Robert. We'll have a great time, you'll see. He lives in a big house in the country. You can see the mountains right from the back porch. They're really something."

The crying diminished to some whimpers.

Tasker leaned down and asked, "Belts on?"

"Yes."

"We're ready."

"Okay."

The helicopter lifted slowly off the ground, then turned and rose into the sky. It made a slow pass over the city at about three thousand feet so Carl could point out the Washington sights to Andrea. That was Tasker's idea, Carl told Karen.

As Carl pointed to the Lincoln Memorial, then the White House and the Capitol Building, Andrea stopped whimpering and craned her neck for a better look. She was coming out of it.

They flew for twenty minutes, landing in Manassas, Virginia. Robert was waiting for them with a car and driver. The drive to Warrenton wouldn't take long, he explained. "We didn't want to draw too much attention," he said. "There've been a couple of times when the president has flown out here in his helicopter. The whole town comes out to the old house to get a look at the man. We don't need that."

"Good thinking," Karen said, her ears still buzzing from the helicopter's noise and vibration.

Robert lifted Andrea up and held her close. "You and I are going to get to know each other, young lady. Did you know I have two horses?"

"No."

"Well, I do. I keep them in town. How would you like to go for a ride tomorrow?"

"Can we?"

"You bet."

Andrea's eyes shone with excitement.

The old Andrea was back. The lump that had been in Karen's throat since the attack finally began to ease.

Like most old houses, the kitchen was the biggest room in the house. This one was furnished in a combination of late-nineteenth- and early-twentieth-century American pieces. A large wood-burning stove dominated one wall, with huge pipes, painted white, that went through the ceiling. A hundred-year-old wooden table and matching chairs sat immediately in front of the French window. The wall coverings reflected the Early American theme of the room. Most of the modern appliances were cleverly built in. Even the refrigerator hid behind rough wooden panels that looked like pantry doors.

The theme was maintained throughout this red brick, high-ceilinged, triple-gabled, two-story former farmhouse that stood alone in open space, less than two miles from the town of Warrenton and bought by the Jamesons eleven years ago. Claire's elegant touch was everywhere, from the gleaming hardwood floors she'd personally refinished to the changed-daily, freshly cut flowers in every room, except the den, which, with its modern electronics cheek-to-jowl with Robert's collection of old and rare first-edition books, sparkled with unsullied nativity, generating a unique, if quaint, warmth.

It was a second home, used eight months a year, its location unusual in that it was so far from the city of Washington, necessitating an often brutal commute. But Robert liked it that way. It gave him an excuse to avoid all but the most essential of the interminable parties and receptions that begged his attendance. And it gave Claire a taste of another time, away from the hurly-burly, the fantasy world that seemed to exist within the Beltway. Here and there, other modern inventions stood apart from the antiques, but they were placed as unobtrusively as possible.

Karen had met Claire once, and then only for minutes, but Claire's greeting was like that of an old friend. She was a senator's wife, conditioned to meeting new people, being pleasant to even the most obnoxious of them. She did it with an unforced naturalness that set Karen at ease.

The Jamesons' live-in maid Ursula took their bags upstairs while the Mondori family huddled in the kitchen with Special Agent Tasker and the Jamesons. Outside, beyond the wrought-iron fence that surrounded the homestead, security people stood guard. Some were uniformed, others not.

"I trust you've eaten," Claire said.

"Yes," Carl told her. "Courtesy of the United States Government. Not exactly airline food. First class all the way."

Claire smiled. "I sometimes think the perks are what keeps Robert in public life. I can offer coffee or tea, whichever you prefer."

Karen and Carl asked for tea. Tasker suggested he and Andrea see what was on TV.

"The house is lovely," Karen said. Immediately, she thought of her mother uttering those exact words.

"I'll give you the tour after we have our tea," Claire said.

She was quite beautiful at fifty, even more so than when she and Robert had married almost thirty years ago. The years had been kind to both of them. Claire was tall and slim, her soft face dominated by riveting blue eyes, framed by brown hair that curled in just above the jawline.

On most women her age, the style would look out of place. On Claire, it looked perfect.

"I'm so glad you're here," she said. "I've followed your career with great interest, Karen. I can't possibly imagine how you must feel after such a dreadful experience, but I hope your stay with us will prove propitious. I so admire your courage."

"Thank you," Karen said. "It's not really courage, more a sense of self-preservation."

"I think not," Claire said. "I've admired you from afar for many years. I can't tell you how pleased I am that you and Robert have finally buried the hatchet. Family is so important these days, don't you agree?"

"Yes," Karen said, her gaze drifting to Robert. "Family is very important."

The attorney general arrived with a small entourage at nine. Andrew Williams, a former federal judge rumored to be seeking elected political office at some time in the near future, was a handsome, outgoing man with a spotless reputation. After a round of introductions, he and Karen retired to the den to negotiate. Carl took Andrea up to bed.

"Thank you for coming," Karen said.

"Not at all. Under the circumstances, it is I who should thank you. If we can work this out, and I have no doubt we can, you will have done us all a great service, Ms. Perry-Mondori. Why don't we start by determining exactly what your client can contribute to our investigation."

"Fine," Karen said, delighted with the man's straightforwardness. "With documentation backing up his personal observations, he is prepared to testify that a group comprised of officials from the CIA, FBI, DEA, and other agencies is directly engaged in the importation of illegal drugs into this country."

"He has documentation?"

"Yes."

"Go on."

"The profit from this enterprise is in the range of five billion dollars annually. My client thinks this money is being used for purposes that may not be in the national interest. I've just learned from Special Agent Tasker that you're aware of the money and that it's sitting in banks. Whatever the true status of the money, it would seem that my client's interests and yours converge.

"My client will testify to the criminality of a United States senator, ten Miami police officers, five DEA agents, six members of the Coast Guard, three Customs officials, three judges, nine FBI agents, five lawyers, and six Department of Justice investigators. He has personal knowledge of their activities. His documentation is impeccable."

The attorney general's face blanched. "How many CIA agents?"

"Eleven. That's a total of fifty-nine people so far. There may be more. We've got fifty years of documentation to review."

"How does your client know all this?"

"Because he was personally responsible for most of the drugs coming into Florida for several years. He was the man who made the deals, who paid the fees and kickbacks, who worked with the very people he's now prepared to expose."

"And why would he do this?"

"Because the business is now run by the group I've just outlined. Whether or not they are working independently is unclear. What's clear is that my client is out of the loop. He could have lived with that had they not tried to set him up for years. Now, they're trying to kill him. They almost succeeded in killing me and my family, as you know."

The attorney general thought for a moment. "And under what conditions will your client cooperate?"

"Before we get to that," Karen said, "you must be aware that the charges brought against him will be dropped as soon as the circumstances surrounding his arrest are publicly revealed."

"I am aware, yes. And let me, on behalf of the Department of Justice, apologize to you and your client. Once I'm free to comment publicly, I'll make that apology directly to your client. I hope you understand that while the Department was immediately advised of the improprieties and illegal involvement of certain federal law enforcement officers, it was impossible to prevent an indictment from being brought forward. To do so would have compromised an ongoing undercover operation of great importance.

"Further, it is my intention to seek authorization to reimburse your client for expenses incurred as a result of these illegal acts."

Karen tensed. The man was being overly obsequious, signaling trouble ahead.

She forged on.

"Therefore," she said, "he is not under indictment, faces no trial, and as a man never convicted of a felony, he is free to leave the country if he so chooses."

"Understood."

"Very well. The first condition for my client's testimony at any hearing and/or criminal proceeding is that the people he is about to expose be arrested and held as material witnesses until such time as my client has concluded all of his testimony. He fears for his life. He doesn't want any of these people walking around loose while he's testifying against them."

The attorney general took a deep breath. "Well, you've certainly started with a toughie."

"I know. The problem, sir, is that we're not dealing with common criminals. We're dealing with people within various federal agencies with access to enormous resources. Considering what's at stake, my client has good reason to be concerned.

"As I mentioned earlier, Special Agent Tasker's protestations to the contrary, it's conceivable that money gained from the sale of these drugs is being used to subvert national policy. That's so dangerous as to be inestimable. For that reason alone, I submit that the import of my client's testimony is vital to the national interest. When it comes to the national interest, there are several precedents wherein individual rights have been subjugated in the interests of justice."

"You've done your homework," he said.

"I hope so."

"You're forgetting one thing. And I refer of course to the Justice Department's own investigation. To be candid, Ms. Perry-Mondori, that investigation is about to conclude. We've gathered enough evidence to proceed without help from your client. I'll grant you that his testimony would make our case stronger, but we can live without it.

"Sadly," he continued, "the results of this investigation, of which you know very little, forces us to confront the fact that far too many trusted government officials have broken that trust, and the law, in their greedy quest for money and power.

"I expect it will take us two years to conclude whatever legal proceedings are brought against those who've participated in this wide-ranging conspiracy. To arrest and detain those people now, before our own investigation is concluded, would not only trigger outrage in the legal community, but would alert those outside your client's purview to what lies ahead, giving them the opportunity to not only cover their tracks, but leave the country.

"In truth, we're being premature here. And

while the Justice Department will gratefully accept whatever information your client is prepared to give us, we cannot, and will not, jeopardize the work of hundreds of devoted law enforcement officers who have toiled mightily to break this case. In the event your client cooperates, we will certainly place him in the Witness Protection Program and offer whatever other security we can. Unfortunately, we can do no more."

"So," Karen said, "what you're really saying is that the Justice Department is selective when it comes to which laws they choose to abide by and which they choose to break."

"That's not what I said at all."

"Sure it is. But, as always, it was expressed in politic-speak."

"I came here to help you," he insisted.

"Of course."

Karen leaned back on the sofa, digesting the attorney general's words. In Washington, politics was everything. Politics was more important than God. No one in power was going to let a major disaster be exposed by some headline-seeking criminal defense attorney representing a now-minor Mafia member.

Not if it could be prevented.

If there was ever to be a full accounting, it would come as a result of hard work by dedicated federal law enforcement people eager to clean up their own mess. That was how it had always been, always would be. For to avert the attention away from internal vigilance would be to diminish the importance of the government as a whole.

The attorney general knew the media would lionize Angelo Uccello, make him a hero of sorts, and that was unthinkable. The attorney general, now representing the Administration more than the Department of Justice, was gambling that Uccello would refuse to testify unless this initial condition was met.

Uccello, when discussing the drug business with Karen, had used the analogy of professional sports. He'd said this was the bigs.

Indeed.

This was bigger than the bigs. There was no room for minor leaguers in this game.

"I'll discuss what you've said with my client," Karen said, her disappointment undisguised.

Clearly, the attorney general thought he had won this opening skirmish. It showed in his eyes. "Good," he said. "While I'm here, perhaps you'd care to discuss your other conditions."

"Not at this time, Mr. Attorney General. As Mr. Uccello's attorney, I'm obligated to place my client's interests first. Your position will come as a blow to him. Unless he can get past this, there's no point in us discussing anything else."

He smiled. "Please don't misunderstand. In no way do I want to leave you with the impression that the Justice Department doesn't appreciate your client's position or his magnanimous gesture. We do. As I said earlier, his testimony would be tremendously helpful to us. It's my earnest hope he will see his way clear to do the right thing. We'll take every precaution to ensure his safety. I appreciate the fact it's his first concern."

Karen stood up and extended her hand. "Thank you, sir. I'll be in touch."

"I'm glad we had this opportunity to meet," he said. "I hope to hear from you soon."

"You will," Karen assured him.

23

Angelo smiled knowingly when Karen reported on her conversation with the attorney general. Strangely, he seemed almost happy, as if being right was more important than staying alive.

They'd given him a room in the officers' quarters, furnished in Marine green, spartan, but comfortable. The small room stank of cigar smoke. Uccello was leaning against the metal headboard of a small bed, his hands behind his head, his gaze directed at the ceiling.

"So, what do you want me to tell him?" Karen asked.

"Tell him to go fuck himself," Angelo said.

"Seriously."

"I am serious. He's blowin' smoke up your skirt, Counselor. Bluffin' all the way. Without me, they got zilch. It's like you said, they want the credit. Besides, they don't want all this comin' down at once. They want to take them out one at a time, drag it out, take the heat off. They're hoping I'll get hit."

Karen opened a window to let some of the

smoke escape. "We can't wait them out, Angelo. He said it might take two years to see this through. You can't stay here that long. Neither can I."

"He's counting on that."

"So, what does telling him you won't cooperate achieve? Nothing. You'll still be a marked man."

Angelo sat on the edge of the bed and shook his head. "You're not listening, Counselor."

"No? What did I miss?"

"I tol' you he's bluffing. This so-called investigation of his? Small stuff, like always. The only people who really know what's goin' on are the ones on the inside. I was on the inside for a long time. They weren't ever on the inside.

"What brought down Gotti? His own man, that's what. It wasn't the feds, and they'd been workin' on John for years. The families have been under the gun ever since that double-crossin' bastard Kennedy was president. But it took people on the inside to screw it all up, not some candy-ass FBI agents.

"With this deal, you got the CIA runnin' the show. Who better? These guys are experts at deception. They're in this for the money. With the kind of money they drag out of Ramirez, they can do what the hell they want. You think they're gonna let anybody get close? No way."

"I still don't understand what you're trying to tell me," Karen said.

"Okay. I'll lay it out for you. You tell him we

ain't gonna talk to the committee. Period. And that's all you tell him. Then, we all get out of here. While we're somewhere else, you have your people in Clearwater hold a press conference and release everything. Let those vultures run with it. They'll build such a fire under the Justice Department's ass they'll all be runnin' for cover. And they'll have to act."

"I thought we agreed that was our last resort," Karen said glumly.

"Changed my mind. They're playin' games, Karen. I got no more time for games. You offered them a deal. They said no. That's it."

Karen stared out the window. "So, we go on the run, is that it? We hide out somewhere until we think we're safe? And when will that be, Angelo?"

He gave her a pained look. "You have a better idea?"

"Maybe."

"Let's hear it."

"Okay. If we do it their way . . ."

"What way is that?"

Karen stopped talking and paced the floor for a moment. Then, she turned to Angelo. "I'll get back to you."

"What's goin' on?"

"I want to talk to Robert."

Angelo threw a hand in the air. "You're wastin' your time."

"We'll see."

*   *   *

Robert and Karen sat across from one another in the comfortable den of the old house. For ten minutes, he'd been reading the documentation Karen had given him. From the expression on his face, he was shocked.

"Did you show this to the attorney general?"

"No. I told him the documentation existed, that's all. He never asked to see it. In hindsight, I'd say he knows all about it."

"And you think it's politics, that he wants to orchestrate the hearings."

"Either that, or . . ."

Robert shook his head. "Impossible!"

"Is it? Given our history the past few decades, is it that outrageous to consider the possibility that the CIA is operating with the approval of this administration? That once the drug task force realized they could never really stop the drug traffic, the administration decided to profit from it? Is it really that much of a reach?"

"I refuse to believe it."

"I'd like not to," Karen said. "Perhaps it's not true. At this point, I don't know what to think. But facts are facts. You have in your hands documentation from Angelo Uccello that he personally paid tens of millions of dollars to over fifty individuals, all of whom are government employees."

"But some of these people are dead," Robert protested.

"So what? It details a pattern, Robert. Take the three CIA agents he dealt with in 1992. Only one of those men is retired. The other two are still with the agency. None of the three live lavishly. So what happened to all the money? Tasker says it's in offshore banks, that these men did it on their own. Really? Why would a man on a pension live in near-poverty if money was available?

"As far as I'm concerned, he was working on behalf of the agency. I'd like to see how he handles himself as a witness."

"So would I."

"Well . . ."

"I'm thinking."

"Well, think fast. Fact is, Angelo's end of the drug business was less than five percent in the late seventies. All the families were involved, and even then, they only controlled part of it. Now, with consolidation, you've got one gang bringing in at least half of all the illegal drugs coming into this country. And this gang, with the help of federal law enforcement officers, is moving to eliminate all competition. The amount of money involved is staggering. The scandal is mind-bending."

"What exactly do you want me to do?"

"I want you to hold a press conference. I want you to stamp your imprimatur on these documents. I want you to be the one who blows this open."

"Without consulting with the committee?"

"Yes. I realize it's bad politics, but I'm not interested in politics. I'm tired of the posturing, the lies, and the stupid little games. I can't hide the rest of my life. I won't."

She rose from her chair and sat beside him, placing her hand over his. "This is where we find out how deep this goes, Robert. I don't know who the bad guys are anymore. Do you?"

"I thought I did."

"Well, don't you think it's time we found out?"

He put the documents on the coffee table and leaned back. "I'd like to suggest something."

"Yes?"

"Let me talk to the attorney general. I'll tell him what we're about to do. I'd like to give him the opportunity to reconsider. After all, you did come on like King Kong. He didn't see this documentation. He was probably too taken aback to have thought it all out."

"Do you trust him?"

"Absolutely. There's no way the administration is involved in this sad affair."

"How can you be so sure?"

He smiled. "I know these people, Karen. They may be as greedy and grasping as the rest of us, but they're just not smart enough to pull this off."

"I'll have to run it by Angelo."

"Okay. If he agrees, I'll talk with the AG. I'll give the AG twenty-four hours to agree to your client's demands. And I'll tell him what happens if he fails to agree."

Karen stood. "You realize what happens if you're wrong, Robert. An airplane might fall on this house accidentally."

"I'm aware."

"And you're still sure?"

"Yes."

"All right. I'll call Angelo."

24

Erwin Partridge, the chairman of the oversight committee, was a chubby, bald, bespectacled rustic from North Carolina. A member of the Senate for six terms, he reacted like a giant moth whenever the TV lights were turned on. His arms fluttering like wings, his jowls quivering like Jell-O, he was the very picture of vitality and outrage. Off-camera, he liked to put his feet up, sip Jack Daniel's, and exchange tall stories with trusted friends.

But here and now, he was all business. The committee, not taken seriously for years, had been forced to procure a much larger room for this hearing, one that would accommodate the legions of media people who'd requested credentials. No one knew exactly what was going to happen, but they knew it was important.

Conducting lightning-fast raids over a three-hour period, the task force arrested over a hundred people. All were held without bond on unspecified charges. The list of those arrested included CIA agents, DEA agents, FBI agents, judges, Customs officers, Justice Department investigators, Miami police officers, the junior senator from California, and Juan Ramirez himself, along with thirty of his associates.

The raid on Ramirez's house was covered on television. Three heavily armed helicopters hovered above the house as four armored personnel carriers sent tear gas bombs and concussion grenades crashing through every window. In seconds, it was all over. Ramirez and his gasping-for-air associates came out of the house clutching their throats and begging for mercy.

His lawyer screamed for justice.

He was ignored.

The country was in an uproar.

The word was out that this hearing would explain those arrests—and more. The morning TV talk shows, with their pathetic parade of misfits vomiting a litany of misery into millions of American homes, had been swept from the airwaves in favor of what promised to be a sensation of another kind.

"The committee will come to order," Partridge bellowed, banging his gavel furiously.

The room quieted.

"Before we hear from the witnesses, the chair wishes to make a short statement."

The audience could hardly wait.

"This hearing has been called to investigate allegations brought to the committee's attention by the attorney general of the United States. Under his authority and direction, and at the specific urging of this committee, the Department of Justice has been conducting an investigation designed to root out those responsible for the importation and sale of illegal drugs throughout this great nation.

"The investigation was lengthy. It took the combined efforts of members of several law enforcement agencies. Most important, it was successful. Through the efforts of this committee and the Justice Department, I am pleased to say that we have struck the largest blow in history against those who would flout the laws of this land. The chair wishes to thank those who risked their lives in the service of their country, those engaged in a war every bit as dangerous as wars requiring the services of our uniformed military personnel.

"The men and women who worked to bring this investigation to a successful conclusion wore no uniforms. In fact, most of them worked undercover, many of them for years. This has been a long, dirty, and secret war. A significant battle has been won.

"Never again will those engaged in the drug business feel comfortable, for this investigation is the best kind of proof that we in public service will leave no stone unturned until the last drug trafficker is behind bars.

"The chair calls the attorney general of the United States to the witness table."

The second round of negotiations between Karen and Attorney General Williams had borne fruit. Robert had acted as a mediator, and he was very good at it. As with all politics, there were compromises on both sides. Karen and Uccello agreed to let it be known that Uccello had come forward with his offer of voluminous diaries and potential months of testimony after being persuaded to do so by members of the drug task force. Angelo signed a declaration to that effect. In return, all his demands were met.

After the swooping raids, the price of cocaine doubled overnight. But only the most naive would accept that these arrests were but a temporary interruption in the flow of illegal drugs into the country. Where there was demand, there would always be supply.

The attorney general took up the first day of the hearings, outlining the complexities of the investigation and its results. Angelo, with Karen sitting beside him, testified for the next three days. After that would come the directors of the CIA, DEA, FBI, and other agencies involved in the Justice Department investigation. Most of these men would be confronted with questions requiring an explanation as to how members of their agencies could have been involved in such a conspiracy. Clearly, many careers were on the line.

The hearings were expected to last at least a month.

But on this crisp fall day, Karen was with Angelo Uccello, his initial testimony over, as he prepared to depart for a safe house in a small Arizona town.

"I want to thank you," Karen said.

"For what?"

"You know what."

"What could I do?" he whined. "After the guilt trip you laid on me?"

Karen smiled. "I've been thinking. This is what you wanted from the first day you hired me."

"What makes you say that?"

"A lot of things. For one, you were framed so clumsily, any good criminal defense lawyer could have blown the case apart."

"You sell yourself short," he said.

"I don't think so. For another, it was your idea that I have access to your diaries. That makes me think you wanted them to come to light."

"You said you needed evidence," he argued.

"True, but you could have given me selected excerpts. You went all the way."

He shook his head. "You're all mixed up."

"Am I? What about the people you placed across the street from my home? Without them, I'd be dead. So would my family. I think you did that because you knew what was going to happen. You wanted to make sure I stayed alive so I would eventually contact my brother. That was the whole idea from the beginning. You knew you could trust Robert. You checked him out. You used me to get to him, right?"

"It's your story."

"Yours, too. You knew Robert couldn't work

directly with you. By hiring me, you figured I'd eventually be forced to turn to him. Very clever, Angelo."

He stood in front of her, lighting a fat cigar. He blew some smoke toward the ceiling, then smiled. "You think whatever you want. Just remember our deal. When I come back here for the trials, you're my lawyer. I still don't trust these creeps. Not even your brother."

"After what he's done?"

"Okay. Maybe your brother is an all-right guy."

Karen grinned. Then, her face somber, she said, "Thanks again."

"No problem. You take care of yourself."

"You, too."

He stepped from his room and climbed into a waiting car. Angelo waved once, and then the car drove off.

Karen got into Bruce Tasker's car for the ride back to Warrenton.

Karen was filled with mixed emotions as she and Carl started packing for the trip home. Claire was entertaining Andrea. The two had quickly become fast friends.

The worst was over. The Mondori family had its life back. The biggest question in Karen's mind was whether the family could remain in a house they loved. The house, according to the people who'd repaired the damage, was now free of all vestiges of a night of terror. But Karen wondered. Would the memories of that night ever fade?

In the antique armoire in Robert's guest room, live television coverage of the Senate hearings played softly in the background.

Carl had Karen's laptop in his hands. "You want to check this, or carry it on the plane?"

"I'll carry it on."

He started to hand her the machine, then stopped.

"What is it?" Karen asked.

Carl sat on the edge of the bed. "Look at this."

"What?"

His attention focused on the television, where file footage of Angelo Uccello played while the hearings took a recess. Carl stared for a moment, then shook his head. "Nothing—let's finish packing."

"It's not nothing," Karen argued. "That's the second time you've started to say something to me, then stopped."

"The second time?"

"Yes. A few days ago. In the hotel. You gave me this funny look, then brushed me off. Something's eating at you. What is it?"

He didn't answer, just stared at her laptop. She sat beside him and put her arm around his shoulders. "Carl?"

"I hesitate to discuss this with you."

"Why?"

"Because it might cause you pain. You've suffered enough."

"I don't understand," Karen said, her mind whirling.

"Let me be succinct," Carl said. "I could be wrong, but I think I know who your father is. If you want to drop it right there, I'm game."

Karen's eyes grew large. "What on earth . . . how?"

"I've been running things through my mind for some time. Just now I saw something that practically confirms my suspicions."

She glanced at the television in confusion. Angelo Uccello was speaking to the media after one of his earlier acquittals, stabbing his index finger skyward in a familiar gesture. "You saw something about my father—on TV?"

"Look, we can drop it."

"Not on your life."

"You're sure?"

"Tell me what you've been thinking—what you just saw."

"Okay. You said earlier that Uccello hired you because he knew you would lead him to Robert."

"That's my guess, yes. He denies it, but I think that's what was on his mind."

"Okay. Let's say you're right."

"So?"

"What would make Uccello think you'd go to Robert? If he knew you and Robert were related, wouldn't he also know you two were estranged?"

Karen thought for a moment. "How would he know anything about our relationship?"

"You talked about that earlier," Carl reminded her. "You said that you and Robert had taken steps to make sure your records did not indicate a familial relationship. Those steps are taken only by people who really don't like each other. As well, there's never been any media reference to your relationship with Robert. So, if Uccello knew about you and Robert, how did he know? And what would make him think you'd go to Robert? You and Robert hadn't spoken in years. For all Uccello knew, Robert might have been a bitter enemy. Uccello couldn't possibly count on you turning to Robert for help."

"You have a point," Karen said.

"Let's set the issue of Robert aside for a moment. There's also the matter of your relationship with your mother. Another can of worms. You hadn't seen her in years, then, all of a sudden, she comes to visit. Why? She says she wants you to drop Uccello because it's an embarrassment to her. We already talked about that being a lie. So, in truth, she came to see you, and only because she wanted you to drop Uccello as a client. No other reason."

Karen's hand flew to her mouth. She could sense where Carl was headed.

"Then," Carl continued, "Robert shows up in Florida. His story is that he's had a heart attack and wants to kiss and make up in case he drops dead. I don't mean to be harsh here, but that's essentially what he said."

Karen nodded numbly.

"Okay. I saw Robert's reaction when you mentioned Uccello's name for the first time. His response—although momentary—seemed strange for someone with no connection to Uccello. Suppose Uccello knew Robert from the old days? Suppose they *still* know each other? Suppose Uccello trusted Robert, wanted to make some arrangement with him, and it was Robert who suggested Uccello hire you, with Robert eventually becoming the intermediary? But there was a problem. You and Robert have never gotten along. Robert tells Uccello. Uccello tells Robert he has to find a way to bridge the gap. So Robert comes and sees you."

"But I contacted Robert first—"

"Because you were smart enough to follow the logical course of events. Once Uccello retained you, you played right along with their plan."

"My God."

"You see, it just wouldn't look right if Uccello and Robert were perceived as pals, so subterfuge was needed. Uccello trusted Robert for some unknown reason, and Robert knew *you* could be trusted. What better way to get the right parties together?"

"Okay," Karen said, "but that doesn't explain why Mother would come up to Palm Harbor to stick her oar in. She never discussed the case with Robert. Why would she come and see me and . . ."

"You see it now, don't you?" Carl said.

"Maybe. Mother was afraid I'd get to know Uccello a little too well? She wanted me away from him?"

"Give the woman a cigar."

Karen shuddered. "This can't be true. There has to be some other explanation."

"I had hoped so—until now. But the TV file footage broadcast a few minutes ago showed a close-up of Uccello from an angle behind the witness table. Uccello has a small port-wine stain, shaped like a star, behind his right ear—just like yours."

Karen's hand flew to the mark behind her right ear, usually hidden by her shoulder-length hair. "Angelo Uccello my father? I can't believe it!"

"The matching birthmarks could be coincidence, but too many other factors can't be ignored." Carl tapped his index finger on the laptop. "The man is a mobster. And yet, he posts a guard across the street from our house to keep watch over you. Does that sound like a father or a client?"

Karen closed her eyes.

"The answer might be in the files," Carl said softly.

"Angelo's diaries?"

"Exactly. They go back fifty years. And remember, it was *his* idea you have them."

"So?"

He took her hands in his. "You told me that your mother was very cruel to you when you were a child. So was Robert. You were a bastard child in your mother's eyes, someone who would always remind her of the mistake she'd made. But Robert had no reason to hate you. Unless . . ."

"Unless what?"

Carl tapped the laptop again. "Why don't you do some checking? Take a look at Uccello's entries for the time surrounding the date of your birth.

Unless, of course, you'd rather leave things alone. If you like, I'll delete the files and never address the subject again. It's up to you . . ."

"No," Karen said. "I want to know. But my hands are shaking too much. You do it."

"You sure?"

"Yes."

"Okay." He lifted the laptop's cover and switched the machine on. "How do I find the file?"

Karen couldn't look. She stared out the window as she gave him instructions. Carl entered the year, then the month, and finally the day. "Nothing," he said. "It says the file is protected."

"What's the file number?" Karen asked.

"3888440."

"Okay, go back to DOS, to the C prompt."

"All right."

"Type PGP, then enter."

"Done."

"Now type PGP, backslash, the year, backslash, the month, backslash, and then the numbers 3888440."

Carl entered the data. "It's asking for a password."

"The password is 'imperfect justice.' "

"Okay. It's asking for it again."

"Same."

Carl entered the data. "What now?"

"Go back to the file and bring it up normally. This time it should be readable."

After a few more keystrokes, the file appeared

on the screen. "Nothing," Carl said. "No reference to you or your mother."

"Try the next file number. I was born late in the day."

"Okay."

Carl decoded the next file, brought it on screen, then read it. From the length of time he was taking, Karen knew he'd found something. Her entire body started to quiver.

"You might want to read this," Carl said, putting his arm around her. "Then again . . ."

Karen turned the machine so she could read the screen. As her heart smashed against her rib cage, she read:

"Well, Martha had the kid late last night. A girl. Don't know what she's going to call it because the bitch still won't talk to me. I was up there all day yesterday and nothing. Went back today. Still nothing. Pisses me off. I offered her money so many times I can't count and she won't take it. No damn use. She took the money I left at her place last month over to the Salvation Army. Made a point of telling me that any money I give her will go to the same place. I told her I want to be responsible. I'm not trying to run away from this. I'm not trying to make trouble neither. I know it's my kid, and so does she. But she won't give an inch. She says if I ever try to see my kid she'll kill me. Can you beat that? I'm working my ass off down here bashing in skulls and this bitch is saying she's going to kill me. Christ! If I had any balls at all I'd slap her around some. But I can't. She's the mother of my kid.

"I'm glad it's a girl. I might go a little crazy if it was a boy. I like boys better than girls. Maybe with the kid being a girl, I can get this out of my mind. One lousy night with this bitch and I got such trouble. She was the worst lay of my life. Only happened because she was drunk. Hadn't been laid in years. And then her asshole son walks in on us. Jesus. A thirteen-year-old kid standing there watching his mother with her legs in the air. Musta been his first time.

"I'll make it up to the kid. I'll wait a few months, then talk to him. I got the gift. I can settle him down. His mother is a different deal.

"This never should have happened. I don't need this. If Sal ever finds out, I'm in deep shit. So this is it. The bitch don't want to see me, that's it. I just got to learn to forget about it. That's all. She don't want my money. Fuck it. Move on, Angelo."

Karen turned off the computer and closed the lid. Then, she lay on the bed and stared at the ceiling. "The other entries are there—spanning two decades. Uccello kept his word. He made friends with Robert, kept in touch. Your theory may be right, that he and Robert set me up for this case from the get-go."

"You okay?" Carl asked.

"No, but I will be."

"My guess is Uccello never intended you to see those earlier files."

"I agree. When Angelo and I talked about reviewing the diaries, he knew Len and Sharon would be doing all the scut work. Even if they came across the references to my birth by accident, it wouldn't make sense to them."

"It explains a lot, don't you think?"

"It explains everything," Karen said. "Why mother hated me, why Robert hated me . . ."

"Are you going to . . ."

"Never. Only you and I will ever know about this. We talk to no one."

"Why not?"

"If Angelo had wanted me to know, he would have told me. It would have been easy. Same goes for Robert and Mother."

"What now?"

Karen sat up. "About this? Nothing. At the age of thirty-eight, I finally know who my father is. I finally understand why my mother and half brother treated me like dirt all those years. They say knowledge is power. Well, I don't feel very powerful, love. Right now, I feel a little sick. But I'll be fine."

"I know you will."

She got off the bed, walked over to his side, and kissed him. "We have a plane to catch," she said. "It's time to go home."